William Holt Beever

The Daily Life of our Farm

William Holt Beever

The Daily Life of our Farm

ISBN/EAN: 9783337414993

Printed in Europe, USA, Canada, Australia, Japan

Cover: Foto ©Andreas Hilbeck / pixelio.de

More available books at **www.hansebooks.com**

THE

DAILY LIFE OF OUR FARM.

BY THE

REV. W. HOLT BEEVER, M.A., Oxon.,

AUTHOR OF "NOTES ON FIELDS AND CATTLE,"
"SUCCESSFUL FARMING," ETC.

LONDON :

BRADBURY, EVANS, & CO., 10, BOUVERIE STREET.

1871.

CONTENTS.

b

May, 1867.

June, 1867.

July, 1867.

August, 1867.

September, 1867.

November, 1867.

December, 1868.

January, 1868.

March, 1868.

INTRODUCTION.

A FEW yards separated from the shore, in a picturesque reach of the resplendent winding Wye, rests a huge boulder, which ages ago must have broken away from a ridge upon the hill-side above, upon which now there are several such gigantic brethren of a sufficiently threatening aspect, and which may be precipitated any day into mid-channel, therein to cool their vast sides after a prickly roll through thickset gorse.

Below this block, in summer time, the divided stream reunites to ripple in a rapid run, within which lurks many a noble fish, both trout and salmon. Upon it, a few stunted shrubs and heather grow;

Frondesque lymphis obstrepunt manantibus ;
Somnos quod invitet leves.

Often has it formed a foreground for the wandering artist's sketch : and oftener an afternoon couch for ourselves, whereupon were strung together such reflections as occurred to us upon the events of the day. From this diary the following pages present an extract

From this huge stone our homestead itself would appear to have borrowed its name, being mentioned in Domesday Book as "Mainavre" (obviously a corruption of the Welsh, "Y Maen yn yr avon," or "the Rock in the River"), and was held from the king in consideration of ten shillings and a sextary jar of honey annually.

It is a twisted, round-about, in-and-out sort of place, our homestead. Such Robinson Crusoe contrivances exhibited in the sheds, stables, storehouses, pens, ponds, and appurtenances thereto. In part we found it so, in part we made it so. It would have been perhaps, in some respects better (pre-eminently as concerns our purse), to have pulled down the old eccentric buildings altogether, and have set them up anew on approved modern principles. But we should not, I am convinced, have had the enjoyment we have now. It is so much more refreshing to pop in and out of all sorts of unlikely places, by unexpected doors and bridges, and sudden short cuts, and find, here a finely-shaped colt or heifer, there a sleek selection of symmetrical Black Diamond porkers, here a wild-duck sitting, and there a hatch of game fowl : all irregularly intermixed and mutually helping to produce one charming general effect, as the tinted worsteds of a Turkey carpet do. Personally, beyond a doubt, it doth yield us a far more varied and greater gratification in our daily, nay hourly, rambles of inspection, than if the lines had been ruled severely in accordance with modern improvement. Large spacious barns, stone-tiled, and straw-thatched, with lancet slits, and iron-stanchioned windows, yards of old-fashioned type, high-walled and wide, suggesting all a period when the owner's wealth was stored upon the premises, and banks were yet unknown : when the housewife spun amidst her handmaidens her lord's attire, and all cloth for household use; when the domestics were born and reared, and wrought and died, upon the premises ; and he was a travelled man who had been twenty miles from the scene of his nativity : when the wines and cake were all home-made, and the condiments compounded in the kitchen: when gold was scarce, and subject to be stored, and the yeoman literally lived off his land: when the witch was yet wont to come down, and toss into high air the haycocks, during the makers' mid-day meal: and when there was no bye-road or ruin untenanted by a ghostly inhabitant of some sort.

The land, meadow and arable, is of fair average quality: some very good, some only middling. Our stock of all sorts has been carefully selected; a good deal at long figures, and from the best sources.

But a main element in our enjoyment of country life is the fact, which it is only fair to record, of our being possessed of a band of servants, male and female, who have been for years well tried, not only during sunshine, but several in the hour of darkest affliction. So that it is really with us only to give an order and enjoy its faithful earnest performance.

So much, then, by way of preface, what follows is simply but actually Diary.

THE

DAILY LIFE OF OUR FARM.

October, 1865.

AT last the blessed rain! cleansing the foul sewers, giving drink to the grass roots, washing mildew from the swedes, reinspiring the croquet lawn, bringing home the wells and refilling the old village ladies' tarred-barrel reservoirs, delighting the young mudlarks—to be led off in screaming terror an hour hence by exasperated maternity—but, above all, dispelling the dread malaria of typhus and cholera.

On the still pool of the river-bend, there beyond the willow, how the glad pellets dance, lightening and darkening in alternate sport! It is even as Byron wrote—

> " How the lit lake shines, a phosphoric sea,
> And the big rain comes dancing to the earth"—

He wrote, however, of his loved lake Leman, little dreaming that his lines would ever be borrowed by a farmer to point the expression of a bucolic !

* * * * *

It is but a short three weeks since the above was written and left. Already how the wind howls around quite winterly, and the lovely October tints are being beaten away, and the general prevalence of colds and

B

bronchial affections warns us how little we can trust
the climate of perfidious Albion! How lovely was the
weather we had previously, in the which your humble
servant, being an Epicurean, revelled—a sort of second
summer without the damp of the like Canadian season.
But the good this broiling autumn did the tillage-
farmer, who shall fairly recount ?—to those especially
who, like my unfortunate self, succeeded to a foul farm.
This is a red sandstone formation, and in the sandy
loam couch-grass seems to thrive luxuriantly, spreading
out most rapidly its bunch of clawlike rootlets, each
one in diameter no less than a full-sized pipe of
Neapolitan macaroni.

The custom of this country is to scarify the stubbles
directly after harvest—an excellent practice, no doubt,
when the scarifier bites, which it will not always do,
and when the ground is sufficiently soft for its tines to
tear up the couch mass bodily. Still, under the best of
circumstances, with this practice many is the rootlet
broken off, and left as a cutting to strike, against the
planting of the spring. The plan of *ploughing in* the
couch I like still less, as that is nothing less than
deliberately setting new beds, and each separate severed
stem of this pertinacious grass will grow.

The plan I find answer best is to take off all but the
share of Woofe's paring plough, and then go down into
the soil some four to five inches deep. The fresh flakes
of the last year's growth are thus thrown, like sods
half-shaken of their soil, roots upwards with scarcely
one cut in the sun, who rapidly does his part in turn.
It is surprising how hard a surface this implement will
break up. Then come the harrows and the roller—the
scarifier afterwards, and then the chain-harrows to roll

into cigarette form, for gathering, the withered masses that strew the surface of the fallow.

And then—what then? what is to be done with the collected heaps? Should we burn? should we cart off and wash as fodder for the horses, as the French and Flemish do? or should we transport them to a heap in the corner of the field, and mix with lime and salt, to make the weed pay penalty as a manure in its turn?

Each plan I think a good one. The burning does, of itself, an infinity of service to the soil. The mineral ashes' left are invaluable, but then the vegetable element is lost, having fled in the smoke of the fire.

As *fodder*, well washed, it is said to be excellent. Is it not what the grass-cutters of India provide for their pig-sticking master's Arab? But the question is whether, having the prejudices of the farm-servant to overcome, it would not be unsafe policy, since of course *he* would take care that it was no saving, as regards the supply of corn and roots and hay; and besides, he would throw out, as rejected by his team, a quantity to vegetate and hold on its mischievous life in the manure-heap behind the stables, thence to return duly to its former haunt.

Then a good plan is it, again, to pack up tight the mass, with a dressing of lime between each layer, to make it a compost for the meadow, that will bring up the young white-clover leaflets thickly for the nibbling of the lambs when the ewes' milk shall begin to wane. But of all these plans, "which be the best?" as a rustic hereabouts would inquire.

Alack-a-day! what should one do? To decide—is it not the most disagreeable necessity of every-day life? Oh! that some one would say, Do this, or that; then,

B 2

having attended to orders, one could comfortably repose; and is not my bailiff in the right when he says, as he often does, compassionately, " Please, sir, I wouldn't be you for anything. When my work's over my mind is free, and I can go and have a pipe upon the stile ; but your work is always going on, and your mind is never free ! "

But from another point of view, the exceeding dryness of the past summer has been very trying to the temper of the cattle-breeder. Whether from this cause, as is likely, or not, anyhow the cows don't prove in-calf, especially if they be at all obese. They should be cool enough, in all conscience, for they have stood for months, half the day, knee-deep in the waters of a swift and limpid river; but somehow they don't hold. I see that Mr. Tanner notices the occasional occurrence of this sad fact, and attributes it, in his able essay just published in the *Royal Agricultural Journal*, to the extraordinary heat. Whatever the cause, anyhow it is a great sell, especially to those who own Shorthorns of price. What with the wife grumbling incessantly about the want of cream, and the certain loss of interest on capital invested, arising from this barrenness, it is really no joke. I have at this moment three bulls in my stalls, and about a score of buxom cows upon the pasture, not one of which do we know certainly to be in-calf.

Writing of cattle brings up a pretty picture of homestead enjoyment that I saw, not long since, in my farmyard. Upon one of the last broiling days, just under the lee of the cider-mill, in a sort of moat, that I keep full in case of fire in the stackyard, there stood, calmly chewing her cud, and just flicking the flies off reflectively from her flank with her tail, an aged white cow, that once, under the training of Culshaw, wrought wonders at the Paris and Salisbury Shows. Swimming around and about her, steering handily on their pivots as a gunboat or the Alabama, were sòme dear domesticated pet wild ducks, popping up and catching the flies from the cow's white skin, and almost before they settled there nipping them off, to her evident relief and their own private satisfaction. It was a delightful contrast for the contemplation of the indolent. The placid, white old cow in the red-marl-stained water, with the feathered fleet of quackers cruising happily around, and doing her kind service, while they fed themselves, and helped to diminish the plague that is quite besetting this district at present.

This fly abomination! Can it be that the hatches intended for next year are being already quickened by the unusual heat, just as we read of the young crocodiles bursting through the crust of hardened mud under Mungo Park's bed in the desert, having had their egg-covering prematurely chipped by that worthy's weight or warmth.

How devoutly do I not hope that it is so! Then deliverance for the muslin curtain and the whitened ceiling which are now so cruelly bespattered and destroyed! Then good riddance of the villain swarm that gathers in the beer-tap and does its best to be swallowed in a dozen household shapes!

But to return to ducks and their effect upon the meat question. How thankful am I not that I took such pains early in the spring to see that the greatest possible multitude should be reared from our hens and ducks! Have we not such an array of the last—such an army of the former, that our neighbouring friends,

with watering teeth, will wonder how ever we can consume them ? and do they not come in convenient now,
to ease the butcher's bill ? and don't they help to swell
the farm profits by being content to fatten on the
trough of steamed decaying potatoes, just thickened
with a pinch of barley-meal ? It is worth while hearing
how we saved so many. The plan is at once so simple
and effective. It was thus: We let the old ducks
make their nests where they would, under the heaps
of fire-wood and hedge-clippings that we had carted
and thrown down along the edge of the pool, purposely
at once to serve as fodder for the oven and to supply
shelter from the fox—both two and four legged—to
the brooding ducks. Of a sudden there were several
missing at their morning and their evening feed. Anon,
some would appear at odd hours, but with so earnest,
bustling a demeanour that one had not the heart to
scold them for their want of punctuality. And it paid
us for our charitable intention in giving them an extraordinary meal, when one morning, passing by the pool,
our attention was caught by the plaintive wailing of a
duckling, as though in distress. We stop to listen and
look : when we notice he has dropped from the bank
above, as his brother just drops in our view, and sets
up at once an involuntary wailing, as though, human-
babe-like, he appreciated not as he should his sudden
morning wash. Gradually the lot drop out, and at last
the fond parent herself flies down with a splash, having
for a while most faithfully devoted herself to the
hatching of her due complement of eggs, regardless
of her infants' cries below, until at length she makes
up her mind to follow, despairing of the vitality of the
one surviving egg.

Parenthetically, we would observe that all sorts of fowl invariably hatch a larger per-centage when they are allowed to make their own nests than when they are *set* by the henwife.

But to return to our duck : just as she proudly sails by through a strait, beside which we are in ambush, with her merry dark young brood in tow, that are veering around so sharp and jumping at the flies, just then we slip under the landing-net and whip out a pair ; then three, and a fourth, and six more, and there is a grand piping in chorus of distressed and affrighted duck juvenility in the covered basket ; and then, alas for the feelings of maternity ! the whole new brood being walked off briskly to the old henwife's charge, our parent duck but takes a header in the dark flood, and flirts her tail and washes, and feels, no doubt, delightfully her change from incubation to her cool native element, and away she sails down the water-side, so enjoyingly drinking up her beakers, if we may use the expression, until her lord and master observing her, there is a chase and a flight, and they are lost to sight ; all ending, however, in her, within a few days, refeathering a nest, and depositing new eggs, and commencing a new term of earnest reproduc(k)tion. Whereas, meanwhile we, the hard-hearted ones, bear off our wailing freight, finally to turn them out into a wire-fenced covered court, where there is an old duck hissing at us over her already almost overgrown charge, which, with this new accession, now numbers forty-odd ducklings. All these, however, during the day she proudly and efficiently attends to, instructing them to paddle in the milk-pan that just floats with an inch of water upon a sod of grass, as well as the

due use of their chop-sticks in the trough of mashed
meal and potato. But at night this will not do:
they die then by dozens, if neglected, from want of
warmth, the old duck obviously being unable to shelter
well above a dozen or so. The duty of the poultry-
woman is to catch all the others, and stow them away
in the back-kitchen in a hamper or covered basket
in some wool, under which is placed a hot bottle.
They are thus in the morning bright and fresh, to
rejoin their indefatigable mamma. We have lost but
few since we adopted this system.

I have just been shown another greatly improved
grass mower. Of machinery I am very fond ; and once
again, as so often before, is suggested to my mind the
inquiry, why won't the machine-makers take fair pains,
and improve their implements to the utmost *before
they bring them out ?*

For their own sakes it were advisable. Not only
would their sale be vastly increased, but the farmer
would have some comfort in buying. I have of late, as
many others that I know, become wary of sinking my
money in useless or improveable implements. I have
had two mowers and two reaping machines on a
small holding, and they were all comparative failures.
The defects we soon perceived, but could not remedy.
Why could not the makers have fairly tested their
model, and, on finding that in work the grass clogged
in front, have improved the machinery at once ? It
were undoubtedly their interest to do so. I have mentioned the mower, but my remarks must be understood to apply to all other new implements. Farmers
get disgusted, and afraid to purchase. It reminds one
of an auctioneer of ponies, the other day. " This is

the most perfect cob of the lot;" and when this was
sold at a good figure, out came the partner, and from the
•lips of the oracle, to our astonishment, " Now, here is a
better." There were a number of his audience who
lost confidence in his statements in a moment. I have
spoken more than once to implement-makers and their
agents upon the subject ; but the only answer one gets
is, "If you only knew the expense and trouble we go
to in perfecting our machine, you would not wonder
or complain." That, excuse me, is nothing to the
point. There should be no gross defect left when you
offer it for sale. If an implement be fairly tried in
the service for which it is intended—grass-cutting,
reaping, and so on—defects that will disgust and dis-
hearten the farmer would be at once apparent and
remedied : after which the sale at a fair price of a
really efficient, simple implement to facilitate labour
would surpass calculation. The gross inefficiency of so
much machinery when first brought out is the reason
why men decline to invest therein. There is always a
very general prejudice against a new implement, and
the least defect consequently gets highly exaggerated.
Let the inventor and the improver take this to mind:
" Don't attempt to introduce until you have perfected
and simplified :" and he would be surprised at the
difference of the haul that would follow.

But I don't like complaining, and hush! there's the
music of the merry beagles across the water : and as
I run to the window, there my friend pops so cleverly
over a quickset on his cob! and is waving his cap,
that I must be off, to show our bantlings the fun.

Rat-a-tat! rat-a-tat! on the round pebble pave-
ment with the ashen tail of a pitchfork ; the remon-
strative query then jerked out from a very low depth
in his throat by a short chubby lad—age unknown—
" Now what the mischief are ye after ? " followed immediately by the vision of a large sandy Skye scuttering
up the yard with his tail close packed behind, in mortal
terror of a being whom he regarded only as his too
harsh washerwoman, upon occasion of orders from " the
missus ; " young Breeches being convulsed meanwhile
with laughter at his enemy's discomfiture. Such was
the complication when we appeared around the corner,
in search of a marvellous sample of winter oats that we
had heard of, and which we wished to obtain the like
of, for sowing.

" Hallo, Bundles, where's your master ? "

" Guvnor, sir ?—just gone out ; here 'mediately, sir,"
replied our friend, with finger to his cap ; and at once
he was hissing most earnestly, as though nothing had
happened within the month to disturb his equanimity,
over the hind legs of a huge black carriage-horse, whose
downset ears told of tricks played off when he was left
to the lonely mercies of our young Pickle.

Save me, say I, from a lad in the stable, unless there
be a head groom, most smart and steady, over him.

The oats were certainly a glorious sample ; but, on
further thought, we decided to put barley in when the
spring comes round instead, as it will give us one more
chance of annihilating what couch sprouts may have
foxed, and yet be living in the fallow, the cleaning of
which we wrote about in our last.

The uncertainty of the root crop has been great in

these parts. Some who sowed swede seed with their mangold-wurzel, with the view to having an occasional turnip to fill up where the mangold seed failed, have magnificent specimens to exhibit, not a whit the worse off, as far as mildew is concerned, than the main crop sown many weeks later, the bulbs of which are small, as a rule. About this district the farmers, in fear of mildew, don't much like putting their swede seed in until June. This answers well in what they call a dropping season; but when, as the last, a parched and sultry season and abundant fly follow, they are sadly out. Their frantic efforts this year to replace by repeated sowing the gaps left by the ravages of the grub and fly were desperate, but I am glad to say strongly rewarded here and there by a fair crop of green-top and hybrid. The best swedes in the neighbourhood are growing upon land that was heavily lined last autumn: perhaps not only that the plant likes lime, but also that thereby a considerable store of extra moisture was retained in the soil.

Our mangold crop was sown at two periods, with a longish interval between—at the first in a strong piece of ground, once cultivated as a garden, and consequently a deal richer than the generality of the farm, the soil of which we pulverised devoutly, then in the drills deposited a heavy allowance of rather fresh but excellent and wet stable-manure. The seed was sown by a manure-drill, with a compound as a bed for it, down a pipe in advance, of ashes and superphosphate well mixed (about 4 cwt. of superphosphate to the acre). Hot weather succeeded; but the under-soil was sweetly moist and the crop came up grandly, regular, and rich of hue.

Our other plot was put in later, on a portion of plain

arable land, well pulverised and dressed with salt; and in the drill there was deposited a thick pudding of dark, pulpy paste, which the spade cut as cheese—the result of twice turning the winter-stored manure-heap that had been carted on to the adjoining headland.

On this piece the fly played old gooseberry with the plants; and we thought it was all over with them entirely (a neighbour fairly ridiculed the plot), when behold! the fit took them: the leaves sprang out, the solid bulb increased, and they never looked back again. The lines are thin here and there, it must be confessed, owing to the ravages of the fly and grub during the plants' infancy; but such roots as survived are the admiration of the adjoining farmers, and their superiority I attribute altogether to the heavy salting the land got (the mangold being of sea-side origin), and the burnt-toffy-tinted, gum-like, residuum with which we lined each furrow.

Of two facts, then, we are convinced more than ever —viz., that roots like their manure-food soluble, not strawy; and that salt is essential to the satisfactory development of at least the mangold-wurzel.

At the late picturesque Tewkesbury Show, where the competing charms of the cattle-yard, flower-show, regatta, and two bands were delightfully combined for the enjoyment of a butterfly crowd, on a right sunny day—such a combination as we wish all cattle-shows could be—we were lounging by the river-bank, awaiting the return of some racing four-oar crews in gay attire, when we were accosted by an old friend—one of the smartest of men, who makes to succeed whatever he may take in hand. We had not met for a long time; and our chat was protracted. His last words, however, were, "Now you must mind to come and see my roots. You must know, I pride myself upon growing the best in England. I have twice won the cup, and mean to try and do so again this year."

Before many moons had waned, it chanced that my steps drew near to his farm. He was not at home, but his hospitable lady was; and she, curiously enough, and clearly without collusion of any sort, after the first few moments' conversation, said, "You must really see our roots before you leave; for George prides himself upon them." Well, we went out, under the guidance of a strapper from the stables, across a meadow to the field. At first we saw little, and were disposed to be disappointed; but, having advanced a short way further, we were astounded—so astounded that we dared not quote dimensions on our own unsustained authority, so wrote by an early post to the gentleman himself for an account, which we subjoin, and for the accuracy of which we pledge ourselves implicitly, he being a most exact and careful man.

MANGOLDS.	Girth in inches.	Height from ground to neck of root. In.	Length of leaf from neck. In.	Total height. In.
Long yellow . . .	20	22	20	42
"	18	28	23	51
" . . .	15	30	18	48
"	18	24	21	45
Yellow globe . . .	34½	11	19	30
"	30	15	21	36
Long red . . .	18	21	18	39
"	20	17	20	37
Red globe . . .	27	10	24	34
"	28	10	25	35

5lbs. seed per acre drilled, half new and half last year's seed.

His letter communicating these particulars is dated
September 23rd. One amusing portion one cannot
resist quoting. "On being questioned last year at the
show-dinner what nostrum I possessed and used, which
enabled me to beat everybody, and having just taken to
the hounds (a few farmers being present at the dinner
who objected to our going over their land) I told them
that beyond the mode of cultivation usually practised, I
could only attribute my success to the fact of my making
all my arable land my exercising ground for my hunters,
and recommended everybody to get their land, on which
they wished to do something extra, well trampled in,
which, if they wished it, I should be glad to assist by
bringing the hounds over it." He mucks heavily about
November, after scarifying the wheat stubble in the
autumn, there being, I expect, a large portion of *dog-
dung*, in which the bone element is said to predomi-
nate ; ploughs in January, then dresses broadcast with
6 cwt. of salt and 6 cwt. superphosphate per acre.

But, botheration, here comes the cook again! Whatever shall we do ? What with trouble on the neglected
soil without, and the vermin-visitation within, oh! dear,
this new farm !

> "There is nae luck about the house,
> There is nae luck at a'."

Can you, dear people, can any one of you give us some
recipe—a really effective recipe—to get rid of cockroaches ? Aren't we entirely in despair ? Didn't we see
them the other day by dozens wallowing in the flour-
bin, and being fished out of the barm that had been
unfortunately left uncovered through the night ? And
are not their dismembered limbs all through the loaf—
a leg here, a wing there—until it absolutely crackles

like shrimps in the biting? The only consolation is
that soy is said to be made from cockroaches, and soy is
wholesome.

But aren't we entirely in despair? I emphatically
repeat. Haven't we bought patent medicines by the
score of packets? haven't we strewn everywhere the
rind of peeled cucumber? haven't we scalded myriads
as they scamper about in the darkness of the deserted
kitchen? haven't we intoxicated and drowned whole
milkpans-full in beer and sugar? but still there is the

> " Whispering with white lips—' The foe !
>   " ' They come ! they come ! "

Haven't we had in a hedgehog that did abundant
benefit, until unhappily he ensconced himself for the
day between cook's blankets, which she painfully found
out by the feeling of her trotters, when she went up
and tucked them in for an afternoon siesta? The poor
hedgehog has been a sore subject ever since. They are,
though, perhaps somewhat less numerous than they
were.

When the female household has retired with tucked
raiment, shuddering frames, and little screams, as ever
and anon they crack an unhappy wight that has been
wandering up the back-stairs, then begins on our own
part another sort of destruction—a raid in slippers that
are more slippery before the day is won. The horde is
certainly less numerous than it was—so many of the
old ones have gone in search of crumbs down the fatal
glass pitfall of the wooden trap. It is certainly comforting of late that, instead of the extended black
masses which did swarm over the floor when the kitchen
door was opened suddenly, there is apparent now rather

an infant army, with here and there an old fellow—a
sort of Dominie Sampson—as though left in charge,
who gets up vainly a jog-trot across the boards as we
approach.

An army there is surviving, however, and that, alas !
will grow, of all juvenile ages—some tiny as fleas ; some
the size of a wheat-corn, up to the three-parts grown.
You may see them playing rounders by myriads on the
hearth—then in we dash and crush and squash; and
away down crannies and into cracks, under fender convenient and the drying chips for the morning fires;
away and away do we slipper and slide, until there is
left for her who cleaneth up the floor the realization of
those exquisite verses, which you may read for yourself
in the Ingoldsby Legends, commencing—

" But a sombre sight is a battle-field, &c."

After all, it is most tiresome ; so please do, some one,
kindly send us a recipe that shall consign the whole
sort to oblivion straightway.

I see that one farmer gives, as a new accidental discovery of a specific against diarrhœa in sheep, the
crushing of acorns with their allowance of corn. Is it
that acorns are binding as oak-bark is ?

Again, in this county of Hereford, the feeding on
acorn and oak-leaves has been pointed to as a cause of
bovine disease. Whatever it may be in professors' eyes,
anyhow the acorn harvest of this year is of eminent
use. Our Southdowns, who gather them under the
oaks upon the lawn, most certainly enjoy, and seem to
thrive upon them. I have thought, once or twice, that
it made them cough, as indigestible food will a child.
The breeding sows roam about with matronly grandeur,

and most certainly approve the feed, besides doing us
personally much good, by burying a lot in furtherance
of future trees. We buy them also, at 2s. the bushel,
for the fattening pigs, who most amazingly delight in
the change. Of exceedingly fine Spanish chestnuts we
have a vast abundance, that is equally appreciated by the
animals and partaken of freely, both cooked and raw, by
the human household also. Filberts and walnuts, which
were plentiful the last, have quite failed us this year ;
and the smart little squirrels seem to have followed in
their wake. Our last year's store we kept in large
earthenware pans, in the cellar ; and they were deliciously juicy up till May, when the foolish gardener
exposed them to the sun, and they dried, sprouted, and
were spoilt. No apples of any sort—not enough,
verily, to grace even our autumn desserts, which would
be sadly scanty if it were not for the profusion of fine-
flavoured grapes that have ripened in and out of doors.
But of apples, not any—not even of the tasteless cider
sort, enough wherefrom to crush out a short half-cask ;
and—will you believe it ?—only last year it cost us all
but £7 to pick up the superabundant crop on these
very orchards, at the rate of 1d. per bushel. And yet
I did my trees well. I had them scraped of the moss,
and washed with soapsuds, and duly pruned, and the
turf around the butts raised, and a thick coat of
twelvemonth's-old compost of lime and night-soil· laid
on—a plan which a great grower of American apples
recommends as infallible—and yet no produce ! There
was abundant promise, certainly, in the shape of pink
and snowy blossom ; but the blight came, and a sort of
grub that withered up and rolled each leaf : a canker
about the root of each young fruit that bit it off, so

c

that the lovely budding—a very sea of blossom—came
to nothing after all. Nay, and worse still, even they
that did *not* thus

" Unbeseem the promise of their spring,"

—the ripened apples—they do not keep ; there is that
within, which preys upon the damask of their cheek.

Would that this failure of the apple crop were a
turning point in the cider nuisance question ! The
quantity these native people drink—no matter how
vile, how muddy, or how sour—the destruction it is to
their energy, most sure forerunner of rheumatism,
grand cause of constant listlessness, and ultimately, too
often, of mental alienation :—it is the very curse of the
country ; for, after all, they value it no more than
water, and scarce thank you for the giving : but of this
more again. I am thankful that I have been followed
by Welshmen, who do not appreciate the drink any
more than Herefordshire would their potatoes and
buttermilk, that most delicious of all food to the born
Cymry. The worst is, they do not associate enough
with their Saxon neighbour. Yet, hereabouts, is it
scarcely English. The names of places bespeak their
old nationality, and at the post-office there is a notice
in the language of ancient Britain.

But somehow or other there seems no affinity at
heart between the respective races. They run distinct,
as the waters of the Moselle down the enclosing but not
intermingling Rhine. And yet, after all, one cannot
be quite vexed : there is a something comforting in the
clanship that yet undoubtedly keeps up its head amidst
the natives of the Principality. Travel anywhere you
wish, and, if English, you will get, I fear, but scant

courtesy, and that measured by the guinea; but speak a word only in the native tongue, and it will draw forth at once, not only a welcome, but the best of fare and the heartiest reception. I cannot tell how, but certain is it, that years of interchange with the Saxon have not brought about anything like such a fusion of the races as the intermixture, which has occurred commercially and otherwise, might have fairly been predicted to produce. The Cymry in their country are yet as distinct in regard to passionate feeling from the Saxon as the wild-eyed pony of Merioneth and the quick cob of Carmarthenshire are from the stately Lincoln black. An amusing illustration of this strange feeling towards the Saxon is recorded to have occurred at a well-known ford in Glamorganshire. A rider in haste rode down to the river, attracting the curiosity of a countryman, who was ploughing alongside, and whose counsel the stranger solicited as to crossing. "All right, go on you." A gravel bank lay before him, which dropped down quite suddenly into a pool of considerable depth. The ford followed a half-circle of solid footing around it. One step forward, and the poor horseman was aware of the trap. At once the steed was swimming, and his rider immersed by the strong action in danger of being kicked out of life altogether. Blubbering and spluttering, he spoke out.strongly to the giggling onlooker, who had his plough upon the turn, and it was luckily in Celtic that he spoke—somewhat vehemently, we doubt not, as the local tradition records. But whatever he did say or did not say, anyhow instantaneous and effective was the help rendered, as by one who knew the danger and the mode of deliverance.

"Fy nghalon anwyl i (my darling heart), why for you not say it was Cymro? you was just be drown!" Anyhow, that afternoon the stranger was well tended, if ever, his raiment dried, and raisin-cake forced upon him to repletion. But now, as I feel, kind reader, that I must have pretty well pumped out your patience, and as there's some one knocking at the door, I will say for the present Fare thee well!

November, 1865.

AND so they are not cockroaches at all! they are simply black-beetles; at least, so my charming sister-in-law says, and to what she says I am bound to defer, as, although she cannot quite decidedly scold, yet she comes of the same stock as those who might.

"They are not cockroaches at all; the cockroach is brown, not black." If it had been my wife she might have added, "stoopid;" but as she was only my sister-in-law, and is very charming, she only bit her lip.

"Keep a tortoise," she said; "he'll eat all the black-beetles up." "Keep a tortoise!" I repeat; "why won't one of these cider-drinking rustics do as well? they have most tortoise attributes that ever I heard of, in perfection, and they might like his food." My charming sister-in-law didn't quite know how to take this, and so looked serious, and the other way: her near relative might have said "stuff!" or something worse. But suppose, I reflected further and aloud—suppose the tortoise were a pleasant tortoise: why, then you see there's cook, and it might not pay to have a nice cook and a pleasant tortoise together in the kitchen. Then suppose he were to turn out an unpleasant tortoise.

"What a very disagreeable idea, Henry! I wish you wouldn't." Wouldn't what, my charming sister-in-law didn't say; but having gone to the extent of this rebuke, which, under the circumstances, was undoubtedly stern, the conversation soon ended, and yet not before, with her usual amiability, thinking she might have hurt my feelings, she promised to do her best to obtain for me the loan of a real live tortoise, which is at walk just now at her gardener's, belonging to a neighbouring gentleman's family who are away. "And so good night." (Exeunt all but the black beetles).

Again, the bright hopeful morning; though, as I watch out of the window while breakfast is being brought in, there is a mist upon the water below and the distant landscape. Ever and anon a leaf drops dreamily from the oak and ash, while the willow is pensively pendent with full foliage yet. The pheasant crows amidst the bushes on the slope; the wood-pigeon dips from tree to tree across the avenue, or wings her rapid flight away; the nut-hatch is busy creeping up the bark of the acacia, and the rooks caw quite cheerily in their settlement.

I do not know that I ever like the rooks so much as when they come back about this time to their haunts, as though to look up the condition of their lodgings. The sound of their cawing is so social amidst the darkness of this November weather. How stupid it is that the farmer will assail them with poisoned grain, as they do undoubtedly even yet, despite the fine! They must blink their most ordinary intelligence to do so, if they would only watch for a short half-day the inestimable benefit those same grave birds do them, so earnestly stalking up the furrow behind the plough, and devouring with gusto, amidst other pests, the larvæ of the dart-moth, the daddy-longlegs and the cockchafer, whose ravages, if unchecked, upon the root and wheat crops, are so fearful.

A very different bird was yesterday under the house, but too far off for a shot, although we had well nigh attempted one, at the instigation of that worst cause of war, a woman's wish, his grey wing being coveted as an ornament for a riding hat. Poised for an hour or more he stood there with wet feet, watching the shallows at the turn of the river.

There had been a flood a few days before, when the wild Welsh mountains poured their contingent into the impetuous Wye, which sinking as rapidly as it rose left shoals of coarse fish with an occasional salmon stranded in the hollows of the bank.

This feed had attracted our friend the heron, as it had many other human pirates before, in whose track he found it safest to follow.

What a rich deposit those alluvial waters leave ! That shining coat of slime, which looks so nasty wet and so scaly dry, yields yet upon that island strip an earlier crop of fodder for cutting than even the winter vetches. It comes again to mow, and is grazed, after mowing, quite down to the quick, when the adjoining pasture is neglected, notwithstanding an abundance of keep that seems sweet and ample, being close grown with trefoil and clover.

Is the benefit rendered by moles equal to the mischief they do ? I see they have been busy on the meadows. I don't quite like to order their destruction ; and yet, when they come boring under the slopes where you cannot roll, one gets, it is to be confessed, sadly sore. One fears that they are not there for any real good to ourselves, but that it is only their lines of Torres Vedras for them to fall back upon when the flood rises and sweeps across the meadows, where they are luxuriating at present, it is to be hoped, on wire-worm. And a pace they can go, too, when terrified, as you may find with a terrier any day. The way the French tested their speed was ingenious. Poor animal! deprived of sight, he is keenly alive to sound. Well, they marked the working of one across a flat, and in each mound of earth thrown up they stuck down a reed with a flag attached. Having done so with some half-dozen, men were put with watches along the run; while another, stealing on tip-toe to where the sod could be seen moving from the excavation that was proceeding, blew a horrible hulla-baloo, such as an aggravated French musician alone could devise, beside his burrow. Back in terror sped the mole, unsuspecting, down the run, in his consternation inadvertently precipitating the reeds; so the time between the fall of each was taken, and the fugitive's pace ascertained to a second.

I lost two lambs last night. They were lost in some degree from unintentional neglect, I think. The shepherd did not, being elsewhere occupied, attend to the strong purging they exhibited as soon as should have been. Some more showed the same symptoms to-day. I was afraid that I was to suffer from this new disease, of which Mr. Reynolds discourses so ably in the last number of the Royal Agricultural Society's *Journal;* and I ordered them the treatment he pre-scribes—viz., to be moved on to an old pasture, and to be furnished with plenty of sweet hay and bran and crushed peas. But more than this. To those which were disordered I had administered a large teaspoonful of carbonate of soda and " cordial powders" (so delicious they smell), which came in my medicine-chest—treatment that speedily stopped the scouring by, I presume, correcting the acidity of the stomach. Then on the two that died I had a *post-mortem* examination. The butcher could detect nothing, nor could I (I am afraid of the V. S. bringing rinderpest on his shooting-jacket); so I had to concur with my friend in the usual intelligent verdict under such circumstances, " What could it have been ?" " Why, sir, he had pain." " No doubt of it," we grumble inwardly, devoutly wishing, for his stupidity, that he might just have, for a few minutes, about half the disorder himself, as the cabman in *Punch* desired, when the astounded old lady would inquire what was the matter with the drunken man in the gutter.

Yesterday afternoon, as I was going in the direction in search of a rabbit with my gun, I relieved the bailiff of his task of driving up a pet Southdown flock of Jonas Webb's best sort, in which I invested at a well-known Essex sale the other day. We were short-handed on the farm, owing, I suspect, to the cider curse; and the mangold-wurzel was being stored. They would scarcely leave the meadows for the hill-side under the house, going grudgingly along, picking and nipping as they passed, and so shy of the gateways that they would not advance through for ever so long, trying all they could to hark back, as though they feared a trap, until the youngest and leanest made a movement to spy round, and seeing no cause to intimidate, went on. Then they all passed ; and so across

another field, and through a wicket to the slopes.
Then didn't they prank and charge along this way and
that way, darting squib-like ; then, of a sudden, at full
gallop back, as a cock-pheasant preparing to roost
sprang up, with a loud cluck ; onward again ; then
pell-mell, half-affrighted by the rustling fallen leaves,
until, with noses bent down, and keenly searching, they
pegged into what I think has been an undoubted support to them against ailment, this sickly season—the
abundant Spanish chestnuts. And here they had another fright. A porker with his tail cocked, who had
been rooting under a tree, by caracoling in a sort of
zig-zag fashion that was meant to be playful, and most
loudly snorting, gave us all (it came so suddenly) a
sort of turn, as the cook says, and which irritated me
so much that I gave chase to the ignoble cause of my
intimidation. I was sorely tempted to have given him
a pellet in his hams, such an unconscionable run up-hill
he gave me. He could not, assuredly, belong to my
fold ; but alas ! after all, he did, and to see the villain
make boldly at the wire-fence, and not top it, as the
deer do, but go through it with a twist and a swing,
and a squeak at the scrape it gave his deserving hide !
" What security is there, after all, in wire," methought,
" when a beast like that makes game of our best work-
manship in such style ?"

All hands were busy to-day, on our next neighbour's
land, drilling in the wheat, when an outcry was heard
in the distance. On looking up, there came along, at
an alarmed sling-trot, a poor doe, that had clearly
escaped from some one of the adjoining parks, and
whose innocent hours were now numbered. There was
a small crowd after her, and our farmer himself did all

he could to get her into his yard, but she was too wary; and when he fetched his poaching piece, she went off too, quite wide awake, with that chamois-like, jumping step that you may see the Welsh mountain-sheep do when suddenly alarmed. Dear, elegant thing! it was not all fun when you sprang so lightly over the park-fence. Your life in the woods hath been a short one, and, I doubt not, scarcely a merry one. By the way, this reminds me that I saw, the other day, an equal amount of contempt shown by a deer for the wire-fencing to which our huntsmen object, but of a different sort to what the porker showed. I·was cantering to see a friend on business. The road across the park was bordered on both sides by a wire-fence. The mansion stands

> "Upon a hill, a gentle hill
> Green, and of mild declivity, the last,
> As 'twere the cape of a long ridge of such,"

and which is washed on three sides by the winding Wye. Under the wide-spreading branches of an aged oak, amidst a thin bed of withered fern, lay an antlered herd, with that restless movement of ear, and horn, and tail, that characterises their repose. But just as I approached, one sprang up, and making right up-hill for the wire fence, which was higher than any gate, to the horror of the hack I bestrode, came calmly flop down upon the carriage drive before him. The poor horse knew not quite what to do. He would fain have swerved round had I allowed him; and when, con-strained by bit and heel, he came back to the fore, he was trembling all over; and why was it? He had earned laurels in an Irish steeplechase; but he clearly did not like this apparition in his path. Possibly he

may have dreaded an encounter. And how he shook
all over, and was scarcely quite relieved when the stag,
quietly stepping across without noticing us, went over
the upper flight as well, up-hill too, and at what seemed
a tremendous disadvantage : this time just clearing the
wire with his forelegs, but coming down heavily upon
it with the hind ones, in such a way as would have led
a careful rider to make keen research. Yet the spotted
buck never minded it the least, but simply went full
charge at a dark one, which we now saw for the first
time, and who was apparently an exile from the herd.

Rattle !—clatter !—clang !—clang !—and our thorough-
bred was nearly wild with terror or excitement at the
antler engagement. We trot off in fear of mishap to
ourselves, in case our steed might be blinded by fright,
and victimize us both upon the fence. Mrs. Hemans
could scarcely have been between wires on a steeple-
chaser, when she viewed a like delicious scene to com-
memorate it afterwards in those immortal lines :

> " The stately homes of England,
>   How beautiful they stand !
>   Amidst their tall ancestral trees,
>   O'er all the pleasant land.
>   The deer across their greensward bound
>   Through shade and sunny gleam,
>   And the swan glides past them with the sound
>   Of some rejoicing stream."

Returning across the park, when once clear of the
wire, I found such mushrooms as I longed to carry
home. Alas ! we have dug up the spawn repeatedly
from a meadow that yields thickly a most delicious
annual crop, but comparatively tasteless is the produce
grown from this same spawn in the house under

cover. Is it not that the manure may be too rank? I see in a review of Sowerby's book, in the *Times*, they speak of many vegetables being ruined by over-manuring, and the absolute necessity that exists of denying all such forcemeat to the finest flavoured grapes of France, which are grown upon the bare shingle. We noticed this year, that the white grapes which ripened out of doors had a flavour some degrees superior to the house-grown. Or perhaps it is that the fairies dance not under roof, and that, consequently, you cannot establish on your foul indoor compost, those bright green rings that mark the footing of their midnight revels, and which are the only parts of the meadow that ever yield a mushroom at all.

> " Oh, a dainty life doth the fairy lead :
>   She roameth at night in the clear moonlight
> O'er silvery lake and verdant mead.
>   She chooseth right well
>   Her tiny bower;
>   Her house is the bell
>   Of a cowslip flower;
>   Or she rocks her to rest in the dewy rose,
>   When the gentle gale from the sweet south blows."

March, 1866.

" HERE we are again !" to quote the simple words with which the inimitable Wright used nightly on his appearance to convulse the audience—as a bad penny returned. The fact is, that since the time when last we met, " I have been roaming," not only " where the meadow dew is sweet," "but I'm coming, and I'm coming " with the sawdust on my feet. What a lesson this is to one not to procrastinate! It seems but yesterday that I wrote, and it is four full months since.

If you let the stream but once catch your bows, you will find it right hard to recover your course. How sadly easy it is for us farmers to be swept behind our work ! and yet the main profit of our business depends upon our being smart, early, and punctual.

But for the sawdust. It was gathered during a protracted and eager study of the curiosities of Bingley Hall—of Mr. M'Combie's black ox that was bent down in the back, as though he bore the weight of all Scotland's honours — of Mr. Crisp's prize pen of Black Diamond sows, one of which exhibited such wondrous breadth of beam that we doubt if even our excellent friend himself, set on all fours, could present a better back—of intelligent Mr. Allender's juicy-looking and apparently unfairly degraded pen of porkers—of fearfully priced pouter pigeons, and most human-looking bull-terriers. The London show I could not visit, and am consequently thrown now upon the topics of my home experience.

I am always a great advocate for salt—salt (refuse, or if possible, fish-salt) upon the mangold fallow, for mangold-wurzel is a sea-side plant — salt upon the layers of the manure heap—salt (rock-salt) before the cows, and for the flock upon a covered tray (only mind the ewes in lamb don't have an overdose, or abortion will occur)—salt in my horse's manger, and salt upon my children's victuals ! But of brine beware ! didn't my young hopeful a few weeks since come running into the room where I was bent upon the digestion at once of my breakfast and paper, with the horrific intelligence, flop out in childlike earnestness, that " one little pig was dead," and that the other would be dead directly, too, Robert said." And this, of the pair that

I had reserved for their beauty and high lineage to perpetuate the breed! They were the only two produced at her last farrow by their dam, now some fifteen years old. She is one of the three original "Black Diamond" sisters, that came of a lucky cross at Butley Abbey, the descendants of which, in the hands of Messrs. Crisp, Sexton, Barthropp, and Stearn, have been so wonderfully victorious at the various shows. For her last three families she has had no milk whatever. The first, which we attempted to feed on cow's milk with a bottle, all died of constipation. Of the second farrow, half died, although dosed repeatedly with castor oil; but the remaining four we reared on a mixture of warm milk and Glauber's salts: they turned out beauties and prizetakers. The next time she had but two, which were reared likewise on this nauseous compound, but whose sad fate I am about to record.

Hurrying out at once, sure enough I found a very melancholy exhibition—one little fellow twisted in and out of the bars across the iron feeding-troughs until he was clay-cold, in the shape of the letter S, (it must have been done in the throes of an intensely sharp agony,) while his only brother lay foaming at the mouth and writhing as if he were mad. My first idea was that they had been wilfully poisoned, but I banished the thought at once for want of foundation. The vet. was sent for (a grave invalid, but a local authority in his profession), and was wheeled in his carriage up to an outhouse, where the bailiff made, under his directions, a *post-mortem* examination of the deceased. Decided inflammation throughout his internal arrangements. "Do you know, sir, can they have had any brine by mistake? I've known that happen, and have this

THE DAILY LIFE OF OUR FARM.

31

effect." "'Pon my honour they might, for anything I
know, but I'll ask;" and I pounce at once upon the
cook, a gentle obliging creature who would do no one
any harm.   She had lately joined, however, and it was
unfortunately as the vet. surmised.   The pickle-tubs
left by her predecessor had been emptied into the pig-
wash.   Poor thing! she was so horrified at what she
had done, that scolding was out of the question.   Scalding water for a bath we decided on instead : and castor-
oil to be taken internally, and turpentine rubbed well
into his stomach externally, and an occasional clyster.
By dint of such continued care for some days the
youngster was brought round; but, alas! blind.   He
has not since recovered his sight; nor ever will he, I
am informed by that eminent authority, Mr. Frank
Buckland, who knelt enthusiastically down in the straw-
yard, and, with help of the cow-boy, who held on by
both ears, made careful inspection of his luminaries,
notwithstanding a most cruel squeaking that the
affrighted brute kept up.   "Amaurosis : he'll never see
again ; but he's none the worse for breeding.   I should
like to have his head to examine some day."   "Certainly, let's cut it off at once ; I've got another boar in
the sty, and he's good pork."   "Oh! no, no!   I mean
when you kill him in due course."   And so the piggie
was released, unconscious of his late imminent risk, and
groped his way along the wall, like Tennyson's cavern-
wave, to where his drowsy comrades lay.

Taking a round this morning to inspect the gardener's work, I was surprised to see the surface of the
grass-plot in the neighbourhood of some Portugal
laurels, all bristling, a couple of inches above the
ground, with the stems of the last year's decayed blos-

soms. "It's only the worms, sir," remarked my companion, with an indifferent air. But methought there
must be a reason for it, which I should like to discover. One knows the beautiful provision whereby
Nature secures the enrichment and accumulation of
soil through the worms drawing down leaves, curled as
an incipient cheroot, into their burrow. Each plant is
a compound product of aliment drawn from the air and
soil : these two, philosophers term the vegetable and
mineral elements, of which (when you burn a leaf or
stem) the vegetable flies off back to its native air in
smoke, and the ashes remaining form the mineral portion. Obvious, then, is the benefit of the worms
drawing thickly down the falling leaves, whether to
line their apartments, or to supply their larder, for the
same reason as mankind ploughs-in green growing-
mustard in preparation for wheat ; but whatever could
the meaning be of these *long stalks* being hauled
gradually down ? Were they to chew, as celery, or
be stewed, as rhubarb ? Or were the fibres to be bent
into crinoline-hoops for the lady-worm ? or be fitted as
handles to chibouques for the gentlemen ? or, to prop,
as pillars, the piazza of some subterranean Parthenon ?
or to be woven into gabions against the invading mole ?
Whatever it meant we are puzzled to this moment, as
it was only in the neighbourhood of this one bed of
shrubs that the phenomenon occurred. It must clearly
be an "ile" region of some sort, of which a lucky
colony has been making the most. Alas! that their
days are numbered ; for we cannot, after all, allow the
untidiness of their earthy deposits (" worm-casts," as
they are called by White, of Selbourne, who pronounces
them, being " the worm's excrement, to be a fine

manure ") upon the lawn to continue. Their normal
enemy the throstle already begins to hop, listening,
along the sward, until his quick ear informs him of
their immediate vicinity; when down he drives his
beak, and, with many an impatient shake, draws
out, writhing, a prey, rich as marrow, for his enjoyment in the bush to which he flies. But we have a
more wholesale mode of ensnaring them than that,
as we have a more wholesale customer for their consumption in the salmon-pool there below. Our plan is
to water their haunts with a strong solution of quick-
lime, when they are up, like lamplighters, on the
surface at once ; and you can sweep a heap together,
to take down to the river, where you will see the
dark form of that sovereign fish cleave the water, as
lightning, to the enjoyment of his accustomed meal.
Pounding the surface of the ground with the flat of a
spade will bring them out :—whether they are consternated or not, and imagine an earthquake is going
on, I don't know; or whether they find their dining-
room walls come toppling around their ears, and so
hurry to escape by the lobby.

"Pappy like shorthorns ? " was an inquiry jerked out
in a high key, as he hung his head on one side to look
up, by a little one whom I gratified this morning by
allowing him to hold my hand, and canter along at
my side as an imaginary horse to the farm. "Of
course I do, darling, or I should not keep them." "So
does me : me don't like them 'ed cows at all with
white faces, nor Miss Eglantine " (that's our governess)
"don't neither. Her told us so in school-'oom this
morning. Her likes shorthorns best, 'specially 'omans"
(romans, that is, I presume, roans). "Those red ones

D

with white faces are good cows, darling; only pappy had the shorthorns first, and doesn't care to change." So it is that the shorthorn obtains precedence among the uninitiated by its variety of tint and shape. And (a partial witness) I say no wonder. I have just been through my sheds, and return with a sense of pleasure that is only saddened by recollection of the dreaded rinderpest. What lovely little things the calves are— red, white, blue-roan—clustered picturesquely together as a bed of tulips! There is but one drawback. Would that they were always calves and yearlings, and never grew to that advanced matronhood when in ordinary breeding condition it requires more than the eye of the passer-by to appreciate their points of beauty. But our further discussion of cattle we must defer until at least our next instalment.

And here's the bailiff come for orders for to-morrow. Why, really, I don't know what to say. Only Monday last, it was so spring-like; the air so warm, the sun so bright, and the birds quite lively with their songs in every thicket. But there are symptoms of renewed bad weather, for listen how the wind howls already at twilight through the trees; and just now, as I cantered home from my distant farm, I could not but note an angry ripple rushing up the stream in foam, and a tempestuous period only can be meant by that lovely background of lemon-tint, which throws into such bold relief the crest of pines upon yonder distant ridge of hills. "Well, then, suppose you thrash out the barley in the barn to-morrow: get the machine oiled early, and I'll be down to look on." [Exit bailiff.]

And now there's no good fretting, and in the supper distance there is a delicious dish of richly-embrowned sausages (a food which none but he that fed the porker can be safe of), and an old friend coming to partake. Meanwhile, just one oblivious pipe, and ten minutes' fruitful rumination.

March, 1866.

I WAS cantering home after dark the other evening, when I had to pull up at a turnpike-gate kept by a lonely, lame, old man. As the door opened, I saw a plough-lad, absorbed in the contents of a slate, at a small round-table in the middle of the room. I was curious, and found on inquiring that the poor fellow came to improve himself after he had done his master's horses up. This anyhow was satisfactory, and a hint to me not again to abuse the cider-drinking inhabitants of our neighbourhood too indiscriminately. I tipped the teacher a shilling, and galloped on delighted.

An illustration of what mind can do, combined with will and means, you may find recorded by Mr. Caird in his able work on "English Agriculture," as occurring on Lord Hatherton's estate at Teddesley, near Penkridge. I will quote it for the sake of those who may not have access to this valuable volume :—" The ease with which a constant supply of water for driving machinery may be obtained, is well illustrated here. A bog, 30 acres in extent, left unplanted in the middle of a plantation, having been considered irreclaimable, was thoroughly drained. Besides the surface water, some strong land springs were tapped, and the whole conveyed by main drains to a reservoir a few acres in extent, whence the water is carried underground about half-a-mile to the farm-buildings. The drainage of this swamp, and that of 140 or 150 acres more adjoining it, gives an ample supply of water for working machinery of 12-horse power every day throughout the year ; and, before the lands were drained, this water was not only lost as a motive power, but did immense injury by stagnating beneath the surface, and extending its chilling effects to every portion of ground through which it slowly oozed from its source. At the farm-buildings to which the stream is conveyed, a mill-wheel, 38 feet in diameter, is sunk into the solid sandstone rock to such a depth, that the water discharges itself into it ' over-shot.' The tail water is taken from the bottom of the wheel by a tunnel driven through the solid rock for nearly 500 yards, whence it is conducted into channels for irriga- tion. When the mill is stopped, the water between the reservoir and the wheel, which would otherwise run to waste, is conveyed by pipes to the different yards and buildings for the use of the stock, from which any surplus finds its way to the meadows. The purposes to which the water-power is applied are these : It turns two pair of stones (one as we saw it grinding wheat, the other peas) ; it grinds malt, works a circular saw, a lathe, a chaff-cutter, and a thrashing-machine. The whole of these can be worked at the same time, though in practice that is seldom necessary. It has been in operation for several years, working every day, and all day, summer and winter. Independent altogether of the improvement of the land by drainage, and the sub- sequent use of the water in irrigation, its direct value as a motive power is estimated to exceed £500 a-year ; and that was obtained by a total expenditure of about £1,700. In a multitude of cases, a similar power to this could be as easily got, which at present is suffered to stagnate in the ground, or, if collected in drains, then heedlessly allowed to run to waste; for there were no unusual facilities on this estate for obtaining a supply of water. All that is required is procured from the drainage of about 200 acres of land. It is carried in earthen pipes along a gentle declivity, and with very little leakage, about 600 yards from the reservoir to the mill, and is then discharged through a tunnel; the whole distance, from the reservoir to the outfall, being 1,200 yards, and the total fall being about 50 feet."

An instance of somewhat kindred experience was related to me recently in casual conversation by a neighbouring gentleman, whose original profession as a soldier, and subsequent success in intelligent agriculture, remind one rather of the late Sir John Conroy's performances. We had been speaking of lime-water having been found accidentally in Cheshire to be a remedy for rinderpest, when he remarked that it is quite possible that it may turn out to be the longed-for specific at last; for that in Ireland it was the household medicine of the peasant for a disease affecting cattle pastured on bog-lands—a sort of paralysis that seizes the limbs, but which is effectually cured by repeated doses of lime-water. The reason for this is probably that the bog-pasture and water are inordinately deficient in the lime element that is required by the system for the formation and support of bone. The local name of the disease is "crupawn." But what I wish to mention, by way of hint to the young farmer, is, that this gentleman, having observed and reasoned on these facts, found an opportunity to purchase at a

comparatively low figure a considerable tract of bog-
land, above which a stream ran along the side of a
mountain, on which there were here and there accumulated, amidst the granite boulders, mounds of " lime-
clay "—that is, very finely comminuted limestone
embedded in clay, and turfed over as the rest of the
hill-side. His plan was to direct the stream to the
base of these, which the floods gradually undermined,
until whole masses fell, quite colouring the torrent.
These charged waters were then spread by carriers
over the low-lying bog-land beneath ; the heath, &c.,
on which arresting the flow caused a gradual deposit,
that in the course of about three years produced a rich
carpet of clovers. The property he was thus enabled
to sell at a profit of fifty per cent. in a very few years.
It was a common practice in Ireland to haul lime on to
such surfaces; but the expense was usually too great
to allow of profit in the improvement. That which
deserves credit is the seizing an opportunity that had
escaped so many. It is easy to copy, but not to ori-
ginate, although the mind may be awakened considerably by the record of such cases. With that view I
write.

To revert to rinderpest. It is to be hoped that this
compound of onions, &c., so nobly made public by Mr.
Worms, may prove an antidote to the ruinous plague.
Most undoubtedly effectual for stone in the human
species is onion-water ; a recipe for which we have to
thank the Arabian medicine-men, I believe.

Curious is it how superstition lives in England. My
Celtic country I had supposed to be the fastness of ghost
stories. There, there is no flood-gate, where some unhappy spirit stays not, charmed by local enchantment

to remain, "so long as holly's green," or "till he has counted the sands of the sea."

> "I remember, I remember, how my blood was made to creep
> By the stories and the stories of my nurse, destroying sleep."

But to think that in this enlightened time, with the railway ventilation of old homely mountain-bred fancies, one can find such as the following!

A poor fellow, of whom I will say only that he was twenty-four, and the ferrywoman's son, fell backwards from the boat a month since, just a short half-mile from this. Twice he rose to the surface, but there were none to rescue. He could not swim; and the flood was chilling, from its mountain element of snow. His sister had been drowned, under similar circumstances, a few years ago. But can you believe it?—a fact notwithstanding. His brother and associates (men of forty years' experience) put quicksilver into a new-baked loaf, committed it to the flood, and ran along the river-bank to watch where it would stop in its whirling course, because there, of necessity, would the body be found! However, the loaf outran them, and was lost to sight. The point of disappearance—as a fair critic I am bound to add—was in the immediate neighbourhood of a cider-drinking shop. This plan having failed, they determined to suspend their search for the missing body for three weeks, *because it was three weeks before they found the sister!* Well, of course, the search having rested, and having been resumed that day three weeks with a will, the body *was* found, "sanded up," just below the spot where he was drowned; and to *spiritual powers is it attributed* that the body was then recovered! Are we advanced, gentle reader, on

the fable of the appeal to Jupiter by the carter with
the wheel in a rut ?

Heigh-ho ! oh, this dreary day ! The rain-clouds
sailing overhead with a horrid threatening look, that
keeps us ever on the watch ! It is positively as fatiguing
as sentinel duty in an Indian forest, where, if you wink
a second, you run the chance of being tomahawked ;
and if you keep up a sedulous wakefulness, you are no
less a victim to exhaustion. It is so wearisome to
work ; yet is it worse to idle. What ever shall one do
during this damp, wretched time, that is so depressing
to the human species—so somnorific to the feline and
the canine ?

But here comes the postman. Hark his wet horn in
the distance ! So I must perforce conclude ; and after
that—not the deluge, for I don't drink—one hour of
unmitigated delightful sleep, for the merits of which
see that interesting volume, "Diary of a Lady of
Quality," as related with respect to Napoleon, Pitt,
Wellington, and others more worthy than your humble
correspondent.

March, 1856.

WHAT a glorious frosty morning—a right hard black
frost, with its determined glittering shell upon the over-
flowed pool—a kind of lagoon, as they would term it in
Venice ; none of your humbugging white frosts, that
pinch the turnips, scour the sheep, and disappear in-
gloriously in most despondent rain, but a splendid, in-
spiriting, real old-fashioned frost. Long life to your
honour, for the ploughed clay-land's sake, not less than
that we long to air our skates !

The birds twitter merrily ; the vagabond robin's voice pre-eminent, for the selfish tramp knows his time is come, and that kind gentle ladies will feel a morbid compassion for this most spiteful and pugnacious of all birds, and will feed the " poor thing" with the finest of crumbs, just as in turn they will pet that love Ned Careless, of the Prince's Own. "Scarlet fever" in both cases, *n'est ce pas?* When will the ladies learn wisdom? After all, would they be as charming if they did ? The willow sprays glisten gaily in the sunlight, but are as still as possible. Their long lithe fingers are, I believe, frost-bitten, if they could only confess it. They took off their winter gloves, and assumed " spring goods " too soon. Anyhow, their demeanour is hopeless and sad enough, despite their bright attire.

Halloa ! Look—there's a punt adrift, and left to its own devices, for I can see no one in her. How she veers and flounces down stream, like little missy in her first crinoline—now this way, and that way—so gracefully undulating all ! But there's something always to be learnt from everybody and everything, so I'll just watch this rejoicing craft's career on the flood, for I have been often puzzled in my boat to know which way the current actually does flow.

Ah ! I notice. I never knew that turn before. How exceeding capricious—so short and sudden in its change ! no wonder that with the lapse of ages this wayward river hath wrought itself such an eccentric course : whereupon it hath been christened the " Winding Wye."

But swifter and swifter borne along, the object of our contemplation has ceased to twist, and with her bows bent down and her whole length craning forward, as a

Daniel O'Rourke filly making play for the Oaks, she is gathered up for her plunge into the rapids, where the sentinel salmon will be startled at her approach.

> " Morn on the waters, and purple and bright
> Bursts on the billows the flashing of light;
> O'er the glad wave, like a child of the sun,
> See ! the tall vessel goes gallantly on.
>
> *   *   *   *
>
> " Onward she glides amidst ripple and spray
> Over the water, away and away !
> Bright as the visions of youth ere they part,
> Passing away, like a dream of the heart."

Ah ! would that all convict transports—for you will recognise Hervey's lines—were empty as the punt we watch ! How it relieves one to know that there is nobody to mourn that vessel's flight, save her owner, the old ferrywoman, who will forget herself a trifle, if common rumour malign her not, as she mounts her jolting donkey-cart, to try to intercept the fugitive at the next turn, which, reached in twenty minutes by the road, it costs the stream two hours to attain.

And now the rapids are past, and her career is tranquil as, to borrow the celebrated image of the swan on Loch Leven, she "floats double, punt and shadow" along the smooth reach below the castle. Some small boys, who are hacking firewood off a fallen apple-tree, get up a cheer ; but otherwise, all is calm around as we bid her adieu, and turn to think whatever we have been dreaming about the last half-hour.

My life is brought back by the crackling of a block which the servant has thrown upon the fire, and the painful coughing of an Angora cat upon the hearth-rug —who ever heard before a sound so distempered ?—so

I must go out for a stroll, to clear my brain and cheer thought.

Curious is it that I may not yet forget the river, for up comes the bailiff with an "If you please, sir, I didn't like to disturb you; but it's all right." "Why, now what's all right?" And I have recorded with becoming gravity an accident that befell my pet colts last evening —the darkling thorough-bred Welsh Galloways, too, that are to make my fortune. It was an accident that might have been serious. Having been sent from one farm to another for change, they became too jubilant, and when driven to water, not appreciating the different aspect of the current from what they had been used to, they plunged out of their depth, and were swept at once into the middle of the swollen and icy flood, to the horror of the lookers-on, one of whom fortunately had presence of mind to run along the bank, keeping them off as they attempted to approach the too precipitous sides, while another galloped a pair of half-bred cart-horses to a ford several hundred yards below. It was terrible, I understand, to see the three being swept along, with hardly their heads above water, and in the fear of each moment being their last. They fortunately drew to the horses at the ford, and so were saved. "Please, sir, you'd never have seen David, or Morton, or Welsh, again." "Why, what's the matter?" "Oh! if the fillies had been drowned, they had made their minds up to be off over the mountain." "Well, as they weren't drowned, and I want to think, just go and wet your whistle in the servants' hall, and then meet me on the meadow there. But first, have they taken cold?" "Oh! no, sir; they dried and clothed them before they came to me." "Lucky for me," I thought, " that they had been handled early, and so allowed themselves to be clothed."

I wanted to see the effect of a palisade of willow staves, which I had driven in close as Robinson Crusoe's fence into the bed of the river against the bank where it was being undermined, to fall in masses away when frost came. The work had been done some months ; the stocks I found had taken root, and were surmounted by a growth of light osiers, which sway as bulrushes with the stream, not opposing it so far as to produce a back current, but inducing a settlement of the mud with which the winter floods are charged. I had been told that nothing would prevent the encroachment of the river but a stone bulwark. I am inclined, from what I see, to persevere with the willow stakes, only taking care that the heads be not allowed to grow too stiff, so that the river can take hold of them, and by swaying them to and fro, and loosening the roots, do more harm than good.

It may be delightful as it is profitable in many ways to have a range of alluvial meadows with their rich grasses and clovers for the summer enjoyment of your herd and flock ; but it is not all fun in winter, even if you can keep your stock upon them without poaching the ground. The other night we turned out about eleven o'clock, to see a friend off. The moon was bright, and to our consternation we saw a silver sheet of water spreading rapidly as we looked down, swallowing up patch after patch of pasture. There had been no signs of the river's rising before dinner ; but our Wye, as Sir Walter Scott wrote of Lord Lochinvar's love, just " swells like the Solway, but ebbs like its tide," so I had to rush down to awake the bailiff, a willing fellow,

who is always ready for anything at any time, and a
couple of other men, who had scarcely time to drive up
the stock on to higher ground, when the river had
devoured all in sight for some hundred yards each side.

But this subject's chilling, and by your leave we'll
change it; for I feel already half "dead of tea-leaves
and snow-balls" as the jury found of a teetotaler-
suicide.

Colder yet, one might fancy the young lambs were,
this precious keen weather, on the open park, and yet,
to see the pack lark in bundles, and squib about
beside their grave mammas, it's clearly no such thing.
Those that have been left out altogether seem to do
better than the lot that has been driven in at night.
There is certainly plenty of shelter behind the furze-
bushes if they chose; but I see them now, as though
despising it all, gathered for the night in a flock together, just to leeward of a small tree, with nothing to
screen their nodding heads from the cutting night-air;
one thoughtful matron did certainly interpose her body
between them and the blast, but she had no sooner
fallen into her first sleep than a playful youngster performed a hornpipe on her head, which had the effect of
making her retire to a quieter suburb.

At what a distance one keeps from one's herd. It is
quite dreadful to think of Shorthorns, seeing how remorselessly this plague pursues its unresisted way.
Yet no specific! Where will the matter end? The
least tear-drop coursing its sad way down a heifer's
face, the slightest indication of arched back or dry nose,
how anxiously does one contemplate with an apprehension unknown of old!

"Why ever you call that stuff a farm diary, I cannot

conceive ; why, there's not a word of farming in it this week," remarked the wife of my bosom at our matutinal meal.

"Pity she hadn't got her tongue burnt with the fish!" we mutter inwardly, as we notice a sudden start back of the head, and a settled frown, that fungus of matrimonial life which appeareth only when the rose-leaves of the honeymoon are about half reduced to mould.

Whereas our outward utterance is, " Well, I will, my dear, for the future *be more practical and less poetical*, as I hinted to your papa, when he seemed to want the settlements loaded a little too much at one end, like a Donnybrook shillelagh." "Yes, pappy," chimed in a youngster ; "why don't him write something about shorthorns ? Me thought him was going, him said oder day ?" Well, my precious Herefordshire prattler, so I meant to do; but it's not altogether now the cheeriest of subjects. What a fright one got the other evening, when the unthinking servant startled our siesta with the "Please, sir, David's come to see you!" Whereupon the over-anxious Master David nailed one further with the announcement that "the bull was bad ! " Eh ! my eye ! what didn't I give for that said bull ? and to think his turn is come ! But happily not the plague symptoms, so far as I can make them out from the various printed directions. Can it be a cold, or what ? We prescribe an anti-inflammation treatment, and dispatch back the consternated youth to sit the night long by the couch of his treasured pet. When the coveted morning came, after an anxious night of startling dreams, with a foreboding heart I bent my steps to the further farm, meeting the affrighted youngster at full gallop on the bailiff's hack, to inform me that his patient was worse, and that he had found out it was something in the hind-leg, and not a "touch of the kidneys" as he suggested last night, when he begged vainly for a diuretic dose. He had had the forethought to have the boiler filled with water, and a quantity of mallow leaves thrown in, should fomentation be directed. The bull was down, and couldn't rise for some time. At last he did, and there were clear indications of a sprained hock. I had feared "black-quarter" as I hurried on with the lad. Now, the buckets of hot-water were brought, and an old horse-rug torn up, soaked, and applied steaming, until he soon began to shrink and notice. "Can't I go to the doctor, sir, and get something to make him eat?" "Eat be bothered; do you think you'd care for your broth if you were in the pain that he is in? Just stick to the bathing." We could not manage to tie the rug round the hock, as the least uneasy movement of his huge muscles shifted it. At last he lay down, unluckily upon the wrong side, and then, silly thing! began groaning piteously at the superfluous pain he gave himself by so doing. I just touched the tender part of his thigh behind with the boiling-hot liquor, and an instinctive wince brought the limb released to the position we wanted.

I send the lad to his dinner and take his place awhile, most industriously keeping up the fomentation. I didn't quite enjoy it, I must own, in that old cow-house, with masses of dusty ancestral cob-web swaying over-head, such as a wine-merchant would be delighted to have grown along his cellar-ceiling. One bovine companion groaning on this side, another half-snoring drowsily on that, the white cat coiled up in the hay, the Irish muck-spreader nodding in the root-house, the wind howling through the rafters, and dark sleet clouds threatening above; a broken lantern and a tin labelled "poison" on the shelf, an inviting halter suspended by a peg; the only lively individual being a bold brown hen that had taken advantage of the door being ajar, to advance in gradually and scratch beneath the manger.

I did not quite enjoy it, I may own; but still duty's duty, and I was unremitting in my attention, until I was rewarded by an abatement of his complaining, and an occasional attempt to chew his cud. "Come, he'll do now, my lad; and as you've satisfied the Minister of the Interior yourself, just gather a handful or two of grass by the hedge in the rick-yard, to see if he'll pick it. That's all right; now come and take my place, and I hope it will be a long time before you present yourself so suddenly to me again as you did last night." "I hope so, indeed, sir; but I was so nervous after Norman."

This referred to a sad tale; for you must learn, young reader, that farming's not all fun, especially just now. This same poor lad had galloped up, the day before the bull's attack, through a snow-storm, the flakes of which descended off his rough coat in small avalanches on to my study carpet, to say that "Norman had something the matter with him—he thought the staggers." Having directed him what to do, I followed as soon as I could to find the poor horse stretched out, devoid of life. What an awful nuisance! For he was just six years old; a fine Welsh cob, grand in harness; and about to be got up for sale. Well, I could think of nothing, except that he must have had an attack of colic, which ended in inflammation, not having been taken in time. "I am sure it wasn't that, sir," the lad burst in; "for I was with them at 12 o'clock last night, after I left the ewes, and he was quite well then." I could say nothing, but await the arrival of the V.S., to make the *post-mortem* examination that I invariably insist upon in the case of any death upon the farm.

The knife had scarcely cut through the skin when a torrent of blood rushed out, and finally a clotted mass slipped by. His courage had killed him, poor fellow. He had ruptured a vessel, probably impaired in its coating some weeks since; for, despite the best feeding, he kept getting thinner, so that I had just begun to suspect worms. Lay him under the sod: £40 worth of as gallant stuff as the Welsh mountain-side ever reared! His only fault was that in harness he must always do the work of both, and so probably he brought about his end.

And now, as we've launched upon a sea of troubles, let us record further, that, in our absence a fortnight ago, the bailiff sold a cow which had been put up to fatten, because she began to neglect her food. She was by Usurper (13,929), and had once been sold for a hundred guineas. I bought her barren at an auction for her exquisite hair, flat horn, and general style, in the hope that a change of home might restore her fertility. Alas! it did not. She never proved in-calf during two years, and when the butcher killed her, she was found "full of matter" (as I'm told), whether from some old injury or not, I don't know. Anyhow, the money was returned: I am a poorer and a wiser man. I shall know better than to speculate so for the future. But just to look at the other side: for it's a blessed pro-

E

vision that two thoughts cannot simultaneously occupy
the same box : the one always kicks the other out. So
if you ever get sorrowful, just bethink yourself that
there are lots worse off than you at that minute,
and that there are thousands may-be who would be
glad to step into your shoes, with all their pinching
points.

Didn't an industrious farmer near this, the other day,
lose two out of a valuable team by drowning ? He had
sent them to work some land on the opposite side of
the swollen stream ; and at dinner-time, being left to
themselves, the whole lot unhappily attempted to stem
the stream, with their harness on, being attracted by
the sight of their stable on the other bank ? And
didn't a neighbour of his, last week, lose a horse,
harness, cart and all, overbalanced into the same wild
river ?

And has not the terrific plague been, as yet, kept
fenced a dozen miles away from our homesteads ? And
are not the ewes producing fine lambs, and, many,
couples, on abundant keep, and, as yet, without loss of
parent or offspring ? And haven't we found a beautiful
bright spring just a foot below the surface, where we
had not suspected its existence, and which only requires
a pipe laid down to lead it to a point of great service
in the steaming-house ? And haven't I got a chatter-
box along-side, who would never allow one to be dull,
if one wished ? At this moment he has the paws of
the skye-terrier upon his knees, looking so repentant
with her melancholy eyes, while he inquires as to a
visit made here this morning by a son of hers, which
we had given to a neighbour.

" Now, didn't her invite Photo to come here to-day ?

Tell the truth, Viky: me won't scold.   Yes, her did,
me know."

"Be off, you young mischief there.   I can't write
while you chatter."   And off he trots, with his affectionate follower cantering in orthodox style after him,
having one hind leg tucked up as though to save her
boot.

Bless their little hearts! one cannot watch and listen
to these prattlers without feeling somewhat gladdened
under the worst of circumstances.

The other morning as I went to pay my visit of inspection to the stables, hearing peals of childish laughter,
I turned into a spare loose-box, where I found my
juveniles convulsed by the woful countenance and the
uncertain steps of a pair of fat puppies that they
had put to take a constitutional along the Shetland
pony's shaggy back ; the fond parent, Vic, looking on,
and wagging her tail, and trying to show (whether she
told the truth or not I don't know) that she quite
approved of their diversion, having, no doubt, an ulte-
rior view to toast-and-milk in the school-room.

It was a beautiful sight to see her and her little
plump dark-tan rough family when we first found them
after she had littered.

She had been howling and barking for several days,
until she disappeared altogether.   We had begun to be
uneasy about her, when she was seen walking calmly to
the back-door, considerably reduced in outward show.
After refreshment we followed her back into a wood,
where, under the tangled roots of a wych elm, she had
dug herself a nest.   It was in a fine situation, commanding a lovely view.   And here, incessantly barking
at imaginary enemies, she kept watch and ward over

E 2

her precious charge, until they were able to crawl
about pretty respectably of themselves ; when they
were moved, lest the over-fondness and nursing of the
children should annihilate them ; as, when once they
had found out her retreat, which we kept a secret as
long as we could, there was no end to the interruptions
they gave them ; yet all amiably received, as we should
scarcely have expected, by the mother.   It is astonishing to see how dumb animals will allow children to
interfere with them—disarmed, it would appear, by
their very artlessness.   That above-mentioned Shetland, tricky enough towards the full-grown, will yet
allow any treatment—the handling of her heels, the
pulling of her tail, and all other torture which their idea
of grooming may suggest—without moving a muscle,
as though mesmerised by their touch.   Bless their
little hearts ! they'll grow rather expensive in a while
though.   The thought appals, and I desist once more.

April,.1866.

ALAS ! my Reader, how sad I always am to meet you—
not but that I believe you to be uncommonly pleasant
company : rather doth my sorrow arise from recollection of the irrecoverable weeks and months which waste
away between the periods of our correspondence.
    First and foremost amidst my thoughts there ap-
peareth a vision of that bright treasure (of which I made
mention in my last)—the unexpected spring we discovered beside the foldyard.   Alas ! it hath not proved
altogether an unmixed good ; for a branch line, which,
in sinking our well, we failed to encircle and intercept,
has worked a bolt-hole by a treacherous seam into the
basin of the foldyard, which we had hitherto fondly

imagined to be sound, having had it excavated out of
the live rock.

How we discovered it was thus : One morning, on our
rounds, we were surprised to see a usually snow-white
call-duck, that carries her head proudly erect, and is
possessed of just that amount of *embonpoint* which was
the special admiration of the First Consul, all dyed of a
deep purply brown tint by the watermark from her bows
around. At first, methought she was but in the fashion,
and, after the example of her betters, in approved
coquettish style, was stepping with her upper plumage
reefed, just so as to exhibit the dainty petticoat beneath
—in her instance, it must be allowed, of an unwontedly
sober hue; but, then, she's a dear, darling, retiring,
little duck, somewhat slow, perhaps, on shore, and superior to vulgar display, even while afraid of being behind
in the fashion. Well, she waddles on, and is lost to
sight, evidently not quite happy in her mind, as the
bailiff generally remarks of any agitated animal ; when,
wonder on wonder ! behold my pet white shorthorn cow,
dark buskined to the knee, and having a most unortho-
dox muzzle ! There is the old white pony, too, which
must have slipped down, being rather shaky on his legs,
with a large dark stain upon his quarter, that reminds
one of old days, when we wicked lads, at a hard-hearted
boarding-school, used to lay a trap of black cherries on
the bench in a dim corner, having first set a decoy pic-
ture-book upon the desk for mamma's pet, the day-boy
in his superb and superfine light moleskin trousers.

And the pool itself is not the pool of our pride and
delight—the pool that we had excavated with so much
trouble for the refreshment of our kine and the delecta-
tion of the ducks. It is a water bewitched ! Whatever

can have happened ?   We call the bailiff.   He looketh,
and is of a surety surprised; he kneeleth, and from
hollowed palm behold he drinketh! (Thank you, that'll
do—don't pass it on, please) ; and his decision, after the
fair test, not simply of a gulp down, but after a deliberate rinsing of his mouth (most audibly expressive),
he pronounceth gravely, " Well, sir, I've drank worse.
There's many a time I'd have been glad of that, ploughing."   " All right, but it won't suit me, and if you go to
the glass you'll see your palate now is as dark as a
Dandy Dinmont's; and your missus will think you've
been chewing her black-currant jam on the sly." Well,
but to be serious, this won't do.   We must find out the
reason.   By steps we trace the mischief to an illegal
overflow of the foldyard, owing to that above-mentioned
incursion of the spring.   It has clearly something to do
with the bark that was deposited from the tan-yard as
an absorbent substratum for the muck-juice.   Well,
then, we must be cautious lest there be poison in this
liquor.   There is nothing for it, but we must let off the
pool—oh ! and that too which it has taken so many
months to fill, and at a season when the rainfall is due
to decline.   I mount my hack, and hurry to the tanyard,
where I am informed that there is luckily nothing
poisonous in the drink, but that the fluid now is a deep
and permanent dye—that some lime must have got to
the tannic acid.   At once the whole process is intel-
ligible ; for one feeder of the pool is the wash of a
neighbouring road that is repaired with limestone.
What a wretched bit of superfluous trouble do we owe to
this meeting of the waters ! But I can stand it no
longer, and, despite the malt-tax, must drown my care ;
for was it not my favourite resort at sunset to watch the

pet wild-ducks disporting themselves in grateful enjoyment? and I was just about to plant for them such a
nice sedge corner, where the flies would accumulate for
the tiny ducklings to peck at.

But to adjourn to the other side of the farm, there is
an alluvial bank below our garden terrace, the gathered
deposit of rich soil frayed away by floods from upward
shores. On this, in summer time, a luxuriant crop of
various plants sways gently in the backwater of the
hurrying stream. Here, at eventide, as you lean over
your boat, you may watch the promenade of many a
lustrous fish, which in our Wye it is far easier to behold
than to ensnare. Of late the water has been clouded ;
but one evening last week there was an assembly of
village lads upon the shore, and next morning there was
a rumour of unwonted success. We determine to try
our luck as well. At last a nibble, clearly, by the float.
We pull ; but what a weight ! Hurrah ! he's a good
one, whatever he may be. Draw gently, for the line
may break. Now he is pulling, and no mistake ; and
now—woe's me, he's gone ! What a horrid sell ! I feel
disgusted and desponding, and am about to wind-up,
when again a full weight as ever. He's on again ; coming
up, too, gradually. Hurrah ! after all—but again no
sign—he's gone—it's disgusting. I'll be off. We wind
away at the reel, when again a most tremendous pull,
and a renewal of our apprehensions for the line. Again
a slack, and again as quickly a tightened strain—he's
surely some pounds weight. Come away, then, at all
risks ; I can't be bothered any longer ; and our friend
floats up—what think ye? Why, nothing more nor less
than a small dirty flat-fish, who had produced all this
excitement by alternately setting himself upright against

stream, when he became weighty, and, when exhausted,
sliding obedient to the hook. A flat at both ends, might
not Dr. Johnson have remarked, in improvement of his
well-known definition of a fisherman ?

But on the adjoining meadow I notice there will soon
be a bite sufficient for my precious Shorthorns. Wherefore precious? for did I not once speak lightly of the
breed, as a transient thing of beauty soon to pass away ?
The lapse of years has, however, shown one that there
has of late sprung up a line of farmers so fond of the
sort, and so skilled in their cultivation, and further, too,
that the breed has in it so much promise of ultimate
deep milking, as well as fat-producing, that I believe it
to be now as firmly established in the taste of the
nation as cricket and the thoroughbred horse. What,
then, should the young farmer do ? Buy Booth or
Bates, and nothing else ? Why, most certainly not;
unless you wish the breed indeed to wane and dwindle
away. Get fixed in your eye one special type of form,
such as you may have noticed to have already obtained
(as Disraeli said of Peel's quotations) the meed of public
approbation ; then, at the sales of really well-descended
stock, buy such (not too hastily nor too numerously)
heifers as you see of the stamp you love—almost everyone has his own ideas as to the exact form requisite for
beauty. Then purchase a bull of noble alliance, and
the offspring of parents that are known to transmit
their type and likeness strongly. There is much in this.
Your object should be to try and breed up a herd of one
particular style. So Sir Charles Knightley acted, in his
successful aim at a fine shoulder in his animals.

It is folly and nonsense to get together for breeding
purposes a herd of all sorts as regards shape and cha-

racter, even though they may be stated to come of
purest Booth or Bates. Whatever you do breed, try to
breed them as like in outward fashion as a handful of
beans. Uniformity of fashionable style, so engrained by
long and careful cultivation that their young can be
relied on to appear (with rare " misfits ") of the same
character also, is, I consider, the mainspring of a successful herd, both as regards show prizes and a good
auction average. Long pedigrees, of course, you must
have to exhibit. But I find I have struck a subject
which might fill a volume, and my allotted space is
being visibly lessened. I am sorely tempted to be off,
too ; for see now the rain is over, and the sun is out
again, and the yellow-green arms of the willow glisten
as young snakes under its renovating influence.

The intermission of shows this year will, I trust, do
good by obtaining the release from forcing-diet of an
extra number of choice animals, which, so far as breeding
goes, would otherwise have been sacrificed. It is very
sad that the first prize breeder is obliged to spoil the
reproductive powers of so many of his herd in order to
keep up the prestige of former successes. The fact is,
the buyer must see what the raw material will be,
polished. I believe the plan of exhibiting in store, or
at least in reasonably fat condition, was once tried in
Suffolk ; but the thing did not do. The pleasure-
seekers comprehended not the real merits of the
animals : they looked only for the beauty of a plump
condition.

What a battue we had among the black-beetles last
night again ! I wish some one would kindly suggest
a mode of exterminating the disgusting horde. For
months, owing to their non-appearance (do they hyber-

nate ?), we had fondly hoped that they were gone for
good, having bolted in despair or disgust, as Buckland
says rats will ; when one hot night lately, during the
small hours (to use an Irishism), as we were taking our
round to see that all was safe, we found the kitchen in
parts positively black with them again—and such enormous brutes, too ! It is inconceivable that the young
fry we used to thin can have so grown, or else there is
room for considerable retrenchment in the flour-bin.
However, in we rush, and lay about us with an extemporised weapon, a golosh ; a grand implement, we can
assure you, for it doubles back to fetch them out of the
deepest corner and the most unlikely ledges. How
they did scamper along at a glimpse of the light (but it
was no use), under the wood-basket, and the duster,
and the coal-bin ! All of which having been lifted in
turn, down we came with a fatal crush, that soon sadly
defiled the kitchen boards. But there was a stone
recess alongside the fireplace, a sort of cul-de-sac, into
which a legion fled ; and it was pitiable to behold them
after the first smack, how they dashed and leaped
around, and met our gaze at the one only outlet, and
retreated, and how the veterans were resigned and
quiet. It really went quite against our heart to kill
them thus helplessly cooped up ; but then there was
the remembrance of the food they spoil, and so the
slaughter proceeded, until unenviable indeed was the
kitchen-maid's washing-up in the morning. And the
missus hears, in confidence from the cook, that master
must have been as quick as a cockroach himself to kill
such a number. One old fellow amused me much : he
lay upon a ledge, ensconced behind the skirting-boards,
with just his head and horns out—unless the candle

approached near, when he at once drew back—deliberately watching the slaughter of his clan with apparently the most imperturbable coolness. The next morning, however, he was found dead on his shelf. It is possible that he was the moneylender of the community, and sorrowing for his bonds had expired of a broken heart.

A problem often suggested to my mind, the solution of which was of great importance, recurred again to-day, as I watched a new Samuelson taking its trial trip across the lawn. Why is it that a sward of coarsest fibre, or, rather, of coarsest stems, will rapidly be overgrown by a clothing of the dearest little white clover when once a mowing machine has been brought to use its cruel, crushing, bruising energies upon it? I have not only noticed it myself, but I have stated the fact to others who have found invariably the same result. I have now on this red sandstone formation acres of weak grass, which I should be, oh! so glad to see interspersed with an enriching element of trefoil and clover plant. Would that some recipe on a large scale could be found to answer.

> " Oh ! many a time I am sad of heart,
>   And I haven't a word to say,
>   And I keep from the lasses and lads apart,
>   In the meadows a-making hay,"

when I take cognizance of the benty stuff that one has to put up with after all, and when I recall how zealously and repeatedly I have harrowed and sown with the most approved " renovating mixtures " these selfsame ungrateful plains. Come up it will as a rule, but it seems as if it could find no resting place for the sole of its foot ; for in the course of a very few years, or rather months, the coveted shamrock development disappears,

just as it will if dressed with too liberal a dose of liquid
manure from the fold-yard reservoir. A compost of
lime and earth induces certainly an occasional tem-
porary settlement of clover; but the plants are rare
and, as the raisins in a school pudding, at duelling
distance apart. Whereas whatever be the nature of the
soil and the texture of a lawn submitted to the mercies
of an ordinary mowing machine, quite surely, and
almost before the moon has waned that dawned upon
the experiment, the desired plant will thickly appear.
Whatever can be the cause? Is it that the bruising
of the strong grass-stems debilitates and discourages
them? giving room for the advance of a timid plant,
which, indebted to Holland for its distinctive appellation, yet most certainly partakes not of the failing
attributed to the people of that country by Canning, in
his famous poetical despatch to Sir Charles Bagot:—

> " In matters of commerce, the fault of the Dutch
> Is giving too little and asking too much."

Anyhow it would be most advantageous to us farmers
if the machine makers would put their heads together,
and invent some implement that would do on a large
scale for our pastures what the mower does for our
lawns.

The increase of canine madness alarms one. Having
a team of nice terriers, and abundant rabbits to work
them with, one gets daily alarmed lest something should
happen to oblige their extermination. It is satisfactory
to know that caustic potash applied at once to the
wound is a specific against the poison of the rabid animal's fang. I have always a bottle-full in the house.

How marvellous is the gift of scent! How it struck

me, particularly one morning some weeks since, on our approach, out shooting, to a place that seemed likely to hold game, or at least a rabbit. Not he—this pet terrier, with a touch of spaniel in him, as good a dog as ever was shot to—he will not look. With a single half-sniff he canters by ; and when you call him, once, twice, rather sternly this time, he comes coaxingly up ; but when you "hie" him in, such a reproachful look he directs you, such a deprecatory glance of his melancholy eyes, as though he would fain say, "Now, you wouldn't have me stultify myself by doing more ; " but, as man should, being master of the creation, when we insist, then in he goes, and sniffs and searches, but makes no sign of the hoped-for presence, and the place is clearly void. The keeper hints that after the last night's storm no creature could be expected to lie in that cover under the falling leaves and boughs. Then, doggie, as you feel constrained to pat him, and say, ·" good dog ! "—then don't he wink his eye internally ? and don't he keep on bobbing around, and altogether looking so delighted as though, while feeling he must be civil for his victuals' sake, still he were very much inclined to ask his master " Where ever were you riz ? " " Who's who in '66 ? " or any other such like intellectual but insulting query. We on our part are glad of a diversion, and so we charge, "Hie on, lad," and he leaves us to reflect not only on that old stern inquiry where instinct ends and reason begins, but also more deeply upon the marvellous gift of scent, which engaged our pen above, and which again falls tame beside the sense that guides the condor of the Andes from beyond the horizon long miles to a feast upon the failing mule. Then comes a further reflection. These animals must have some compensatory attribute, or their lives would assuredly be miserable.   Our own nasal organs are too sadly appreciative of the disagreeables in life already, we think.   What then must the victims of these so much subtler olfactory nerves think ?   This same bow-wow got a nip he didn't like last night.   He is of an inquisitive turn, and as he was following the bailiff's wife home just before dark, he must needs go out of his way to explore the cellars of a huge boulder that, rolled down from the mountain behind, has come to anchor, in ages gone by, upon the orchard slope.   He is a plucky fellow, and doesn't insist upon weight for age in a street quarrel ; but this time he cried sadly.   The fact is, either a fox or a badger, both of which abound about, must have caught him by the collar and shook him well, for he had no wounds to show.

Such a beautiful fox was brought to me last winter, that had been caught under a rock upon the hill above the house !   He was tracked over the snow to his retreat ; a bag with a hoop in it was then put against the opening, and a piece of lighted candle on a stick introduced through a treacherous chink behind, which so affrighted Master Reynard that he bolted into the sack and his captor's arms.   He had not been caught many hours ; but it was amusing to note the old rob-ber's resigned, or rather indifferent, way in which he laid out his head on his paws, just turning an observant eye only, if one moved.   He struggled violently, and hung back desperately when his chain was pulled.   His coat was so richly tinted—a lustrous red-brown—I almost longed to keep him as a pet ; but then pets accumulate, and guineas don't, so I allowed his trans-portation to a neighbouring hunt.

" Oh, my dear mother, do let me alone ! I've got to finish this writing by post-time."

She is leaning over me, enlarging on the past, present, and future (as the respected old Athenian poets used to say) of some party that I really don't take the least interest in, inasmuch as I don't know who it is.

" Well, I'm going." And as she goes, in her energetic laudation of some one whom she has been praising the last half-hour, but whose name escaped me, as I cannot, like the First Napoleon, talk, write, and listen at once, I start at her emphatic whisper, " He's a man that drinks nothing but water."

" My stars be thanked ! I don't. I have already too large a per-centage of that precious element in my natural system, if one is to believe the explanation of analysts. Water's a very good thing in its place ; and I wish it wouldn't leave us so treacherously as it does sometimes, in summer, on these red-sandstone rocks.

Alas ! that poisoned pool I spoke of in my last ! We have had to let off the main part of it, after all— it had grown so foul in tint and taste. My bailiff, being of a thrifty turn, had it guided on to a plot of cabbage-plants, all of which I now expect to see brought up to table as guiltily dyed as the bone of madder-fed poultry is said to be.

And the dear little ducks are dropping in daily—a yard further down, by the way, than they need have done—from the hatching-nests under the thorn-heaps along the banks. We have already a good store, and have been hitherto successful in the rearing. It makes one's teeth water to think of the Sunday dinners a little later on.

I had been cantering through my ewe-flock yester-

day afternoon, to note the growth of the lambs, when
I got a message that some strangers had come to view
the bulls.   This makes me tremble lest they bring the
dreadful rinderpest upon their garments in some sub-
tile form.   The worst has not, I believe, yet come.
Only the other day there was an order signed in this
district for the removal of some cattle, on the declaration of two respectable farmers, one of whom had *not
seen* the stock of which he testified.   What must be
the result of this loose—if, indeed, honest—action?
I was informed of this by the magistrate who had to
countersign their witness.

How lovely the pear-blossom has been! but the
apple is not fully out yet.   The cherry-trees are
laden; but the berries, Gardener predicts, will be but
a scanty tribe. ·The wall-fruit might be better; but
I dare not think much of that, having forgotten to
have the walls duly pointed with new mortar.   "They
be all full of herrywigs and all sorts of varmint; and,
lor! these trees they be no manner of good.   I've been
averdepoising ever so long what's best to do with
them."   But, as the gardener's getting thus even
warmer than his hothouse, there's no "averdepoising"
for me.   I'll just make up my mind, and be off for
a gallop in the cooler climate of the riverside.

March, 1867.

"Once more upon the waters!—yet, once more!
And the waves bound beneath me as a steed
That knows his rider! Welcome to their roar.
Swift be their guidance, wheresoe'er it lead!"

It's all very fine—this beautiful quotation from
Childe Harold; but the fact is, we are not upon the

waters at all (except metaphorically); it's rather that the waters are upon us, and, upon the whole, not doing us unmitigated good. The floods are out, and have been so, off and on, since the choleric Welsh hills sent down their surging torrent of ripped-up old ice raiment and superfluous mud broth. In faith, we could have well spared those everlasting mountains their gift of old clothes; for it's sand mainly, and not a Nile-like deposit of alluvial loam, that they have shipped down to this (the lower) estate.

And right good reason I have personally to be dissatisfied with the dressing. For just a week since, indulging in a matutinal digestive cheroot, there caught my eye the dark form in the distance of a colt lying somewhat more heap-like on the hillside than suited my idea of repose. Hailing the gardener, who was busy with the rhododendron bushes close by, I inquired his opinion. "Heigh!—Hurroo there!" he shouted— with a power of stentorian lungs that I quite envied —by way of awakening the animal rather than replying to his master. And, sure enough, it raised its head thereat, but painfully and appealingly, it struck me. "Him be only sleeping in the sun—I seed 'em ever so many times so. Him be only a gammoning."

However, as I am not wont to be quite so easy in my mind as that, I desired his attendance on a visit to the suspected. It was as my fears augured. We found a pet pony, that had carried the blue riband in a competition of thirty, all broken out into a sweat, and trembling violently, while ever and anon she cast an anxious imploring glance towards her flank. Colic, methinks, or inflammation. "Him be bad, sir," broke in our estimable melon-shaped servitor; "well, I'd

F

never have noticed him." Of course you wouldn't,
methought, but didn't say, as he is excellent in his
place, and has no charge of the live stock ; but why
did not the labourer who feeds them notice something
wrong ? But there's no use talking or reflecting on
this point. Of course if he did he wouldn't be a
labourer on twelve shillings a week. That's all I have
to conclude. However, we stir her, and she rises. We
lead her home, and dose her for colic, the symptoms of
which presented themselves. But she was a pet, and
so we did not trust our private medical treatment, but
dispatched a messenger for a "vet." of considerable
local reputation. He pronounces it "a stoppage," and
dealt with her accordingly. She rolled and groaned,
and was no way relieved the livelong day. Two faithful fellows sat up the night beside her. At midnight
I saw her apparently no better, and as yet not relieved
by action of the medicine. At six I get a glad message
from the bailiff that the desired movement had taken
place, and that the filly was decidedly better. I see
her at eight, and find her standing with water running
from her mouth. She laid her head affectionately
against me, as if to ask, "Can you not relieve me ?—
I do feel so bad." But, after some petting, I had to go,
and, on my return at twelve, expecting to see her a
trifle brighter, I found her in the box, laid out cold and
stiff, and the attendants gone. She had fallen and
died almost the moment I had left her. And this was
all from her breaking out in a fit of high spirits from
her proper pasture to a meadow, which, left with a long
coating of autumnal grass, had got thickly strewn with
this pestilent sand from the river's overflow, and which
had lodged heavily on the poor creature's stomach.

I did not before know the risk of leaving long grass upon the fields that the waters invade. It seems that it is, however, no unfrequent cause of death in this district, especially in the case of sheep and kine.

But there's no use crying for shed milk—we must make the money up somehow—by cutting off the beer, or the French plums, or the bonnets, or somehow. To change the sad subject, let me remark, as an old tutor, that children cannot be taught the modern languages too soon. French, Italian, and German, they should learn almost from infancy, if they are to learn them at all, when the elastic organs of speech can modulate unerringly each syllable, and the ear is quick as accurate in catching sound. But, unfortunately, the fry don't appreciate these advantages, and, moreover, are difficult for foreigners to manage. So, as a last resource parentally, we offer a prize for him or her who shall earliest learn to speak the most French. Even as we write, behold a result. A six-year-old Pickle, who has been allowed by request to spend an hour in pappy's study, and has been reclining upon the sofa, apparently in a state of brew, for some time—an indication, we trust, of future authorship—breaks out at last in a tone of weariness that is intended for our ear, while he would affect that it was not either : "*Ah! cher moi !*"—the obvious translation of which is, "Oh! dear me!" and the only parallel to which we know is the Frenchman's rendering of the Shakespearian "So woe-begone"—"*Si triste allez-vous en.*" But there is another anxious youth just come up to report progress— the lad that has the charge of our shorthorns and sheep. He is "consternated " by the daylight vision of a fine fox seen twice yesterday crossing a field, where our earliest Jonas-Webb Down lambs are billeted with their mothers. This comes of living under a gorse-covered hill upon the verge of a forest, which the county hounds don't care to visit. This must be the Reynard that I too charitably allowed to pass unchallenged a month since, when stationed at an advanced post in a cover which was being beaten for pheasants.

I was half-inclined to let drive at the red robber when he trotted so confidently and listeningly along the main path, within thirty yards of the keeper's house, and close beneath my lair. "Ah! would you ?" " Vulpecide!" &c., &c. Oh ! yes, I hear; but if the region be such that hounds cannot hunt it, and your ducks and chickens go, why, what then ? But we won't discuss it, for we have hunted ourselves, and we know the arguments of old, and have let thus much drop, just for fun, to disturb any chance venatic reader. Upon the snow we could trace the villains close around the house and buildings, and yet we abstained even from dropping a ham-bone in their way—a *bonne bouche* which as certainly promotes their disappearance, as a meal of salt meat will make a monkey gnaw his tail.

But writing of stratagems reminds me that the poachers are about after the pheasants, to be disposed of for breeding purposes, and this obliges an incessant look-out. The most favourite modes of taking them in this district are by catching their necks in a noose—a knot on which prevents its being drawn too tight ; or by strewing grain that has been soaked in spirits in their runs, and then arresting them under intoxication ; or, the third way, by scattering tick-beans about, each one strung upon a bristle—the effect of which is that the unhappy bird, unable to swallow the berry, owing to the bristles projecting out on each side his beak, falls ultimately, gasping, an exhausted easy prey for the concealed poacher, who then just draws the bean back by the bristle ends, and has an affrighted but uninjured prize.

Yesterday—blessed day that it was for man, bird, and beast—there was such a number of the hens running coyly about the shrubberies, with a mate or lover gorgeously plumaged in attendance, as though upon the look-out for lodgings. So warm, so deliciously April-like was the air, only wanting the perfume of later spring. The speckled thrush hopped in and out, too, amidst the ivy-leaves, and the nuthatch was busy upon the bark of the willow, where they annually breed. Ever and anon a splendid salmon leaped out upon the reach below the house, making one long for the expiration of the current fence month, so gaily glancing back to his dark home, his path being quite visible under the surface by a line of silvery sheen. The bees, too, awoke, filling the greenhouse with quite a lively, sociable buzz of industrious occupation.

Talking of industry, I am reminded that co-operation between employer and employed is the order of the day. As it affects us—the question being, How can it be adopted upon a farm ? In two instances it answers certainly well, and I should be glad to learn how the system could be extended further. Being a good deal given to exhibiting at shows, I have found it to my advantage, as Joseph Ady would say, to share the occasional success with those who have the care and keeping of the stock exhibited. Instead, then, of a traditional half-sovereign, I have adopted the plan of insuring the cowman's life, so that he shall receive £150 when he is sixty years of age; while, in the event of his death before that period, his family will reap the benefit at once. I allow him to exhibit—retaining just an ultimate voice—what he pleases, but without waste, as I ascertain for myself from the corn and cake book. The policy premiums annually he must pay from money won as prizes, or, that being insufficient, out of his private pocket. The consequence is that my stock is always in excellent condition, and the prizes taken make a good slice.

Another extension of this principle to the affairs of the farm is to make a pig at Christmas a part of the bailiff's wages—the least of the fattening pigs. The obvious consequence of this will be that he takes care that the whole lot are made as big as they can be. And, now, sir, for your story. I shall be much obliged to any gentle reader for a hint as to further use of this belauded system.

My bailiff and an assistant labourer have been busy the livelong day in renewing the pile of heaped-up brushwood beside the pool, where our pet wild-ducks make their nests every year; and I am glad to say that the dear, grateful little creatures show an evident and admiring appreciation of the service. There have been a series of graceful minuets upon the water, the sober-tinted matron bowing coyly to her mate, who bowed again. One or two, moreover, I have seen attended, clearly, by fond swain, affectedly inspecting the interior of the dead-leaf-carpeted recesses between the twisted tree trunks that were laid to keep the mass of superincumbent hedge-clippings from pressing quite to the ground—inspecting, as engaged young ladies might a block of houses, with an earnest quasi-business air that they believe to be profoundly effective,

but the main issue of which is not that they succeed
in attaining any great bargain over shrewd landlord or
demure landlady, but that they impress the future
spouse with their exceeding power of connubial
economical management.

I am quite longing for the arrival again of the
delicious spring mornings, when we shall see once
more the lively little black broods sailing after their
proud parents right down into the jaws of the narrow
channel, where we shall whip them out with a landing
net, to be brought up by a foster mother within doors ;
their mamma proceeding, after a few days' widowhood,
and sundry excited splashing gyrations, to refit her
downy nest amidst the thorns.

Our impertinent friend, the fox, is so persevering in
his visits to the homestead that we shall have to chain
a terrier close beside this settlement, and only hope
that Reynard may not come to appreciate the exact
value of the chain, and so despoil us after all.

By the way, there has been another fox brought to
grief the last week amidst the crags across the river—
a human fox, whose incessant and omnivorous depreda-
tions have for some time annoyed the neighbourhood,
successfully baffling discovery. His habitation was a
small cottage, pitched under shelter of a long beetling
range of picturesque inaccessible rocks, with the boiling
river just below, and with no ferry but their own boat,
for a long distance. The consequence was that their
family were at once aware of any alarm, and had time
to make things safe. However, it came about, last
week, that his master, a neighbouring farmer, who had
long been wearied by the continual mysterious disappearance of multifarious articles, boiled fairly over

on finding a fat sheep missing from his fold. Suspicion
pointed, and the police managed with difficulty to
circumvent the stronghold, where they found, not the
lost mutton, but two whole cartloads of stolen property—wool, wheat, tools, oats, barley, sacks, &c.,—a
hoard that must have been accumulating for months, if
not years. We ourselves lost, last year, during the hay
harvest, when all hands were busy at a distance, a
mountain wether and a ewe that were fattening for
home consumption on the field just opposite this depre-
dator's den, to which at the time we vainly sought a
clue. That hill-side, so lovely in the sight of the
tourist, with its hanging, ivied, castellated rocks, where
the jackdaw and the hawk tribe haunt its soft brown
beech coppice and nut covert, is unhappily dotted over
with the small freehold cottages and garden plots of
" squatters," a most lawless set, that are the terror of
all respectable people within reach. These " forest "
fellows are up to anything, from banding to poach
pheasants, to burning down the buildings of any
gentleman who may object and dare to convict them.
Only this afternoon I observed in the distance an old
fellow in a smock, sitting on a rail where he should not
have been, and not sleeping very sound either. I at
once took up my glass and read distinctly off every
lineament of his precious countenance, as it changed
under the evident quick workings of a not over-com-
fortable conscience. At last, clearly deeming it to be
all serene, he slipped stealthily off, and along under
cover of a hedge between him and the house, stopping
ever and anon as if to examine a snare. Ourselves, we
slip down too upon the lawn, and along an orchard
slope, and through the chestnut avenue, until we attain

a hollow beech tree, within which escreened we direct
our glass upon his movements at easy rifle range.   I
would not have had his feelings for something, so
guiltily restless were his glance and movements.   At
last we fancy we can distinctly observe him setting a
snare in our fence, although he stands upon a neighbour's ground.   No—he has been watching someone
on tiptoe.   Now, what does he ?   He is busy twisting a
hazel rod, with an astonishing amount of handiness
and exertion for so old a craftsman.   Then he steals on
—Ha, ha! we see ; and we are out of our sentry box
and across the meadow before he turns, to be aghast :
just caught in time before he could commit himself by
appropriating a load of newly stacked cord-wood beside
some trees that have been felled.   I didn't envy him
his feelings on the occasion, nor did I spare my threats,
to his infinite consternation.   " By goby, him be cotched
well," observed our plethoric friend the gardener, in
confidence to the missus ; "him's not a going to be
searching maister's ground again in a hurry."

This reminds me of a clever mode of arresting three
poachers single-handed, which I learnt from an old
friend, a distinguished county chief-constable, a sports-
man also of the first water, to whose harriers I used to
whip-in as a lad in the holidays, on those wild North
Welsh darling hills, with their miles of turf-gallop,
interrupted only by just jolly low stone walls and dykes
—now, alas! being gradually enclosed for cultivation.
At once seize the nearest, and handcuff him around a
sapling.   The others will run—catch the first, slit down
his trousers before and behind with your knife, and cut
off his braces ; then make after the third, whom, if
reached, handcuff also to embrace a sapling oak.   You

may then readily get up with the owner of the disabled raiment, because you will find he cannot run fast holding up his things, and he is averse, as much to meeting the briars *sans culottes*, as on the other hand he is too much attached to his vestments to leave them behind : lead him off to a safe place, with or without admonition by the way as your taste and judgment may direct, and return with help to release and secure the other pair.

Well, our young French scholar has been trying it on again. All conversation in English during meals being prohibited to the boy, under a fine, there was distress one day, on the appearance of a novel pudding, upon which cook had tried her 'prentice hand, and upon the ingredients of which of course they must needs speculate. "*Du fromage*," remarks one ; "*Et du beurre*," interjects another ; "*Et du sucre—et du lait*," adds quickly a third ; "*Avec toute suite*," with philosophic gravity chimes in our juvenile : which phrase, upon his being called upon to explain, he interpreted to mean "with preserves." Having that morning heard "*tout de suite*" in the schoolroom, from native predilection he had straightway translated it to mean "all sorts of sweets ;" and being hard up for the appropriate rendering of *jam*, he gave his generic idea of it in what he conceived to be unimpeachable Parisian. A fair equivalent for which I remember a friend of mine at Oxford, who was fonder of his hounds at home than the pursuit of classic lore in the University, inventing, when hard up in the school for the Latin of *pan*. "*In re aliquá*," he bravely wrote, with more self-congratulation than clearness of meaning.

But to return from literature to the purely agricultural. I am determined to breed no more horses—at least until Mr. F. Buckland can persuade the nation to partake of horse-steak; in which case I expect there would be more horses bred, and so a better field for selection; when the screws could be made into soup, to which no suspicion could attach, as does to the dark details of the Mugby Junction mixture. At present it is too much of a lottery. You don't know what you may get; and when you do get a nice one, it either dies of unjustifiable inflammation, or, as did a good four-year-old of mine lately, jumps too pluckily at a monster fence, slips on the frozen bank, comes down with his eye upon a hedge-stake, and is brought home literally at half-price. Heigh-ho for horseflesh! Writing of Mr. Buckland, I wonder he does not give us, in his amusing paper *Land and Water*, a description of his swallowing a young frog, to which experiment he was induced by seeing some rustic Arabs do it by the village pool. The moments preceding execution I remember his describing as being so fearfully long. "I thought he'd (from his position on the Professor's lingual ornament) never jump," was his description of his uncoveted experience.

This fine weather has enabled us to get the oats sown in good season, as the expression is. We only hope that the price of this cereal may continue at its present elevated pitch. Our difficult, rough, side-lands may then give us a fair return for what their tedious cultivation costs.

There is a noisy conclave among the rooks this morning. The resolutions before the house must be interesting. They have been wheeling in the air for some time, filing off in the far distance until quite undiscernible by the naked eye; then coming back in shoals

full drive, before you could turn about or whistle, to
settle down, thick as currants in a Christmas-pudding,
upon the tall beech-trees right opposite my neighbour's
fallow, who marches about, gun in hand, in evident
apprehension, behind the drill that is depositing wheat,
not a whit grateful for all the good they did him,
picking up the larvæ, while the ground was being
ploughed, but only anxious to pot them vengefully,
wholesale, now ; of which beneficent intention they are,
however, sufficiently aware, and so they look on list-
lessly during the pauses of their debate, ever and anon,
with a sweep, uprising, should he discharge his weapon,
again to wheel, advance, retire, as though

> " Forming swiftly in the ranks of war."

To-morrow, at sunrise, my good friend, shall be the
retributive foray.   Now they will not spare you, as they
might have done had your ingratitude been less transparent.   Have your supper light, then let your night-
cap orders be :

> " You must wake, and call me early ; call me early, shepherd dear !
> To-morrow 'll be the plaguiest time of all the glad new year."

Shall we, or shall we not ? that is the question.
Well, the fact is, there has occurred another great
invasion of moles, not a whit the less, apparently, for
the subtraction of the lot we paid some coppers a-head
last spring, to see strung upon a willow wand.   I very
much doubt whether we shall take any measures against
them at all this season.   Their runs are certainly detri-
mental to the light-soil meadows hereabouts ; but, on
the other hand, you cannot kick over one of their
mounds, without finding within the crustaceous *débris*
of many a mischievous grub.

What a number of Short-horn sales appear on the
horizon! Whatever will the upshot be? what the
average of Mr. Bett's herd, or the Marquis of Exeter's
celebrated stock? Shall the furious fighting of Towneley
be repeated? or a determined, earnest bidding, as
under the pouring rain at Fawsley? Certain it is that
the fountain-heads of the purest blood must be kept
untainted, wherefrom to replenish and repair the
weaker springs and compound mixtures of the ordinary
farmyard herd. Yes; and there is chivalry in England
to do it. The purest high-born families of the Shorthorn are now as interesting and valuable as most
blood-horse stock; while the love of them is as deeply
ingrained in the hearts of their many agricultural and
aristocratic admirers, as is the love of cricket in the
affections of the English nation at large. Shortly we
shall see. It is a turning-point in the tide of pedigree-
herds, of which we anticipate a golden issue.

May, 1867.

WELL, I have about made up my mind respecting the
moles. My bailiff informs me that an excellent hunter
has offered to keep our invasion down for a halfpenny
an acre, if I will supply him with new traps. This
looked so much like a trap for myself, that I have
informed mine excellent helpmate, who is not a 'coon
of the first water, that we will let the host alone, and
study consequences with a view to future action. One
fresh line of hillocks I noticed yesterday, thrown up
across a wheat-field put in after clover ley. They cross
the brow, however, where I have noticed the plants
look feeble for some time past, so that I have hopes

they mean me real service, especially as the rooks begin
to settle on the same tract too.

Our birds, bar blackbirds, which after repeated expostulation I have allowed the gardener to wage war
on, not altogether so reluctantly either, as they have
to my mind a sneaking element in their disposition;
always haunting the low branches of the bushes, mis-
trusting one's approach more than any other of the
feathered tribes, and not only that, but screaming an
alarm to the whole neighbourhood as they start off
through the brushwood—our birds, I say, selves and
nests, we religiously spare, only trusting that we may
not be ultimately disappointed of the benefit they are
said to work by the extermination of the insect hordes.
Our cocks and hens about the homestead are a nuisance
upon all fields but the pasture.   They have such an
aptitude not only to scratch and roll where they
needn't, but to nip off the green seedlings, turnip,
cabbage, &c., as soon as they appear above the surface.   I cannot comprehend how Mr. Mechi finds them
do him such striking service as he says they do.

The mention of seedlings brings to my mind a curious
circumstance related to me lately by a clergyman who is
successful in gardening.   Last autumn he cut down the
stalks of a bed of Jerusalem artichokes, and threw
them at random upon the rubbish heap.   The other
day, having occasion to excavate the lower strata of
that deposit for stuff wherewith to condiment a flower-
bed, on removing the undecayed artichoke stems, he
found to his astonishment a tiny bulb attached to every
joint of the stem.   One knows that once planted this
root is difficult to exterminate, but it was a wrinkle to
find that the plant had such extraordinary reproductive

power, which one might be thankful to find belonging to some other orders of vegetable.

"Never heared of sich a thing afore," was the simple commentary of our pumpkin-shaped gardener; an occasion which I took care to improve by remarking, "I'll tell you what it is, old fellow—this ought to be a caution to you when you get an extra suck of cider at the hay harvest and get snoosing under a cock : I shouldn't wonder if you were to get up, some day, with a new-born brat hanging from every joint, knee and elbow—an accession of fortune that neither you nor the parish might be thankful for; so just accept the moral, and don't slumber during working hours, harvest time, or otherwise; for I expect that bass-matting in the tool-house may have an especial tendency to promote such an undesirable growth if reclined on of a wet day, the more so too if a pipe give additional forcing heat to your system."

It was an opportunity of reminding him that (whether he indulges so or no) his master is up to a trick or two —a conviction which we trust may spread its beneficial influence throughout one's dependent people.

This same old ally informs me that Jerusalem artichokes "bean't of no manner of use for pigs ; him have tried 'em ever so many times, raw and biled, but the monkeys moots 'em out." I listen, as of duty bound, to mine faithful help, but notwithstanding resolve inwardly that I shall adhere to my purpose of planting a rough arable hill-side (too sandy to make a pasture) with this same esculent, which requires so little cultivation, and I will see whether we cannot induce in our porcine possessions the same delighted appreciation that one has of them oneself upon the dinner-table, and be content that in the interval he should deem me, as he doubtless will for my pains, a Jerusalem pony.

Our hill-side tract it is not all fun to cultivate. Some parts, all rough with boulders of a kind of pudding-stone—a conglomerate, hard as iron, of semi-opaque pebbles, out of which are wrought the cider-millstones of the country, we resign to the gorse and fern, being thankful for the game they shelter during shooting season. Delightful is it to sit there of a summer evening, cheroot alight, upon one of these blocks—which once formed the bed of the ocean, and are now upheaved to be the highest ridge of the district, commanding a full view of the whole farm—and watch the tints, various as hues of the dying dolphin, reflected upon the level reaches of our lovely Wye.

Other upland patches afford nice picking for the flock, but not such as one meets with on the wild Welsh hills. It is in the very centre of one of these that there bursts out the eye of a spring (as the Greek and Welsh so beautifully term it), " clear as crystal and cold as charity." Close beside it is the twisted stem of an antique wild crab-tree, under which we propose to erect shortly a grotto, and just beyond a hazel copse, on which we gathered last season some bushels of the sweetest nuts.

The spring itself we shall utilize as follows: First and foremost it will deliver its sparkling jet, fresh filtered from the internal cavern of its birth, into a circular basin of rough-hewn forest stone, from which the drinking supply of the house will be fetched. [As regards this, I must record one friend's remark, " Faith, it's a beautiful liquor ; a bottle of it sealed would last

one a life-time."] The basin's overflow will feed a
shallow reservoir, cemented and gravel-strewn, with an
occasional deep hollow upon which will be piled a few
irregular pieces of rock, so as to afford shelter to the
fish, of which a regular supply will be kept for the use
of the house, being constantly replenished by netting
the river-pool below. This reservoir there will adjoin a
flat bed of the crisp brown-leaved watercress, escaping
from which the exhausted current will be allowed to
soak indolently into the turf of a winding gully, to
be planted with willows as a pleasure-ground for the
pheasants.

The period of enjoyment in this summer-house seems,
however, just now a long way off, while we contemplate
the deep snow-carpet so suddenly spread, and listen to
the wind so discontentedly howling at every crevice.
Comfort now for the stock is only in the sheds and
boxes, which, all fresh laid with sweet straw and fern,
quite realise one's idea of brute creature enjoyment,
To leave the poor things cramped up and shivering
upon the fields were, one might fancy, the height of
cruelty. The wild breeds on their unrestricted feeding-
grounds find plenty of warm nooks under rock and
tree wherein to spend the dull tedium of such a season;
whereas thoughtless man exposes to the pitiless blast,
between open hurdles, or on a wind-swept, hedgeless
meadow, the flock and herd that he has comparatively
enervated and rendered tender by cultivation. To a
certain degree they may undoubtedly be habituated to
exposure, but it is anyhow waste, seeing how warmth
conduces to fattening.

Habit—what a thing it is! There is nothing like
being used to it, as my charming sister-in-law remarked

G

the other day, on coming down to welcome our party,
with a face beaming more than even usually bright
from the exertion, as she explained, of tearing up strips
of calico by her baby's ear, because it started at the
sound of an accidental rip. By dint of this same habit,
I was once enabled to discover the delinquency of a
groom, who, first-rate hand when he chose, unhappily
did not often choose, and, who having fallen into the
service of an epicurean, soon began to give sundry
symptoms of neglecting his work. After he left me I
found that at a previous place (how is it that, like
Parisina's maidens, so few will help you in time of need
with a hint ? whereas, after the catastrophe, they one
and all overflow abundantly with, "Ah ! that's just
what I expected !" "I knew that would be the case !"
&c., &c.)—however, to return, I found that this fine
fellow, being in the service of a Cheltenham dowager,
used to clean only the side of the carriage that was
next to the door as he drew up. To return further :
suspecting him of being addicted to lift his little finger,
one summer evening I rode slowly along highway and
byeway by every neighbouring public, soon detecting
his various haunts by the deliberate stand my thorough-
bred made against the passage to the cider-tap. When
I had consolidated the charge sufficiently to bring it
home, he was, I heard subsequently, much puzzled to
know how I could have gained my information so accu-
rately, and would doubtless, had he had the chance,
have wreaked his vengeance on the dumb detective.

As I was watching some peas being put in, the other
day, a smarting hailstorm and heavy wet came on,
which sent me quickly under a tree and my umbrella,
despite the supposed hardening with which one's

matutinal cold-bath is credited. Meanwhile, there stood, calmly watching the operation, a young broad-built son of our village Vulcan, who has not seen his sixth birthday yet, notwithstanding the chill rain-pour, without a symptom of uneasiness. I almost think the rain never pierced his raiment, scant as it was. The soul of fire he inherits may possibly have helped his endurance, multiplying or neutralising—which you please—the usual effect of a driving sleet-shower. Blessed habit again, methought!

How deep again lies the vein of early attachment to agricultural affairs. This last week only I have spent long happy fleeting hours in the company of one who is now a distinguished dignitary of the Church of England, and an earnest promoter of all that is good and charitable. He can number seventy winters in the snow upon his head ; yet there are few young members of his profession who could outstrip him in energetic beneficial service to his fellow-creatures. Now, in the intervals of work, there is nothing he prefers by way of relaxation to a talk about shorthorns—a small, but goodly herd of which he reared at the period when Mr. Berry and Mr. Bates were at their zenith, his anecdotes of conversation with whom are as entertaining as instructive ; as are also his comments upon the forefathers of our stock—Belvedere, Pilot, &c., a small volume of which I deemed it worth while to note down at his lips. How delighted he was too to scan and discuss the points of the type of cow that I have selected as my model.

I had with me a portfolio of clever and singularly truthful sketches in oil, done by my friend, Mr. E. Corbet, which I always carry about with me by way of consolation when from home. It is a plan I commend to my shorthorn brethren, for the twofold reason that they will like to look back in years to come upon the materials of which they so carefully compounded their herd, while again it will be a public benefit to have attainable for study the lineaments of many a famous ancestress otherwise known only through the written record of her pedigree. We would most of us subscribe heartily, I doubt not, could we obtain a pictorial idea of the early celebrities—Sockburn Sall, &c.—so very few of whom are to be found in the *Farmers' Magazine* or *Herd Book*.

Right glad am I to hear that Mr. Carr is going to give us an enlarged reprint of his essays on the Booth sort. Would that some competent person would compile a clear reliable account of the other great breeder's experiments and experience.

Did I not, in my last, register my determination that I would breed no more horses ? Yet, what shall I do herein ? I have just had returned by a friend, who has hunted her the past winter, one of the grandest timber-jumpers in England (her grandam by Touch-stone, too), lame—quite lame. I am tempted to cross her with the Stockwell blood, and make her pay her way by work upon the farm. Foolish I feel I am ; but what can one do with a pet of wide celebrity for her performances in the hunting field ? And am I not con-vinced, moreover, after repeated trial, that, too gene-rally, half-bred horses are useless upon a farm, unless they be considerably advanced in years, and you can put them under the care of a regular, good, steady, intelligent fellow, who will never leave them standing by themselves in the plough or cart ? The risk attend-

ing their use greatly exceeds any advantage their speed
may give. To suit the ordinary labourer, you must
have the regular plough-horse as fast walking as you
can obtain, but there must be no galloping or impulse
to start off in him. The fellows who can manage
spirited horses at agricultural operations are usually
of a sort that should not be on a farm at all, if they
had given their skill, head, and ability a fair chance.
Should you find them after a team, sadly be it stated,
there is too often reason to suspect a penchant for
public-house entertainment, a course of which some
day or other mischief will inevitably come. One good
smash of cart and frightened horse takes the gilding
off a long slice of farm work. A big or broken knee, a
disabled vehicle, and shivered gate (if not worse), nay,
even the anticipation of such misadventure, yields too
many a pang of discomfort for the wise to adopt the use
of such a team. But then, no one is wise at all hours,
the Latin grammar teaches; and in regard to this
grand mare, one feels an unwise wavering of purpose.

"What do you advise?" asked a young officer the
other day (an old friend and pupil) : "I am thinking
of getting married." "*Don't* by any means ; think of
the horrors of a wedded life in a marching regiment,
seeing that you are not a man of fortune." "Oh! but
she's such a nice young girl," he replied, with evident
disappointment at my counsel. "Very well, then ; do."
And I sent him away delighted ; and to say truth,
I don't think he did so badly after all. But we are off
the rails. Is it do or don't, as regards this favourite
huntress? Time alone can show.

Alack-a-day! the morning hath returned, and with
it a new unrelenting fall of snow. There is nothing

for it but steadily to forge our way onward in its teeth,
foddering and littering without stint. But we are in
for a misfortune, I fear. The bailiff just informs me
that our pet of all the pet herd, a short-legged, square-
built, but most elegant cow, bred by Sir Charles
Knightley, and possessing in a high degree the characteristics he aimed at—the breadth of back, the shoulder
sloping as that of a race-horse, the small refined head,
broad-browed, with short, flat, waxy horn—shows symptoms of being burdened with a dead calf: that calf
which, if a bull, we had intended to be the father of a
future generation. Every care has been taken of her
during gestation. She is within a fortnight of her
regular time, and has milk in her udder; but the signs
that present themselves are unfavourable. We can
only hope.

Bad cess to the period! Again there is sorrow and
consternation through the household. A favourite half-
Angora cat (a property of the nursery) is brought in
with both fore-legs smashed in a vermin trap, a fate we
have ourselves been long anticipating, inasmuch as my
lady had begun to be neglectful of her household duties,
and to go a-gipsying. There was nothing for it, but to
put an end to her misery. Her habit of lapping up the
milk with which the children supplied her was peculiar.
Instead of applying her tongue directly to the surface,
she dipped her paws in the dish, and then sucked the
same with very much the air wherewith Augustus
smoothes and twists his moustache. Of our crops we
can say nothing, as they are simply out of sight. But
here comes an old friend, one of Wellington's aides-de-
camp at Waterloo, trudging over the snow, to have a
game of billiards, with slippers in his pocket, but

nothing on his feet but two pair of woollen socks, which keep them dry and warm, a dodge he learnt in Canada.

June, 1867.

WELL, it's over now; but it was a sad job! Two fine bull-calves, one a rich roan, had to be taken away from the Sir Charles Knightley's cow piecemeal, being locked in an inextricable embrace. Luckily we have saved the mother, but it is questionable whether she will be of any use as a breeder again. So it is that, if disposed to be sad, as I am now—having got up very early to finish off some writing—one might exclaim with Moore,

> " Oh, ever thus from childhood's hour
> I've seen my fondest hopes decay."
>   *   *   *   *
> " But when it came to know me well
> And love me, it was sure to die."

It is a bright sharp morning, and the birds are very busy arranging for the wedding. I see, however, that a pair of starlings have taken violent possession of the hole in the willow where our friend the nuthatch has annually reared its youthful family. This cannot be allowed; but how to set matters straight is the question, without shooting the enemy, which certainly must not be done. We'll try what pulling out the cradle continually will effect.

I see my neighbour's hopeful returning from an early walk with a victim in his mole-trap. He will not believe me that the glossy little fellow could do him any service, " Him was a mooting up the clover; " and now him will have to be skinned to make a purse for our young acquaintance's occasional halfpenny.

Poor little Vic got into a trap yesterday. She was wise enough thereupon to raise a loud lament, which drew the children down to the spot at once. Since she usually canters after them on three legs, it will not much matter to her, except that she cannot change the favoured foot as she is wont to do, being a thrifty matron and given to saving shoe-leather. One cannot explain satisfactorily to her that she ought not to interfere with the gardener's traps, as her nose leads her involuntarily along the rabbit's track. Luckily there was a good deal of moss strewed upon the teeth, which eased the pinch. She never said a word about it, I noticed, when she was lifted into the box where her puppies are. What a constant source of delight the fat little fellows are to the children upon the lawn after school! They straddle along and bark so affectedly in their feeble cracky way, while the fond mamma looks on approvingly, wagging her tail in perfect confidence. She is wary enough, however, in her generation. She has doubtless discovered that it is worth her while being civil, inasmuch as many are the tit-bits she gets quietly dropped to her at the nursery breakfast. She seems thoroughly devoted to them in consequence, and follows them everywhere; whereas to ourselves or any grown person she gives plenty of sea room. As there is a goodly pack of her descendants now, I hear some talk of a hunt to be organized, the trail of a red herring being led over some fences and a part of the common. Who started the idea? I don't know. I only know that our young French student charged a deep, narrow, muddy ditch the other day, on the old Shetland pony. She being, however, too wise to shake her joints, the youngster took an involuntary header over her into the

mire, out of which he scrambled shivering and all but
in tears. Cry, however, he did not, at the remonstrance of his indignant elder brother, who immediately
remounted the wee one, and sent them over flying, with
a circus flourish of his hunting-whip that consternated
dame Shetland, and drew the sun out after tears on the
jockey's triumphant April face.

Well, it's busy with the "taties" we are upon the
Farm. Of this inestimable esculent last year we grew
about double as many bushels as I expected to use ;
but, owing to an attack of dry rot, the ranks have been
so fearfully thinned that we shall barely have enough
left for seed. Potatoes in every shape and guise—
potatoes roasted, potatoes boiled, potatoes in their
jackets, and potatoes peeled—they are a delicious food
altogether ; and reader, gentle reader, did ye ever taste
them in combination with butter-milk ? Oh ! it makes
my teeth water at this early hour of the morning, to
think of it. If ye have not, then order in a snow-white
bowl and a jug of the precious drink. Then peel the
ragged jacket of a mealy specimen, and smash it up
with your spoon in the basin. Then pour in a small
quantity of milk, just enough to cool the vegetable ; in
a second or two again pour on a lot, and then peg in.
Oh ! the delicious sensation, passing description, with
which a cool spoonful with its potato-island passes down
the thirsty throat ! Oh ! then for the gullet of a crane,
as that party mentioned by Aristotle wished, to prolong
the happy taste ! There is but one drawback—it is
a very bilious food ; but there is a way of meeting this
difficulty. For about a fortnight you may indulge
yourself with this diet, but then possibly a headache
may loom in the distance. The way we do is, on the

thirteenth day we take a dinner-pill, and start afresh.
That's what our Yankee friends term "licking natur'."
The butter-milk must be made by churning milk and
cream together.   When the cream only is churned, it
is too oily and rich.   On a wild Welsh mountain-side
how often have we made thereof a repast a king might
covet, followed by a slice of barley-bread, all thickly
coated with the sweet golden butter the glen-grass
yields, when one has spent the morning fishing all too
fruitlessly upon the sunny tarn.

Halloa, there! there are half-a-dozen wild pigeons
busy picking up the peas I had strewn for the pheasant-
hens which are building underneath the laurels beside
the drive.   Their turn will come, however, ere long.
Every spring we secure a large wire-house full of the
young ones, which grow very fat in confinement, and are
ready at any time to furnish a *recherché* dish when a
friend drops in.   The way we manage is thus : Having
found a number of nests, we tie one leg each of the·
young pair, passing the string through and under the
nest.   Thus fettered the old birds will continue to feed
their offspring until they are full-feathered, when the
tree is scaled and we transport them to their new
quarters.

I see a prediction in *Land and Water*, respecting
some river, that the coarse fish-supplies may be short-
ened this year owing to the floods ; the spawning fish
having miscalculated and laid their spawn upon the
meadows, where it will perish when the waters recede.
We have been interested in the overflow of our noble
Wye, having indulged a fond hope that a stray salmon
or two returning home during latch-key hours might
have got stuck in an unexpected fence.   As yet our

anticipation has not been gratified, although last winter
a fine fellow of about 9lbs. weight was found embedded
in the ice, in a gutter upon the meadow, to which he
had retired probably in the condition in which Sheridan
was found, when with " unerring instinct " he gave the
name of Wilberforce to the watchman that disturbed
his damp slumber. This fish was in good condition,
and was eaten by a labourer's family. At some period
of his existence he had been indulged with a charge of
shot, which had spotted him smartly.

Local experience is of vast value to every farmer. Of
course it is not to be supposed but that the tide of ages,
in its ebb and flow, has left a deposit of various quality
upon the minds of different districts. Last autumn we
recorded our intention to leave the clover-plant after
harvest unfed, expecting thereby to have a superior
spring show to our neighbours', whose practice it is to
gnaw the crop right into its heart, with sheep and even
horses turned on to pasture. Their argument is, that
they cannot get the light soil sufficiently firm otherwise. I hoped that a good rolling would effect this
sufficiently. I see now, however, that their maltreated
fields are, as regards thickness of root, although not
forwardness of growth, far in advance of mine, and yet
my land was well dressed.

One more wrinkle for my note-book. I see the rooks
have fastened upon a beech-tree before my window,
from which they are snapping off twigs with their
strong bills, for architectural use in the tall oak beyond. I fear that beech is destined, or it would not be
so brittle. It is curious that several of our finest
beeches have died during the last eighteen months.
There has prevailed some unpropitious influence—the

fat gardener attributes it to some frost he recollects. I see some authorities write of whole plantations dying off, and attribute it to "an electrical or pestilential blast." It must have been the comet, I conclude. I wish he'd fold his tail a little closer the next time he approaches our earth. By the way, what can be the language of the brutes? Last week the young terriers had two joints each severed from their tail point. The first one operated on yelped a wee trifle as he felt the incision, but sadly, as the executioner applied a touch of lunar caustic to help the healing of the wound. The next brother tightly folded his tail between his legs underneath him on being brought out, as the schoolboy spreads his hands to protect the threatened part, having evidently learnt from his brother's voice what was going on. He was pluckier during the pruning, but winced and wailed under the application of the caustic, kindly meant as was the dressing on our part.

Puppy number three was yet more enduring, and only "weeked" once as the lunar was appreciated. The nursery was horror-struck at the mutilation, and stood aghast at the man's recital of the agonies endured, which our careful bailiff judiciously enlarged upon as being the fate, in one way or another, of all naughty children.

Another wrinkle for me, which, as it comes from my better half, I am evidently bound to believe. The room is deliciously perfumed with the lemon scent of a coronella, of which I have despoiled the green-house show. Moved to my room, I found it disappoint me in the paucity of its fragrance. I concluded that it was vexed by its transportation from its bright garden abode to the region of musty books. My wife comes, however, and throws up a window (she is very fond of throwing a light upon the subject; I often expect that, in an excess of misplaced energy, she may some day, inadvertently, of course, make me see a multitude of dancing stars); whereupon immediately out comes the imprisoned delicious sweetness. This is a return for a dodge I taught her, which if you promise to be grateful, gentle reader, I don't mind telling you. It is that you can preserve a bouquet for a long time in its freshness, if you cut off daily the stalk ends and put some camphor in the water. Talking of water, the dissolving snow has carried away cartloads of the surface of one of our sideland fields sown with oats, tearing up extempore channels with reckless force. I hope the oat-seed may prove acceptable to the cray fish in the brook at the bottom.

Another botheration for which we have to thank our light sandy soil is that it works up into the ewes' claws, eating right into the quick with an effect as irritating as unsolicited advice.

Having just strolled around the premises, I have been greeted more than once with a half-playful "If you please, sir, you were before me this morning; but you'll not be again." .I reply, "How is it that whenever I do make one of these forays, I invariably am before you?" Be it confessed, *sub rosâ*, that I do not often make them, preferring, as a rule, to read late into the small hours. An occasional upset of this sort, however, acts medicinally on the men for some time to come.

This lovely April morning the bees are busy amidst flowers in the greenhouse, into which they travel by the open door. Alas! that they know not how to stoop so as to get out again the way they entered! "Them fills theirselves so much, them forgets the road," is the gardener's solution of the difficulty. "I puts out as many as I can, but I finds them continually dead about in heaps." It is a pity that the industrious swarm should suffer so, but whatever should we do? It is time to be painting the boat, which has rested the winter through upon its carriage in the barn. The salmon-fishing licence, price £1, has just arrived; our pools swarm with fish, but they don't often care to take the fly; whether it is that we are too near the sea or not I don't know. They possibly have their baskets of prog along with them, which last them until they reach the upper waters. The greedy old dowagers in their descent take freely enough. But the fresh-run clean fish are mighty daintiful as regards the baits we present for their acceptance.

Owing to the late severe weather, our chickens' coops are a positive workhouse, the surviving individuals of ever so many separate broods having to be clubbed together to make out a charge for a solitary hen. The ducks are not over-industrious, laying an egg now and then, as the whim takes them, while the turkeys have not commenced at all. Geese I never rear, having plenty in the household. I was much amused the other day by the performance of a bantam which I had purchased, being exceedingly tame, from an old woman by the roadside, for the children. One of the little girls was sitting on the grass with the bird in her lap, on a nest of hay, which she had seductively twisted, when lo and behold, after an agony on the bird's part, which the child took for a fit, there was produced a new bright egg. Whether the bird was pleased with the attention paid it, and wished to gratify its mistress, or happened to be caught at the right moment, I cannot say; only what did actually happen, as a faithful historian, I record.

"I'll bet all papa's Shorthorns," uttered in a most indignant tone, was an exclamation that startled me the other morning as I descended from my dressing-room. "And pray what are you going to bet my Short-horns for?" "Oh! papa, only that I could lace my own boots ever since I was five years old." The fact was, there were a pair of them busy putting on their boots, seated on the lowest step of the staircase; and upon our young French friend declaring that he must go and get his laced by the housemaid, who pets him, he got rebuked as above by his more independent sister.

To go on with Shorthorns, however, there was much food for instructive reflection at the sale to which I referred. The herd, numbering some fifty head, con-sisted of very various elements. There were old cows of great value, but very different in appearance, which had been picked up at long figures at some of the cele-brated north-country sales, and which this day the representatives of very eminent breeders had travelled many hundred miles to recover, at whatever cost. There was a grand red bull, bred in Yorkshire, or wonderful style and quality, and meat to the hocks, with the very important defect, however, of being rather short-quartered and high over the tail—a defect inherited by almost every one of his stock, which is one proof more, if such were needed, of the impres-siveness, as regards likeness, of long-descended cattle,

and the necessity of using none but the most symmetrical as sires.   There was a small tribe offered
with most attractive names upon their pedigree, but
exhibiting throughout a marked Ayrshire look, especially about the head.   Generations back, their ancestress was doubtless a cow of that sort.   Murder will
out, and this was an instance of it.   The old lady
must have had a strong character of her own to have
perpetrated it so far down.   The average was about
£50 per head, young and old; which, considering how
many were ancient and profitless both to the butcher
and dairy—how many, again, viewed as ordinary stock,
were worth at most a ten-pound note a-piece—was
surely a paying price.   However, upon this the opinions
of the wise will differ.   The conclusion I arrived at,
and which is confirmed by accumulating experience, is
that any one possessed of an artistic eye for points, and
sufficient capital to keep on a growing herd for some
years, by regular attendance at the distinguished sales,
and uniform use of one stamp of male, may ultimately
bring to the hammer a number of nice things, as like
and level as a handful of beans, and which will yield
him a precious *quid pro quo*,—may, in fact, " make
Shorthorns pay."   By the same rule, if you go in recklessly, and buy, without reference to a particular type,
something of all sorts, as you get a chance, provided
they are of the Bates or Booth sort, you will only have
to lament the low return when you clear out.

What a nuisance these new floods are!   I had
thought that all danger of any more was gone; but
there's no trusting those wild gullies where the Wye
rises; and what rattles down upon us here as merely
a smart April shower will most probably up there be

such a disheartening down-pour as made the mud-pudding in which the Prussian artillery stuck on their way to Waterloo, when the Duke kept looking at his watch every moment, and it was so nearly all up with the hopes of the gallant long-pounded English army.

A week since the water had begun to "fine," and one evening we went down to a famous salmon-run with full fresh paraphernalia, bent on doughty deeds ; but, after an hour spent exposed to a sprightly breeze, we had to return home as darkness fell, without having been indulged with even a sight of a fish, but having caught a violent cold.

Oh! the tortures of that neuralgic night! It was impossible to get a single wink of sleep until I had plastered my temples with a mixture of powdered ginger and whiskey, having applied a strong dab of the same in brown paper to the nape of my neck. It is an excellent remedy, but the ginger must be keen : stale, it is of no use. As regards toothache, it is worth knowing that there are two sorts—the one dependent on cold, the other arising from acidity in a hollow tooth. This latter kind (the toothache of children) may be instantaneously cured by a filling in of carbonate of soda. It is just as well first to cleanse the cavity, and dry it with a pinch of cotton-wool, as a dentist does in preparation for stopping with gold. You may readily know which sort of toothache the patient is suffering from, if you press the pulse tightly at the wrist. The pain being neuralgic, it will be momentarily arrested by the check to the blood's flow ; whereas if it be local toothache, owing to the presence of acidity (late sweetmeats) in the hollow, this squeezing of the artery will not affect the sensation.

II

Reader, gentle reader, it being just after supper, I am lavish of pet receipts; and, having last time told you of the mysteries of that delicious compound, potatoes and buttermilk, to which we poor farmers, in these sad times, must fain so often have recourse, let me now give you a hint of another stunning amalgamation. Upon your plate lay a slice of rich cheese, which pare, and work up to melting mood with your knife, used medical-spatulalike, by help of about one-sixth part of butter. Then, taking the castors in hand, pour out and sprinkle on your product, of the contents of each bottle — vinegar, cayenne, black pepper, Worcester sauce, anchovy, oil, salt, mustard, catsup, and what-else may offer. Beat up and mix well. And the result? Don't ask me, but try. Our teeth are watering already. Try it, my lads, if you never have done; and be thankful to him who has given you the receipt for "crab," or, as some term it, "all-around," from the simple mode in which the source of its excellence, the condimental reservoir, is used.

But we must really get out-of-doors. I shall be glad when the ash-bud bursts, and there is a good sub-stantial bite upon the meadows again. I am thankful that we have an abundance of mangold left, and a good stock of hay—this latter not of the best, however. From a variety of causes, it was allowed to grow too old before it was mown.

It scarcely seems so, but it will soon be a year since a jolly young friend of ours saluted us as follows : "I'll tell you what it is, old fellow—if you don't cut this field soon, you'll just be making toothpicks for your stock, instead of fodder. It will be no better than straw." He was right in a good deal. If one pretends

to make hay, let it be done properly, as all things
should be done, in their turn and place.   But as for his
comparison to straw, I would it might prove no worse !
Why, cut wheat-straw, mixed with pulped roots, and
left to stand awhile, is as good provender as can be—
super-excellent, in fact, if sprinkled with meal and a
wholesome flavouring of salt.

Straw, indeed !   Our youthful adviser can never have
read old Drury's interesting volume, in which he shows
how, if you steep chopped wheaten straw in cold water
for some hours, it will form a jelly, which, mixed with
meal, is most nutritious.   " Anything that makes a
jelly is good," how often have I heard from the lips
of a capital feeder !   Don't abuse the straw, then ;
and what's more, save it a little more rigorously in
your foldyard.

By the way, as regards this, let me give you a
wrinkle which we accidentally obtained, but which
may be deemed serviceable, having met with the decided approbation of more than one distinguished
agriculturist who have lately done us the honour of
inspecting our stock.

All around our cattle-yard we have an open shed ;
but, from shortness of material and hurry, we were
enabled to put a manger along one side only.   The
consequence of this is that on three sides there is
always a dry lair.   The cattle get a habit of standing
about and trampling near the manger, which soon
reduces the ¸bedding beside it, ¸however often fresh-
laid, to a wet mess ; whereas in our yard, by this accidental arrangement, the straw upon three sides lasts
clean and dry a week.

To return, however.   It is certain enough that hay

H 2

from which the seed has fallen is not nearly so nutritious as that on which it was saved half-ripe ; witness
the Australian plan of cutting and drying oats, for
winter use, before the seed is full. *Apropos* of this,
I remember, some years since, visiting the farm of one
of our greatest and most intelligent living agriculturists. He took me, after other sights, to see a batch
of six prize cart-mares, fat as butter, and frolicking
about the fold. At the expression of my exceeding
admiration he smiled, and took me to the corn-bin,
wherein he showed me only grass-seed. Being a
man of substance, and always wide-awake, he gets
many a good bargain such as does not drop into the
mouth of every passer-by.

Grass seeds will not vegetate, as a rule, the second
year. A neighbouring speculator, having been unable
to clear off his stock within the season, was glad to
take what he could get for the surviving store, and
that was, if I remember well, but a shilling the sack.
On this the team fattened—whether profitably or not,
you can calculate, my reader, for yourself.

The gardener is just beginning his noisy, clattering
avocation upon the lawn ; and, as I am in the humour
for revealing pet receipts, let me tell you of another
very useful one, originally discovered by a professor
of chemistry at the University, who took pride in
the improvement of ˌthe˙ fellows' grass-plot. I need
scarcely describe to you that industrious weed which
so persistently disfigures our slopes, to the displace-
ment of fine grasses—the plantain (its name how
suggestive of delicious West Indian breakfasts ! but
its use, so far as I know, in this country being confined to supplying canaries with a change of diet on

its stem of seeds). Having watched for a hot day, cut off the crown, just under the surface, with a sharp, thin knife, and drop a taste of the tincture of iodine upon the bleeding root. The sun must shine upon the execution, or it will take no effect.

How delighted the children are now, every day, upon the advent of either a foal, a hatch of chickens, a calf, or late lamb! How they hop and skip about, and beg it may be theirs, at least in name! The only young thing they don't seem to affect is a litter of pigs; probably, although they don't confess it voluntarily, because they so often get dubbed themselves, by the nurse, with that appellation, when they bring themselves in from bird-nesting to dinner all tattered and torn and bemired, as if they had been drawn through a ditch, "And everything quite clean put on, sir." If they could but know the delights of their age, with no thought beyond the hour, a rainy day their sinking market, an empty plate their stunned exchequer, the morning lessons their bad investments—sorrows which glance off at pudding time, as arrows from a polished casque! How delightful would it be, if we old people could sometimes, in a like degree, strip ourselves of the mouldy arras of our cares! It would be as a butterfly coming forth from the grub. It would be like taking one's aching brains out, and plunging them in spring-water, as one feels a longing to do sometimes —a process to be considered on a par with sitting in one's bones only, on a hot day, as Sydney Smith suggested.

Talking of aches, with one more medical hint I will conclude this paper. Several of our young ones, and the Missus herself, have been wise enough lately to get their fingers pinched in a closing door. I need not

tell you how agonising the sensation is; but what I do
tell you is, Rush immediately, open mouthed, at the
writhing sufferer, and hold its arm high up in the air.
The pain will cease at once; for the blood is arrested
in its flow by the artery being compressed against the
bone (it runs under an arch), near the shoulder. Have
hot water brought at once, into which dip the wounded
hand : and keep the temperature as high as they can
bear.

July, 1867.

"THAT 'ere be the Glory der Die-John," remarked
Mr. Melon, the gardener, as he saw me arrest my step
before a fine rose in the greenhouse; and, as he spoke,
he proceeded to pinch the unhappy florets of a young
geranium.

"Why, whatever do you do that for?"

"Oh, them be the beggar, the green fly!"

"Well, what do you do to get rid of them?"

"Oh, smoke 'em, sir—smoke 'em, when there's nought
else to do."

"Well, you'd better be quick about it."

"Oh, I'll do it to-night. I thought to do it last
night; but there was that 'ere batch of taters kept me.
Them be the beggars to breed, they be. Why, they be
great-grandfathers in four-and-twenty hours!"

This set me a-thinking. Can these creatures realize
all the hopes and fears, delights and pains, of this
mortal coil—of food, sleep, pleasure, travel, toil—all in
that short period? What a concentrated existence!
Or do they live a life within our life, and have years
rolled up in one of ours, days with their own night, and
sun and moon distinct from ours, and appreciable only

by their own peculiar senses? Mystery on mystery! How, on every side, there teem proofs of an almighty superintendence of this *world*, the Greek equivalent for which is "well-ordered arrangement," and the Latin "neatness," or rather "neat," as our excellent preacher told us last Sunday!

Well, I have just brought home for this faithful dependent a choice assortment of fancy geraniums, to his great delight.

While making my selection, a stray question led to an enthusiastic outpour on the part of the seedsman (who is very eminent in his line). You may learn something from every one, if you keep your ears open, and let him discourse on his pet subjects. The great Burke's version of this idea was, you will remember, that no one could stand with the passer-by, to shelter from a shower, without gaining instruction, provided, un-railway-traveller-like, he took the trouble to talk at all.

To return, however: "Why don't you amuse yourself with this, sir? I know a gentleman who has made thousands by it: he got forty pounds, the other day, for one seedling."

I pricked up my ears; and he gradually instructed me in the mode of mixing the pollen of one flower with that of another, by means of a camel-hair brush, taking care that the bees have not been before one at the particular blossoms, and covering the impregnated flower, until it seeds, in a muslin bag. Won't I cut up one or two of my indulgent spouse's caps!—unbeknown to her it must be. But won't she thank me when she sees the brilliant floral effects of next season? and won't I then tenderly try to tap the plethora of her cheque-

book, supposing mine to be, as is likely, most agricul-
turally weak? The seed of this season, sown in June,
will send up its plants to flower next year. But, after
all, consider the taste and skill that will be required to
produce a lovely combination!

"Then, sir, you must take care to choose plants of
good strong habit to operate upon—plants, too, showing
quality, and true in shape; and then, sir, you'll find
that you must beware of the best varieties, as they are
internally unhealthy, having been bred in-and-in too
much. That's the way they get the fine tints."

Why, what, after all, methought, is this but Shorthorn breeding, without the preliminary outlay, and
consequent precariousness? Both pursuits exert the
same fascination that attends the chemical compounding of elements. The one, however, may be followed
in a cottage with a rood of garden attached, whereas
the other requires capital, and acreage, and ample
accommodation.

Having drifted to Shorthorns, I remark that my
prediction has come true, and that there has been
found in England the chivalry to buy up at a price
that implies the careful keeping of the blue blood of a
breed that is gaining favour every day. But, as we
sped down to Preston Hall in "the special," we involuntarily reflected at what a discount this famous stock
would be, if the crowded train should happen to be
smashed by an accident. What prices! My neighbours and friends have never ceased to meet me openmouthed ever since I was known to have attended the
frightful auction. What a sight it was, too, as the sun
shone out, and the busy train went by, to see a "Grand
Duchess," only calved last March, come hopping and

skipping around the ring, a mossy-coated, substantial youngster, showing exceeding quality, in two minutes knocked down to the name that boasted "Exquisite" (Lord Spencer) for 430 guineas.

"'Spose that 'un takes to scouring?" growled a butcher at our elbow.

True to his instincts, Mr. Eastwood secured for a moderate sum, one of which I noted "a small head, very racing-looking—stepped like a thorough-bred—a strong loin, and short level back;" and then came a white one on the scene.

"I'm not prejudiced against white, sir," confidentially whispered an unknown but shrewd Shorthorn authority behind me, from whom I sucked between the sales, parenthetically, many an anecdote of the earlier crosses and favourite families; "and I know that Joe Culshaw considers that colour to have turned out some of the best and truest-shaped things he ever had to exhibit: they are hardy enough too, sir."

And this bidding, I assure my friends, was not the bidding of novices or nincompoops. Grave, stern calculating countenances of canny Scot and serious Saxon, masked many a brain that might on occasion serve even a Chancellor of the Exchequer. Tenant-farmer, peer, banker, brewer, baronet, and manufacturer—all and each were ably represented on this famous day, to which men went down under strong excitement, as to the fight at Farnborough. I am considered no longer, I am thankful to think, the unmitigated lunatic they did think me, for drawing at the fountain-head, and I shall henceforth dilate with satisfaction on the beauties and the pedigree of the white, red, and roan. But Shorthorns, avaunt! or I shall dream of ye!

" What a precious nasty mess this fold be in !" murmured a good but slow labourer just now, in our
unintended hearing, as he vainly endeavoured to push
his barrow laden from the calf-pens, up a yielding
incline of accumulated muck ; "and them pigs be
always a mooting it."   .

" Come, you wouldn't say that if you were a turnip
grower."

" Nay, sir, it be rare stuff for that job."

" Very good, then ; just get your pike and level that
heap, then lay yonder board upon it, and you may
wheel any amount on it without difficulty."

Intensely dull is the lowest order of the bucolic
mind : the monkey that used puss's paw to fork out
his roasted chestnuts from the fire, were a professor of
political economy, beside so many of our labouring
population, who believe, even in this enlightened age,
that the ugliest local hag is a witch, and account for
every death of stock upon the farm with a " Please sir,
him had a pain."

The fact is, I consider pigs in the fold-yard do an
immensity of good by breaking up and compounding
the mixed strata of the manure pan, reducing it to a
pulpy state, fit for transportation at once into the root
drills, without being robbed of its moisture and spirit,
as it is so much through evaporation when turned in a
heap upon the headland, not to mention the saving of
labour.   And the pigs, too, they do very well for themselves somehow in this employment.   The juices may
feed them as mud fattens the carp.   The waste of cake
and corn, too, they secure.   This reminds me that from
stress of work lately, we have not been able to crush
the oats as I like to have them done.   The carters,

from some cause, prefer them whole, and as I see no
alteration in the teams' appearance, I have not inter-
fered, for it manifestly will pay better if I find that the
allowance keeps the horses fresh and blooming, at the
same time that there are a porker or two sustained on
such grain as runs the gauntlet of the equine internal
mill.

"Time will show, sir," as our honoured bailiff invariably answers when I shock his understanding by a
suggestion or description of some new-fangled machinery
or mode.

Since I wrote the above I have begun the green-house
experiments. Having tied in the shape of a cross two
pieces of light wire, looped at the four ends, and laid
them upon a circular piece of net, through the border
of which and the loops I had run a fine tape, on drawing its ends together a tidy cap was the result, with one
of which I encircled each geranium boss that I operated
on, so effectually fencing off the bees from confounding
my experiments.

What pleasures of anticipation will overhang those
boxes of seedlings next year! And if only I should
manage to turn out something triumphant, then I'll
sell it for a lot, and buy, say a new bull-calf, or a brooch
for the Missus, or better still, perhaps, bank it. Ay!
that's just what I'll do. I find that the winter floods
have left a rich deposit of no less than four to six inches
in depth, where an island is gathering upon a gravel-
bed at a bend of the river; but the grass already considerably overtops it, being just ready for the first
cutting. A great treasure are these two acres of Nile-
like vegetation. There is plenty to eat and plenty to
trample, the summer months through, in the fold-yards;

making a goodly store of manure for autumnal dressing without the aid of straw. Thanks, then—my profoundest thanks—to the kind upper regions that load our loved Wye with this precious fertilising matter, and save our pocket the unsatisfactory purchase of so many tons of " artificial."

There is some advantage beyond the beautiful scenery it affords, in living upon a side-land. The turnpike road, of necessity, is made and mended with limestone ; the washings from which, as they come conducted in small rills along our orchard pastures, being allowed to wander from fixed points at their own sweet will, develop and foster an under-carpet of clover which fascinates the Southdown flocks, keeping them devoutly to the watered spots. Without this aid there would be but a picking of weakly grass.

We have two fields of wheat this year, the history of which is very different. The one was sown on a rye-grass ley, which had been closely fed with sheep and cattle for two years, having received besides a heavy refresher of some patent grass-manure—the beneficial effects of which, I am bound to say, I never saw. This plant started well, and then reverted, being for weeks a sickly growth—so much so that I was once half-tempted to plough it up. Once, during a morning ride, I found a regiment of rooks in grave investigation of the thinner places. Taking care not to disturb them, I see now the service they did me by their wire-worm lunch. The field was rolled with the heaviest Crosskill, still for some weeks the plant was puny and consumptive. It has lately picked up, and is now advancing at a great pace, promising to be of fine stature after all. It reminds one of the curious way in which some stunted children

have been known to take a start, and spring up to good
size, after confinement to their beds with measles, or
other infantine complaint. The fact is, I have been
taught that it does not do to turn down these light
loams with too much growth upon them. The clod
won't lie flat, do what you will, and dries too ˙quickly
too—so that when the young wheatling has sent its
foraging fibres through, they get starved in the hollow,
and only revive (none the better for this check) when
they manage to grapple the under-soil again.

The other field started oddly, and has never met with
a reverse.   It will be a grand crop, with cane-like,
branching stems, and heads, I hope, in unison. Although
close adjoining field No. 1, it has a strong admixture of
marl in its composition, and is considered a sulky soil,
difficult to work, by the native population—a delightful
contrast, however, in our eyes, to the sticky, impractic-
able clays we had upon our Welsh farm. This field was
well dressed with fold-yard muck two years ago, and
sown with wheat.   The frost managed to get at it and
nip its roots ; the crop was consequently thin, but the
grain was excellent.   It was accidentally over-ripe when
cut with a machine, and shed a good deal. The stubble
was pared for autumnal cleaning, when—lo ! and behold !—a thick covering of wheat came up, despite
gleaners and pigs.   It weathered the winter so well,
and was so strong by the time the ewes went upon it,
that I have allowed it to stand ; and a grand harvest I
anticipate, which I shall take care to have cut in good
time.

One short word more and I have done.   The other
morning, having seen a mouse in the mushroom-pit, I
inquired of Melon what the tortoise-shell cat was about ?

"Oh! him be *blowed*, sir!" "Blowed! What do you mean?" "Why, you see, sir, when you gave orders to have them poachers trapped on account of the pheasants, the very first night why ours gets nabbed and breaks both her legs, so as it was a mercy to put her out of her pain. Well then, says I, as the worst is come to the worst, we must get summit out of you; so I skins her for a cap, and I slits her in two or three places, and hangs her in a bush by the brook, where the cray-fish do mostly congregate. There the fly soon settled on her, and, now they're hatched, the maggots do flop out beautifully, and you'll have a nice dish soon." "Save me from such," I exclaim, with an involuntary shudder; and, being now myself somewhat blown, conclude.

And so it was a mistake altogether, and the experiment came to nothing. Certainly, most certainly, the experiment did come to nothing, but it was only for a night. With the bright morning I was in the conservatory again, as a giant refreshed, having during the dark hours, by lamplight, investigated all the sources of information upon the subject, hitherto latent in my library. And to save such among my readers as may be equally ignorant from error in their practice, let me premise that the first day when I set enthusiastically about my novel task, I simply took one flower, the colour of which I thought would blend happily with a second selection, and showered the pollen or yellow dust upon it. I was greatly wrong, however, and that performance must lead to most uncertain results, being simply what the unreflecting bee does; wherefrom, while it allows occasional beauties, still a multitude of hybrid deformities arise. Such a kaleidoscope mode of operation will only accidentally answer. The line and plummet way of proceeding is, first fix upon the florets the tints of which you may imagine, from study of the theory of colours in some such excellent treatise as Chevreul's, will tastefully combine with those of another plant of the same genus, be it geranium, azalea, pansy, &c. Catch the bud as it is opening, just before Sir Bumble Bee attempts to worm himself in : open it gently, and with a pair of fine-pointed scissors nip off the heads of the stamens before the pollen has powdered them (they break off quite readily at the merest touch). If you would be sure of having seed, as there is some uncertainty in these fancy flowers duly ripening, operate as I have described upon every floret in the pelargonium boss, and then encircle it in a bag of net strained over cap-wire, bent transversely. The pistil, or female organ of the flower (being a dark stem in the midst of the stamen bunch) is not ripe so soon as the stamens or male portion. Watch your charge narrowly, and in a day or two you will observe that the pistil has opened its button head into spreading antlers like the horns of a butterfly. It is then covered with a gummy deposit, to which the pollen dust will adhere. Now, with a fine camel-hair brush, apply the farina off the stamens of the other flower to it. Cover up again, and leave it. The flower hath now performed its office. Very shortly the petals will fall off, and the seed vessel appear in full stature. Now set up the plant in the sun to ripen, and you may with comparative certainty look forward to the production of a new variety next year. Before the horns of the pistil open, there being no gummy dew, the pollen will not adhere. Hence the wisdom of the natural arrangement. The stamens

attain their full growth, and being thickly strewn with
the yellow dust, overhang the pistil, whose opening
they await until the least gust of wind shakes a shower
over it, that is most certain to adhere on the sticky
surface ; or a bee, with his hairy legs and ecstatic
movements, does the same service.   Old Melon is delighted, and thinks me a mighty genius for my pains.
His imagination had never wandered forward from the
common practice of the hot-bed and cucumber frame to
the like mysteries of greenhouse cultivation.

There was a loud chattering and avine scrimmage
the other morning upon the lawn, when a villain of a
jay came and dived into the dark recesses of an Irish
yew, quite near to the house, and whipped off the
frequently-inspected eggs of one of the children's nests.
They have ever such a number of them everywhere
about, of which one little boy, I think, almost dreams.
They are not allowed to take any except the blackbird's.   I found, however, the other day, a "collection"
of eggs, blown and laid carefully upon bran, in an old
toy-box.   Of course, this would not do, being nothing
less than open mutiny.   On inquiry, however, I found
that mamma had been a party to the transgression,
inasmuch as she could not resist one youngster's argument, that he was sure that it made the birds industrious to take toll of a solitary egg.   It was impossible
for her, without injury to the youthful mind, to
condemn any move that fostered industry ; so the
youngster innocently triumphed.   To return, however,
to the jay: the children have several times since the
fracas found an egg laid in a flower-bed or on the grass-
plot—once that of the missel-thrush, once that of the
turtle-dove.   Their idea is that the jay has dropped

some of his spoil: mine, that the fond parent had mis-calculated the distance home. The birds upon the lawn afford us endless amusement: the starling nimbly working after worms; the thrush and blackbird, with head depressed and ear on one side, as if in detection of a grub's subterranean excursion; the fly-catcher hover-ing and alighting in turn; the selfish, detestable robin —and, behold, now too a rarity—why, no less than an individual of the large woodpecker species, with gor-geous scarlet head and yellow breast. How he stoops so awkwardly (being quite out of place off a tree), and bends and digs in with his hard long tongue! How comes it that he has resort then to the feeding-ground of the throstle? Is it that his stomach is out of order, and that he has a sore tip to his tongue, which makes his usual task of tree-boring painful; or is it that he requires change, as we human beings take salad and the dog chews couch-grass? Look out, my brilliant, for there are hawks about, and you may have one down upon your broad back in a moment, making havoc of your plumage in savage eagerness, despite your shrill cry.

But here comes one of the little girls.

"Well, and what brings you here?"

"Oh! I want to go out with you, papa, if you will let me, and lead Juno."

"Well, but where's your sister?"

"Oh, she's gone out with Miss Eglantine: she likes going with her" (this was in an earnest, thoughtful, half-sad tone and way,) "because she thinks she gets better luck."

"What do you mean, darling?"

"Oh! I don't know: she's always more fortunate

I

than I am. And I'm sure I don't want to go out with
the governess. I get quite enough of her in schooltime."

Well, that's not quite a right feeling, and I don't like
this symptom of incipient superstition, that draws one
to think of swimming witches, when if they floated
they were guilty and burnt; if they sank they were
drowned, and so in both cases conveniently cleared from
the community. However, we'll set out and see how
the oak-stripping gets on in the plantation I have to
thin. Having arrived upon the scene of operation, the
black pointer tugging at the leading-rein all the way
with a determination to get on, that I cannot believe to
have given absolute pleasure to my little companion—
(she never murmured, certainly; but perchance her
dignity forbade it)—we seat ourselves on a rustic
bench in the wood, hard upon the spot where the busy
band is engaged. How amusing it was to watch the
lads climb monkey-like up the slender stems that sway
to and fro with their weight, as they peel the uppermost twigs or chip away with a hook the obstructive
sprays, chattering all the while to one another with a
twenty-tongue power! The lowest five feet or so, a
grown man just hacks around, and then strips the
bark, which parts with a wheezy sound from the wood, if
it run well (as they technically phrase it) in shape like
the cricketer's leg-pads. Then against the tree a boy
places his ladder and mounts. When we arrived the
gaffer was engaged in making one of the rough ladders
they use for this purpose. It was a good yard wide or
more, the side-pieces being straight limbs of a peeled
sapling, the three intermediate steps hazel wands, their
ends being thrust into holes extemporised by the point of

the woodman's knife ; the top and bottom steps were,
however, peculiar in being made with a twisted hazel or
honeysuckle vine. The reason for this was obviously
that when the ladder is placed against a tree this twisted
supple step forms an arc, which slips not as a stiff
smooth step would, but which holds the more firmly
the greater the weight upon it, as the greater the strain
upon it the more it bends towards the shape of a semi-
circle.

Curious is it that these simple men have learnt in
practice a fact, the theory of which it belongs to
the highest mathematics to explain.   It was very
delightful to sit there and watch the swift progress
with which, locust-like, the lads shifted from sapling to
sapling.

The subdued sunlight shot gleamily through the
thick foliage, producing an exquisite alternation of
most lovely light and shade as it fell, fancifully broken,
on creeping bramble, the bursting bracken, and the
twisted brushwood tangle, tinting all with such delicate
exhilarating dyes, as would baffle the pencil of the
most skilful artist, whether he dash in a general effect
after the brilliant, dreamy, suggestive style of Turner,
or contortedly copy each sprig and leaf with the feebler
disciple of the pre-Raphaelite school.

Could the photographic apparatus give colouring, as
it does the network of underwood, one might hope to
see such delicious effect reproduced ; but not, I fear,
before then.

My eye! what an amount of cobalt and opaque white
would the fair lady-sketcher vainly daub upon her
board, in frantic faithless imitation of that wondrous
atmospheric ethereal effect which those blue-bells so

simply produce, intermixed with a copse's under-
growth.

But the marker's dry. Well, to be practical, let me
record what the woodman taught me. A good oak
coppice is reckoned to pay about £18 in sixteen years,
not reckoning the trees that are left standing. The
plantation we are thinning is about twenty years of
age, has been thinned once, and will require thinning
in about ten years again. It is calculated to yield
about 1½ tons of bark to the acre, besides the sticks,
which are worth a shilling each, one with another, and
will come in for valuable fencing, hop-poles, and the
like. The present price of bark is about £4 10s. the
ton, and the stripping costs from 27s. to 30s. the ton.
The peeled saplings must remain standing until the
winter. "If you was to cut them now, they would rip
in the sun, so as you couldn't cleave them nohow."
Then it requires an artist to decide upon the best
period for taking the bark into scale, and he must have
his wits about him there, I'm informed, so many are the
customary allowances, so crafty the tricks of the trade.
"I remember when I went in last year with your'n, sir.
There was the foreman; him was a-bobbing about with
his toe under the scale. 'Stand off,' says I, 'and you
shall have your weight, never fear.' There be dead
robbery oftentimes, sir, in a bark-yard."

Oak should be planted about four feet apart, and
thinned ultimately to forty trees the acre, in order to
grow timber. Well, then I consult him as to a bit of
rough side land (arable ground), that it does not pay to
cultivate for ordinary crops, whether he would advise
my planting it with oaks when the time comes. "Oh
no, sir—larch; them do pay so much sooner. Bill, you

remember that bit of a rocky breast near ——, that was planted with larch as thick as it could stand—in nothing much better than stones, too. Why, they had to carry the soil here and there, to have place to plant in. Why, that 'ere bit of wood sold for £320 by public auction. There was some from forty to fifty feet high, and about four feet apart. Them was used for sleepers and rafters, and the tops came in for fencing stakes (all the dead 'uns I was to have, for to carry home to my lodgings). That was a thing that would come in for any market, and it was a regular timber merchant that bought it. Bless us, what a game the haulier had to get them away ! They was packed so close, and felled this way and that way everyhow. But it was a good price, that was."

And so larch planting, when the season comes, shall be our little game.

His opinion about orchards is, that you cannot have the trees too thick in reason. " If you mean to plant an orchard, plant one. It must be a blow then to kill the bloom upon all." An odd phrase he used once " Says I, I'm not going to be cattled about any longer,' which he explained to mean worried, as a herd is, being jostled against each other on their way to market. Another good phrase I heard the same day from a preacher's lips, who spoke of his having some good " swivels." Fishermen! whatever can they mean ? Why sermons on general doctrine, that will do to attach to a variety of texts and endings. The mention of sermons reminds me of a sad scene last Sunday morning. Overnight, the children, who had been especially anxious that I should visit their beds to say ' good night," were full of wonderment and praise of a nest of young birds that the cowman's boy had brought them.

"Do you know, papa, they are only just fledged, and they sing beautifully already!"

They supposed them to be young martins. In the morning, the first thing, they brought me the chirping nest in a dormouse's cage. One "poor little thing" had forced its way through the wires during the night, and was dead.

"Listen, papa! how they sing!"

"My darling, they are hungry, and calling to their parents, who can't hear them. They are sure to die. What a naughty boy he was to take them."

"Are they martins, papa?"

"No, they are young water-wagtails, I think. Put them out on the lawn there, and see what they will do."

Just then the school-room breakfast-bell rang, and away they scampered to their meal. Meanwhile, the poor birdlings sat in a heap, crowded together, as one used to read the Babes in the Wood did, chirping sadly, but apparently strong. "Well," thought I, "when the children return, we'll try to feed them." I had not been gone five minutes, when I returned to find one quite suddenly dead and stiff, and two others gasping their little lives out. What a sad sight it was! and then to think how many human birdlings there are, even this minute gasping their poor short lives out, under the torture of illness or cruel parental treatment! When the children returned, we got some small cater-pillars from the lime tree; but they would not take them; and the four surviving innocents sat up against each other, and chirped so sadly, as though they felt they were deserted. "Poor, poor little things," said our youngest, with wet eyes. And so the human birdlings sat round, and keenly felt for the sufferings of the nest that was intended to please them. Hereupon the man came with a small worm, off which he severed a piece. Then tapping their beaks, by some magic manipulation he made them open them, and then he popped the worm in. In an instant the first fed took flight a few yards, to the delight of our French youngster, who clapped his hands and cheered. Then it was caught again, and the rest fed. "Oh, they'll do now! Take them to your pantry, and feed them soon again." Perhaps we may save what remain! But alas! on our return from church, we found them all dead corpses. Good cook, in a fit of misjudging benevolence, had crammed them with crumbs to death. And so the next day they were buried, and their grave planted : and now the very fact of their brief existence is lost in that facile forgetfulness which is a characteristic of children, and which is a blessing, nevertheless, to be coveted.

I heartily wish those runaway icebergs in lat. 45 degrees, would move on, that are credited with causing this inclement weather. My clipped sheep are all shivering under the fence—small blame to them for it. In fact, I'm shivering myself, and must be off to get a warm.

August, 1867.

WELL, the proof has come! The excellence of the pudding is found in the eating. Although, some weeks back I was apprehensive that I had erred in diverging from the regular local practice of feeding down the young clover in the autumn and spring, with a view to consolidating, as it is thought, the soil through the treading of the stock, I am rejoiced to ascertain, now that harvest has arrived, that no one in the neighbourhood has anything like such "seeds" to mow. The gang, strong men as they were, fairly groaned under the weight of work, the gaffer declaring that they should not get their 2s. per day. One shrewd old neighbour, who is never above learning, and by observation of whose excellent practice I have certainly been greatly instructed, has determined to follow in my wake for the future. All honour, however, to him by whose hint I profited myself. Years ago, when I first took a fancy to farming, among the books I perused was "Nesbit on Agricultural Chemistry," an excellent little volume of the sort. I must then have been struck with the sentence, "Every leaflet upwards has a rootlet downwards; and if the leaflet be taken off, the rootlet will not grow," for the fact has stuck as a burr to my memory ever since. I have to-day referred to the passage, which I find in its entirety so useful and interesting, that I transcribe it for the use of those who may not have the work itself to refer to. Mr. Nesbit writes: "Now what does the clover do? Every little leaflet which it shoots up into the air sends a rootlet downwards, so that in proportion to the upward growth of the clover is the downward growth of the root; and when you have taken the clover away, you retain, in the shape of roots, several tons per acre of valuable vegetable matter which, by its slow decomposition, affords nutriment for the narrow-leafed wheat; so that by employing in the first instance turnips for the barley and clover for the wheat, you accumulate in the soil a large quantity of material absorbed from the air, for the benefit of the after-crops. This may be clearly seen, if you consider the difference between cutting clover and feeding it off. It is generally believed that a man who feeds his clover off, with a little oilcake, &c., will get a better crop than one who takes the hay. I know I am here treading on tender ground ; but, at the risk of being accused of heresy, I will aver that the man who spends his money on oilcake, feeding it off upon clover, is committing an error, unless he can realise benefit in the shape of mutton. If you cut clover at Midsummer, and let it grow again, and then take another cutting in the autumn, you will afterwards obtain a far better crop of wheat than you would secure by feeding with oilcake, unless you choose to go to an enormous expense. Every leaflet upwards has a rootlet downwards, and if the leaflet be taken off the rootlet will not grow ; so that if the sheep be fed upon the surface, the under-production is diminished. In exact proportion to the increase of the upper, is the increase of the lower ; and if you are always feeding-off the former with sheep, you will have but few rootlets below, and the small amount of nutriment you give in the shape of oilcake will produce little or no effect." He proceeds to relate the issue of an experiment that was tried for him by a friend in Northamptonshire. "A field of clover was divided into two parts. The whole was cut at Midsummer ; half was left to grow again, and the other fed off. In October two pieces were staked out as regularly as possible, all the roots dug up, carefully cleaned and weighed. The result was, that where the clover had been cut once and eaten once there were 25 cwt. of roots per acre ; and where it had been cut twice there were 75 cwt. per acre, being a difference of two tons of

roots per acre," which, containing so much nitrogen as
these roots do, constituted an exceedingly good dressing
for the wheat crop to follow. The whole of this little
volume is full of the most valuable information for the
sucking agriculturist.

Talking of oilcake, the other evening, as I was watching the gang busy cutting the "seeds," I happened to
remark how much the manure showed that came from
the boxes of the best-fed animals. One of them, who
until recently had been in the service of a notoriously
cross-grained farmer of the neighbourhood, who treats
his animals as ill as he does his human *attachés*, said
that if he does ever get a ton of oilcake in, he gives his
shepherd out one piece daily to be divided amongst the
flock. He is of opinion that half-an-ounce a day is
plenty for a sheep, and that if a portion of the lot
should consume more than their due proportion one
day, it will only make the rest nimbler at the troughs
the next feeding time.

Walking the wheat-field yesterday on which I had
observed the rooks so busy in the spring, I find that
the stems have tillered out gloriously to cover the weak
spots, and that, in fact, the plant in that portion of the
field looks almost healthier than in any other. We had
a *battue*, however, of the young rooks the other day,
which, made into tarts, were pronounced excellent by
those who ate them. It was surprising how quickly
the old birds moved off all their offspring that could
fly, into some elms across the river, beyond our reach.
The very day the firing ceased they seemed to comprehend how matters stood, and returned, notwithstanding
that several young scions of the noble family lay dead
in the various nests to which they had managed to

flutter when only wounded by the shot. Paley, in his interesting work on " Natural Theology," remarks upon the wonderful provision of Nature, whereby the sounder a bird sleeps the faster gripe his claws take of the perch. This seemed the case, too, with the wounded rooklings.

There had been a small hawk about for some days, which we desired to exterminate, seeing that the young pheasant broods are abroad now. I fancied I saw him alight on the topmost branch of a silver fir, fully eighty yards off. Taking aim, without the least expectation of success, I fired, and brought down, sad to relate, a lovely turtle-dove, one pellet having pierced the brain. There was, of course, much reprobation of this slaughter in the nursery ; and they were right too, although the time is approaching when the pigeons will have to be warned off the pea crops.

The rook-skins I have cured and stuffed, to be hung *in terrorem* over the ripening fields. One shrewd friend, who is free to acknowledge the benefit these birds do by destroying the grubs, is rather "riled" that they let alone eleven acres close to their and his abode, which are alive with wire-worm. My conclusion and mode of consoling him is, that the prudent colonists reserve that nearest home against a rainy day, just as one keeps an extra five pounds always in the house against difficulties unforeseen, through wife's bonnets, &c.

But I can write no more. A pet half-Alderney, a magnificent milker, has, despite precautions taken, fallen with milk fever, as her mother did before her. The ailment is clearly constitutional. This implies retrenchment of cream at the approaching strawberry period, no less than immediate sorrow and sickness of heart.

September, 1867.

IN quest of fresh ideas for the improvement of practice and the enrichment of pocket I set off duly for a week's hot study amidst the stock and machinery of the Bury show-yard. It was, indeed, hard sultry work ; and if it had not been for the repeated pleasure of falling in with old friends, and a frequent drain of the sherry and claret flasks which kind-hearted exhibitors kept for the encouragement of customers' wearied spirits, it might have been hard times with our excellent self. The absence of the cattle classes took away much of the interest that usually attaches to the bucolic part of the scene. The pigs were cubic in form, and fragrant as ever, alongside their sticky meal troughs. The Black Diamonds were forward as their best friends could wish upon the prize list. Of sheep, the Southdown classes were superb ; at the same time I protest against Lord Walsingham's sort being considered to have the true character that Ellman loved about the head. The nose he approved was straight —Grecian, if we, may borrow an illustration from the human feature, rather than Roman. The Goodwood ewes, with their oval frames, long lashes that gave their grey eyes a dreamy look, and gentle faces all thickly nightcapped with soft wool, are beautiful to behold, as their flesh is delicious to eat beyond all other.

To enjoy it, however, in its sweetest, juiciest state, it is the meat of a three years old maiden ewe that you should kill for the table. " It will eat like a pheasant," was the description given to me by an old breeder of the sort. You direct your butcher to send you wether mutton as a precaution against being served with joints of a tough old matron ewe. The three years old maiden is quite another thing.

It was a great treat to saunter through the machinery department, having beforehand marked upon my catalogue the articles I desired to inspect; the consequence of which is that I have already arranged several alterations for the improvement of my implements, which will ensure a considerable saving in time and power.

I was amused to see the heterogeneous geological specimens that under the attractive name of "coprolites" were tastefully arranged on the specimen stalls of the artificial-manure makers. It gave me a considerably stronger idea of the value of the limestone road mud, which undoubtedly contains very many elements quite as manurial as those crushed materials can furnish. By the way, one more proof of the value that any burnt stuff has, in ensuring a good clover crop. It has been said that, if a building were burnt down and left, white clover will soon spring up and clothe the ruins. Anyhow, this last spring I had the wilderness adjoining our pleasure grounds uprooted of its nettle and rubbish growth, all of which was burnt in a heap upon the outskirt. The surface of the cleared ground was worked fine, and sown with Dutch clover. Scarcely a plant, however, has come up, probably owing to the overhanging shade, except alongside the ash heap of the burnt weeds, where there is an abundant crop. I shall, consequently, redouble my efforts to accumulate ashes to mix with the bone-manure on my turnip land, having an eye especially to the clover that will follow in regular succession.

How murderous hot it is! There must be thunder somewhere, and it is felt with its effects in more ways than one. Just now, taking my usual nocturnal nursery rounds, I came upon the boy juveniles in their broiling bed-room. Yet they were boiling over with boisterous fun and larking in all sorts of ways. Just arrayed in a sheet each, they lay and tossed and chaffed, and frolicked one with the other, and were "cheeky" above measure, as their elder brother observed confidentially to his mother, with whose pony-carriage whip I, finding it opportunely in the hall, made my silent way up the back stairs to their room, the door of which was open. I found them rolling in their respective sheets upon their elder's bed. Catch a weasel asleep you won't, nor will you readily find our young French friend off his guard. One eye out somewhere he must have had ; for immediately, when I aimed at them a quiet cut, as much to awe as to afflict them, the sharp youngster, by an effort getting undermost, upturned his brother's—not his head—so as to intercept the flick, and then rolled, roaring with delight, off the bed and underneath, there enjoying to the uttermost the juvenile's discomfiture and astonishment. The youngster squalled, of course ; whilst underneath the bed crowed our French friend.

The wail has, however, caught the doting mother's ear ; so, while little Benjamin's hurt is being looked to, we have urgent private affairs with the bailiff, to whom we confide our earnest feeling that a fall of rain, if it do damage to the corn crop, would be of inestimable service to the roots.

The swedes I find a splendid crop, on my return home, upon that land which I described to have been pared after harvest last autumn, the couch being then allowed to grow into a thick surface-mat that was the laughing-stock of my neighbours. When it came to be worked, as I had calculated, no rootlets had. pierced beyond the cut sod; while, through taking care to work the land in favourable weather, I secured no less than nine waggon-loads of ashes, which, having been soaked in their thirsty state, before rain fell, with liquid manure from the tank in the fold-yard, I drilled in along with the seed (Sutton's Champion), over and above a good dressing of muck, also ploughed-in wet.

How singular, however, in the management of a root-crop is the value even of a single day! Whether the weather be more favourable at one time than another, or whatever it may have been, anyhow it is astonishing to view the difference in the growth of two breadths upon land equally well dressed, the only difference being that a few hours intervened between the sowing of the one and the other.

The value of water to the flock must be greater than I ever suspected. A friend has a flock of sheep running upon a withered, bare, trefoil stubble, where, to the naked eye, there would seem to be little or nothing to eat; still they are in excellent condition, and merry enough. The way he accounts for it is, that they have access to a brook at the bottom. Just opposite to where I am writing now, too, there is a large herd of Hereford cattle in capital trim upon a very naked pasture, besides that half their time is spent standing in the river. I shall at once order some nice low tanks on wheels, which were exhibited at Bury by

Burney and Company, and hope by consequence henceforth to render my dry side-lands more prolific of
mutton.

November, 1867.

"REALLY how time does pass," remarked my charming
sister-in-law (who has come to us for a visit) just now!

"Of course it does," I replied, "or how else could I
have this dear little tit of a niece asking 'Terries,
pease, untle,' meaning grape-berries all the while,
although she would (but for a fault of enunciation)
have termed them cherries, when this said niece was,
as the racing men say, nowhere not so many months or
years ago?"

Anyhow it's no good philosophising after one's with-
drawal from acquaintance with the University, where
such studies not only lent to the passing hour the
charm of that highest mortal pleasure, keen intellectual entertainment, but further fitted the mind, through
practice, for gladiatorial contest with the world's craft.

"If you don't take care, young man, you'll be pretty
soon out of your depth," I hear some dreadful voice (it
might be one's wife) behind me exclaim. So I think
too; and before I go further, would simply remark, *en
passant*—having had the idea awakened—that if ever
youthful agriculturist (for such only we write) should
wish to cross a river by swimming, there not being a
bridge in the vicinity to help you, and you should have
to carry a gun across, or some such load as you may
desire not to wet, just throw your handkerchief over
the hollow of your hat, and tie the four ends underneath. Hold on by the knot, and you will find yourself sustained in the stream as by a buoy.

It is not quite to the purpose of this paper, which is *really* to be regarded as the record of wild Robinson Crusoe experiments which actually take place regularly upon our small estate ; but, having fallen upon the subject of swimming, let me further advise the sucking farmer, that if he be called upon by the force of circumstances to assist in saving a drowning person, let him always endeavour to get behind, and put his hands under the armpits of the drownee. He may then, with comparative ease, and without danger to himself, propel the body forward to the shore ; whereas, if he advance in front, he runs the risk of being tightly clasped, and of so being incapacitated from doing any service, while he runs the risk of being finished off himself. These secrets I learnt lately from a friend, who has been instrumental in saving many lives ; and I put them in print with the hope that they may be beneficial to others.

But I pass from swimming to the real business of the farm. What a sweet season we have had for clearing the stubbles ! On this light sandy loam, which is as hard as a road in dry weather, but soft as wife's words before quarter day in wet, it is delightful to see the sharp-pronged cultivator tear up the astonished couch-grass in great flakes, and deposit it drying in the sun. Success is everything ! Soothing as syrup to the babe is it to see an experiment in agriculture answer. Having been used until lately to a sticky, matted, just-cooling gutta-percha sort of clay in South Wales, you can guess, gentle reader, the satisfactory sensation of having thus simply to deal with the corn crop's deadly enemy, instead of having to cut it up and plough it in in winter, to be fetched up in spring, on trust that there be no

K

insidious sets left for a new plantation. How glad
one feels to traverse the swede drills, and find only a
timid black grassling here and there, scarcely daring to
put in an appearance, being assured that its term of
existence is limited to the brief period that elapses
between its venture on the surface, and the time when
the first frost shall have so far burnt the turnip-leaves
as to allow a clear passage of inspection between to a
boy with hamper and fork! Thank heaven! these last
rains have made the layers cut like gas-pipe before the
plough, their previous dessicated condition having been
favourable to the hauling out of manure; so that we
hope we have a glorious prospect of a wheat crop for
next season. May it so happen, we devoutly trust,
for this present exaggerated value of wheat is not
altogether of advantage to the farming interest, while
it is pregnant with deep care to the community at
large.

But really we have scarcely time to dwell upon the
future—we have been and are so fully occupied. Our
local show is at hand; and for the sake of filling the
yard, which is a main feature on such occasions, we
have made over a score of entries. All this delightful
morning through, notwithstanding the landscape attraction of the brown and yellow fern-clad hill, with the deep
blue rippling river below, and the ancient grey rocks
above, where abound colonies of rabbit, pheasant, hare,
and partridge, we have been most delightfully occupied—
we do not hesitate to say so—in handling and selecting
various assortments of sheep, until, I declare, one's
hand got so thoroughly greasy, that one had only to
pass it through one's hair to be prepared for to-morrow
(Sunday), the only drawback to this dressing being

that one may detect, further towards midnight, the
grip, just across the back of the neck (where, shepherds
tell me, their hunting-grounds usually lie), of a disagreeable, flat, exploring customer.

The pigs simply snore, and await their fate. Washed
oiled, transported on wheels, it is a matter of utter indifference to their porcine highnesses whether they win
or lose—whether their owner and fond feeder be ruined
or not in their preparation.

Since our return home from the sea, there has been
much of literature in the house to interest one, but few
books more than Mr. M'Combie's "Cattle and Cattle-
breeders," and Mr. Carr's little volume on the Booth
race of pedigree Shorthorns. The first, written quaintly
enough, abounds with much that is gold to the young
farmer, being the mental deposit of an acute thinker, a
practical salesman, and a plain-spoken, honest man, of
long years' experience. Our copy is lined and interlined
most abundantly already.

The second is an able treatise upon its subject, and
should be in the hands of every breeder. I would we
had such a record of other eminent herds, instead of
the "all shirt-collar" histories with which we have
been hitherto favoured, and which are paralleled only
by the late railway-trip estimate of England's crops.
Mr. Carr's book is ably written, and shows him a
master in the art of breeding Shorthorn cattle—an art
of no little importance henceforth, it may be fairly
expected, if we are to judge from the issue of recent
sales.

What we want now is a counter demonstration on
the part of the Bates men. The late Mr. Bates once
proposed a meeting of contemporary authorities, for the

purpose of setting down in print what was known of pedigree origin, but without success, as I will relate in my next, being just now unable to lay hands upon his letter.

December, 1868.

BLESS the day that Her Majesty came forth from the affectionate retirement with which we all so sincerely sympathise, even while we regret it, to be a competitor upon the agricultural lists of England, where her excellent husband was formerly so fortunate. Happy may the omen be of her winning the *first* prize in the *first* class, as we were glad to notice. There was not an exhibitor upon the ground but would gladly have cheered her success had she been foremost in every class, even with that loyal spirit which prompted the M'Combie so gracefully to make his Queen a gift offer of his most grand and laurelled Scot.

Of the show itself I must remark and moralize another time. There has been so much to tell the untravelled natives hereabouts, since our return, that one is well-nigh sick of the remembrance — ovine, porcine, and bovine. A fund of new ideas, and a whole curiosity-shop of new, not over-expensive inventions I have brought down for adoption in the improvement, I trust, of domestic affairs. First and foremost, then, did not our rich deep-milking household Alderney die of milk-fever in the summer ? and ever since I've had no peace because I have not afforded to replace her. But you know—I need not tell you—Christmas time is a jolly time, and there's a good deal of that jollity depends, you will remember, upon the humour and the arrangements, culinary and other, of the *placens conjux* (apple-cheeked matron); so, you see, having regard to such seasonable gratification, I determined to inaugurate civilities, and so I frowned at myself, just a short minute, and then put more notes than I dared to think of in my pocket, and buttoned my coat up, and started ultimately, with a pleasant sense that I was about to do my duty, having made inquiries before-hand as to his stock, of the honey-tongued importer of this fancy breed. Well, I saw what there was to see, and I returned to a grateful spouse. Grateful! and for what, I should like to know ? Why, that she had for breakfast this very day, such a delicious roll of fresh butter as she hadn't tasted for ever so long, and of such a golden tinge, too ! There's nothing like those Guernseys for the production of the precious pats ! And she made herself so agreeable, too, I didn't know what to do, that I was afraid she might ask to see the cow. But I didn't give her time for that, and during the intervals of talk I coughed somewhat—journeys leave such a disagreeable (this time I may say convenient) lining of comminuted foreign material (not so dusty a phrase that, I think) in your throat, and then I sucked again of the nice saturated toast, and we were mutually gratified, and, at last, as I am the quickest feeder, I got off with an excuse ; and here I am, gentle reader, at your service for the moment. Whatever shall I do? Ah ! may she never find it out. But I'll tell you in confidence, only don't try to do the same, for perhaps your wife won't be so easily satisfied, as a fellow-passenger in the train, to whom I had revealed my intention, remarked, apprehensively, having regard to his own help-mate.

Well, then, to make a clean breast of it, how do you

think I did it ?   Why, I'll tell you ; I went and bought
one of the butter-making implements, which, for the
sake of such as may be ignorant, as I was of the
existence of this household treasure, I will endeavour
roughly to describe.   You have a pewter cylinder per-
forated around, for half an inch at the bottom, with
small holes ; this cylinder is fixed in a frame, with two
extended elbows that rest on the sides of a tub filled
with cold spring water, in which the cylinder is immersed
just over the holes.   Into the cylinder you throw a
lump of butter, it matters not how rancid or salt, and
you squeeze it down by means of a screw piston.   First
spurt forth the imprisoned globules of foul water and
butter-milk ; then follow, as a cloud of maccaroni, a
mass of spun-out butter-threads, as really sweet as
when in earliest infancy the lump was gathered from
the churn.   This mass you leave for a few seconds to
harden in the chill water ; then sprinkle it with salt,
and beat it into pats of exquisite grain, by means of
the ribbed flat wooden trowels which dairy-maids use.
The effect is really wonderful.   What we next did was
just to tint it with an atom of golden syrup—the Irish
put sugar into their butter—and it was served up and
mistaken for a true Guernsey yield.

     And now, having invested in a keg of Cork salt
butter, and a ha'porth of treacle, by connivance of the
cook, I am clear of the rocks, so long at least as I can
defer her ocular appreciation of our new treasure, with
regard to which event I can only hope.   I know, at
least, that until Christmas is gone she will be sufficiently
occupied ; so, on her busiest morning I shall relieve my
fretting mind by this pleasant remark, " Bessy, dear,
you've not seen our new butter prize : won't you come

now ? " to which won't there come the nice reply, " Not to day, Edward, dear, but when our visitors are gone " ? And then I shall emerge along the passage with a mingled feeling, containing somewhat of hope, that when she *does* discover, she will duly appreciate her husband's inventiveness ; for have I not saved a twenty-pound note in the transaction, and may she not want a bonnet or so when the spring fashions come out ?

We have to-day commenced operations for utilising, as I described, the spring upon our hill-side, and in course of the work came across an effect, which most may know, but which had not certainly occurred to my mind before. I found out that if you want to obtain a pan of clear drinkable water, in the very heart and in defiance of a muddy river, why, having safely moored, just sink up to the lips a stout floatably-inclined tub, having holes bored in the bottom, which should be strewn a few inches deep with gravel, having a coating of fine sand a-top : through this the exploring water will ascend, being determined, as its human superiors, to attain and keep its level ; but having in this instance, as a pauper casual, to suffer cleansing in consideration of its lodging. Simply, in plain words, the water that will rise in the tub will be purified and transparent, and a contrast to the muddy stream outside its oak-stave barrier. You may fill your kettle therefrom with delighted impunity.

But here comes the charcoal-burner, whom I have engaged to turn into this useful material the oak boughs which were intended to have been sold for cord-wood to the tin-works in the Forest, and so, for to-day, adieu.

January, 1868.

For the life of me I cannot set hands upon the letter of old Bates regarding Shorthorns, which I promised to quote. Somewhere it is safely deposited, and will certainly turn up, unless our hopeful hath, in the absence of his fond parent, made spills thereof. This cannot be, though: the colt is better trained; so we will hope and proceed.

" Farming this land, sir," said an observant old neighbour to me lately, as we stood upon an arable slope of light brashy sandstone soil, " is like farming a sieve," strewn with some temporarily absorbent material. Just so long as you can secure the use of the layer in an inebriated state, you ensure a paying crop of grain; but then the virtue is so evanescent. There is a tide in the affairs of—soils, &c. Once let the occasion pass, and your seed-bed is worthless as the vapid draught of a three hours' uncorked soda-water drink. So have ingenious spirits grown salad vegetables, such as mustard and cress, on the surface of moist flannel. The great secret of managing this soil is, soak it well and sow it soaked: certain then will be the remunerative return. "Ah, bless them clay lands," he continued, " on which the clover thrives so bountifully; we can't get it no how on these rubbishy side-lands, leastways as a permanent resident. It's a hop-and-go-one plant with us at best—now here and now there a leaf. Dash these light soils! them quite beats me, they do." Dash them! we remark remonstratively, in regard to the increasing vehemence of his expressions—dash them! pray with what? "Dash, sir? why excuse me, but I meant it metaphorically. However, as you ask me the question, dash them, as the gardener does his young pear-tree stocks, to keep the sheep and rabbits off, with a coating of thick muck-mud, and in that plaister-compound sow. It is in the production of this prolific compost that our heavy Cotswold flocks pay to fold, so much more than the sweet juicy Southdowns of which you are so fond."

I have been much interested lately in the study of an adjoining estate, which occupies, as it were, a peninsula of some miles in extent, all but surrounded by the winding of our wayward river. Raised from the bank on either side, it has for its highest part a ridge of sandy gravel, pounded pudding-stone, and the like ; while in the very next field there is a wide bed of blue limestone marl, and just beyond, again, a red sandstone layer. This present height has clearly once been the bottom of an estuary, subsequently heaved up by volcanic action ; and these so different soils are simply deposits made by the tide at different points of the shore. It is strange to think this now, as one stands, gun in hand after game, amidst a grand grove of old pines, like the wood of Ardennes, which stud the ridge as spines upon the back of a monster lizard species, and feel the cutting wind sweep off a landscape reaching away in view of a good fox-chase. Fortunate, however, is the proprietor, for he has there closely accumulated the materials of a rich soil, which only requires to be mixed by a master hand, as his is, to ensure success in the growth of a cereal abundance. By dint of carting the blue marl, during the slack season of the dark months, on to the gravelly tract, he has given it a fertile consistency that has this year enabled it to throw $44\frac{1}{2}$ bushels of wheat to the acre, and that in a district where we are thankful to obtain 33 as a rule. The money-value of this single crop was equal to forty years' purchase-money of the fee-simple of the ground itself, taking the rent as it stood when the farm came into the present cultivator's hands. The stubble is now being ploughed about ten inches deep, and will be again dressed with the marl; the consequence of which will be that, after the frosts have done their part, there will be a permanently-established loam of golden value, within forty yards of the pit from which we neighbours haul a hungry, sparkling, quartz, gravel, to strew upon our garden-walks.

The burnt surface of an old, foul clover, or rather couch ley, which I had pared and just done brown (mind, the red-brick tint is a sign of lost strength, owing to the fires having been too vehement), in large, slow fires, built on a pile of thorn-stumps that were excavated from a hedgerow which I have found it expedient to level, with a view to dividing the farm proportionately for rotation of crops, I find, as I had anticipated, does admirably under the fattening pigs, in a bay of a disused barn. There is already a thick floor of fat stuff, richly soaked as a Yorkshire pudding (for I had it hauled in during sunshine, in a thirsty state), which, pulverized, I shall drill in with the turnip-seed, thereby escaping the ruinous artificial-manure drain. One effect took me by surprise, al-though, of course, had one given the matter a thought, it was an effect simply to be expected; and that was that, whereas, before we used these ashes to strew the floor with, I found it impossible to approach the pig-lodge, much less to stay near it any time, owing to the pestilent effluvia that met one's nasal organ, why now the most delicate lady might stand by, and admire their sleeping highnesses, without the least offence whatever,—this desirable result being due to the deodorising quality of the charcoal-dust pervading it, and which came of the thorn-stubs that I mentioned above as built in for fuel, to start and help the fire. You may really stand, now, right in the centre of the sties, and be as unaware of the vicinity of an animal whose only fault is his smell, as though you were in your "parlour, counting out your money."

I shall take the hint, and, for the future, use plentifully an agent so easily obtained, the value of which is so great, as I see by a little work on "Antiseptic Treatment," which I had recently forwarded to me, bearing on this very subject. A few remarks therefrom, which interested and taught me, I quote, in the hope that they may be equally serviceable to others : "Farmers should never deeply cover up manure, so that the air cannot freely unite with it ; for if the air have not a free circulation within the manure, it perishes, and produces more injury than advantage." "Farmers should always·mix burned earth, peat, or charcoal with their stable manure, as charcoal retains the essential properties contained therein, and prevents its escape until it is ready to be put on the land, when the sun will liberate it." "Charcoal put into a tank will purify the water." "Farmers who raise stock should mix charcoal plentifully with their food." "Charcoal strengthens and heals the mucous membrane throughout the alimentary canal, and increases the power of the digestive organs, healing any unhealthy condition existing there : it prevents worms generating in the stomach, and absorbs the putrescent gasses by which they are generated, and they consequently die." "All kinds of stock will freely eat charcoal and salt mixed with their food, and they will greatly increase in weight by the free use of charcoal." I have long known that it answers well to keep a heap of cinders in the corner of a sty. Pigs will crack them like nuts, and chew them "to their advantage," as Joseph Ady would say. Our author further recommends the top-dressing of potato and hop plantations with charcoal or peat (charred I presume) as a preventive against blight and the fly. Charcoal put into a glass of water with an acorn or root will prevent the water from perishing or becoming putrid, as it would otherwise do, and the acorn will grow therein and become a small oak. "Should a joint of meat smell when put in the pot to boil, if a piece of charcoal be put in the water the meat will become sweet." "A piece or two of fine charcoal put into a parcel of game will preserve it sweet." Should "a joint of meat smell, rub fine charcoal on, and it will turn it sweet." "Again, florists and ladies who love beautiful flowers should always sprinkle charcoal on the soil, as it will create in the flowers the most delightful hues and brilliant colours."

The discovery "of the uses of charcoal in the various forms of disease" our author disclaims, and attributes to Moses, who has "recorded its virtues in the scriptures;" inasmuch as he directed the Israelites to put on sackcloth and ashes when they had "brought themselves into an unholy, an unhealthy state of body. The sackcloth was an open coarse kind of linen, and the ashes were burned wood, commonly termed 'charcoal.'

This had a healing and restorative effect on the unhealthy body, by changing its impure conditions." I remember Mr. Frank Buckland making a similar remark with respect to Mr. Moule's patented earth closets. Did not Moses send the Israelite with a spud out into the wilderness? And so there's nothing new under the sun.

The gardener has just shown me several pots of young pelargoniums, the result of our hybridising last summer. I wish I could just hook and haul in next June for an hour, that I might see what sort of blooms will reward our labour; I should then ease it to its place again amidst the hot months, for there is much of winter enjoyment yet due that one were loath to spare ; e.g., the Christmas parties, the gallops across country, and the afternoon saunter on our freshly-littered fold. But by the powers! I must be off; for there is an uproar in the nursery: and when I get there I find the two youngest boys, despite the cold of this frosty night, larking about and playing like kittens, as naked as they were born ; but at the sight of ourself there is a bound to the bed-clothes and a dive into night-shirts and a plunge into sheet-lane, as though they were aware that therein lay their only chance of an effective rear-guard ; and so we could not but laugh ("in'ardly, werry in'ardly, my lord"), and tuck them in, and return to our toil in the study.

"Good news from home!" the bailiff has just hurried up to say that at last, after much waiting, we have been rewarded by the birth of a heifer-calf from a valuable Towneley cow, which upon the spot we christen Lady Culshaw, in consideration of her belonging to the eminent Joseph's favourite Barmpton Rose tribe, and of her not exhibiting a black nose, a tint to which we always understood him to be averse until the recent turn of his Oxford studies.

AND so I am roused from my literary slumber by a round shot falling right at my feet and splashing me with splintered fragments. A printed enclosure with the Clitheroe postmark! I regret if a playful remark respecting black noses and Culshaw's "Oxford studies" has given annoyance to a gentleman so urbane as I have uniformly found Mr. Eastwood. Opportunely enough, however, it brings one to the discussion of a subject which it is high time to have set at rest. The black nose upon a pedigree Shorthorn is an unpardonable blemish at present in the eyes of the breeding world. That it should be so, thanks to the Yankee, who objected of old to any but the "raw nose:" else what harm could that be which is simply a relic of ancestral inheritance from the celebrated Galloway heifer and Chillingham herd, which were used so freely in Collings' alloy, and which is continually reappearing in the oldest and best strains (some, great Royal-prize-takers) of the pedigree stock, as every breeder knows? Names I will not give, as I have no wish to depreciate any gentleman's herd. I will only remark that Belvedere had the defect latent in his composition, and that the Chilton cows abounded with it. The oldest breeders in private converse make no secret of this objectionable nasal tint cropping up occasionally under most unlikely circumstances. From a scientific knowledge of the dip of strata, Sir R. Murchison amidst the Ural Mountains

predicted the finding of the Australian gold fields. By
an analogous acquaintance with the elements that
underlie the famous Thorndale bulls, it was long ago
predicted by a celebrated living Shorthorn authority
that an occasional black nose must crop out in that
stock. I was not myself at the Havering Park Sale,
but have certainly been repeatedly told by competent
authorities that Baron Oxford had undoubtedly a
smutty nose. Mr. Eastwood did well to have an in-
quest in the matter, and we will devoutly hope that
the shadowy dim spot which is allowed to disfigure
the luminary may not spread nor re-appear in his
progeny. But as America started the fuss by objecting
to "black noses," let it now make the amende honor-
able, and confess itself hypercritical in the first instance.
The emancipation of the Black has been of late their
praiseworthy mission. As regards Mr. Eastwood's
herd, be they tainted all in this terrible manner, still
would they fetch by auction, I do not hesitate to say,
the highest average that has been ever obtained.* The
gentleman who founded the first Towneley herd, and
who never meddles with stock of any sort without
gilding it, will not suffer from what really is only a
vulgar prejudice. I do not mean to say that it would
not be better if we could eliminate the dark stain
from our herds; but seeing how deeply it impregnates
them, I do not hesitate to state that I for one should
not decline to breed from an animal of excellent points
and fine quality, if his family be distinguished, even
though he may appear to have carried printer's ink in

* It is gratifying that this prophecy has been fulfilled : 181 guineas
the highest average known, having been the result of his recent sale
(June, 1871.)

his scent bottle. But to settle the matter more immediately and thoroughly : Messrs. Eastwood and Culshaw
—are they not, in the Shorthorn world, of authority to
set fashion even equal to that of the Empress Eugénie
or the Parisian stage ? " Let there be golden hair,"
and there was golden hair. " Let the eyelids be tinted,"
and the eyelids were tinted. Her Majesty had only to
ordain, and the thing was done. Let our leaders be as
resolute, and declare that at least the quadroon tint
shall not condemn a bovine beauty. And as we are
upon the subject, let them issue an edict further that
the white colour shall be equally costly with the red
and roan ; for have they not proved, in the course of
their distinguished victories, that the white heifer is
usually pre-eminent in loveliness of shape, in grace, in
wealthiest quality ? Again, are not the very richest
roans often the offspring of a white cow ? Such, at
least, has been my own private experience. To say
that the white are more delicate is simply not fact, as
anyone who likes may prove for himself, and as the
most experienced breeders and feeders readily allow.
To depreciate the cream hue only serves the purpose of
a few far-sighted buyers. That Mr. Eastwood is superior to this prejudice is proved by his using that grand
white bull the Hero. Speak out, then, upon these
points, Messrs. Eastwood and Culshaw : your determination will be law.

Having written so far upon the subject of Shorthorns,
let me conclude this paper therewith. First, I would
avow that my first experience of pedigree Shorthorns
made me freely condemn them. I unhappily got hold
of an invalid sort. There is, however, no occasion for
any beginner to do this. The store of sound stylish

tribes is now so great that anyone possessing judgment and sufficient funds, may soon stock his boxes and fields with a collection of animals which shall be a source of unceasing pleasure to him, as of undoubted profit.

Foremost amidst delights is the gratification arising from chemical studies and experiment. The breeding of shorthorns affords this delight ; for, allowed that you begin, as you should, with cows of a similar type and exalted—I had nearly written "fashionable," but that fashion must alter with success—pedigree, there is subsequently no little to be done by judicious crosses and selection in *keeping up* of the *form you approve;* for in that respect every different breeder has his special tastes.

Just for amusement, I ran over, last week, to see the conglomerate herd belonging to the late Mr. Packe sold. Arriving at Loughborough by the first morning train, it was very hard not to take a peep at the Quorn, whose meet was within a mile of the town, as I was informed by my host. However, duty carried the day ; and so, after having satisfied the claim of the Minister of the Interior, I trudged three miles to the farm, wishing heartily that I had brought my waterproof, heavy-metaled farm-boots, instead of a gim-crack, elastic-sided pair, that looked like yawning under the influence of the slush of a damp morning. However, arrived upon the scene of action, and before anybody, save some half-dozen neighbouring farmers, I had ample time to cast my eye around. The cows looked exceedingly well, in good beefy condition, as though they had had their calf-meat kept upon them rather than that they had been barley-mealed for the sale. They were a lot of very fine cows, and,

L

being so numerous, and representing so many breeders, afforded a good study for the tiro who could have an able Mentor to point out the characteristic points of each.

There was a wealthy-looking grand-framed cow of the Marjoribanks formation; there were the elegant, aristocratic-looking maidens of Sir C. Knightly's moulding; a useful, thick-fleshed, big, matron, bred by Jonas Webb, whose artistic hand, had he lived only a few years longer, would have established a famous kind for both butcher and dairy; there were a few specimens from that keen judge, Mr. Wetherall, with the true ring of his stylish Silver Bell sort; there were a few square-built cows of the much-belauded Waterwitch tribe, bearing in their dewlap the mark of old Vanguard, but with the most cantankerous horns that it is possible to conceive. Above all, however, were the lovely massive Towneley Butterflies. "Them's the pick," I heard a master-butcher remark to his fellow, as with a dainty movement the celebrated White Butterfly wound her way amidst the herd over the bedding of deep muck, to a sweet lock of hay in the corner of the manger, beside a heifer that had recently calved, and to which she whispered, I doubt not, in her own considerate gentle way, a few words of matronly counsel, just as a Marchioness of thirty years might over the cup of tea she was sipping, by way of company to the young Lady Maud, whose reclining attitude and pale features were significant of a recent interesting event.

The average, so far as I could make out, was about £37 for the cows: but there was a general feeling that "if Strafford had been there," there would have been a vast improvement in the prices obtained. "That Tattersall of Shorthorns," as the auctioneer of the day handsomely termed him, would certainly have lifted several lots considerably, if only by recounting the story of their blood. But I had to get away to catch the train, only after all to find every bed in Birmingham occupied, owing to some neighbouring races, and the coffee-room crammed with sundry coteries of hoary experts and downy-lipped would-be turfites, who were undoubtedly buying their experience.

And so, in pleasant company of some experienced Shorthorn breeders, I took the night train, put on a double suit of clothes, and lay down for a restless journey between sleeping and waking, to arrive at home some hours before expected, and so to realise fully in the bright glances that succeeded first surprise the truth of the poet's exquisite lines :—

> " 'Tis sweet to hear the watch-dog's honest bark
>   Bay deep-mouth'd welcome as we draw near home :
> 'Tis sweet to know there is an eye will mark
>   Our coming, and look brighter when we come :
> 'Tis sweet to be awakened by the lark,
>   Or lull'd by falling waters : sweet the hum
> Of bees, the voice of girls, the song of birds,
> The lisp of children, and their earliest words."

Now, if I were Lord of Dunrobin Castle, and for reasons sufficiently obvious to you all, I dare say I should particularly like to be Lord of Dunrobin Castle, I should prefer of the article bovine most decidedly to cultivate the shaggy West Highlander, with its long lithe cubic frame, sharp-pointed horns, and uniform type. To see a lot of such, brown, black, dun, upon the fern-clad park slopes by the wild tumbling cataract, and amidst the heather-brake (the whole my own property too), would afford me, I must

confess, unmitigated pleasure, and would lead me often
in admiring contemplation to their vicinity, only provided the lord regnant of the herd should not too
curiously reciprocate the attention : as the having to
" tree it " for an indefinite period, especially towards
the luncheon hour, might not be equally delightful.
But as I am not, nor likely to be, the master of
Dunrobin Castle, I must cast about and see what sort
of cattle will best suit my taste and pocket as an
ordinary agriculturist upon a small scale.   Well, then,
will the juicy Devon do ?   Aye, right well, my lad, in
the shape of cold roast sirloin with pickled onions, and
mashed " pratees."   It is a lovely little breed upon its
own clovery pastures.   Again : the mossy-coated Hereford cows.   It is a pity that the best breeders of this
stock don't try more to keep clear of the hard-skinned
smooth ones.   A rare herd might be got together in
this county of Herefordshire, by picking here one and
there one—often, too, out of a small lot almost by the
way-side.   Both Hereford and Devon do best, I think,
upon their own soil, better perhaps than any other
sorts there.   There is a virtue, doubtless, in their
being natives of the district, just as the Suffolk horse
does better on the bean-producing clay-fields of the
eastern counties than in a damp turnip district.   But
why drift on in this way to the expected declaration
that for all purposes one deems the cosmopolitan
Shorthorn the best cattle to keep ?   Why, simply to
ask whether some one cannot put an American pump
into the auctioneer's head, and draw forth a stream
of the information we breeders desire.   We desire it
sadly.

The blessed spring is at hand again.   One sees it in

every glance of sunlight, and feels it in every breeze. There's Master Tom-Tit, the long-tailed, flirting with his cousin, Miss Blue-Tit, whom he has taken in to dinner upon a willow-spray, as he hops about, and busies himself to pick out for her delicacies from underneath the bark ; while on the lower branches there's quite a juvenile party of the small tit's fry. Two young squirrels from their nest, which hangs like a ball in a neighbouring birch-tree, have been gambolling around the trunk, bobbing this way and that way, and cutting over the tall box bushes, as if it were a race-course, no more ruffling it than would a breath of summer air. Then our industrious, lovely, nut-hatch has returned too. She has gathered, and we trust enjoyed, all the filberts we had pinned around the hole in which she annually builds her nest. There's a rabbit too—the gardener says, " Confound him ! " flicking his white tuft contemptuously in view, as he deems it best to bolt under the bough of the laurel fence at our approach. Master Reynard we don't scent about, although during the snow he made a frequent circuit of the very house, and actually had the audacity to kill a hen-pheasant close underneath the windows. A wood-pigeon, reared from the nest last year, that got loose from the aviary when the fat gardener went in to fetch a board one day, and was not smart to close the door, hangs very melancholy about the woods. She hopped so leisurely beside me the other morning, that, not knowing of her escape, I concluded she must be a wounded bird, and tried fruitlessly to catch her. Since that, while a pigeon-shooting match was going on in the meadows below us, upon the other side of the river, she flew up from somewhere below, and nestled as if for protection, behind an oak bough, close above the children's heads, where they were standing to look on. I hope she'll find a mate, and build near the house. During the frost and snow a pair of water-hens came up, and fed regularly with the pheasant upon the lawn. With the return of softer weather, they have discontinued their visits.

I am sorry to see that Mr. Frank Buckland has pronounced decidedly against the introduction of horseflesh upon the table. Certainly if the taste, as he states, at all resembles the smell of steaming hunters at a check, it must be inconceivably abominable as a viand. Surely, too, there would be great risk of a glandered specimen being sometimes served up, the incipient symptoms of this disease it being impossible to detect. It certainly would have led to a considerably larger number of horses being bred, if a filly whose forelegs were too fine could have simply been sent to the shambles as first-class beef. It would have much diminished the great risks of breeding which deter all but the most enthusiastic lovers of horseflesh now from keeping a brood mare.

This reminds me of a piece of luck which befell me the other day, not before I wanted it, considering some equine losses that I experienced two years since. I attended, quite casually, the sale of a small mountain farmer who had notice to quit, and picked up a rare specimen of a sort that I have been long looking for— a short-legged, square-actioned, spirited, Welsh cart-mare, about fifteen hands in height, or just under it, with quarters that one might play ball against, and a back that would carry a cradle steadily, with a sweet head, a tan muzzle, and short cannon-bone, heavy in foal, too : a most temperate worker, and so fast that, being matched with a colt, while I was looking on, she walked right up with her nose into the neck of the driver of a Suffolk team before her, so that the lad had to ease them, and wait for room : all this, too, gentle reader, for the sum of £11 12s. 6d. ! Congratulate me, and hope of her as was once aptly said of Lord John Russell, in Eastern language, that her shadow may never grow less. I trust that, although aged ten years, with luck she may prove the ancestress of some valuable teams. Her late owner has gained considerable celebrity as a winner of silver cups at local ploughing matches, this mare being one that he generally used. A colt of hers went for £37 ! It was a bit of rare luck. The spectators were not thinking, until it was too late to bid.

There have been considerable losses hereabouts among the lambs of last year upon the turnips. In the worst cases the disaster has been clearly attributable to their having been starved during the autumn, so that their system could not stand the change to forcing food. In one case the lad was giving the pen too wide a range. One or two had fallen several nights in succession. Orders were issued that they should only have turnips between ten and four, but plenty of hay by night. This stopped the plague at once.

I have had a recipe sent to me for the making of sloe wine, which is said to be an excellent specific for the scour, being of course strongly astringent. Carbonate of soda and ginger mixed strong, the dose being about a wine-glass at a time, I have never found to fail. That acidity in the stomach, which is the cause of its excessive looseness, is thereby corrected.

By the way, being in the humour to communicate recipes, you will doubtless have tried the old plan of getting grease out of cloth by laying brown, blotting, or other absorbent paper upon the spot, and pressing it with a hot iron. A far better plan, as was shown to me the other day, is to hold a piece of red-hot coal with the tongs close above the stain ; you will see the grease apparently issue out in steam. I have always found that the ironing of paper left a something still inherent in the cloth, which was attractive of dust, and *showed* very shortly. Under this latter process, the obnoxious element vanishes like a well-rattled fox. *Experto crede.*

Curious is it how practice sharpens natural ability. One has heard of a man having an eye for a horse ; but to-day it occurred to me to find a man with an eye for a needle. One of the servants having a bad whitlow, I had pricked it for him, and threw the instrument out of sight as I imagined between a drinking trough and the wall. The next day, having to repeat the operation, I remembered where I threw the needle, and looked for it, but in vain. The coachman, seeing me stoop, said, "Oh ! I have the needle, sir." I could not have thought that anyone would have noticed it thrown there ; but I found a solution. The man had been a tailor, and took to driving, as his health suffered from too close confinement to the house.

More assured am I than ever of the value of rowen for lambing ewes. It is delightful to stand by the tame grey-eyed Down mother, and watch her so daintily make her dinner, cropping first an advanced green blade, now a faded stem, now leaf of sorrel or crow-foot, then a nip of flat-green succulent (I don't know what leaf), mixing them quite as cook does the salad. And the lambs thrive so well with it.   Such a flush of milk the mothers seem to have, and there's no diarrhœa.   It well rewards for saving in the autumn. What a talent Jonas Webb must have had for finding the needle ! I am every day more surprised to con-template the meaty legs of his mutton, and compare them as milkers with my Cotswold flock.

I wonder he never took to pigs. But I had best betake myself to bed, you will suggest ; so, gentle reader, I wish you with Byron's grasshopper one " good-night " chirrup more.

"Painless dentistry," did you say the advertisement was ?   Why, then, now, that's just exactly what I wanted last Christmas, and expect to want about Mid-summer-day.   Now, is there no one of the many existent goodnatured fellows who will not, as poor inimitable Wright used to say, " come for to go for to send for to fetch for to bring for to carry" one of these said clever artists to sustain me under the operation of " draw " to which I shall shortly be subjected ?   I should be so thankful if it could be done.   How thank-ful I cannot say.

Having touched upon the subject, let me go further, and counsel, I trust without offence, enthusiastic youth. I am spirited thereto by a recent encounter, from which I have emerged I consider not only scathless, but tri-umphant, with an unconscionable tradesman who had the audacity to try upon me a trick which I can attri-bute only to what they must have judged a juvenile guilelessness of countenance.

Don't you, my lad, if you go into a swell London shop (whether to fit out your bridal, or in any such bashful mood), on giving an order, content yourself with simply entering in your pocket-book the price stated by the airy and self-satisfied individual who shall accompany you through the show-rooms, giving the prices so fluently after rapid calculation with pen from behind his sapient ear. Get the particulars written out of each article that you order, the price it shall be for cash upon delivery, and the time of its certain delivery. To that document get your fashionable attendant's signature appended, " Catchem and Co., per Oily Wideawake," or else the chances are that upon receipt of the goods you will receive also an exceedingly spiced invoice, far hotter than you intended, and which shall curtail you of some reasonable comforts for months to come; while if you go openmouthed to your solicitor, and mean to blow them up bodily, you will find that there is no *locus standi*. They will shield themselves under the simple reply, " We gave only a proximate estimate." So you, my dear, will be beautifully done. *Experto crede !*

I am more urgent upon this point, as there is a noble trustfulness about the mind of youth, which is most admirable and highly romantic, but simply doesn't pay. For many a year how have not we old fellows been prone to half-apologize if we had dared to ask whether " discount were allowed ;" " if such be the cash price ;" " whether it were of the material," and so on. And it is with something of an angry rebound of feeling that one triumphantly demands now from the most self-possessed shopman " the best material for the lowest figure ; and be quick, please, for I'm in a hurry."

No more of the diffidence with which we took our orders as to breakfast, &c., from the college scout, and allowed his intervention with the awful University tradesmen. No more of that : "no, no, not for Joe— not for Joseph, oh! dear, no!" Eh! the smiling of the counter-skipper now, and the bowing, and the desire to serve, and the "hope that you'll recommend us, sir," which, to the vain mind, are of value equal to a redoubled discount.

Smart's the word. Knock the wind out of them first blow—apologizing, of course, for the *contretemps ;* but the effect's produced, and the courteous apology effectually salves.

Water-wolves—water-wolves are we not all ? preying upon each other, rather than "jolly dogs," as one fain might wish, and as we were wont once to believe over devil'd kidneys and a damper, "in the days that we were young, a long time ago."

D'ye see that, young friend; for if ye don't, and have to wait for the spectacles of personal experience, why, then, more's the pity, and our Cassandra self has sung in vain.

But to return homewards. I was constrained just now to steep my hands, feverish from rowing, in a basin of water half-boiling. I had been musing of Shorthorns, and the sweet, darling heifer-calves that have been dropping upon our pastures of late, when, drop! down came a huge spider from his swing, which I had not noticed above me. Poor thing! how he was doubled up at once! Didn't like hot water at all. Must have been married. It was so like what one is obliged so often to do oneself, under influence of the conjugal (tin) kettle.

There hath been a multitude of the spider-tribe about the house lately. They are said to follow the wake of the black beetles, a huge horde of which has overrun us again lately. The beetle must afford rich feeding; for these spiders are a monstrous sort. We have found that strewing the leaves of the elder-tree upon the kitchen-floor causes somehow a diminution of the beetle class. Whether they find the vegetable poisonous or not, I don't know. A confectioner counselled the recipe.

We are plagued by another insect invasion. The evening air hisses with the flight of myriad cock-chafers. Herein, however, our old friends the rooks (to whom we have been staunch under the remonstrance of prejudiced agricultural neighbours) have done us an exceeding service. I could not imagine, yesterday morning, whatever was the matter with the birds. They were in and out among the apple-trees and beeches, clumsily alighting, and staggering along the weak twigs, managing to maintain their equilibrium only by a half-flutter, with their wings up, and swaying after the example of Blondin's pole.

"Them be after the blight, them be," remarked fat Melon, the gardener, as he came up to my window, triumphantly exhibiting a grand Gloire de Dijon rose: "Beant he a beauty, sir?"

"Call him the 'Second of May,' Melon, if you want a name for it."

"Why, sir?"

"Why, because it reminds me of some one whom I saw on that day with his shirt-collar petals all turned down, and a yellowish tinge about the gills."

Poor Melon, who likes a dance about the May-pole,

and a suck at the cider-cask afterwards, hereupon retired in consternation.

"Them be after the blight, sir." And, sure enough, they were in good earnest. I at once had the craws of sundry rooklings (of which a tart was being made for the kitchen) cut open, and found therein a thick débris of the comminuted, half-digested pest, a few of their shiny brown armour-plates being yet unsmashed, which I exhibited in exaggerated stature, by help of the microscope, to our horrified cook.

Bless her heart! she is a good, clean, simple-minded thing. But the mention of her name reminds me. She of late has heard a ghost! In the stillness of the night, a knocking at the door! Too frightened to move, she has simply ducked under the blankets, instead of advancing, as we consider she should have done, to interrogate. Well, of course, this is no joke in a country-house. A place soon has the reputation of being haunted; and then there's no getting servants at all. Well, it so happened that, one night, ourself had got deeply interested in a hideous novel —one of the "Fine Young English Gentleman" sort, which are as keenly rapid in their attractiveness ("sensation effect," it is termed) as a red-herring drag, but which no one ever looks at a second time, for the pleasure of restudying a pet passage of eloquent and truthful worth (as one does with the Waverley lot), and which are only so much "rot," to use an expressive vulgar term, when the literary merits of England come to be registered—when, about the witching hour of midnight, we heard a mysterious "Tap, tap! rap! tap, tap!" It made our blood run cold, we confess; but we were brave enough to explore, and we found—what, I wonder? Why, no more, no less, than simply a death-watch beetle.

Heresy and insubordination in the camp! "You must indeed tell us when the calf is going to be killed, poor dear little thing. It is *so* tame and so pretty," with an air of coy indignation our eldest born little girl remonstrated, sitting up in her cot, as I went to give her the regular good-night kiss. "Such a sweet," coaxingly added another little puss, also leaning out from behind her curtain with a remonstrativeness of pouted lip that was pretty to behold. "I declare I won't touch veal for ever so long," said her sister in chorus. This was all in reference to a fawn-tinted gazelle-eyed Alderney calf that was unfortunately born of the masculine gender, and had consequently to make way for cream and butter. As if they hadn't quite enough of pets already! enough forsooth to ruin any farmer. There's the old faithful canter-on-three-legs Breadalbane terrier, with three fat long-tailed puppies in her wake, as slow-paced as herself. There are no end of bantams, although ultimately I had to send all the poultry from the stable premises to the bailiff's wife at the farm, as the poor hens prone to incubation had been frequently left to their fruitless sitting without even an egg under them, until it was difficult to say which were the barest, their hapless bosom or the board that served them in lieu of nest. Talk of the discomfort and attaching agonies of a seat in Parliament; they are for not a moment to be compared to the occasional sufferings of a brooding fowl in a child's hen-house! Then on the list of pets come cats and kittens in hopeless measure. Woe betide either them . or the young pheasants ere long! A curious incident happened to this special nursery puss last week. She had had left to her one prettily-marked bantling out of the lot born and duly consigned to a watery grave, and of this she was especially proud. Well, one day it was missing, and the poor mother was miserable. The children declared that she had forgotten where she had deposited it. This seemed an extraordinary theory, considering the might of instinct. Anyhow she followed them everywhere in their search about the rooms of the house, the out-buildings, and even through the shrubberies and woodland walks, all to no purpose, mewing piteously the while—whether a note of lamentation, or gratitude, or entreaty, it is impossible to say. At last they appropriated a kitten from a cat at the farm, which with much ceremony they delivered to the nursery puss. She at once took to it, while the robbery or transference was treated with the utmost indifference by the bucolic puss, who trotted about or watched in the stable and cowsheds for her prey just as unconcernedly as if she felt that all had been done for the best, and that her offspring had been fortunate in its promotion to an upper circle.

Well, one morning, about light, some days after the kitten's disappearance, I was awoke by a sad cry, as if of an animal in pain, which seemed at one time quite near, at another quite far off. It occurred to me that it might be that old Melon had managed to ensnare a rabbit, of whose inroads he had been complaining lately, and that it was from this unhappy animal the wailing proceeded. I looked out of the window, but failed to detect the victim's whereabouts. Then the agonized cry drew nearer, until at last it was beside my pillow. I sprang up, and in a closet behind a chest there was the wretched missing kitten, crawling and shrieking as if mad with pain. It must have been there for some days the housemaid declares, and that without making the least sound of any sort. How to account for the circumstance is beyond me, unless possibly it had been in a trance. Anyhow, so it occurred. The nursery puss was delighted to receive her own again from the children, with sundry scoldings to boot, while the farm cat took ungraciously the return of her infant, which our fry decided it was only just to restore.

Rooklings, tom-tits, sparrows, and such like, they have had in quantities, and destroyed by excess of kindness, too, feeding them by force ever so often in the day. Lastly, they have some blackfaced mountain ewe-lambs within a wired enclosure. This last sort doesn't pay on my side. It's all very well for the young ladies to have a snowy pet, with broad blue ribbon around its neck, nibbling parsley out of their hands, and bleating gratefully at their approach. But when these said lambs grow to be big sheep, and in their turn have lambs too, then it comes to be no joke, for me at least, the fond feeder of the lot ovine and human, for it just happens that their pet lambs of the year before last have this year lambs of their own, which are now worth, the chicks hear from the bailiff, some fifteen shillings a-piece. For this sum they have deliberately sued me. Now if this goes on it must ultimately be a serious affair. "What about their keep, my pet?" I appeal in vain. "Oh! you know, papa, they can't eat much," &c. &c. But the subject depresses.

To change the subject : In the river bed below the farm, there is lodged a huge boulder, some five yards square, which when under water is, as the Irishman said, a sign to the traveller that he must not attempt that ford. It is a splendid balcony this hot weather, whereon one can lie wandering in dream-land, soothed, too, as Mæcenas, by the murmur of the flowing stream.

The other day we saw a splash from the shore ; so getting into the boat, we ascended the rock upon the upper side, and creeping quietly to the edge, on looking over we saw beneath us a glorious salmon of about ten pounds weight, resting on his oars, upon the look out for spoil. Dash ! flop ! and having secured the prey, with a quick, brief curve in the flashing water, he was returning to his post when his quick eye marked us, and with a glance of light through the wave he was gone !

What a blessed gift is Sabbath repose ! For the fashionable idler it is an idea difficult to realize; rather in fact, *ennuyé*, tired, tiresome, he wanders from club to club, acquaintance to acquaintance, to the stables, to dinner, to early bed. The right welcome bright enjoyment it really is, fully to appreciate, take a mastership in a school for six months. Teach boys from half-past six a.m. to ten p.m., with rare intervals, when the small deer have their play, and are really more troublesome than while under lesson drill, owing to the scrapes they will get into, their noise, their pugnaciousness, their dirt-pie delight. Eh ! what it was then, to sleep .the extra two sweet hours unstartled by that dreadful bell ! But why particularly I dilate upon Sabbath repose here is that one enjoys it so thoroughly of a summer evening at one parti-

M

cular corner of the sloping lawn, just where it joins
on to a wild piece of the hill.   All nature seems to
appreciate the difference in the day.   The whole air
is so still and warm, and the tints upon the western
sky are so delicious.

The swallows skim fearlessly and frequent in the
upper cloud region.   A bright brown hawk slips idly
across.   Abundant turtle-doves croon amidst the elm-
trees.   The wild pigeons are cooing through the wood.
The incessant rooks are so busy on their tree-tops.   An
occasional pheasant steps gallantly out from the covert
shelter, occasionally escorting a timid hen who has been
up to feed, and seems fearful of returning alone ; while
a brace of partridges advance, pecking up to the very
verge of our feet, where we lie unseen, young and old,
holding our very breath, lest we should disturb the
elements of our enjoyment.

We have had a good deal of trouble with the shorthorns of late.   " Well! and what is it has happened to
your fascinating stock?" some may ask.   Why, in the
first place, the grand cavalier, the monarch Butterfly,
having managed by dint of his great weight, and his
being tied up, to establish a housemaid's knee, it
was judged expedient to remove him into a loose box.
As it happened, fortunately, the place selected was the
bay of a disused barn, where he was strongly walled
in on every side, excepting the door, which he makes
to creak and shake every time he touches it with neck
or flank.   Precautions had been taken in the fitting of
it, that he should not be able to introduce his horn
anywhere.   As his temper is not of the best, and his
eye-balls glare out exactly like those of his grandsire
the Towneley Frederic, I judged it expedient to attach

a cord to the ring in his nose, to run over a small wheel on the beam above, being weighted at the end, so as to allow of his advancing and retiring at pleasure to and from his manger. This was a large stone trough laid upon a bed of masonry. The very moment he found himself at liberty he worked his horns beneath the trough, and threw it high in air with inconceivable strength and savage temper. Down it came again, and right upon the cord, pinning his nose to the ground; whereupon he blared and roared so fearfully that his attendant, in a fright, managed to cut him loose and get out again in time to avoid his resentment. Here, then, was a pretty kettle of fish! For the time, he went positively mad. It was frightful to behold his fury as he wreaked it upon everything within reach. Fortunately there was little besides his bedding and his victuals attainable. He had to be watched continuously, for fear he might manage to overthrow the door; but in a day or two he grew calmer, as he got used to his lodgings; and stealing his opportunity, the herd-boy, having left the door so far open as to allow of his hasty retreat in case of need, managed to pounce upon the animal's tail, to which he clung vigorously, until the beast, having exhausted himself in the vain endeavour to get free, took a look round of curious inspection; whereupon the lad hooked him cleverly with his rod, and the bovine brute was at man's mercy again. He became mild enough on being tied, and I trust now will not have to be done for with a bullet, as I once was afraid. What other events in the herd have occurred I must leave until next time.

Alack-a-day! that one must needs write, sultry

weather or not! It don't matter that one would mightily prefer just to sit down in the now swift, shallow stream of the limpid Wye the day long, listening (if it could be) to sweet music in the distance, and having bird's-eye and bottled perry within reach. It don't matter that the prevailing heat is such—(Bother the comet who will sweep his tail so near to our gasping planet!)—that one could with advantage, as Sidney Smith said, "get out of one's flesh and sit in one's bones for half-an-hour;" but you see, gentle reader, that when one's mind gets on the fret, 'tis like one's wife's talk, or young pop: it must froth over, under risk of an explosion. I am anxious to tell you the result of my experiments: first, as respects the pelargonium seedlings, the history of whose parentage I gave you in a former number. A few have flowered. With what keen anxiety, and almost hourly visits, did one not watch the *début* of that first blossom! It was all I could do to refrain from opening it, *vi et armis*, when the floret had really begun to extricate its petals from the enclosing grasp of the calyx points. I think old Melon did take a surreptitious peep by the help of the grape-scissors, for I cannot otherwise account for sundry marks upon the flower when it did appear, which looked far more like bruising caused by human interference than simple veining due to Nature's pencil. How grievously disappointed I was to find that the flower I had produced by dint of so much painful care, actually came out identical, to all appearance, with one of the commonest sorts that old women indulge with a broken teapot, in their cottage window. "Good-bye," said I at once, with Celtic perseverance, "to this fun;" but behold! the next in size and tint is an eminent triumph, although not so rare-looking a sample as one could have wished. And yet the parents of the first (the failure) are superbly tinted flowers from the stock of about the best grower in England. However, the farmer, if he would succeed in his profession, must reflect over every experiment : and this is what I did conclude, on my river rock and over the sweetest of pipes—Why, you see that's a new proof, young man, if you wanted one, that if you are to succeed as a breeder in the production of fine animals, at all equal to their parentage, you must select for your elements those that are not only symmetrical in form, but whose striking traits and features have become stereotyped in their nature, so that you can safely rely upon "like" being born of "like." More than ever now I appreciate the wisdom of those shrewd, grey-haired men, of whom the auction ring leans forward to take a good look, when the glass runs out, and a small, well-shaped heifer is credited to Mr. So-and-so, at a bidding of many hundred guineas. Besides her own sweet feminine attributes and graceful style of person, her character went beyond, upon a long, stout stock of most fashionable sires. There will be little doubt of her producing beauties. Finally, then, whether you would breed Shorthorns or Southdowns, or any other "fancy stock," you must provide yourself with the *very best* blood, to begin with, *in well-shaped animals* that have a genealogical tree of indisputable value.

It is no good beginning now to start pedigrees. A great and successful breeder, pre-eminent in the prize-list, lately found out this fact, and consequently made a clean sweep of the lot, a grand selection of cows fetching only a few guineas over butchers' price. He was, doubtless, getting aware of what his customers had long since found out, that there was no satisfaction in carrying his new strains on. Himself endowed with rare judgment and taste, he could generally attain success ; but when it came to his elements (only just conglomerate and scarcely baked) being put into less experienced hands, the sad fact occurred that no particular development could be relied upon to issue out. It might be this shape, or that shape, or something of all sorts. Hence, he wisely made a clearance, and will, I expect, now be more fortunate in his prices, when his customers find that the seedlings answer to the parent plant.

There is one disagreeable nuisance to which I am subject. I don't know whether other Shorthorn breeders suffer similarly. It is, that certain gentlemen, exceedingly worthy in all respects but this I doubt not, come and look over one's young bulls. They always select the best, and ask the price. As a matter of course they wince thereat, and reply coldly, " Mine is only a common dairy herd ; I cannot afford that." "Ah! then I'll show you what will suit you at one-fourth the figure. Here's a grand young animal, pure bred, but descended from animals whose owners never took the trouble to enter their stock in the 'Herd Book.' There now, he is as good as any one I have shown you, only excepting his having no recorded pedigree to show." Oh dear no, not for Joseph at all ! The gentleman-buyer wants the best of pedigrees, although his herd is but a dairy lot of cows, and requires this cheap in consideration of that fact. Just look at the logic of it ! Is it to be wondered at that one has sometimes not patience to reply to such application. He never calculates (oh dear, no!) that if, in consideration of his cows' poverty of blood, I charitably sell him at about butcher's price the near relative of a twelve hundred guinea bull, he may the next day pass the animal on at a stinging figure to the enthusiastic cousin or friend who *does* go in for the terribly high-bred kind, because really after all the bull is better than he requires. And if he does make this second bargain, will he remember the first seller? Will he or will he not? Avaunt! I have no patience to write further of such. Let them learn to reason, before they insult the feelings of those who like myself have launched their bark in trust upon a costly deep.

" Poor little Dandy; how sorry he will be to leave his mamma!" This was the sympathetic remark of our Benjamin, in respect to one of the three terrier puppies which is about to be sent to a distance, as of course one cannot be keeping such small deer for everlasting; especially as the lamb question makes one sufficiently sore in regard to the children's pets. Benjamin had not reckoned upon the neighbourhood of his brothers and sisters when this tender-hearted reflection gained utterance. Of course a maternal caress reached him ; but, alas! the agnomen of Dandy stuck, and hath given an advantage to his mischievous brother.

Talking of mischief—unfortunately, one day, a month since, a lady, who had been with the "Missus" inspecting the poultry at the farm, quite casually cast a glance of inspection over the half-door of a loose box in which a young Butterfly of ten months holds his reign. She had a white floating veil on, the flutter of which so terrified the young animal, that he jumped and knocked himself about the box quite frightfully. He has since

given us much trouble. He will not be soothed, and
butts viciously at remonstrance of any sort; whereas,
up to that period he was as gentle as need be. It is so
busy at the farm-house now. Such squadrons of ducklings, each officered by a single matron, dabbling about
as dirty and as short-clothed as campaigners upon a
heap of fresh vetches in apartments damp as I wish
the turnip ground could be. The burnt couch ashes,
of which I carted in quite thirsty some fifteen waggon-
loads last autumn, and upon which a shoal of pigs was
fattened, has sieved out so beautifully fine, and yet so
greasily damp, as to put the bailiff into ecstacies. I am
not quite sure that he did not actually taste a crumb on
the tip of his finger. I trust the swedes may like it.
I have not a seed in yet, nor shall I put any in until
rain threatens. Mildew always punishes our early
sowers. My seed is reposing the meanwhile amidst a
bedding of sulphur, as a precaution against the raids
of fly.

I must—botheration!—but yet I must, despite the
depressing effect of this fearful electrical weather, for
I have promised that I will write. I really hope that
at last the sky has arrived at its bursting period, for
there has gathered during the evening right above the
house, a most matrimonial-looking thunderous cloud,
which I think must needs come down about curtain-
time. What a thing it would be to be young again!
Even at this sultry irritating moment there is a merry
noise from the roost of the youngster boys, who have
bolted the door against the remonstrance of the only
party they fear, their eldest brother, and are throwing
nude somersaults about the nursery floor. The handmaidens are weary, and only feebly expostulatory, for

we are going to have a "leetle" dancing party, and
they have been hard at preparatory work all day.
Oneself is angry, but tied hereat, so that the juveniles
have a fair prospect of being ultimately triumphant.
Even as I write, however, there is a consternated close
cry of "Eliza! Eliza! Eliza-a-a!" as the shrewd
attendant hath turned the light off, and plentifully
applied "cold pig." Pig! that recalls one to the farm
again, and the thought of water, too, is suggestive. I
have been the main part of this day with a home-made
implement tapping weak spots, in anticipation of a
Norton's pump, that I expect to arrive to-morrow. We
have repeatedly struck water, but as repeatedly been
stumped out. There is

> "Water, water everywhere,
> Nor any drop to drink."

We strike a sandbed, and the mixture chokes the
valves. We draw forth the pipe by dint of lever,
empty it on its head of a good thick sedimentary gallon,
replace it in its hole, and, still most obstinate, it refuses
to yield water. The pulling up and down hath made a
puddle of the sides, and again suffocating results!
Then we get dismayed and despair of gaining our object
from this slough. So we strike down a crowbar anew,
and come thud, thump, upon a rock, a soft sandstone
layer, through which we drive the bar without much
difficulty; and then underneath occurs a bed of marl,
which fills the perforations of the pipe; and so we are
effectually done, as we have no further length at hand.
There is no alternative but to desist, and await the
arrival of the genuine article by rail from the Birmingham agents.

Here we left off last night, it being positively too painfully sultry to get on with one's writing. Hand and arm absolutely stuck to the paper, as our ideas stuck resolutely, too, in the clay pocket of our muddled brains.

But, as the Irish song says,

> " 'Twas of a Wednesday night,
> At two o'clock in the morning,"

when, glad sound, through the open window! there was a torrent descending. Good-luck now for the embrowned pastures, good-luck for the mildewed swede-leaf, good-luck for the farm *in toto;* for now, at this hour of 9 a.m., a mist—quite a washing-day mist—covers the face of the whole earth; and there will be a luxuriant growth forthwith. With our abundant sweet straw, there may not, after all, be a dearth of cattle-food, supposing—as there is every present prospect—that we can put in the breadth we intend of hybrid turnips.

There is an excellent plan of quaint old Drury's for the multiplication of food, the secret of which consists in soaking wheat-straw. I cannot lay hands on his work just now; but, if I remember well, his plan was to cut wheat-straw of a short length, and then put it to soak for some hours in cold water, until a thick mucilage be formed. He then boiled it, stirring in a portion of meal. By this means he was enabled to keep a large extra quantity of stock. I must look the volume up, and give his exact words next time.

I have just been called off to inspect a useful new implement which I bought at Leicester, and which, wonderful to relate, satisfies my honest, ruddy-faced old bailiff. It is an ordinary, but excellent plough, which, by the simple alteration of three bolts, can in a few moments be converted successively into a potato-raiser, a digging implement, a subsoil plough, a paring plough and a double mould-board plough.

Having stumbled upon the mention of the Leicester Show, let me thankfully acknowledge what a wonderful opportunity for successful study both of animals and machinery, that tented field afforded to the young farmer. From the shilling knife-sharpener and linen-wrapped refrigerative dish-cover to Howard's monstrous moorland plough and Owen's cataract-pump. There was something at every step to attract and instruct. The Southdown ewes were lovely as ever, with their quiet grey eye and weighted thigh. The snowy Cotswold were a picture, yet suggesting to one the involuntary thought that the loss of one such individual must be heavy, and that, considering the precarious life of a sheep, I should prefer meeting my luck with four small representatives of the ovine species to staking so many sovereigns in a single specimen. There were some grand Herefords, amidst others of vulgar quality. There were delicious-looking Devons and a sweet first-prize Alderney heifer, that capered about in her owner's hand as if triumphantly exhibiting her rosette in gratitude for the indulgence her early youth received at his hand ; but, after all, for numbers at least, the Short-horns had the pull of the show. Of the professional critics there were some who considered this the best show upon the whole of such kind ever exhibited ; there were others who compared it disadvantageously in their mind's-eye with the exhibitions of past years ; but I must say, in accordance with a very general con-

clusion of the practical-farmer-tribe, that the fallow
period, owing to the cattle-plague, if it had produced
no wonders, has heavily accumulated a grand store of
the breed. Lady Fragrant, with her immense frame,
her very table-land of back, her great udder, and most
sweet feminine front, is (deny it who can) the very perfection of a cow. In old time we have seen others
more tubular and beef-suggestive, but we have never
seen a cow before displaying in so high a degree the
characteristics of the milking cow, with fattening promise for the period when the lacteal produce naturally
shrinks.

Again, was it not astounding to see Commander-in-
Chief (who in his stall showed a head too ox-like and a
tail too high) in the exhibition ring, draw himself up
and magnificently look around him with an air that
reminded one of old Comet's picture, and which at
once placed him first amidst a numerous assemblage of
superb old bulls ? It was the sight of the show to see
these veterans pace round—rich roan, red, or white.
We were all glad to find so eminently triumphant
the breeding skill of that rare old man, who was so
hospitable at Warlaby, and we heartily trust that his
mantle has descended on his nephews. I must not
omit to give a due meed of praise to the retiring, quiet-
mannered youth who had charge of these cattle. A more
obliging, civil, unobtrusive lad I never met. His manner
in the ring, too, was a lesson to others. There was not
on his part, as on the part of others who repeatedly
made the bystanders indignant, the kicking back of a
beast's hoof, the jerking up of his head into some pet
position, nor was there the repeated grotesque lugging
forth of his charge before the judge's eyes even when

his turn for inspection was past, and the claims of other animals were being fairly investigated. He left his animals to exhibit themselves with their natural elegance, and accepted his fate accordingly.

The great number of new names intermixed with the old ones shows how the breeding taste is advancing, even as is an inclination amidst the wealthy for mowing-machine and steam-plough.

My paper having come to an end, I would only use the few last lines to remind the beginner that if he wishes for real satisfactory success in the end, he should climb as far as he can upon others' shoulders to begin with; that is, he should buy only animals of the best of pedigrees and the best of shape, an opportunity which is offered him by the continually advertised sales of famous breeders, who are either overstocked, or have fulfilled their term of years.

September, 1868.

I have not been able to lay hands yet upon Drury's quaint work, so cannot yet give the exact mode which he recommends of utilizing wheat-straw. But as I must find it for my own use, I shall make the bailiff, who I suspect never returned it to my hands, have another rout out of his literary baggage.

Assuredly, the labour of collecting leaves in this country to be stored to help out our winter fodder could never pay, considering the price of labour, the thinness of the crop, and the damage that would probably ensue to the tree itself from being over-fla-gellated.

The hint given us that it is beneficial to the plant

to pluck off all the mangold-wurzel leaves that touch the soil, for present use, I am acting vigorously upon. They considerably supplement the contents of the pig-wash tub, and are greedily devoured by the dairy cows.

The gorse sprouts upon the adjoining hill-side I intend using so far as they will go. I shall crush them between the stones of a cider-mill, and then chaff them with a certain proportion of hay and straw, adding a good pinch of salt, an ingredient essential to prevent the hair falling off the fed animals, should they partake too freely of this prickly salad.

Old Melon has just summoned me to view the blossoms of two more of our hybrid pelargonium seedlings. Astonishing is the variety produced from the same ovary; some of the produce throwing back in tint to either parent; some representing the two combined; some going far away to the commonest old-fashioned strains. It is an occupation that I shall not pursue any further. Far more satisfactory is it to go into the professional florist's houses, and take your pick in an assortment of plants upon the verge of flowering, at a shilling a head.

Another experiment has resulted capitally, and encourages me to repeat it, as well because it relieves the hurry of spring-work, as that it enables one to turn what were otherwise waste to account. During October and November last year, following the directions of an able essay in the Royal Agricultural *Journal*, I planted at a depth of nine to ten inches a quantity of diseased potatoes. It was scarcely a fair trial, because all the larger ones had been used for the pigs, and what we picked for seed were extremely small, and had lain in

a heap under straw very thickly strewn, awaiting their
turn for conversion into a mash with meal for the
fattening fowls. Everyone upon the farm was against
me, and thought me simply soft, when I proceeded to
give directions and superintend, as I felt I must
personally, the planting.

It was all I could do to get the furrows opened deep
enough, and the sets covered to a gauge of over nine
inches. They were planted, without manure of any
sort, upon a wheat stubble, the wheat having followed
an old ley well manured before ploughing. The spring-
sown potatoes I put in about five inches deep, the soil
having been limed for their reception. The autumn-
sown were so long in making their appearance after
the spring-sown were up, that I was almost afraid they
would never show, and that I should be beaten after
all; eventually they came, with many gaps I must
allow, but then the seed was very far gone in rottenness, and diminutive into the bargain. They were
dead-ripe a fortnight since, and we have used a great
quantity of them. Mr. Melon is very pleased, and says
that he has not found a single bad potato at any root :
the only thing is, that they are beginning to throw out
little ones ; but this is the pretty universal complaint
of all growers this anomalous season. I requested him
to bring me the bunch off a fair average plant ; he did
so, and I weighed them (they numbered fourteen
potatoes, four being remarkably fine) the morning after
drawing, for he had kept them (not seeing me) in the
tool-house : they weighed 2lb. 5oz., good. The parent
had mouldered away into dust. I got him then to
raise me as good a sample as he could find of the
spring-planted. The produce I kept the same number

of hours that the others were out of the ground before weighing. There were nine tubers, none so fine as the other lot, and the aggregate weight was 1lb. 7oz. This year has of course been an exceptional year, and the drought was disadvantageous to the spring sets, buried as they were only about five inches ; but, on the other hand, it is to be remembered that they had the advantage of lime to keep their skins cool. I am so encouraged by the experiment that, as I take my crop up this year, I shall deposit fresh, in drills already prepared, all the large-sized diseased tubers that we come across, and cover them with nine inches of mould. A great authority pronounces that no potatoes are ever diseased over which six inches of soil are kept by repeated earthings-up; he also says that the disease hits the haulm just at the back of the neck, and that repeated high earthing-up baffles the assault of the blight as it sweeps by. The *rationale* of planting diseased potatoes is this : They are calculated to clear themselves under the soil, of the morbific matter which is in an advanced stage when they are planted; whereas, no potato now-a-days being trustworthy, the great proportion of the so-called sound sets have in them the undeveloped seeds of mischief, which they perpetuate in their produce. But of potatoes enough, most excellent esculent as it is in its place.

To change the subject, I was rather surprised at Leicester to be asked by one of our leading English agriculturists whether I used a donkey upon the farm. "Heavens !" I replied, " I should think I did, of all sizes and all ages." On further parley, however, I found that he did not use the word metaphorically, but literally—that seriously he meant to inquire whether I had a real individual of the *Asinus vulgaris* amidst the beasts of burden upon the farm. He said he could never do without one. A donkey-cart is so handy for everyone to use for a multitude of services, to perform which one might grudge to break a team. The best specimen of the breed he ever knew was at the beck and call of every man, woman, and child upon the estate, who could justify its use, and when done with was accustomed to be turned off at the nearest point to the homestead, when it would set off at full canter, and not stop until it had backed its vehicle carefully into the cart-house, waiting quietly there until some one might pass by and release it, when, with a flourish of its tail, and a sly side-kick, it would canter off to browse. I was fascinated by this idea, and have been upon the look-out ever since—as yet without luck.

The river being full after the recent rains, we went out for a sail yesterday afternoon, and at a bend of the stream came across a beautiful small gull hovering and dipping after the fry, not regarding our presence in the least. I have looked Yarrell over, and, so far as I can make out, it was one of the "kittiwakes," in whose behalf a recent protest has been made. It is astonishing how little the birds regard us upon the water ! Not only does the heron wade contemptuously within fair pea-rifle reach, but the hawks come sailing close overhead from a rock in which they build, and the pigeons wing their rapid way from the corn-fields to the wood, not a dozen yards above or before us. I see that our little Dandy is pacing the hall, nursing a nearly-fledged turtle-dove to which he lays claim, having discovered the nest in a filbert-bush close to the house. He was to have had the pair, but one has disappeared from its

N

shaky twig platform—by courtesy, nest. The young Benjamin's theory is that their mamma takes them out one at a time, and he proposes to restore this one to the nest, in the hope of obtaining the two after dark.

The lodge chimney went on fire yesterday, and great was the consternation of the inhabitants. By dint of energetic efforts, however, it was soon put out, but not before some dozens of hornets came wheeling angrily about the heads of all engaged. They have a nest beneath the tiles, which will have to be taken somehow. We have long noticed an extra abundance of the plague about, and especially upon a young elm, which, whether it has burst itself by over-feeding or not, has anyhow great rents in its bark, through which a sweet-tasted candied-looking sap oozes, reminding one of the Canadian sugar-maple. This tree was discovered by the small boys, and for some days, until I discovered their proceeding, formed a sort of post-prandial hunting-ground, whereon they slaughtered by the dozen, with well-aimed blows of a hazel wand, great blue-bottles, wasps, and hornets. We have been very busy putting in trifolium and rye-grass on the stubbles, and mustard where the turnips failed.

It has long been a case of "Call me early, mother dear," with the swedes, and I expect they will now do but little good. If they persevere in their backwardness I shall simply re-plough, the land being clean and richly manured, and plant wheat when the season comes. "I daren't do such a thing," said my gallant neighbour; "I should have all my tenants following my example." "Another sad consequence of being an extensive landed proprietor," I reply; but surely the farmer can only recoup himself for losses by a judicious ringing of changes. " Anyhow, I'll have a try if I lose my place," as the old song says.

And so to-morrow's the First ! and if I don't write to-night, I know I shall never write again this week ; but I'm so dull at present that I don't know which is likely to be the less killing — midnight article or October gun.

" Now then, Jerusalem ! " as with horror I heard myself, I thought, addressed by a dashing, young, and most self-impressed Bobby, of A 1 area character I doubt not, as I was sauntering down the paved walk before a series of cattle-houses at a recent Shorthorn sale, and looking over the half-doors at the occasional animal within. However the address was not for me, but for a white and most intelligent moke, who was also sauntering down the walk (there being a scent of hay at the far corner), and who at once, upon being called to in this unceremonious way, put himself half round into a repulsive position that astonished his uniform acquaintance, and made the bold policeman shrink closely to the opposite wall, being baulked thereby of the cowardly poke he had intended with his staff for the poor brute's unoffending ribs. A victory to be scored for the donkey ! He was not for sale, or I should have gladly picked up so shrewd a specimen for the farm labours, which I learnt at Leicester can be so successfully performed upon a farm by this, so often abused, beast of burden.

There is a small one—a most tiny specimen—in our village, belonging to the native Vulcan, and which was won by him in a raffle ; but for this one I feel ashamed to offer any price that might tempt to the dissolution

N 2

of a union such as exists between him and Vulcan minor. This last youth is a great, strong, stout fellow, whom it is a wonder to me that the oppressed animal can draw at all, as he does notwithstanding, at a tearing gallop up-hill and down-hill, and often with a load of iron rods upon the cart, in addition to his human load. The other day I employed him to convey my Abyssinian pump and tackle down to a meadow, where I wished to try it. In getting there he missed the gateway, whereupon the lad jumped off, and, with a cheer to his ally in the shafts, and a push at the cart-wheel, sent the whole safely, but shaken, over a deep wide ditch, with a steep bank on the further side, in a style that I can only imagine equalled by Penn's artillery when at Aldershot, as I heard from a brother-officer of his. That gallant officer (whose intelligent daring found at last fair scope in the late expedition against Theodore) made his troop charge, and clear too, quite sufficiently to render the feat a thorough success, a fence that had made the cavalry draw rein.

This village moke of ours is a household word with our children ; for it will drink beer out of a cup at young Vulcan's command, and will rest his fore-feet upon his shoulders, looking him most sympathetically in the face the meanwhile. It will also lie down when he lays hold threateningly of its fore-legs. We all pet it. I allow it the run of my hedge-rows. It has its lodging in a pig-sty. It amuses me often. It seems to reason so.

I am reminded that my Norton's pump arrived duly, and we have had the greatest possible amusement in trying all sorts of spots that we fancied likely to yield water upon the farm. Unfortunately, above the house, where I am anxious to establish a spring, we came incessantly upon rock, and have had to knock up the tube and adjourn. In one place certainly we hit a crevice, a fact that was indicated by the tubes persistently taking an oblique direction under influence of the blows of the monkey, and getting full of water some feet in depth. However, when we screwed the pump on it would not work, and I have since found that we had got into a pocket of clay, wherein it is difficult to establish a well after this patent. But get into a sandbed, and it's rare fun. I have just been examining the settlement of colouring matter in a tumbler full of thick water that we pumped out of a new place just before dark. There is an inch of water, clear and bright enough, resting on a stratum of the oiliest-looking marl, and beneath the marl a stratum of beautifully fine and extremely keen sand, almost too fine, I fear. The sand we desire to strike is of about partridge-shot size. I have already had fifteen pounds' worth of gratification afforded me by that seven pounds' purchase, and there's a lot more coming.

The results of our various experiments, whether they turned out for better or worse, it is right we should record. The swede crop that I had intended ploughing up has begun to spring in earnest, so that we hope we shall have a sufficient quantity to prevent our playing tricks with the regular course of cropping. The mangold-wurzel has swelled grandly of late, and I shall have a really good weighty yield ; but it is curious that a few of Sutton's champion swedes, the seed of which got deposited with the mangold seed in May, although showing a fine bunch of leaves, have at base only a tough long thin radish-shaped bulb, showing to my

mind that there has been something anomalous in the
climate of the past season, especially as regards that
mainstay of the homestead. The ground was damp
enough, and there was plenty of wet hearty muck put
underneath ; still, amidst mangold roots of real grandeur for this year (for it so happens that these swedes
are situated in the best portion of the wurzel crop), the
turnip has failed to develope any succulent growth.
It is a withered wizen-shaped and mildewy specimen,
suffering from what in the Eastern Counties they so
appropriately term " the dry stunt."

Respecting these mangold-wurzel, it is worth noting
that where the women searched for the larvæ of the
dart moth the plants are smaller and weaker than in
the portion of the field which was let alone, out of pure
weariness at the apparently endless labour. Query,
have I lost or gained by that outlay ?

I certainly saved several hundreds of plants from
being gnawed clean through, but is not the general
bulk of the yield lessened by such tampering with the
root fibres during the plants' infancy?—treatment which
at the time, not I alone, predicted would be beneficial
to its growth, inasmuch as it seemed to pulverize the
soil about the seedling so thoroughly. There is one
circumstance about the field that puzzles me. In a
slight hollow, situated about three parts down the enclosure, the marl-bed comes rather near the surface,
and the rain-water lodges somewhat there. The fallow
was consequently knobby in this part when worked in
preparation for roots, and so rough when we sowed,
that we despaired of seeing any come up at all. They
certainly long delayed putting in an appearance, and
came thin when they did come ; but the bulbs that are

there are the finest in the whole field, and would be
respectable any season. Possibly the oily juice of the
marl may suit their taste, or the knobs may have
afforded them such a wholesome shade from wet and
sun, as Jonah found in his gourd. A lumpy fallow is
propitious to young wheat we know—possibly in consideration of the shelter it lends, or of the fresh suck
it allows the spreading rootlets with every shower. I
have at last found out now that industrious dear little
Dutch clover manages to make itself an establishment
in my pasture, that is abused either by excessive drain-
ing or extraordinary sun heat, as this summer, or by
the rigid cutting of the lawn-mower; and which once
attained it manages to maintain through the wide
spread of its fibrous roots. I learnt this lesson on our
slopes this year. They were absolutely burnt up like
King Alfred's cakes, or a fox's tail (?) shall I say, so
burnt that we all, fat Melon included, gave them up as
lost to life. Even these darling little plants found it
impossible to spring in extended growth. They were
content, or obliged to sit, each one stem over his root-
bed, just as you see the Alpine Marmot do before the
mouth of his burrow, in the nursery books on natural
history ; but, then, whether or not from want of exercise in having their range so restricted, and a consequent concentration of juices, they indulged all in a
most dowager-like tiara of seed pods, the contents of
which in due season fell so thickly as to defy the birds—
who, I dare say, got tired of their monotonous diet,
preferring the flesh pots of an adjoining wild cherry—
especially in one spot, along the line of a house drain,
where the sward was simply reduced to a sepia tinge,
they lay as thick as comfits on a confectioner's window,

advertisement cakes' sugar roof, or (to set our meta-
phor in unison with the season)

> " As autumn leaves that strew the brooks
> In Vallambrosa, where the Etrurian shades
> High over-arch'd embower."

Anyhow, this abundance of shed seed took advantage of the first shower to vegetate, and the lawn is
now one carpet of tiny heart-shaped and round leaves.
I argue thus then: the roller, the sheep's tooth, the
lawn-mower, all cut so close or bruise the swollen limbs
of the coarser grasses so, (intense heat, again, being
adverse to their swelling at all) that something approaching to mortification ensues, or, if not quite that,
at least considerable contusion; such as sends them
into the hospital's compulsory confinement, of which
the smaller plants take advantage, so as to have their
little strut upon the stage of life.

I have been obliged to write at a gallop, as the hour
of shooting approaches—an exercise to which I am
rendered almost averse, by the dumb expostulation of
some half dozen young pheasants that have flown up
just now to be fed at my study window. The nest was
cut-over by the mowers in a meadow, and the hatching
was carried out by a half-bred Lucknow-bantam, which,
possibly, from its half-wild Indian tastes and tendency,
stuck more affectionately to its strange offspring than I
ever knew a barn-door fowl do before. Every evening,
when they had grown quite as big as herself, they used
to fly up and perch upon a pole we fixed across a coach-
house, and every morning she brought them round to
our lawn windows to be fed, until one day there was
great consternation in the nursery. The naughty hen

had joined the Lucknow cock (a very handsome young
fellow, I can tell you, too), and was gone into the
fowl-house, deserting the poor little pheasants, as
our " Dandy " explained, with a pitiful elongation
of the word *poor*, that could be due only to his
remembrance of the tale of "the babes in the wood,"
or some such sad recital. Of course, I was pulled,
nolens volens, to see, and there, sure enough, was one
young pheasant already missing, and the others kept
jumping off their perch, and wandering about with
most plaintive cries. The " naughty hen " was brought
back by a youngster, who braved the fleas of the
poultry-house, but all to no purpose. She deserted
them again the moment we had receded out of sight.
Later on, too, at the hour of retiring, to our consternation, we found not a single individual, hen or pheasants,
upon the perch, and so we gave them up as lost. In
the morning, however, they assembled by the window,
to be fed, but indulging in sad notes, such as are appropriate to being first sent to a boarding-school from the
mother's lap, and since then they have found a roosting
place somewhere in the woods; coming about the house,
however, the day through. The young cocks' voices
are breaking fast (they were a late hatch, and are only
assuming their bright attire now), and it seems to me
that the hen could understand them no longer. Else
why be so spiteful to them as she now is, pecking them
away if ever they venture to approach and feed in the
stable yard; whether it be that she thinks them great idle
things that ought now to be finding their own liveli-
hood, or that she is ashamed of owning such a gipsy
lot in the presence of gay chanticleer, for, of course,
in the recesses of her mind, she is ignorant how ever

she came to hatch a brood so diverse to what she expected. Anyhow, I am puzzled by her demeanour, which overlays a great mine of philosophical thought, and the children puzzle me even further by their inquiries.

But my sands are out, and the breakfast bell rings. *Au revoir.*

December, 1868.

How time does gallop ! One cannot get through the half of what one wants and feels one ought to do. I find myself always at the last moment in arrears.

Well, and what have we been doing lately upon this farm ? One of the latest events is my having been fortunate enough to win the prize for the best crop of mangold-wurzel within a considerable radius. The crop was so cheaply grown (in a previous article I gave particulars of the way in which I treated our light soil) that I feel doubly proud. Any one, with a fair purse and good eyes, may buy stock for competition, although it does not follow that he will produce from those pur-chased elements animals equal to the parents ; but I feel—too triumphantly, you will say, perhaps—that to have grown the best piece of mangold-wurzel in the district during this disastrously-hot year with only one ploughing, and having sown about the latest of all around me, is really a feat over which one may fairly smoke a comfortable reflective pipe.

We have had the " Long Firm " tapping at our door lately pretty often. The last dodge they adopted was forwarding a circular of prices which they were ready to give for apples and potatoes " in any quantity " to the various local postmasters, to whom they offered a commission upon all purchased, on the condition of their spreading the inquiry. I sent them a large offer of both fruits, only with the proviso that the cash must come previous to the goods being despatched. Of course, I need not tell you there was nothing heard further of the parties.

We have been all storing quantities of acorns and chesnuts for the pigs in winter, any quantity of which we can get gathered for 1s. the bushel acorns, and 6d. the bushel chesnuts. A high wind that had just sprung up will help the accumulation. Unfortunately it is down stream, so that we cannot get a sail upon the river.

The spring-planted potatoes are, I fear, a great mess. We are waiting for a fine day or two to raise the burden of the crop with Howard's new plough, and so in a certain degree one nurtures hope. A lot of the garden-grown, however, that has been raised exhibits a great deal of rottenness in the state. I am having a piece of stubble deep-ploughed, to set all the bigger diseased tubers at once, as we take up the main crop, and only hope that the experiment will answer next year as successfully as it did this.

We have a number of hands raking up the abundant downfall of dead leaves where they lie thickest in this woodland district, to be strewn with a free hand over a mattress of nut and elm chippings, which are packed in the basin of the yards, after the fashion of the heather couch upon which the Highlanders bore the wounded Waverley. Only pack the twigs close enough, and it affords a most elastic bed for the cattle, even in what would otherwise be wet spots.

The missus nearly lost her best Alderney a few days since, and unhappily I hear that the disease which struck her down, has made sad ravages around us. She was saved, undoubtedly, by the strong dose of salts and ginger, that she at once got when we found her to be ailing. I ought to have put opium in also. That omission the veterinary surgeon (a most able neighbour luckily) did upon being summoned. These little cattle, which are usually tethered upon the orchard sward, were allowed to run free one day. Whether she fed too heartily or not upon the rank growth beneath the trees, or swallowed acorns and such like in deleterious proportion, anyhow she took to scouring violently, sank beneath the pressure of my hand along her spine, and had her nose quite burning dry. It was an attack of what the old farriers called " scouring rot," or " dysentery," but what is now spoken of as typhoid fever. We kept her up with plenty of wheaten gruel, with chopped and melted mutton suet in it, a recipe which I knew to have saved a poor fellow under a severe attack of dysentery during the Crimean campaign. The little cow is now gradually coming round, but continues very weak.

We were recently very much provoked by having a boar disqualified for the prize, in excellent company, at an adjoining county show, as being incapable of breeding, although we have his stock in our hands, and although he was passed by the veterinary of the Royal Show in much higher condition. So much discretion as this should not be allowed to judges. Their business is to select the best animal, and leave all such questioning of disability to the scientific inspector.

We were all delighted that the Didmarton Shorthorns sold so well. They were a grand solid-framed, wealthy-coated, mellow-flesh sort, and would, if they had possessed at more length the fashionable pedigrees of the day, have fetched most reckless prices. The whole affair was well managed. The arrangements, and the neatly-dressed, respectable-looking old servants, with their most intelligent earnest boy-assistants, told of a well-ordered establishment.

I have since seen some purchases made at that sale in strong company, and they quite hold their own as regards style. There was what is so often wanting in herds, but which should be a main object of the breeder, a most marked uniformity of type and character. The young aristocratic breeders, who came out upon that occasion, will find that they have a good foundation to build upon by the help of the more terribly high-bred bulls.

Talking of "breed," the day must come when other originators besides Bates will be credited with the wizard character that we all allow to that great man. So don't be too rash, young breeder, in rejecting first-class animals of long pedigree, even though the elements be not all of the excellent Duchess strain. The exquisite Bolivar is a considerable mixture I think, and yet he will be celebrated.

I want the shrewd Culshaw and the Messrs. Booth to get into these patent American coffins, giving out that they are dead, and after their ascent to the air again to lie perdu in some outlandish district for a dozen years. They will see then how it is only the misfortune of their being alive that is against them; and they will find that they will have to pay fabulous prices to recover choice animals of their favourite strains—as tremendous possibly as existing fashionable relics of a departed breeder fetch.

We are glad to welcome Mr. Thornton's Shorthorn Circular, but to make it really valuable, besides keeping advertisement sheets, he ought to give us slices of the lore respecting the earlier days of this grand bovine race which he is said to possess; reliable anecdotes of the bulls and cows, whose names the Herd Book holds, and particulars of Shorthorn *sales long gone by*. The padding of recent matter, such as we all have for ourselves or in the Journal (*e.g.* the prize list of the Royal Society's last meeting), I regard as dead weight; anyhow, I wish the publication well.

I see the river is rising. The floods descend from the wild Welsh mountains so rapidly on occasion that we can scarcely be too quick in moving our stock.

I dare say some of you will have read Mr. Lord's description of his tour as a naturalist in North America: a most interesting work I may observe. He mentions a tribe of Indians whose teeth are quite worn away from chewing salmon that have been split and dried in the sun, owing to a coating they get of fine gritty sand blown upon them during the curing. This sort of evil, and even more, we, who dwell along the banks of this lovely but insidious river, suffer from. There is a deposit of fine sand left upon the herbage, which not only grates upon the teeth but accumulates in the intestines and kills the animal. After a flood the more prudent wait for the occurrence of a heavy shower to wash off the powder.

Those lovely young pheasants, which I mentioned before, have become so dreadfully tame, that I am afraid they may come to grief. Not only do they fly up to be fed at the different windows, but they have taken to wandering upon the high road. I don't think,

however, that they would allow anyone to catch them :
at least we hope not. Having lately taken to feeding my
own chickens with Latin crumbs, I must now attend
to their meal, for they are hopping and chirping around
me. I hope they may never be guilty of such fearful ignorance as I have just heard of occurring in a
neighbouring somewhat cider-bestricken parish, where,
upon a recent occasion, one child explained a picture
of Cain and Abel to be "Eve a-walloping of Adam :"
drawing, probably, for his idea upon the experience
of his home. The cider question is the curse and
puzzle of this country.

At last we have finished taking up our potatoes
(spring-planted), and a comparatively valueless crop
they are, considering the number of hands who have
been employed in storing them, the ground occupied,
and the sets. We have several waggon-loads of " seedy"
ones, which I shall deposit at once ten inches deep
upon the mangold ground, trusting to recoup myself, as
the lawyers say, thereby next year for the losses we have
sustained through the failure of the turnip this season.
Anyhow a diseased "pratee" is noxious, I think, even
to the gizzard of a pig, that wondrous animal, which
is said even to chew ordinary poisons without hurt.
How splendidly my porcine pets are doing upon the
slopes, they look so full and sleek. Now that the
acorns and chesnuts are sprouting under the fallen
leaves, they seem to possess a doubly fattening quality,
as barley does started. Our children have found out
that the porker of about sixty pounds' weight is the
most delicious eating conceivable. Older, they are apt
to be too fat, and there is consequently waste, both in
the parlour and the servants' hall. I don't know

whether it is good policy killing them so young, and
I have no time just now for an extended calculation.
It is a mode of consumption co-ordinate anyhow with
the genial Mr. Mechi's chopping up his beans green, as
fodder. My remark as to my milking-cows enjoying
the leaves plucked from the growing mangold-wurzel,
has drawn upon me a long letter from a kind-hearted
and shrewd friend, one who knew well old Tommy
Bates. He cautions me against the plan, inasmuch as
he has proved the mangold leaves to be conducive to
abortion. He writes, "Now, as I know from my own
experience, as well as from that of others, that mangold
leaves and the roots also, if given before Christmas, are
dangerous food for in-calf cows or sows in-pig, as being
liable to produce abortion, I hasten to drop you a line.
You may give a word of warning to your friends.
If they be so hard up as to use them at all, let
them be passed through the chaff-cutter, and *largely
mixed* with dry food of some kind, to counteract their
cold watery nature and purging quality. I have for a
long time ceased to use them for stock of any kind,
and now spread them equally over the land, and plough
them in." Of course they are full of nitrogen, and,
therefore, excellent manure. Mangold roots can, however, be used, if commenced with cautiously, before
Christmas without harm, if the precaution be taken of
throwing them, a few bulbs together, to wither in
a corner of a dry barn. A neighbour of mine tells me
that he has failed to get his cows and sows to breed
when they have been fed on mangold. It is no doubt
like tobacco, a dangerous plant if used to excess.
Medio tutissimus ibis, as one used to read in the Eton
Latin Grammar. " If you want keep," my friend adds,

" you will find your swede leaves, if free from mildew, a much less objectionable adjunct ; but these also I always prepare in the same manner, and with the addition of some dry food, hay or straw, according to the age of the animal, and increase or decrease the quantity of the leaves according to the effect upon the animal's interior arrangement. We leave the swedes standing in the rows, denuded of leaves, and time the taking up and storing to suit the cutting of the leaves, always endeavouring to get the leaves consumed, and the roots stored before Christmas, up to which time we seldom have hard weather. We find it greatly facilitates the getting up of this crop to run the plough (without the coulter) under them. They are then, by boys, easily picked and thrown into heaps ready for the carts."

I shall act upon this hint, and employ Howard's potato-raiser under my crop, by way of a trial. In fairness to that new implement, convertible into so many useful forms, with so little trouble, I feel bound to mention that in its first development as an ordinary plough it is a grand success. A gentleman who has always had a good deal to do with the machinery part of the Royal Agricultural Show, predicted, as I sat next to him one day at dinner, and somewhat proudly described my implement, its failure as an ordinary plough. I can only say in reply, that my bailiff offered the loan of it ten days since to a neighbour, who proposed competing at a ploughing match, and in a large entry he won the champion and another first prize. The work was magnificent, I am told. I shall always mention deserved success.

A farmer to whom I mentioned yesterday my friend's

o

counsel (as quoted above) respecting the use of mangold-wurzel, fully confirmed the statement from his experience this year. An Alderney cow, seven months gone in-calf, slipped it only last week, and from no cause that he could ascertain. It was, however, the fact that he had been feeding her of late a good deal upon mangold leaves. We talked about chaffing, and in the course of further conversation he said that he had been sadly put out by " the earthquake about three years since." He had had new machinery to be worked by water, of which a pool served him with an ample supply. After the earthquake, however, the springs on the upper land failed, and the outflow has most provokingly taken a fresh course upon the other side the hill—another of the vexatious uncertainties to which the vicissitudes of the earth's crust subjects the agriculturist.

The winter is coming on apace here. The leaves have gone all of a run, and the wild-fowl are beginning to make their appearance in small bodies. I shot a teal upon the river close under the house yesterday, and disturbed a woodcock upon the gardener's leaf-mould heap. We had a beautiful pheasant hen upon the lawn just now, very much pied, almost white. I hope we shall find her nest in the spring. The tame ones keep as yet so faithfully about the house, and continue to feed out of our hands.

It will soon be time to have the brood mares off the moorland. One pet hunter that I was obliged to turn out last summer, has never thriven at all ; being natu-rally a healthy animal, I have been quite puzzled to know why. Last week, however, the groom showed me that her tongue must, a few months since, have been nearly severed. It has healed now ; but it must have been nearly off once ; as she has a beautiful mouth, I cannot comprehend how such a misfortune could have happened to her.

The Italian rye grass and trifolium that we sowed upon our stubbles have failed in a great degree. The barley-sheddings have come up as thick as a hay-crop, the escaped ears having been so thoroughly torn to pieces, and scattered by the harrows. I have one field nearly a foot high ; I don't know exactly what to do with it. I don't know that the crop would survive the winter, even if I were to let it stop ; besides, it would put us out of course. Again : I don't like to feed it, because the sheep would nibble the clover as well, and that, I am sure, on our light soil, is a mistake. The rank autumnal growth of grass has caused us a good deal of botheration. I caught some ewes, the other day, only just in time to save them, by administering strong doses of carbonate of soda and ginger ; and now we have a valuable cow in a very bad way indeed. The V.S. calls it indigestion ; but it's pitiable to see the saliva running from her lips, and to hear her groaning. He's just going to "prop" her. What that means I don't know, but, as he says that is her only chance, and I'm sure I don't know what to do with her, I leave the business to him and my careful herdsman. It's not all fun, this farming "on times!" To reward my little men, the other day, for very good behaviour over their Latin lessons, I allowed them to go out ferreting for the first time in their lives. It was a very cold day, and late in the afternoon when we started. Of course their little sisters must go too, and it was a fine sight to see them all seated upon a heap of leaves. and holding their pet terriers in their laps (the whole lot

not being worth a fig, I positively believe, if a strong
rat had charged them, although, of course, it would
have been heresy to say so), listening quite earnestly,
as a bunny which had been marked in was heard
scurrying about the runs with the white ferret at his
heels.   Then, when he did come out, and went rolling
over and over unhurt in the meshes of the loose net, I
thought our Benjamin's delight would kill him.   Lest,
however, the chill evening air should give them cold,
they were hurried home.   A neighbour having preserved these vermin a little too fondly, we shall have
some trouble in keeping them down.

We had a narrow escape upon the river the other
day.   It was blowing quite a gale of wind when I went
out sailing with a friend.   The waves ran very high ;
but we did very well so long as we ran before them.
Having to row back, and there being no steersman, in
a very broad reach of the river, we shipped three great
seas in succession, and only just got to land in time to
bale her and prevent her sinking.   Another day we
must weight the stern better.   As we two men were
alone it did not matter.   However, the next gale that
blows I shall enjoy upon the river.   They don't come
too often.

January, 1869.

Cider drinking, is it wholesome ?   Bless me, to see
the rubbish—the absolute mud of decayed fruit that is
committed to the press in certain hope of a satisfactory
drink being produced !   Why, one has read and seen
how carefully, in the making of the best foreign wines,
each mildewed or decaying berry is sorted and picked
out before the juice is crushed—but oh ! to see the

apple heap with which ordinarily the Herefordshire farmer (myself amidst the number) is content—the fruit is gathered and spread eighteen inches deep, and occasionally fenced about with wattled hurdles, then upon these heaps, if you are curious and take a pipe and spend the forenoon sitting on the bar of the chaff-cutter to look on ; why, the geese waddle, and—why, what don't they do ? then the hens pick daintily here and there, and the dirty-footed duck tribe go dabbling in with inquisitorial beaks, and the old sow, too, steals an occasional crunch.

Eh dear ! to think what reversions of fortune the crop has gone through before its yield is committed to the cask, and after all it is really good stuff; very grateful to the senses, especially that one of taste (the liquor being new), and what's more—it's very odd—but the system on an apple-growing soil seems to require it. I am one of those who hold out against the truck plan of paying my labourers so much in money and so much in drink. The arrangement is deplorable. Give the poor fellows their full share of the coin of the realm, and let them buy from your cellar what they feel they require and can afford, and you'll be surprised what a little they content themselves with; and then what a real pleasure it is to you to find that their family is better off, and you are not disappointed when you have a cask a trifle tart, which must be emptied before next year. It is a pleasure to reward men who have denied themselves; and the slightly acetous drink is more grateful to their taste as a rule, and more serviceable to their constitution than the sweet readily-saleable drink. Problems there are on every soil; and a stout problem here is the question of drink. The water of this district, at

least is undoubtedly deleterious, being very strongly
impregnated with sulphate of lime. Very good, then,
the cider-apple, a positive hedgerow weed, the fruit of
which you cannot chew to your gratification, yields the
liquor needed by the human system, that is grown upon
this particular geological formation. The cocoanut is
meat and drink to the fortunate native who lives upon
the reefs whereon its parent tree springs luxuriantly
from a seed that was an ocean waif; buttermilk is the
comfort and mainstay and luxury of the rich meadow
butter-making counties (it's a fine drink too—*experto
crede*); whey, that of the cheese district; and so I've
come to persuade myself that cider is essential to the
native (small or adult) of the apple counties. It is
rather astounding when fry, just as high as your table,
ask for " fourpence a day and their drink," just as it is
to see a female worker in harvest time pack up her can
in her basket as an essential implement for the day's
performance; but under proper regulation I have come
to think it is required. I have given them tea, but it
did not do—beer and it intoxicates; acidulated drinks
I saw recommended in the *Times*, and so to acidised
cider I reverted. The only thing is, observe method in
the distribution. The reason of all this is, of course,
obvious enough to anyone who will take down Johnson's Atlas, and note the various character of the foods
and products of different latitudes; but what drew me
into this discussion was the contemplation to-day of
several cider messes at different stages of development.
After all, what have we not read of the way in which
London bread used to be kneaded, and the moist sugar
squeezed? Nasty enough each one, anyhow.

     It was curious yesterday that a number of thrushes

about the house took to singing quite spring-like upon
the boughs. They are "mum" again to-day: whether
wearied with their exertion, or that they took cold, or
that they have found out their mistake, I don't know.

There was such a glorious breeze on Sunday upon
the river, making foam-crested billows run up the
surface; but it failed before Monday; and now the
flood has fallen some feet, and left the boat high and
dry upon the meadow adjoining her moorings. I am
longing for another run before the wind : danger
despite !

The barley-sheddings, of which I spoke, has been
quite a god-send to us. It is fully a foot high, and
much has gone into premature ear, so that I had no
alternative but to mow it. The clover looks so fresh
and regular underneath, after the mown swathe is
cleared. I am cutting it up with wheat-straw for a
yard full of cows and heifers, and they do well upon it.
It seems a better plan than if I had fed down the crop
a month since, for I should have lost the subsequent
length of growth, beside injuring the clover plant, as I
believe the nibbling of sheep does. So certainly the
lamented Nesbit taught. It quite delights me, every
time I enter the field, to see how regular and thick the
produce is. Every year now I shall certainly harrow
the barley-stubble remorselessly four ways, with sharp-
tined drags, and then put the chain-harrows across just
to cover the seed, which is dispersed from the shattered
ears ; the benefit of which I should have lost too, had
I allowed the bailiff to turn the pigs on, as he desired
to do. The mangold-wurzel has yielded fully sixty
loads more than the bailiff calculated, so I trust we
shall not be short of keep, after all. I am insisting on

the most rigid economy in the use of the new sweet straw, which the stupid or perverse hinds began to strew freely for litter, although there was plenty of last year's straw a little distance away. For the life of me I cannot find old Drury's work, and I forget exactly how he compounded his wholesome gelatinous mess of soaked wheaten chaff and meal. I am afraid the book is out of print.

Having amused myself with it repeatedly throughout the summer in tapping the damp spots upon my several fields, I am to-day about to drive my Abyssinian pump down alongside the highest stage of buildings, into which I shall put pipes if our search for the drink be successful. As it is now the water-supply lies below or on a level with the homestead, and a good deal of toilsome carrying consequently devolves upon the feeder.

Alack a-day! we don't know how to distinguish the pet pheasants from the wild ones with which they have begun to associate, and we are bound to have a clearing now the leaves are off, for the poor bird is so confiding in its mind, and roosts so prominently, that some measure of thinning must be adopted, or our night's slumbers will be incessantly disturbed by the poaching-gun. I think I shall soak some peas in gin, and feed the tame ones, to-morrow, so that if they want to rise, they cannot. We may save them so.

What a delicious scent there is in the steaming-house to-day! The bad potatoes that I didn't want for planting are being steamed and mixed with meal in a vat to force off the porkers, which, up to this morning, have been for weeks under the oak and chestnut trees.

I sat down and eat a lot myself of the whiter sort, as did my labourers for their dinner. Most excellent

esculent ! I shall hope to clear my crop, in the end, of
disease, by this plan of sowing the invalids in autumn.
Some of my friends, who have tasted my deep-sea crop
of last year, and found what a floury lot I obtained
from what was otherwise of little comparative value, are
about to copy my example this year.   The farmers I
cannot persuade.   For some reasons one might, if
selfish, be thankful : but then one musn't be selfish,
and just this moment one's bound to be off : so good-
bye.

_____

February, 1869.

At last the winds and rain have come.   The heavens
have broken in earnest, and the full-flooded river hath
over-run the bank, pouring in, I observe, along an old
ditch (the filling-in of which must have shrunk from
its original dimensions), and at the mouth of which I
shall fix sluice-gates next year, so as to be able to warp
the flat meadows of thirty acres at will, at the same
time constructing a main drain by which to draw off
the stagnant volume of water, which is apt to abide too
long upon the same place.   It is so delightful sailing
over the fields.   There being no stream to oppose, you
positively tear along.   Returning after nightfall, I
steered my boat right over a high flight of rails, and
moored her in a meadow, with the bows tied to a stile,
and the stern to a bush !   There is a grand wind blowing now, and I shall soon be off, so I must make sail
fast in the delivery of my sentiments.

I have been greatly amused by listening to the
recital of the woes of a young agriculturist who has
bought a fine tract of improveable land in Ireland,
but which he farms at duelling distance, being as far

out of reach as he can. About fifteen of his flock, a small sort selected and fed for the picking of himself and friends, the mountain foxes took. Their remains were found in the bog (a storehouse, usually of the peasants methinks I have read, who I dare say on occasions can imitate the depredation of his vulpine majesty, even to the biting and tearing of the wool !). His geese, also, a fine flock as they floated on the bay and river, went too ! But, after all, he has an enjoyable life in the wild West, which I should like much to share if it were not for the family mill-stone.

Our pet pheasants have, alas ! at length shown their ingratitude, and joined the company of the covert-bred, only occasionally coming at breakfast-time to the school-room window. We are all in high glee expecting the return from school shortly of our eldest boy, for whom I bought a singularly clever galloway, fast as a thorough-bred, and a rare jumper; but most amazingly, I have just found out that she has quite lately learnt a trick of turning home occasionally, in which, if she be opposed, she has a donkey-like habit of crushing you up against the nearest wall or fence, as I found quite unexpectedly to my cost the other day, having at this moment my leg from knee to ankle all bruised and black. It seems a stable-boy who exercised her, was in the habit of yielding to her when she first began the bad habit, until it has now become seriously confirmed. Spurs she does not seem to mind, so that I am rather at a nonplus. She was so wonderfully temperate and gentle before this humour came. It is quite delightful to behold how well the cattle and horses do upon the chopped barley-sheddings and wheat-straw in their line of extempore boxes, which we have run up for the

winter with wattled hurdles and oak poles around the
yards. Unless snow comes to beat it down and rot it,
there is several weeks' keep remaining, and so the hay-
stacks are left almost in their entirety as yet. A
terrible thing is it to have mainly consumed the hay
before Christmas, as thoughtless youth is sometimes
apt to allow. I remember, when I began farming,
having a fearful nip of that sort : having to give from
£5 to £7 10s. per ton for fodder for some weeks of the
spring when my own stores had run out. I see old
Melon in a fit of the greatest delight beckoning me
out from my study. And well he may be, for he has
managed to purchase for me a whole cart-load of choice
firs, roses, laurestinas, yew, dahlias, and hollyhocks for
the mighty sum of £1 15s., his own feeding and gates
included ! A young market-gardener in this neighbourhood having become bankrupt several times, upon
this occasion, at the first day's sale, there was little
competition, when I sent Mr. Melon to look after a few
things. I learn that the next day, when everyone went,
hearing how cheaply things had gone the day before,
there was a pretty spirited sale. We may congratulate
ourselves, therefore, upon having taken time by the
forelock. We shall now have some new occupation in
the planting to fill gaps and improve points of landscape. Our watercress pool is a rare success, as we
have an ever-abundant supply quite close to the house.

A London cousin, who was lately staying here, was
much amused at the Robinson Crusoe meals to which
we introduced her. Our own pork, mutton, wild-duck,
pears, chestnuts, walnuts, perry, butter, and cream, all
unbought, and produced upon the premises,—this simple
phase of the farmer's enjoyable existence surprised and

delighted her, making her teeth water in more senses than one.

During this period of flood, the boatmen to whom the salmon-fishery is let, are considerably occupied in netting the pools formed upon hollows of the meadow-land, wherein they take at almost every haul a quantity of trout and " coarse fish " as they invariably answer if you make inquiry, which means, I suspect, anything they can catch.   A winter or two back a salmon ran up a ditch, where it got frozen in, and was discovered by the children, who had been down to skate.   One of the workmen had it given to him, and it was discussed, he told me, with amazing gusto by his little ones at dinner. It weighed about eight pounds and was in excellent condition, having been preserved by the ice.   This pleasurable devoration of an animal that had died a natural death, reminds me of an intention we have of shooting a few chickens instead of bleeding them to death, as the common mode is.   They must assuredly taste less insipid from having been so slaughtered. I fancy I have seen that the plan has been tried before.

I have just had the offer of a large quantity of lime refuse from a tanyard, which, having been used to dress the imported hides, has also a considerable mixture of salt and hair in it.   The price being only one shilling a horse for every load, I shall put a lot on my turnip fallow.

I am sorry to have to record that the clover crop, thick where I planted swedes with home-made compost of wood-ashes, salt, soot, and bone-dust, all saturated with liquid manure, is upon the piece adjoining, of two acres, which I dressed with over five cwt. per acre of superphosphate, feeble beyond measure.   I shall rely more than ever, consequently, upon the home-made stuff, for of the farmer's difficulties I have long come to the conclusion that the artificial manure and excess of labour bills constitute a great part.

Hurrah ! there's one of the missing pheasant hens come out of the bushes with the bantams to feed ! I throw them some small wheat, and she runs up the first to pick it ; but she hops away quite indignantly from the attention of the gay Lucknow chanticleer.

Here comes a workman with a brace of squirrels— " Executed in the very act of nibbling off the tops of a fir-plantation," he says.   I hope the statement is true, for they are very pretty, running up and down the trees, although I am not partial to them, I must confess, when the filbert and walnut crops are ripe.

There is a beautiful hawk floating about, notwithstanding the number that my neighbour's keeper has shot upon the ledges of a rock just in sight of our lawn.   I have given orders to my man to spare him. He looks so graceful sailing amidst the tree tops, as we see them below us ; and we can quite well spare a lot of the increasing wood-pigeon tribe.   " Murder ! Oh ! my—my ! "   I was startled to hear, yesterday, uttered rapidly, and in shrill tones, by an unhappy green woodpecker, who comes daily to feed upon the grass-plot. Master hawk had spied him, and gave chase, which was the reason of the agonised cries I heard, and which were uttered as the foolish bird took his flight, rapidly losing way, across a small meadow.   He turned suddenly, however, into the wood ; whereupon his pursuer, making a graceful, but contemptuous swoop, declined further pursuit, and floated elegantly out in quest of new game.

Just at the children's dinner, there was awful excitement—a boat apparently upset, and another following.
I took out the glass, and discerned the state of things
to be that there was a light punt, with two men aboard,
in chase of a runaway raft, on which another man had
managed to crawl, at imminent risk of his life—the
more especially as he experienced our rapids.   It was
interesting to watch their manœuvres.   How calm and
yet effective their performance ! It reminded me of the
quiet way in which a lad, used to the sort, will coolly
go in and out of a savage bull's box with little risk of
accident ; only a certain amount of snorting rage on
the animal's part, and a trifle of contempt on the boy's.
Here, down the foaming, dirty river, went punt and
raft, waltzing gracefully around and around, while the
men, as calmly as if on shore, were lashing it gradually
together ; which having done, they slipped quietly
along a pole into their punt, the whole three, and with
a skilful scientific tow just arrested the monster's
affrighted gallop, as they reached a backwater, into
which they guided it, all helpless ; and where, in an
instant, it was stranded as comfortably and humbly
as, at this period of my story, am I.

Honour to the brave ! Honour to the benefactors of
Society ! Let me gratefully record the benefit I not
long since derived from a fortunate scientific invention,
for which I paid a few sovereigns, and which has repaid
the investment amply from the comfort and security it
has given to my mind. One bright morning last month
I had been loitering, as is my wont, in my dressing-
room, watching the timid hen pheasants that ran out to
pick up the Indian corn strewn over night for their
maintenance, and having to tap the glass occasionally

to warn off the peculative wood-pigeons which, however
pretty individually, one doesn't care to feed in a gang ;
hesitating more, perhaps, in dire anticipation of that
ruthless torment which the razor inflicts upon the chin,
however much you may have prepared it by soaking or
adoption of other tonsorial counsel, when the man-
servant came running up to say that the lodge was on
fire ! Eh ! My eye ! and this comes of living on a hill
with an abundant river two hundred steep feet below,
along a wooded incline, but not a drop available for
immediate use. " Where is that extincteur ? " I ask.
It was down stairs ; it had never been unpacked. That
undertaking had been continually postponed for the
amusement of the next rainy day. Well, as in his
existing undress Mahomet could not go to the mountain, the mountain must needs come to Mahomet, and
so in the course of a few moments, the man reappeared,
staggering under the weight of a huge package, most
tidily packed in brown paper, and carefully corded.
Being, you must know, of a thrifty nature, and remembering Miss Edgeworth's striking anecdote of the successful archer who had stored a string in his pocket, I
began deliberately to untie the several knots. But
they were more securely tied than usual, methinks, or
I was involuntarily nervous. Anyhow, it ended in a
Gordian severance by the razor that was lying open on
the table, much, I remember, to my increased skin-
torture when I came back from the open air to the use
of its riled edge. Then the wrappings were hastily
thrown off, and a gorgeously painted little metal barrel
stood forth, with a number of tin cases packed about
it, and a paper of printed directions prominently dis-
played, which I began at once to study, not knowing

the proper mode of using the engine. Possibly my demeanour was puzzled, as my progress was slow, when the man, who lived at the lodge, and whose wife and babe were possibly frying all this time said, " Please, sir, I'd better go." " Very well ; " and go he did. Then in a few moments, I had mastered the full purport of the directions, and had artistically emptied in the charges from the tin boxes, and filled the barrel itself with water. The number of cans it took to fill it quite astounded me, as much, perhaps, as you remember the boy mentioned in "Tom Brown's School Days " was at the endless profusion of feathers which were plucked from the duck he had appropriated and was preparing to roast. Then I put it upside down ; then violently reversed it ; then played it see-saw on the edge of the bath, until I became suddenly aware of a most diabolical savour pervading the apartment, and which I was assured must proceed from some orifice in this engine, although I was too prudent to apply Nature's investigator to ascertain the fact. So I simply screwed down the stopper several turns more, beyond the point of endurance I almost feared with each wrench of the key, and then, after some few moments more of aggra-vated agitation (strictly speaking, the preparation should have been compounded some hours), I hurried on my boating dress, and by dint of extraordinary efforts, managed to struggle down stairs with it (to the great delight of my youthful pickles, who came out half-rigged to the top of the stairs to look on, and who saw more of fun than seriousness in the matter) and had it conveyed to the lodge. Exaggeration, I was glad to find. It was only the chimney that was on fire, after all, but that might still be a serious matter. There

was fat Melon on the roof, half-melted, and vainly
endeavouring to suppress the flames with a wet mat
and such like, and there was his frightened assistant at
the foot of the ladder by which he had ascended, in
deadly terror lest his superior officer should be precipitated by some extraordinary effort, upon his head and
crush him, as he would undoubtedly have done, with
the weight of a cider butt.   There was the luckless
tenant, all bewildered and smoke-begrimed, and in such
a condition as his "missus" would certainly not
approve of at breakfast-time.   There was the goodnatured, half-blind, old village carpenter, ready to
assist in any way he could, and his comfortable spouse
offering recklessly the contents of their rain-water
cistern, when we force our way in and find a furious
fire burning yet in the grate, with the terrified builder
of it looking hopelessly on.   You had better get your
baby out of the way, and send Melon here.   Immediately we had put the barrel upon a chair, and quite
nervously, according to the directions, I turned the
cock gently, directing the fuse upon the grate. Splutter,
fizz went a discharge from the pipe, and, darkened at
once, dimly drew back and disappeared the flame ; one
shoot more and the blaze was extinct.   "Now then,
Melon, have you a good eye ? Mind that smoke : don't
inhale it, and direct this pipe up the chimney." He
did earnestly what he was told to do.   "Dash my
buttons, but that ere was a good shot ! " he exclaimed,
with the triumph of a hero, as a great fiery mass came
tumbling down, having been disturbed by the violence
of the discharge, and then being extinguished into
darkness at once.   "Look out for your eyes, Melon !
Now aim again."   He did so, and started back, as

P

another burning fragment came loosened down.   Again and again, and the conflagration was extinct.   Considering that the mixture had been made only a few moments it was really a wonderful performance.   I shall keep the engine now always charged and ready. The theory of the effect is this: the mixture produces in the barrel a quantity of what is known in mines as the fatal fire-damp, so largely diluted with water as to be not injurious to human life, while every drop that touches flame extinguishes it.   I had always before been puzzling myself how I could store a sufficiency of water to meet the contingencies of fire.   No more anxiety on that score.

Honour, too, to another device.   Shorthorn breeders will remember my mentioning once a set of clever oil-sketches of my pet animals that were done for me by Mr. Edward Corbet.   A few weeks since I was applied to from a distance for a young bull.   I sent pedigree and pictures of sire and dam.   The animal was purchased and gives most thorough satisfaction.   How simple the process !

And now let me turn to the farm, more strictly speaking.   The lambing season has progressed most favourably, as yet, owing, I think, to the ewes having been *evenly fed* throughout the winter.

One of Jonas Webb's best sort had, however, a squeak for it as men say, the other day.   She was actually upon the barrow to be killed, and the butcher fetched, when the bailiff's heart failed him.   His anxiety occasionally renders his measures too impetuous. His heart failed him.   She was returned to the fold to " take her chance," and she gradually produced no less than four lambs !   No wonder she was distressed.

A prize cow of mine two years ago produced three calves, which came alive to the birth, but two of which died during delivery. The third is now a nice thick young heifer; her dam wasted for some months, and then died a mere skeleton.

Of course it is a great time for the children. They have no end of pets now, between lambs and calves, and rabbits and canaries and dormice and what not. A few weeks since the two youngsters had been absent for some hours, when they re-appeared all covered with mud. They had found a wild rabbit's nest in a bank, had excavated it with their nails and a stick, and brought home four brown-furred babies, with their eyes still closed. These infants they managed to rear with a bottle and a " baby's tit," as the eldest tit informed me. How long they might have survived with fair care, I cannot say. Unhappily two came to an untimely end soon, the one from repletion, the other from starving. The young feeder had given a dose of milk twice over to the same individual, and so the two suffered ; another lived some days, perishing ultimately from too close confinement, I was informed. The fourth would, I think, have survived all his ills and lived, if his owner had not been himself laid up in bed, when poor bunny got neglected.

The Wye floods have been out and all over the meadow land again, covering the whole with a rich deposit of alluvial mud, and leaving a great salmon stranded, but interrupting the work of our drainers. One sunny afternoon I took the children all out in the boat, to their great delight, and the bright mirror reflecting the rays, it was warm almost as in summer time. What fun we had going across the fences, and

even over one gate! It was the more enjoyable that
there was little or no stream in the outspread waters.
Before I conclude, I owe it to myself to record the
results of the *post mortem* examination of a grand
young boar just killed for the butcher, which won a
prize at Leicester, and several since, finishing up with
a cup at Lord Tredegar's show. Having been fattened
when quite young and then reduced, he retained from
the period of his first obesity a " purse" of skin and
blubber underneath him, which ignoramuses persisted
in calling a rupture. We knew it was nothing of the
sort, having had proof. Besides, the V. S. of the Royal
Agricultural Show found no objection to him. When lo
and behold, at the Gloucester show a wiseacre appointed
as judge actually disqualified him, owing to that formation, in spite of all representation upon the subject!
Another V. S. should have been consulted. A decision
of this sort should not be left to a common farmer or
bailiff, however pig-headed he may be. They have only
to pronounce on the symmetry and quality of the
animals set for their judgment. Breeders knew better.
At Leicester, one of the most eminent of the class in
England wanted to buy him, and during conversation
remarked that he had seen many such cases. My
indignation chokes me.

April, 1869.

I HAVE just returned from a walk by the river side.
It is a favourite ramble of ours, because of the freshness
that we fall in with, as well as that we obtain therefrom
a charming view of " home, sweet home," nestling
amidst the trees that crown the steep overhanging
bank. No matter what time of the day we go down,

there is always novelty; but especially when the sun sets behind the ruins of an old adjoining castle, casting a glow upon the sky and lower landscape, it is delightful to wander there. Just now my steps led me to a point which a grand old heron daily visits. I found there a profusion of emptied fresh-water mussels, and another plump salmon, who had missed stays in the receding flood and been left ashore. The effect of last summer's heat has been beneficial there. A wide extent of gravel, the grey tint of which harmonised beautifully with the grass and water, got plentifully seeded, and is now a bed of young trefoil and clover. I could not traverse the whole, owing to the depth of soft rich mud that the floods have left upon it. In returning by a circuit over the meadow, I was surprised by the number of partridge pairs that I disturbed, arranging about the "marriage lines," I expect. There ought to be an abundance of birds next season. I am always glad when many are left, they do so much good in picking up grubs over the fallows. Some silly farmers are already beginning to persecute and poison the rooks, forgetting the infinite service they did in devouring the cockchafer by myriads in grub shape and full uniform last season. But some selfish, shortsighted beings there is no persuading.

Although most heavily stocked I shall have a large heap of mangold-wurzel to sell, for the late turnips and stubble-sown rye-grass yield a vast amount of keep. The grass seed turned out better than I expected, I must allow. The water-meadow that we made this winter has done wonders for the ewes and lambs, with which, I am glad to say, we have done extremely well, having lots of couples, and in one case a living trio of ewe lambs, and from a Cotswold too, which is wonderful, we consider. Of the four that were born of one mother, only two survive. We have only lost one ewe as yet.

It is good to see that there is an annual show and sale of yearling Shorthorn bulls projected at Bingley Hall. I am quite sure, however, that it would be much better if it were not for, what I consider, the unreasonable condition that every animal must be put up at 20 guineas without reserve. They call it a parallel case to putting a ram up at 5 guineas. At 30 guineas it might be, but not 20. One of the most celebrated breeders endorses my opinion in a letter received this morning. He says : " I quite agree with you about the Birmingham prize list, and cannot see how anyone would like to risk a good animal there, much as the £50 prize deserves a good one." I cannot lay hands on my Dublin show regulations, but I scarcely think that they can have the same rule ; they may, but I doubt it. The show is at least a good move. I hope heartily that it will answer, but for myself I shall prefer to run my risk as a buyer rather than as a breeder under existing circumstances.

The subject of dentition again ! not in this instance porcine, nor involving an indignant protest from insulted exhibitors, and a universal condemnation of professional pretention, but a matter more immediately concerning the human species. I was yesterday just half-way into a post-prandial nap (we had dined early as it was a special half holiday, and the chicks were to have a drive), when the rustling garment of a little maiden disturbed me, notwithstanding that her coy diffidence caused a stealthy approach. After some general remarks, by which obviously like a parent partridge, she assumed to throw me off the scent of her intending anything, she asked me to advance her half-a-crown, on the security of what think you? Why, a loose tooth! They get that amount paid on the extraction of certain difficult fangs, and I find now that she has been patiently working to loosen three, which she values at six shillings, for some days past. As her object was to go shares with a wealthier sister in the purchase of a present for their governess, after due admonition I advanced the cash, with which she instantly made off. I hear that Mademoiselle is delighted to-day, but I notice further there are no operations going on for the undermining of the teeth. Here she trips just along the passage, and I must change the subject, for she is sure to peep over my shoulder unless I stay my pen for a game of romps, which I have not time to indulge in. We have just been sending off in great state a fat little Shetland pony, which has educated two families, to my certain knowledge, and is said to be verging on thirty years of age. He is hopelessly broken-winded, but galloped after the hounds with a youngster on him, the other day, with great gusto. We have another of a larger sort coming on, and in consequence a little friend has got an unexpected present. A companion of his, an old pet mare, heavy in foal, met with an accident yesterday, that might have proved fatal to herself or foal, or both. The youngsters had driven the lot into a corner, confined by wire fencing, with a view to get an extempore ride each; whereupon this unhappy mare, fearing more than the ponies did, tried, but unsuccessfully, to leap the wire, chesting one of the uprights, and peeling off a piece of skin some nine inches square. Happening to pass just afterwards, I saw her with apparently a clot of gore hanging from her neck. Having had her caught, the wound fortunately proved not deep, so I sewed up the rag of skin, after washing the bare surface with calendula and water, and to-day she seems to be going on well. She was a rare racer in her time, and I don't want to lose her yet, although her colts differ much, and breeding does not pay. We had some precious calves born the other morning, which gave some trouble in the delivery. One cow is positively fit for the butcher, and yet they have been feeding all the winter upon only a mixture of chaff more than half straw, with sufficient pulped mangold to moisten it, and a few handfuls of bran strewn upon the feed.

It has just happened to me casually to overhear a discussion carried on between Mamma and one of the young men as to the food supplied to the rabbits, in the course of which, after dilating upon the various qualities of the several kinds of food they obtain, in answer to an inquiry, he gravely informed her that it would not do to give them wheat, because it would " button them up" at once. Mamma was clearly puzzled by such a plain expression for the binding property of this grain, and I left her to his enlightenment, being sufficiently amused by the native eloquence of my son. Yesterday there was great grief throughout the nursery in consequence of a pet ferret having been accidentally shot by the man-servant, who during some sport in the woods, had shot the poor animal as it came hurrying out after a rabbit that had bolted. They had nursed it from its infancy, and it was certainly a very pretty sight to see it with its back arched playfully, jumping

and skipping and squeaking. The last thing I saw of
it was just before they started on the fatal expedition,
when a youngster, whose province it was to carry him
in a green baize bag, took him out for me to admire,
and started him caracoling across the servants'-hall-
floor. They have already arranged to have " his nephew"
from a neighbour's coachman, so I hope that there
will be no great intermission in the extermination of
the bunnies, especially as I have been indulging in a
young plantation, which I have no desire at all that
they should invade. I have caught two ideas lately
from the paper—the one being the making all rainfall from the roofs pass through a box-filter laden with
gravel and charcoal, and put to intersect the delivery-
pipe into the reservoir.

I have hitherto been used to throw charcoal into the
reservoir itself occasionally, as well as to filter its contents before use. I wonder we never thought of so
simple an expedient before. The other idea, which my
man, who is just engaged in brewing, won't credit, is
that a bag of malt and a bag of barley yield as good
liquor as two bags of malt would. I only hope so. I
shall try the experiment on a small scale.

" Blow me, if I'd try a hogsyed fust," was old Melon's
commentary : he having been engaged to assist in the
carrying down of the brew.

I wish some one would tell me a simple plan of
hauling up hay three hundred yards along slopes in-
clining at about forty degrees, where the use of carts
and waggons is difficult, there being no roadway cut,
so as to save one's sending it more than a mile around
the bottom of the hill, and then winding up the mail
road. I have bethought me that something like a

sledge with a deep cradle on it might do.   I should be
so thankful for a practical hint from some experienced
mountaineer.   A capital dodge for going down hill
quick yourself I can tell you: Cut a bunch of rushes ;
grasp the points, and sit upon the root ends : lift your
legs, and .down the grassy incline you shoot like lightning.   So the Welsh shepherds descend steep places.
But it is easier to descend than to climb, metaphorically
or otherwise.

May, 1869.

"'Come home to die!' It's so very sad, isn't it,
papa?" says a little plaintive voice beside me, dis-
turbing one from reverie. "Here we found her close
beside the front-door, just where we used to feed her :
poor little dear," she continued, stroking the glossy
smooth plumage (it was a hen pheasant). Just our
luck ! just the luck of everyone : but another illustration of Moore's sentiment :

> " Oh ! ever thus from childhood's hour
> I've seen my fondest hopes decay ;
> 　*　　*　　*　　*　　*
> But when it came to know me well
> And love me, it was sure to die."

Of the whole batch, two hens only had survived the
perils of puss and fowling-piece, and would even up to
the period of their decease run up at call to feed out of
our hands.

Strange was it, that one day having a friend here
who kept firing under each bird as it rose, at last he
knocked one over. The shot met her as she stooped
in her flight. She was, in fact, one of this precious pair
that had wandered into the wild wood to a kettle-drum

probably with her acquaintance, and on the sound of
the firing made for home, unluckily in a lowered
direction. And now the last is gone! This one was
wont to consort with the bantams, and I had hoped
for a cross. Alackaday! but how came she to die
thus without mark of shot, or spot of blood upon her
beauteous plumage? Her under beak was broken,
and the top one partly split. Could she have got into
a trap that old Melon has for a pestilent rabbit in those
laurels? No, the trap was unsprung. We then decided
that some one must have hit her with a stone, and so
the little ones retire, and the subject drops.

I take a walk; I watch the thrashing-machine beat
out a fine sample of wheat which I fear will still be difficult to sell. Suddenly, as I look on, the recollection
occurs that on Monday last we were in search of this
above-mentioned rabbit, and disturbed a hen pheasant
that was seen to fly right full against the upper story of
the house, and then wheel back into the bushes, these
very bushes whence she crept out to die in the sunshine.
Poor thing! she must have perished from the shock, for
her craw is full of peas. So we will hope that it was not
the pet hen after all. I hear that, fortunately, to-day
this rabbit hath met its deserved fate. Singularly
enough, we have always been free from rats: whether
they don't like the exposure of our situation or not I
don't know, but so it is. I was horrified, then, to hear,
yesterday, that a huge fellow had been seen under the
lodge, regaling himself upon the pheasants' Indian corn.
Very shortly I saw him laid out upon the brewhouse
window-sill, having been caught about the waist, by a
trap of Mr. Melon's. Surmising too that as hares are
now found in couples, so too, might rats be; he set the

trap again last night. This morning it was missing. In amazement, with his assistant and the man-servant, he tracked it through the bushes. "It's one of the long tailed uns," says the servant. "Bound to be," echoes Mr. Melon. "Here he be," shouts the assistant-gardener in advance. "Stop, then, a moment;" shouts Melon, panting with the exertion of struggling through the bushes. "Kill him, Melon;" shouts the man-servant, waiting outside with his gun cocked. "That I will; I'll hit un," eagerly threatens Mr. Melon. "Gosh, it be ours!" suddenly he exclaims, as he nears the spot, in an altered tone. "Never mind, hit un;" shouts the man-servant, who is a wag; mimicking his expression. "Eh! but what'll the auld ooman say? give it now, this chance;" so saying, he slackens the trap, and out darts away the affrighted animal. "But if him come again, by jabbers, I'll kill un. Gosh, him did jump though; him knowed him'll never have another chance," he said, relating the circumstance to me! stooping his fat form, and half covering his mouth, in an agony of suppressed titter as he spoke, his sense of the fun of it overcoming speech. I have not remembered since to ask him whether the rescued valuable took home scars or not, and whether he got better or worse off with his life's partner himself.

He was up and away before me, watering his plants in the porch this morning; and as for his day time, I am afraid to approach; he is so pleasant—so wondrous pleasant—with his "Please, can't we have some peat hauled noways!" or some gravel, or some salt, or some pea-sticks, or some other aggravating article, considering that we farm and want the horses.

Now, even the wisest will sometimes go wrong, as the

old Eton Latin Grammar duly cautions us.   In his
anxiety to force on the young fry, my shepherd (usually
most cautious) went and penned the lot upon some
sprouted turnips, straight from grass, without having
subjected them to a novitiate.

We have been so lucky with the sheep that it was
quite vexatious to hear of the death of a ewe, " found on
her back."   He might as well have given the regular
old senseless answer " had a pain."   Riding by that part
of the farm I saw the reason at once.   Why he did such
an imprudent thing I don't know—wool-gathering I can
only conclude.

Referring to wool, I wish it would run up.   We have
managed to get saddled from one cause or another with
three years' clip, beautiful lustrous fleeces too.   Few
things delight me so much as to contemplate the clothing
of a pet ewe that one has reared through so many generations.   " In the days when we were curly" will be
remembered as an expression of the ex-Premier's
(meaning " the days when we were young, a long time
ago "), which his own collection of glossy spirals probably put into his head.   I never fail to recall it when
I inspect my flock.   It was a shrewd remark of an agricultural writer lately, that the long-wooled sheep suffer
more from rain than the short-woolly sort, whose fleeces
might be described as of an African type.   I notice quite
a broad band down the backs of the former kind, as
carefully divided as any dandy's locks, and where the
pitiless storm can pelt in with disastrous effect.

But on second thought may not this strip of skin
become inured to the action of the elements as the peri-
cranium of the Christ's Hospital youngster does ?   This
brings me to another puzzle.   How is it that birds

escape the evils of influenza, a chill, and so forth, flying hotly around and about, and then just settling on an exposed branch in mid-air for their nocturnal slumbers? I suppose they can close and open their plumage like Venetian blinds at will. I wish I wore feathers—or rather I wish the children did! how much cheaper and more satisfactory it would be for us fond parents! and if they would only perch to sleep instead of requiring new rooms to be furnished, that would be better still, and if they would go under the bushes and nestle quietly on a rainy day, why that would be best of all. I am in the way of being reminded to-day. The youngsters are just indulging in an exclamation on finding only one side of their toast done. "Her sweetheart is dead," they explain to me. But what I am reminded of is the high art of a clever groom I once had from a hunting establishment, who, though capable of anything in the way of turning out a horse, became gradually too indolent to attend to his duties. He went from me to the service of an old dowager in Cheltenham, where his idleness culminated in his using thought and pains to clean only one side of the horse and carriage—viz., that which was next the door on driving up. Another illustration of abused intelligence! Chicks again; how they do interrupt one! this time to announce the fact of a robin having actually made a nest, and laid five eggs, in a neighbour's garden house. Wondrous fact, setting forth the precocity of the season; but to take a philosophical and thoughtful view of the subject—will this said robin after the first brood is hatched consider herself a widow, and set out her weed-ornamentation for a second catch; or will she impose upon Squire Redbreast the maintenance of a second lot?

Some gentleman reports in the *Journal* of the Royal Agricultural Society that he never found his stock to do so well as upon chaff, three parts straw to one of hay, sufficiently moistened with pulped wurzel and left to warm in a heap. It has answered famously on our farm this winter ; and I shall follow up the plan even when there is an abundance of fodder. In fact, when that is the case, it is difficult to keep one's men from so stuffing the racks, that the animals get gorged and saucy, and a large quantity of the food is wasted. A little, often supplied so as to be well digested, is, of course, the secret of successful fattening. Having by a division of common land come into an accession of meadow, we have been taking measures for its improvement. There being one portion covered with rushes, and where the hay crop was always stunted, of course it was decided that this should be drained.

Often as I had walked it over, it was not until the leader of an experienced gang pointed the fact out, that I noticed the existence of a cup-like hollow there. When the cutting tapped it, water ran freely, but fortunately, no springs were found. It was merely the soak of the winter floods which could not get away. The expenditure of a very few sovereigns thoroughly corrected the evil.

A curious accident has happened to a foal, some three day's old, which, owing to the severity of the weather, was kept with its mother in one of the yards. It was strong and lively over night, but was found stone dead in the morning, with its dam standing over it. From some cause or other it had sprung and struck its forehead full against a post, killing itself on the spot. It is the very mare that had so narrow an escape over the wire-fence. The children are, of course, greatly cut up, but I am not very sorry myself, seeing how young horses accumulate, to be after all so unsaleable. It is a good excuse, too, to issue the death-warrant of the dam, which, an excellent mare in her time, is long since past work. One of the boys employed to watch one of the wheatfields has had, I find, great trouble in keeping away the rooks. On hearing this, I walked the piece, and, at the root of several yellowish plants, found wire-worms. No wonder our friends were so pertinacious. The moles, too, had scented their prey, for I found no less than five traps set for them, which I at once sprung. We ought rather to be thankful that nature's remedy is so promptly applied upon the appearance of disease in a crop. Poor old Melon is in a terrible state of mind. His son, whom he educated as a gardener, obtained a good place lately, where he was in sole charge. He was sent with a cart to fetch some articles which his master had purchased at a neighbouring sale. It was a bitterly cold day, and a chill struck deep into him. He lies in most excruciating agony from an attack of rheumatic gout. If, instead of riding, as lads are so prone to do, lightly clad, he had used his legs, he might have been saved this torture.

I have a report of the delicious crooning of the turtle dove having been heard in the woods a few days since; but I doubt it. It is rather soon for the arrival of the dear little stranger. The bailiff just now made a remark to me, which has often occurred to me before: " I wonder some one doesn't sow charlock; for the minute the sheep get a new pen, they pitch into it before the turnips."

One field of swedes came up so slowly that it was

doubtful whether they were worth thinning. I ordered
the operation to be gone through with, however, as it
had been begun, and, thanks to the mild winter we have
had, there came up a fair quantity of small bulbs, which
have been of great service to us. Some of the young
charlock escaped the hoe, and last month raised a
flourishing top amidst the swede rows. I was sorry that
any had been hoed off at all; for the sheep clearly preferred them to the swedes, as the fly is said to do when
they are in their infant stage.

Thankful are we that the late sudden inclement
weather hath taken its departure. For the last few days
it was impossible to believe that we had been sunning
ourselves but a week gone by, so pleasantly the day
through, upon the open lawn slopes. The poor willow,
that looked so lovely in the fresh fulness of its pendent
foliage, got its tresses nipped by that treacherous on-
slaught of keen frost, and old Melon predicts its having
had a squeak for life itself.

What a variety of disaster the agriculturist has to
struggle against? Here, now, is corn down with a run:
and will it go no further, I wonder? And we must
thrash for straw; and six of our best lambs have perished
in the course of a couple of days—some, I think, from
the shepherd's incautiously introducing them too suddenly into an exuberance of young grass, and one at
least from being sanded up, as a pony of ours was two
years ago. The Wye flood leaves a deposit of sand upon
the adjacent herbage, which has a deleterious, if not a
deadly, effect upon all stock that grazes it before it has
been well washed with rain. One of the little girls' pet
lambs was found dead, too, in that hot weather; from
apoplexy, I suspect, or "braxy," as the Scotch shepherds

Q

name a disease, the symptoms of which are similar. Of course I was obliged to look out for a lamb to replace the pet. I had not long to consider whither I should bend my steps, for the little ones themselves, observing a dead ewe upon the hill above my farm, at once ascertained the fact that there was an orphan behind. On my riding up, however, to propose the purchase, I found that the owners had found a foster-mother for the infant. Close adjoining lives one of my men, who has been long laid up with the effects of a bad cold, or rheumatism in the blood, as the doctor tells him, from cider drinking. His father feeds a few mountain sheep upon the hillside. This last winter, he told me, a number of them died, and now a fatality has arisen amongst the lambs of the survivors. Of course I was anxious to know why. He explained that the effects of the late excessive heat was to drive the ticks off the ewes on to their offspring, on which they crowded in such numbers as to weaken them excessively, if not deprive them wholly of life. " They suck their vitals out," the man said. Besides which, in biting to relieve the torture of their limbs, they manage to swallow locks of wool, which is fatal in itself.

He said he had the skin of one at home which had been literally eaten through by these pests. I was incredulous, and so he fetched it. I never saw such a sight. Although it had been stripped nearly a week, there were the parasites, weakly crawling about as thick as currants in a school Sunday dumpling. Ugh ! it makes one shudder to recall them. Of course the dams had never been dipped in the autumn. Such a prudential process had never entered the head of the fatalist owner.

This morning I stepped down to see how they got on

with the thrashing of a wheat-rick I found an Eton boy there, armed with a saloon pistol, and attended by a retriever, on the watch for rats. One he had shot as it dived about in its endeavours to escape through an adjoining pool. I was called away to inspect the young bulls, which were starting for their promenade, and my attention was asked to the back of one, a favourite. It was literally one mass of inflamed bumps. I had his back fomented at once, and the herdsman then extracted over thirty huge gad-fly grubs from the poor creature's hide. No wonder he was ticklish to handle. Some of them had festered. The other calves seem all to have escaped. I don't know whether the fly has a taste for pedigree, for this was out-and-out the most transcendently ancestral of the lot. From the window, I have just watched through a glass the drawing of the salmon-nets below—for this turn without fruit. The river is so turbid, however, that it is probable a large catch may blunder into the meshes before night. I saw a man catch a fine fellow out in a coracle one day lately when the south wind blew softly. He used only a short rod, about the length of two pea-sticks, to the handle of which was attached an inflated bladder. He kept paddling himself leisurely about towards the tail of a strong current, and casting across it until a fish struck. He then threw the rod into the water, and it was drawn down by the victim, ever and anon reappearing, when the man paddled up to it and played it so long as he dare, throwing it off again as the strain became dangerously great. Thus, after a while, a fine fifteen-pound fish was made to drown himself, and was then drawn up in triumph upon a strip of sand. We were all down to look on. There was very little Latin done that day.

I see that in Scotland there is a raid being made upon the " pigeons and crows." The former right well deserve it, and the latter, too, should be kept within bounds by shooting; but to poison them is cruel as well as indiscriminate in its effects. You cannot persuade the ordinary farmer of the good they do in keeping down the dor or chaffer-beetle, an unchecked multitude of which in France, not long since, committed such devastation as one has only heard of before a cloud of locusts. I was told the other day of a man who had found his own chanticleer dead upon his field. How it happened, perhaps, he won't tell. It is astonishing how that piece of wheat has freshened from which I mentioned lately that a boy had vainly attempted to keep the rooks away, and into which the moles worked. I let them do their worst; and that worst I now find to be an excellent service.

And so the Birmingham sale of yearling bulls resulted in a shuffle. We will hope now that the footing upon which it was established will be altered. The fifty-pound prize is sure to attract exhibitors. To compel, as has been attempted, a sale " without reserve," at 20 guineas, must keep all good animals away. It gives the buyer an unfair advantage. I have been unlucky lately in having a large fall of bull calves. I thought I had learnt a secret to ensure heifers, but don't find it answer this year, although it appeared to do so last season.

The nomenclature of our young ones occupying our spare thoughts, one audacious fellow that has a certain head-up-time-of-the-regency air about him I am tempted to designate "Fraudulent Bankrupt" if one could but pack up the two words, German-like, into one.

He has quite the manner and the gesture those vagabonds indulge in.

I wish the old trees would abstain from falling. They involve so much expense in cutting up into logs for parlour use ; and then when they do get burnt the effect they produce individually is so transitory, just a " kiss me quick and go " sort of flame, and a few thimblefulls of ash. Men talk, and with reason, of wood-ash being so excellent an ingredient in manure, but bless me, where can it come from in sufficient quantity ?

What a difference it makes if one can only abstain from feeding down the pasture intended for hay after February 2nd, or even the end of the last year if possible.

A neighbour told me the other day that he never shuts up his meadows until April 1st. I am glad that I did not adopt that line of policy myself this year. We shall have a great portion to mow the next month, and what an advantage that will be in case, as is predicted, we have this summer again the terrific drought of last year.

What famous stuff lucerne is ! We are cutting it nearly a foot high now for the stable ; the vetches being not nearly ready. I have come decidedly to the opinion that it should be sown in drills, although many advocate its being put in broadcast. It is so troublesome to weed it when sown after the latter plan. This soil suits it. The gypsum in the red marl, which makes the well-water so disagreeably hard, is favourable to the growth of this plant.

I hope Mr. Bowly, who has been so spirited a partner of Mr. Rich's, will have a good sale to-day. He has given 500 guineas for another bull, from Captain Gunter, it is rumoured.

June, 1869.

WHAT a pleasant thing is success! I suppose the feeling is pretty much the same under all circumstances. Probably the breeder, who has just sold a calf for 500 guineas, or the Prime Minister, who has just carried a pet bill through the House in its entirety, feels no more elated than I did a few moments since, as I sat down to an eleven o'clock breakfast—toast, tea, eggs, cold boiled beef, and a glass of ale, after watching for some interested hours the disestablishment of weedlings, through the instrumentality of Garrett's most excellent horsehoe.

Faith! don't it cut out right well ; and with not the less gusto, apparently, when it swerves so as to catch a good sweep of a wheat-row. It is a new implement hereabouts, and the men were sadly prejudiced against it. At first there were many difficulties in its management; but at last, by dint of perseverance (that thief of time), we managed to get on pretty well. And all I wish now is to be able to take a short jump forward, and see the effect of this treatment upon the crop ; only I would stipulate for returning to the present point of time again ; the days are so delicious now, with sweet songs of birds on every side, and the fragrant buds and flowers daily breaking.

The bad potatoes I planted last year are beginning to appear above the surface. They are very strong, my man reports. I am desirous of seeing what gaps there are, and I shall not be disappointed if they are many, because I did not manage to do that which I hold to be only fair by the experiment. Instead of having a piece ploughed ready into which just to transport the questionable characters as the main crop is being raised, they were allowed to be some time in a heap, and then were planted after a slight touch of frost. It was not at all what I intended, but we were temporarily over-worked. A friend, who acted on my hint, had his set in due time. I hear of his having been exploring with a fork, being alarmed at their protracted non-appearance above ground. He found the subterranean shoots very strong, I believe. Last year my experience was that the autumn-planted potatoes were later in appearing on the face of the ground, but ripened earlier. I have conse-quently counselled patience. We are all on the *qui vive*, there being an unusual number of extra prizes adver-tised at our local show by the various artificial manure-makers for the best display of roots grown after a dress-ing of their admirable "special," the society itself, too, giving a challenge-cup, without regard to the manure. There is certainly benefit in these public prizes. For a month or more I have had sawdust under my ani-mals, which, after saturation, has been stored in a spare barn, and will be drilled in with Swede-seed between a strip of saturated ashes on the one side, and a strip of superphosphated soil on the other. A dressing of sawdust, wet with liquid manure, has cer-tainly freed an old pasture of its mossy growth. How or why I cannot say, but I think that, mixed with our sandy loams, it may prove a convenient vehicle for moisture, arresting and retaining it throughout the dry seasons we so much dread in this district. We have a good-sized mangold-wurzel heap left yet. The stock seem to do better than ever upon it now. The rye-grass and trifolium sown upon the wheat-stubble which I had harrowed several ways, just to brush the seed in, has been twice fed down, and is now well advanced for cutting; after which I shall expect a tidy show of the green-topped hybrid turnip. I think it right to mention this, because the grass-seed at first disappointed us, and I was forward to blame the sellers who had advertised this plan.

We are very unlucky in the hatching of geese—about forty eggs and only seven goslings, or gulls, as the country-people call them in this neighbourhood. I was afraid that the nests might have been made of hay—a material which conduces much to the rotting of eggs during the mysterious process of incubation. But no, I ascertained that there had been straw strewn in the vicinity of their huts. They had had, moreover, a free run of the orchards and stackyard. They had plenty to choose from, if they had only used their heads; but that of course they didn't do, being geese. They were no better than servants in that respect, whose non-thinking habit, by the way, one would not so much deplore, if, on the other hand, they never took airs. Just before this welcome rain arrived, our tank ran short, and we had to try a number of places, all without success, with the Abyssinian tube for water. At last luckily we struck an accumulation, if not a spring, in a sandbed, and as our good fortune would have it, in the corner of a large cattle-shed, where it is especially wanted, within fifteen yards too of the tank, and, above all, under cover; so that a succession of hands can work it to advantage when it is too wet above head to be abroad. Our water-cresses have been so abundant —so sharp—and all the more delicious that we grew them ourselves. The only fault is, that the spring being in a hollow, it is a regular sun-trap, the bright

mirror attracting the rays of that luminary so as to
force up the shoots to a fearful height; so much so
that anyone unacquainted with the private history of
this pool, would be afraid to chew the lanky vegetable.
I have just been informed that where they grow them
regularly in beds for the London market, they take up
the plants and cut the roots back well in early spring,
then re-planting them bodily. I had this bit of information with a present of brown cress roots from Berk-
shire yesterday. But then these overgrown, out at the
elbow, short-kilted specimens of my own, they come of a
brown sort to begin with. I planted them quite brown.
Their first offspring were of a quadroon complexion,
their next a paler sort, and so on until they have at
last attained that delicate tint which is reckoned dangerous to live near on a drawing-room paper.

How confinement tames! Else how am I to account
for a thorough-bred mare so given to bucking that we
were obliged to throw her out of work a year ago, being
mounted the other day by the cow-boy (without my
knowledge in the first instance) and ridden, without
attempt at mischief, all across green fields and under
orchard boughs. She must be longing for a ticket-of-
leave, and trying to impose upon her keeper. A year
ago she finished up, having thrown everyone else I
don't know how often, by depositing myself upon my
side on a low wall, and injuring my rib. I had mounted
her, after some idle time in the stable-yard, where I
had no room to fight her, and endeavouring to get off,
got helped, and more forsooth, viz., physical damage in
that quarter whence man's helpmate originally sprung.
From that day she had been in a box. I have now
given the lad *carte blanche* to break his head, and

further encouraged him by the promise of five shillings
if he bring her tame for our post-luncheon canters
again.

Ah! there now! How jolly it is to hear the cock-
pheasant crow so comfortably to his patient spouse
upon her nest, a "courage, madame, courage," then
flapping his wings in triumphant anticipation of the
numerous brood he is soon to superintend! We look out
at the window, and there the luxurious rascal is close
by, and he sees us, and just hides his gorgeous head
behind a plant, so we won't disturb him. We have a
snow-white pair shut up for laying ; but as yet we have
not been successful in obtaining any eggs. I hear old
Melon's voice shouting objurgation to the children.
The fact is, there run the little girls with their pet
lambs just along the standard roses, nipping the leaves
too frequently for his patience. In place of the lamb
that died I managed to obtain a mountaineer—black
with white ears, and a white tip to its tail, more like a
kitten than a young sheep. It was frightened and
troublesome at first : it has now come to "take its
bottle beautiful" I am informed, and will follow its
owner, if chaperoned by the elder-born Southdown pet.
Braxy has ceased to trouble my flock after their removal to shorter grass on an old pasture, but I hear of
numerous losses about the neighbourhood.

July, 1869.

I AM sadly afraid that we shall have very thin hay-
crops. I hope to mow next week, having got down a
new Wood's machine. This is the fifth mower I have
had. I bought one of Wood's some years since, when
they were first introduced into the country. It was a

"combined" machine, and the cutting bar was made of ash; hence the severance of the stems was not close enough. This I sold, and have since had three others. by various makers, bought second-hand at sales; which, I would suggest to the young farmer, on the strength of my accumulated experience, is a very treacherous plan. It is far better to pay a few extra pounds, and get a fresh implement. You can never know the exact condition of the article, and the repairs soon mount to an awful height, without either obtaining for you any satisfaction in the end. On our strip of alluvial soil there is a succulent crop of nearly two feet in depth, intermixed with great patches of docks. The leaves of this plant I shall dry and store like tobacco, to steam periodically into their original dimensions, and mix with meal for the piggery. Fresh boiled, they constitute an admirable element of the wash-tub, and are much esteemed by the cottagers. I am so afraid that we shall smash up many a partridge's nest, they are so thick upon the ground. We have a lot of pheasants just hatched under "a silky:" the eggs came to light on the removal of some apple-tree prunings for fire-wood. It was very amusing to us all that the silky old gentleman must needs keep watch and vigil by his patient spouse, sitting with stupid inexorability alongside in her box. The little lads are of opinion that he is a muff, and dare not face the other bantams without his wife's skirts to run behind when threatened by an adversary. Perhaps he cannot fight. He has the funniest way of walking—a most exaggerated ultra-gallic gesticulatory kind of movement, reminding one of the defenceless hop of a fettered donkey, when he is forced off his steady domestic paces by the challenge of a neighbour.

It is curious that a guinea-hen belonging to the adjoining farm has gone off into the woods, whether mated with a pheasant or not we cannot tell. For several evenings she returned later and later to her roost, as if unable to make up her mind under temptation. One evening she never came back at all, and ever since she has kept to the plantation. One could understand it if she had been reared where they are in the habit of turning this bird out amongst the pheasants ; but she was hatched from stock that has led a steady farm-yard life for years. It must be a wild instinct cropping up accidentally in her mind.

The winter river-floods having made great inroads into one part of the bank, we are raising stone close to the river-bed, a few hundred yards away, to protect the wearing part. It proves of a harder nature than we anticipated. Where the layers are excavated we make a series of runs and retreats for the quick-eyed trout, so as to multiply our angling stations. Over the packed stone I propose to scatter mould, and sow therein the running "Agrostis stolonifera," of which I have had a sack down from a seedsman : a consignment, by the way, which gave my young bailiff a strong fright. He was busy overhauling the various packages when he came to this, and was struck by the appearance of the fine diminutive seed. Plunging his arm clothed with woollen in, he drew it out a brown mass, as if a swarm of small flies were clinging by it.

"Do you know what seed that is?"

"No, sir ; it's a funny sort."

"Well, it's couch."

"Couch!"

And he dropped the sack in horror.

" Please, sir, I thought we had plenty of that sort;"
and he tried, but in vain, to brush his sleeve clean.   It
so happened that he was busy with the mangold ground.
Next day I observed that he had undergone a religiously
thorough change of raiment.

The regular growth of the several crops is showing
now markedly the divisions of our re-arranged farm—
small fields having been thrown together and hedges
stocked up.   It is very satisfactory to read so plainly
deciphered, the result of one's careful calculations.
Most fascinating of all pursuits, after all, is the improvement and farming of an estate, however limited in
extent.

An event, which I had often longed for, has just come
off. We had no house-martins building under our eaves.
I used often to remember with what delight one was
wont, as a boy at home, to watch the elegant motions of
these beautiful birds, as they swept up and down in their
twittering flight.   Last autumn I was consequently glad
to see a pair commence constructing their habitation
against our present residence.   It was, however, so late in
the season, that I concluded they must have made a mistake in their reckoning.   After a while, as if disgusted,
they went off, and were soon involved in the annual
migration.   I gave the pair, I must say, little credit for
judgment.   I thought it might be probably an ill-con-
sidered runaway match, or perhaps that a widow had,
after much manœuvring, managed to entrap a wary old
bachelor.   Anyhow they had not given due considera-
to their housekeeping cares, it was clear; when, lo and
behold ! this spring, what should I see one fine morning,
but my fair friend and her partner essaying the security
of a tiny mud lodge, which was all they had managed

to erect last autumn ; she twittering what were evidently very sweet injunctions to him as he swept up on radiant wing, taking rapid flight at once, and returning soon with what appeared a mud pellet, for which he got the dearest of prettily mouthed acknowledgments. It made one's teeth water, I confess, to note the eager and yet so refined billing and cooing of that industrious pair. The habitation rose rapidly tier by tier (not without attracting the wistful eyes of our youngsters, who have "no martin's eggs in their collections," and which they won't have as regards this particular pair), and the bride is now clearly engaged in important considerations. See, then how we misjudge them ! Their imperfect performance of last autumn was a proof of foresight. The exterior of our house is so smooth as, I think, to afford no temptation to a martin of average enterprise and industry. This Romeo, however, was possessed of an engineering turn, and so he took the precaution of making a safe foundation beforehand for his future dwelling. It gave one a lesson not to be too ready to pronounce ill-natured judgment on the proceedings of a neighbour. I notice now another pair beginning to survey the locality : they are clearly birds of taste, for there is a lovely view therefrom, and I shall not now be surprised or sorry if the whole lodge be divided into building lots.

I have had occasion latterly to observe in several instances that short animals lengthen out at different periods of their growth. I remember being struck by that rare judge, Mr. Eastwood, giving a stiff figure for a short, compact red calf. I wondered at the time whether it would always be stumpy as it then was. Late experience has shown me that both in cows, and pigs, and sheep, short animals occasionally grow long as their youth progresses.

I have just had a young quickset hedge well cleaned about the roots of encroaching grasses, bindweed, and other intruders. Some hints I took from a Magazine at the time of planting, answer well. A trench one foot deep was cut, and six inches of good straw manure trodden in. Upon this, six inches of mould were thrown, in which the thorn was planted. It has certainly reached this precious store, for it grows with astonishing vigour, and looks eminently healthy. A neighbour tried the same plan, and has excellent promise. Another neighbour has a quickset hedge all choked with grass and weeds. It looks exceedingly feeble with this " old man of the sea " stuff clinging around its neck ; but he will not clean it, because he says that there are certain tiny fibres which start from the roots to the surface in search of food, which he would so exterminate to the damage of the plant itself. Half-choked as it is, one cannot wonder at the straggling foragers being sent up from below in search of air and aliment, which, it is my idea, it need not and would not do if kept rid of its destructive incubus. I know that upon a farm which I hired I had a quickset hedge, one part of which had been planted much later than the rest, and was not one-third its height, being choked at the base with weeds. I had it cleared, and in a year the difference of height between the two parts of the fence was not apparent, and yet my neighbour who will not clean his fence is an experienced and able horticulturist.

The thoroughbred mare has, like all ticket-of-leave animals, begun to forget her promises, and to plunge and play tricks as of yore. She has not yet, however, precipitated young Vulcan ; for I insist upon his having a roll of cloth before him on the saddle. I think that, after all, I shall convert her into a brood mare, being by that rare stout sire Daniel O'Rourke.

We are much interested in a railway tunnel which is being driven through the hill which I have often mentioned as being of a composite order, and, by its outer coating of pudding stone and inward limestone, suggesting the idea of having been once at the bottom of the sea. As yet, however, there have been no wonders developed : only strata of plain sandstone have been cut through. The coverts where the pheasants build being interdicted ground to the youngsters, it is astonishing what a number of small birds have elected to build within the shelter of these bushes. I don't know what the boys wouldn't give to maraud there ! There is a pair of kingfishers close at hand, too, the whereabouts of whose nest is a waking care to them. I could not imagine how my hurdles got stuck about the orchards in every direction. One day I found a little boy hauling one upon his back along, which I observed him set against a tree. He then climbed it, managing thereby to reach the first branch, and was soon exploring the topmost.

I thought I saw an otter the other day with his nose just above water, and his soft lithe figure occasionally undulating with the stream. I approached on tiptoe. It was the brown leaf of a water-lily which we planted last year bobbing in the current, and the stem we saw waving below. We hope to naturalize them in the Wye if stupid tourists would only let the blossom alone now at first.

August, 1869.

NEVER was implement so kindly treated. Housed in full readiness for action so long before, and oiled and sharpened, and finally conveyed tenderly to the field, before even a villager was stirring, and while the dew hung heavy upon the serried trifolium stems ; if it did not cut satisfactorily then, why all I have to say is, that I don't know when a machine could choose to cut at all.

> " Did ye not hear it ?   No ; 'twas but the wind,
>   Or the car rattling o'er the stony street ;"

It did make a startling row, too, down the sleep-opprest village, sending a spirited old blind carriage mare, that was one of the pair attached, almost wild at the jingle behind her.   Nor was it long before my neighbour's shepherd came, looking scared enough, along the path behind us, with his boot-laces undone, and his wits scarcely awake, having been aroused before his time by the unearthly sound.   Once at work, however, it was delightful to ourselves to find it do its duty effectively ; so that by the time the sun was fairly hot, there were some half-dozen acres laid low.   By changing the horses and knife every three hours, we got twelve acres cut before night. It was delightful to be independent of the itinerant gangs of mowers, who are more extortionate, more thirsty, and more sleepy than ever this season.   We soon got half our meadow grass down in addition to the clover, and had the Swede fallow being rapidly prepared at the same time, and that without an extra hand above our regular complement.   Unhappily our success made us saucy, and by sauntering a day too long, when

R

we had the crop ready for harvesting, we have got the showery weather down upon our last five acres. It is in cock, however, and we shall steal it on to the mow during the intervals of sunshine without much hurt I hope. It is a lesson to us, however, not to loiter, however well advanced, another year. I am so delighted with the excellent work that machine has done in its mowing capacity that I have sent for the extra apparatus for bringing down the grain crops. They must not be allowed to get too ripe before we commence operations. One can cut too soon, however, I know from experience, no less than too late. Last year I had one field reaped full early. The sample was so full and bright while it stood in shocks upon the field, that I thought I had attained a perfect success, and that the sap remaining in the severed stem would sustain through the ripening process the grain in its becoming *embonpoint*; but, alas, it withered sadly, and was a disappointing sample to look at in its flow from the thrashing machine, although it came to scale unusually heavy. The straw was, however, deliciously greenish and sweet to chew, and being cut up with some barley sheddings, kept my stock in excellent fettle for some time. By the way we learnt another lesson from these barley sheddings. The regular clovers having comparatively failed, as I mentioned on a previous page, we worked the stubbles every way with sharpened harrow-tines. Then sowing trifolium incarnatum and rye-grass, we covered the seed by help of chain-harrows, and rolled the bed down hard as ever the heaviest Croskill could compress a sandy loam. Behold, the shed contents of the scattered barley ears were spread evenly in every direction about, and threw up a luxuriant fresh growth. This, when a foot or more high, we mowed for chaffing for several weeks into the mid-winter in the case of one field; another field, the " seeds " sown upon which were intended for permanent pasture, we did not thus persecute, but allowed the barley crop its way. The consequence is, that now at mowing time we have had a grand crop of clover, rye-grass, and barley upon the field mown, whereas upon the petted land the barley had half died off, smothering the young trefoil, &c., beneath its shade, and so injuring the "seeds" that we shall have to plough it up again. We have a crop of autumn oats that has been in full ear for nine days or more, and which we hope to get cleared now in time to replace it by excellent turnips. During mowing, fortunately, we never cut across a single nest, except a landrail's, although we found several, both of partridges and pheasants, in the adjoining fences. One pheasant hen allowed me actually to lift her off her nest. She must have been one of a lot petted about the house through the winter, or she would have been more terrified at the approach of man. Her eggs were hatched by a Friesland hen, and are at this moment enjoying a feed of ants' eggs that I have thrown into their pen. We have had several barrowfuls of the large black ant imported from a neighbouring common for them. This large sort does not breed or build within our grounds, and won't stay there, for some reason, when imported. Possibly, like bees, they may have a Lady Superior, whom we may never have managed to secure. So the mass gradually wing or crawl their way back, weighted though each one be with an infant in swaddling clothes, the juicy contents of which are so beneficial to the youthful pheasant.

These black fellows, however, are terrific looking, and I think frighten the young birds. They certainly are not agreeable to the white silky bantam ; for when we first introduced them to her pen, and she began maternally chuckling to her young charge to peg in while fortune favoured, it somehow sadly happened that a pirate or two of the lot managed to get up into what ladies would term her "panniers," and so irritated or alarmed or otherwise incommoded the old lady, that in a frenzy she hopped and flounced wildly about, unfortunately thereby managing to kill two of the wee things of which hitherto she had been so splendidly careful. She has ever since evinced great alarm at being shown one at all. And certainly they are ugly-looking fellows, and when they sit as they do, if you arrest their course, as if to show fight, our youngsters say it is to beg for their lives ; they assuredly suggest to one that they would be very awkward to sleep alongside, and might certainly be expected to annoy the gizzard if swallowed in their ferocity alive.

In one pheasant's nest that we found in a hole beside the river, a partridge had deposited two eggs. The young ones, partridge and pheasant, broke shell the same day. Now this is curious, as a fact of natural history, inasmuch as there is a week's difference in the incubation of the two birds. Can it be that the birds calculate and have a common language, so that the partridge finding herself possessed of a greater quantity of eggs than she could well cover, lent a couple to her neighbour whose stock was short ? Anyhow they are hatched and feeding under one coop now upon the lawn.

I have been obliged to turn the thorough-bred into a brood mare. She never managed to precipitate the young Vulcan, but she danced with him one day so much that her swelled legs did not allow of her being mounted for some time again. Having, moreover, persuaded him and some other youngsters upon the farm, who make an extra shilling or two now and then, to insure their lives so as to receive 100*l.* when they come to be fifty years of age, that sum in the event of their dying sooner being paid to their relatives, I thought it might be hard upon the insurance office if he continued his horse-taming, so I gave orders to desist, getting myself now too old to encounter a steed in fight for mastery, which might some day have been a necessity if I had resumed her services as an afternoon hack.

We have been busy getting fresh water mussels off the gravel bed beneath the house for a distant friend's aquarium. The mother-of-pearl lining of their shells is beautiful. I am tempted to keep a few, in the hopes of obtaining British pearls, if the naturalist's theory be correct that a pearl is only an accumulation of matter thrown out by the fish, a sort of gummy tear-drop to relieve itself of the irritation caused by an extraneous substance within its house or eye. He says that if a pearl be split there is generally sand, or something within. Will any lady try her chaplet and see ?

How exquisitely graduated is the supply of nature ! How gentle is the preparation of the air for the soaking that our thirsty earth desires, and which it will have ere long ! Following hot, scorching days, that made our hay almost before we knew it, there has succeeded a delicious coolness of superincumbent atmosphere that is grateful as fanning to the feverish cheek. And just the slightest dusting of fine rain hath occurred, as it were, to break the fierceness of thirst, and prevent the

soil taking a too hasty and unwholesome gulp when it
gets the chance, the consequence being a fine mist, which
covers the face of the whole earth, as we read it did
in the first days of the Creation. So it is that we poor
weak men cannot imitate the grandeur of the Almighty,
the plan by which supply is adjusted to want in the
fairly-used economy of our world.

You will have read those exquisite lines of the noble
poet's in reference to Lake Leman—

> " Is it not better, then, to be alone,
> And love earth only for its earthly sake ?
> By the blue rushing of the arrowy Rhone,
> Or the pure bosom of its nursing lake,
> Which feeds it as a mother who doth make
> A fair, but froward infant, her own care,
> Kissing its cries away as these awake. "

Beautiful and touching they all are, but it was for the
sake of the last sentiment that I have quoted them—
" Which feeds it as a mother." We have no power to
feed as nature feeds. How vile an imitation would the
fizzing shower of the water-cart be of this gentle damp-
ing and sequent greenhouse climate which the infant
mangold is experiencing in anticipation of an abundant
draught duly to arrive.

" Nobody knows," but I cannot say that " nobody
cares "—quoting poetry again ; though in the shape
of an epitaph on a favourite hound in Delamere Forest,
which runs thus in its entirety—

> " Bluecap's dead, and here she lies :
> Nobody laughs and nobody cries.
> How she shares and how she fares,
> Nobody knows and nobody cares."

Dear old Vic ! the bandly-legged Breadalbane terrier,

she was so self-satisfied when her long-threatened
accouchement was over.   So comfortably she lay, with
her nose upon her paws, along the hot kitchen-floor
before the fire.   I never knew so persistent a breeder.
She might be fairly ranked with Lord Granville's
" rabbit and curate."   During the night she had cleared
a lodging out beneath the wood-stack, and there the
children found six little black-and-tan puppies, which
became, of course, prime favourites at once, and were
brought out upon the lawn between every schooltime
to sleep beside them as they read story-books reclining
on a travelling-rug, while the old parent stood by
wagging her tail gratefully, and quaintly pricking her
ears in acknowledgment of the notice her babies got at
head-quarters.   But these six were too many both for
me and the mother, and so there are only two left
beside her now.   She went hunting up the straw with
her nose, the children say, on her first noticing the
deficient number ; and they too have been rooting up
every one with inquiries as to " where the pups are
gone."   And one smiles, and another don't know, and
altogether it is unsatisfactory.   Some dirty, young,
mis-shapen wild pigeons, which have been just brought
up in triumph from the wood, will, I dare say, heal the
wound and take the place of the dear departed.

   We have been very unlucky with a beautiful brood
of fifteen young pheasants.   One after another and
three at once they began to droop their wings, and we
could not discover why.   Then they pined and died, not
having suffered from " gapes " nor from any cause that
we could discover by a post mortem examination, unless
it was that they were worn out by a plaguey insect
visitation.   For during our investigation quite a swarm

of lively, angry, saffron-tinted lice ran out from amongst the plumage on to one's hand. I ordered some wood ashes to be strewn under the foster-mother, and the other little ones are alive and doing well.

We are just in consultation whether it would be expedient to move the eggs of a pheasant who only just saved her head yesterday by ducking down from the scythe of a gardener, tidying up the grounds. The children have a bantam desirous of sitting, but then she has chosen so dangerous a site for her nest. It is amidst the ivy, on the top of a high wall, beside the stable. They propose removing her to a more favourable position : but I tell them that ladies, especially little ladies, are perverse; so that I lean rather to leaving the hen pheasant to run all risks on her own account. Whatever could have happened to the temper of the Silky I don't know, but one evening about roosting time she began to deal kicks and blows on every side to the unhappy pheasant brood that she was entrusted with. Old Melon, who has sympathy with young ones, having a sweet little girl of his own, made short work of this business by ousting the old lady herself, taking her degradingly by the wings, and pitching her over to the dung-heap beside the stable, where her twisty-legged lord was investigating his supper. The old pair met affectionately, and she the very next day showed her industry by at once depositing an egg. The poor little orphans crouched together like babes in the wood, and the next day they went wailing so plaintively over the kitchen-garden, although Melon fed them repeatedly with fat morsels from a decaying crow and hedgehog, that he keeps specially for their delight. That night they crouched all in a circle in a parsley-bed, and the next night I don't know where they went. An occasional one reappears amongst the strawberries, as our young human blackbirds report, letting out the secret of their own misdemeanours in their anxiety to report progress of the pheasant babes.

Just returning from a stroll to see how they are getting up stone in the river bed, I passed a labourer cutting thistles, who depones to having seen thereabouts a brood of two sizes with a hen-pheasant, some of which came quite tamely towards him at call. I trust, therefore, that they have found comfort in their orphanage. There underlies this history a problem. The very day that Silky showed so cantankerous a disposition I understand that one of the children found a young wild pheasant amidst the hay on the meadows, and put it, being of equal growth, with the Silky's charge. Whether the gipsy preached rebellion or not I cannot tell; anyhow she stayed quietly enough with her newly-found brothers and sisters until late in the evening, when she was met running and flying rapidly down the hill towards the meadow where she was found in the morning. Possibly the young garden lot got their disposition infected by her, and so disgusted Silky. Anyhow, I have faithfully related what I know of their history, and now I hope that there has occurred the grateful finish of the young gipsy's having introduced them to her mother, and that they will find health and enjoyment in encamping, as nature intended they should, upon the open.

We are excited and delighted to find what a clean sweep has been made of the Eastern Counties challenge plate and money by a young bull bred on our farm. We are going to have a spree on the strength of it.

An own sister to him was born the day he began his victorious career ; to which, coming as his dam does of Lord Ducie's Seagull tribe, we have given the name of Kittiwake.   There was one hovering along the shallows of our river not long since ; beautiful bird from the ocean that it is.   If I believed in Home's mysterious communication with the unseen, I might, perhaps, read her visit as prophetic of the coming Seagull success. " It is nought ; it is nought," said the buyer of that young hero, when he had obtained him.   Anyhow, I am glad that the gentleman made a paying investment. The animal was nearly slaughtered in London, and only escaped quarantine through being conveyed on to a farm half-in half-out of the proscribed district. The jugglery that saved him I trust we may never need again.

November, 1869.

How this sharp, frosty air is bringing off the leaves ! and already the pheasants have learned to wriggle themselves into the close ivy foliage, for warmth sake I presume, as, alas ! ere long they will assuredly take to sitting too exposedly upon the bare oak boughs.   How the morning water in the bath makes one involuntarily whistle, having plunged in, as one takes blue pill, without daring to reflect for fear of cowardice supervening. But, the ordeal sustained, one is rewarded well in an improved capacity to resist cold.   There is resident, not far from here, an old man who takes an early dip in the river every morning, winter and summer alike, without regard to the " weather permitting " clause of the more soft-hearted fox-hunter.   He declares that he enjoys it, which one might scarcely conclude from his usual appearance. The strangest thing is that he is a skilled cook, and consequently spends much of his time before a tearing fire. We know, from the experience of Russia, that it is pleasant, without being prejudicial to health, to roll out of hot water into a carpet of snow; the reverse process of going out cold into warmth being, however, conducive to catarrh. Be careful, consequently, young friend, not to rush to the hearth when you enter within doors, half-frozen, from a journey. Stay about the coldest rooms until your system thaws, and approach the fire only gradually; otherwise a cold will be the certain consequence of your imprudence.

By way of caution, I would mention here that as a boy I remember a gentleman, a solicitor, who, being a bachelor, had his little box and garden of roses in a sunny nook amidst the rocks some two hundred yards from the wash of the sea-wave, at the lower extremity of the Bristol Channel, whose practice it was to emerge soon after daylight every morning in dressing-gown and slippers by a side door into a solitary walk that brought him down quite unobserved to his bath amidst the crags, over a series of which the tide dashed at its height, and within which, retiring, it left full many a limpid pool, wherein the bright red sea-weed floated, and the skittish shrimp larked or poised at pleasure. This person became, at a comparatively early age, stone-deaf —an infirmity which the doctors attributed to what they termed his abuse of bathing. The sound of water brings to my mind those lovely swans again. They are here once more, regaling themselves upon that precious American weed, which has managed to spread itself now, I presume, into nearly every English stream. I am told that it is an excellent manure if mown and hauled on to the grass, which is more than can be said of its kind generally.

Since I wrote last there has been a furious flood, and, to my delight, the elbow-arms of my jetty-piers are quite filling-up with a rich alluvial deposit from head-quarters. The experiment becomes deliciously successful.

We were in decided luck while staying at a seaside town in North Wales two months since. A friend and myself were sauntering along a road by the mountain-side, watching at once the spreading tints of sunset along a distant range of hills and the curious effect upon the calm silvery surface of the sleeping ocean produced by the quick diving and ultimate reappearance of several flocks of fowl, to which it seemed a matter of indifference whether their home were on the billow or under it, so carelessly did they divide their time between cruising above water and a sudden protracted incursion under, after the broad countless shoals of fish with which the whole bay teemed—when all at once, quite close by, a horse neighed and raised up such a beautiful pony-head, with broad front and lustrous large eyes. "The very horse I want!" I exclaimed: for the farm required a new team. "Just wait a moment till I return!" I found him in a bit of a grass yard inclosed with boulders from the mountain-side, nibbling quite patiently at the short turf, tied only by a cord around his neck to a spray— it was literally no more—of a Scotch fir tree. A child of a few years of age only was sitting near, apparently in charge of him. "Whose horse, my boy?" we inquired in Welsh. "Father's: he's there." Whereupon we saw the man reaping a small field of wheat. After a few moments' inspection and a trot along the adjoin-

ing road—for he proved to have come of a celebrated
trotting Anglesea breed—delighted with his sloping
shoulder, flat foreleg, and compact build, I had bought
him for but two-thirds of what an English breeder
would have asked me for an indifferent gelding. He
proved to be the pet sire of the neighbourhood, and the
pedestal of the cottager's fortunes, while, as luck would
have it, I fell in with him just as his owner, who farmed
some twenty acres, being overstocked, was at his wits'
end for provender, not caring to buy, and having consumed all his home-growth. My friend was much
amused by what he called my precipitation in buying,
and said that he had for the last three months been
engaged in the purchase of a carriage horse, which he
had got all his friends to examine for him in turn.
No wonder that he was long in making up his mind.
There must needs be heresies under such terms. My
noble little fellow is but fifteen hands and an inch high,
and proves quite a gem, so tractable and so strong, that
the only mischief is that my people persist in putting
upon him more than his share of draught. Having also
fallen in with a couple of deep-barrelled, short-legged,
active, dapple-brown Welsh mares, I shall now have the
gratification of breeding a colt or two of a taking stamp,
at least so I am elated enough to think.

What a thing to stick that weed the charlock is!
Give it but its toe in the soil, and it will make good its
hold as effectually as a stranger limb of the law would
do amidst the deeds in your strong box. I had ever
so much pulled and hoed out of a crop of swedes
upon a piece of ground which we have not yet had
time thoroughly to expurgate of its latent seeds. The
least fibre, however, attaching to the mould seems

to sustain this plant in full vigour, although in fallen majesty. After all, if it is not allowed to ripen, the sheep like it amazingly.

How hard it is! I spent to-day the best hours of noon in a saunter, hoping to obtain a few birds for the enjoyment of a kind old lady; but, although they have been undisturbed for weeks, I saw no signs of a feather. Yet, hard lines that it is, just as I take my wonted walk before nightfall, up start in succession some fifteen cock-pheasants at my very feet; then a hundred feet beyond, upon the meadow, such a nice covey of plump partridges, and from beside my jetty a wild-duck. Hard lines, I emphatically repeat. Where could they have been all the day? "Hiding, dear, I suppose, from this dreadful cold," is all the comfort and explanation I get from my feminine adviser. Tidings have just reached me of a rascal being deservedly caught. A gentleman, in South Wales, had bought and farmed improvingly a rough estate, adjoining which a fellow farmed some hundred hired acres of mountain land, and who was of that cantankerous nature that he could never agree with his neighbours, but took every opportunity of increasing his own keep by encouraging his sheep and cattle to stray on to their ground, especially where there might happen to be good pasture. This game had gone on, to the annoyance of everyone, for some months, despite repeated notice, which was only answered by insolence, when, at last, his things were sent to the pound. The charges were paid; but as these unprincipled fellows will always manage, there came another side of the picture. One morning, while shaving, this gentleman got the disagreeable intelligence that twelve of his heifers had been caught upon the farmer's land,

and were now pounded in turn.   But the bailiff was a shrewd fellow, and when the case came into Court he showed that the knave had over-shot his mark.   He had, unfortunately for himself, chosen a frosty night for his operations, and the servant employed to help him walked with one foot " in."   Singularly enough, the County Court Judge, before whom the case came, had spent some years in the backwoods, and was enabled so to put many pertinent inquiries which would not have occurred to an ordinary magistrate.   Suffice to say, the knave was convicted, and had to pay for his rascality and malice, to his considerable chagrin.

We have just finished thrashing-out a wheat rick. How jolly it is to watch the fowls and turkeys, and especially the industrious ducks, some half-immersed even in their search after stray grains in the winnowed chaff, and then going occasionally for a drink at the pool, which they gulp down in such epicurean style, throat up, and long beak extended, reminding one of the glutton in old history, who wished his gullet lengthened in order that he might better appreciate his soup !

A friend has just turned in who has taken no less than thirty-eight beautiful grayling upon a run of gravel below the house.   How tantalizing it is to hear of such success !   There is always something wrong with the water or the tackle when we find time to throw a line. His idle days he does not count, however.

But here comes a woodman for orders respecting a new plantation, and my sands are run.

Hurrah ! hurrah ! a glorious flood rising fast, a foot an hour or more, and of such capital consistency, thick with imported matter as pea-soup, and the dear jetties

(I have just been to see them) not budging an inch, but in substantial dignity all calmly repellent of the outside vehemence of waters ; while above them there reposes a quiet body of entrapped billows, which are sulkily disgorging their burden of alluvial mud, to add another layer to the growing subaqueous bank, on the slope of which, distinctly seen when the stream clears next summer, the flock will graze, while, as the white steer of Clitumnus, it admires its own loveliness in the fluid mirror beneath. But the air is damp and raw, and I hasten up into the fire-lit dining-room, and despite the vehemence of my last week's preachment rush straightway to the hearth, attaining at once condign punishment in an uneasy sense about the nasal region that is suggestive of catarrh in the head. The chicks I find there, all deeply immersed in their books ; all so deeply that they give me only a grumpy answer as I disturb them successively with a kiss or mild pinch. But one is thankful, notwithstanding. Half the secret of high collegiate success lies in an early love of reading general literature. Educators will always tell you that they can do wonders with a lad who has always loved to pore over volumes, whereas there is no use in cramming for a competitive examination one whose turn has been absolutely and only for foot-ball and taws.

We are busy at the homestead, or rather there are masons and an engineer busy putting up a steam engine; a beautiful little toy of a thing which will but just cut chaff and crush oats, and be an awful amusement on a wet day, as one will sit by and smoke and watch its industrious evolutions, or roast an occasional potato in the ashes. No, that will not do ; because, of course, one must have all the latest inventions carried out, and I am told by an ingenious and pleasant clergyman (a well-known inventor) that if I keep a pan of water under the fire-bars, not only will it tend to the preservation of the iron, but by some wonderful resolution of gases it will make the coal last at least double the time it would otherwise have done under ordinary circumstances. I forget how many gallons of water he uses daily under his own study fire. He mentioned also a trial he made with Dorsetshire shale or some such stuff, which is very difficult to burn at all. How that he and a friend, by help of this water dodge, managed to set a piece on fire which after ignition for no less than thirty-six hours, had yet left in it enough of oil to allow of their writing their names with it, after cooling, on a white surface. Very well; then I can't roast my potatoes in the ash-pit, that's poz.; so I shall just rake out a few, and do it outside, being wilful as a woman. This dear delightful little machine, it seems to have been a good deal knocked about; there's a brass neckband here and a screw there all wrong, and this is broken, and that won't work, and the days are terribly foggy and short. I hope I shall not be ruined before it is finished putting up, and that anyhow it won't serve me as the sofa did its buyer, who was of an uxorious cast of mind. When it came home to the thankful spouse, why it made the carpet look quite dull, and then the new carpet made the chairs shabby, and the new chairs quite spoilt the cabinet, and so on, until positively this handsome present of a sofa cost its benighted purchaser two thousand pounds. To apply the moral: Why, if I am first to buy a new boiler, and then to fit up a new house for it, and then to get a mill and an improved chaff-cutter, and so on to everlasting, why I shall be wishing the engine altogether at Jericho

s

instead of finding its locality, as I anticipate now, a pleasant haunt upon a dirty day.

After all there's something very human about its arrangements. Why, there's the governor — that's myself—what a regular, wide-awake, steady old performer. Then there's the boiler — that's the school bills and butchers'. Then there's the waste-pipe—that's cook. Then there's the alarm whistle—that's the housemaid. Then there's the throttle-valve—that's the Monday morning inspection of the books. Then there's the elegant, sweet, smoothly moving fly wheel—that's mamma, who so quietly gives a gentle impulse to the straitened action of the too cranky governor's performance!

"Quantity of muck you make, sir," just now observed to me a neighbouring farmer, who turned in to have a look at my Christmas beef. "Of course, sir, and so you'd better do, instead of keeping some half-dozen cows for the dairy in a district where it don't suit— hard-hided enough and of only blue-milk reputation." I watched a field of my neighbour's this year, which has more than ever confirmed me in the impression that "artificials" are only a gin-and-water dose; that they rapidly go through the soil, after extravagantly stimulating it, and leave it very depressed. Next to my plot of mangold wurzel there was carefully prepared a small ploughing for the same crop. They gave it only a heavy dressing of a recently-invented "artificial," which was well harrowed in, and the surface brought to an exquisitely fine tilth. They lost their mangold season, however, and had to put in swedes. What a luxuriant crop of dark leaves covered that field in September, with a fair promise of bulk too! whereas a neighbouring swede plant, sown on a thick muck dressing, was half consumed by the grub. Time went on, and the leaves began to dry, when the bulbs too (fed on artificial only) turned out knotted and thick-rinded and small, not yielding in weight nearly so large a result as the muck-sustained lot, despite the ravages of that horned pirate, the dark moth's son and heir, while in juicy quality there was no comparison. Hurrah! then for the dung-heap of the stall-fed kine!

December, 1869.

To be or not to be, to lie fallow or not to lie fallow, that's the question. It does one good, though. As in the land the rootlets, so in the mind the thoughtlings, in consideration of the soil's rest, are grateful. But if you will take my word for it, I am glad—right glad—to meet again. And as for matter—as for stuff to say—you cannot believe what a lot I've been storing, if you will only be patient. First of all let me record the delightful experience of yesterday. It had been pouring torrents all night and throughout the forenoon—torrents of rain, with wind and lightning fearful to behold—just such weather as baffled so terribly the advance of the Prussians to Waterloo, making old Wellington squeak for it—and the hot-tempered river, already peat-stained and choleric enough, began to rise furiously, to my joy!

Joy indeed!

" Wherefore rejoice ? what triumph brings he home ? "

Why already his subdued wave acknowledges sullenly the success of the plan we have been adopting to prevent his undermining our meadows, as he has for several years been employed in doing, to his satisfaction, and that too of sundry landowners down-stream to whom he has been gratuitously presenting unexpected " surplus."

You will remember my mentioning our busy operations raising stone in the river bed for the purpose of repairing the bank. Well, just as we had carted it a short distance, and were about to commence reparation, a young engineer officer came on a visit, whose brains, as he is clever and an enthusiast, I determined to utilise.

Having walked him down our deep slopes to the scene of action, he at once pointed out, as really is the case, that, however carefully we might face the bank with boulder-stone, still the insidious undercurrent would continue to eat away its base until some morning the whole slice would slip down in hopeless consternated débris into the triumphant tyrant's jaws. He also forbade our building out piers down stream, the effect of which he showed would be just to divert the current a few yards, only to return exasperated in what is termed a " backwater," to an assault upon the soil below the stonework. Instead, he directed us—and the simple idea at once recommended itself so forcibly even to the gutta-percha-brained labourers employed, that they threw themselves with a will into the work—to build out at intervals of a hundred yards, and at an angle of forty-five degrees *upstream*, half-a-dozen thick walls of a jetty character sloping down from the level of the bank to a stone's thickness on the river bed. He selected the most projecting points of the bank to throw them out from. The result of this work is, that the stream gets caught irretrievably, and there is an elbowful, so to speak, within each jetty, of dead water, which acts as a buffer against the intruding torrent, directing it to move on just round the corner. There is no more undermining —no more eating of the base.

Already there are indications of a slimy deposit where before the tale was of abstraction.

It was the success of this plan, then, that I preferred to watch yesterday to partridge-shooting. And there I sat, so doing, with my gun beside me, on a sod for some hours. For is not success sweet in all sorts and cases? Whether it come by demolition of the Irish Church, by the looking into a loved one's eyes, or by the staving off of a cantankerous, greedy river. There is no difference in kind, as logicians say, only in degree. Quality the same, sir, only a question of quantity as might be written reflectively on comparison of a peasant's home-happiness with that of the Baron banker.

There is another matter in which I have been recently interested, the results of which I will record, having had several inquiries in consequence of my former statements on the subject. I refer to the autumn planting of the diseased potato tubers. Last year, through the waywardness of the man who had received the order, and owing to my absence from home, the diseased tubers thrown out of the crop on raising were left in a heap uncovered through a slight frost. They moreover fermented, and when planted were to a great extent half mud. The consequence was that very few plants appeared above the surface in the spring. Hoping on, I left them, until fairly frightened by the gardener's remonstrances that we should have no potatoes whatever for the use of the house unless I did something quickly. It was long after every one else had planted their spring crop that I gave the reluctant order to plough up the ground, and we planted the small round tubers reserved by the gardener out of the crop which I had raised the year before from diseased plants. Three weeks since we stored our crop, a most prolific one, of mealiest roots, free from all symptoms of disease. To-day and to-morrow I plant nine inches deep, or rather with nine inches of soil on them, the small ones of this crop, which were carried under cover and spread thinly until wanted. What a saving of trouble in the spring time is it to be thus forward! A friend who tasted our potatoes last year, and was informed how I grew them, was quicker on the feather than myself, following implicitly my own directions to replant at once the diseased tubers, as they were taken up, in ground ready prepared for the purpose. He has a capital crop, with some, but comparatively few, gaps, while the weight at the roots is considerably greater than in the case of the spring-planted. He had not finished taking the crop up when I saw him last. I will report progress when I know.

Another gentleman's gardener, who doubted my recommendation to plant the diseased tuber, still ventured to put in some sound, or apparently sound, seed, as I recommend, late in autumn, with nine inches of soil overhead. He reports that the produce is much heavier than that of the spring-planted in the same field. Here again is a fact in favour of autumn planting which my gardener, whom I rejoice in having converted to my side, has just gleefully mentioned to me. In a plot of outside garden which I allow to a man-servant, he managed to leave a potato-tuber behind in the ground when the crop was raised last year.

This struck out so manfully in the spring that the gardener persuaded him to let it grow on. It came up between the pea rows. The only extra nursing that it

got was that during the very hot weather one bucket of
water was thrown over it. The result was that twenty-
six tubers were taken up, seven weighing over a pound
each. I have two beside me which have been laid on
the pantry shelf for some time exposed to the sunny
air. The biggest were all cooked. My tape, however,
measures these to be in circumference across ten inches,
lengthways one foot. The whole produce of the root,
old Melon tells me, was thirteen pounds of excellent
mealy tubers. The sort is called hereabouts the Scotch
York. Since writing the above I am thankful to have
finished the planting of an acre during beautiful weather,
in a kind bed. We are now busy with the walnut harvest. What brown fingers and stained nails the juveniles
display ! while at any moment of the day they can produce from their stores in pocket or drawer any reasonable amount of delicious kernel, chestnut, filbert, or
walnut. There is old Melon's boy up on a slight bough,
waving to and fro before my window at this moment
while I write. The old man got an awkward fall from
a ladder some three weeks since, and is more wary of
climbing.

The cook is busy in the preparation of fruit after a
plan of which we knew nothing until a French lady
taught us some days since. She divides into quarters,
subdivided again, such of the huge apples and pears
(which we are wont to store) as have fallen from the
tree, and, being consequently bruised, would not keep
in the usual way. I had the precaution to allow a
considerable growth of grass under the trees, so as to
save the fruit as much as possible in its collision with
Mother Earth. These quarters cook bakes in the oven,
as the sun is not hot enough now to serve our purpose,

and they are then hung up in paper bags, in the store-
room, to be decocted, when wanted, after the various
modes of fruit preparation that sweet ladies are profi-
cient in.   Such dried parcels are a great help to the
larder of the French peasant in winter time.   Quite a
Robinson Crusoe idea, is it not ?   You remember how
he stored his grapes.   By the way, I have just had a
youngster translating a passage for me out of a Latin
Robinson Crusoe, some interesting old Friar having
converted our old friend into that guise, a volume of
which was picked up for me in Paris.   It is surprising
how rapidly boys progress *con amore* in the unravelling
of a strange language when the subject interests, being
already familiar to them.   How they roared with
delight as, dictionary in hand, and grammar beside
them, they made out that old "Robinson did not fall
out of his tree that night, but slept calmly until morning !" the point of the passage being improved by the
sight of old Melon before our window, limping and
groaning whenever obliged to stoop, owing to his late
mishap as related above.

There are symptoms of a hard winter, in the fact
that yesterday some twenty missel thrushes were hover-
ing over and dipping into the Irish yews upon the
lawn, taking a feast of such delicious berries therefrom !
A whole wedge of wild geese passed overhead yesterday : but the most beautiful sight of any is to watch
five lovely swans that have found their way up to the
pool in the river beneath our house.   How they revel
amidst the American weed, a great plantation of which
has sprung up quite lately therein !   And there they
sail so smoothly, and yet in a spirit of such suggestive
wildness, up stream to a gravel-bed beneath the bridge,

where I fear they have a pâté of salmon-spawn, descending thence so grandly with the flood, for their afternoon feed upon our bank again! Where they sleep I don't know : what I do know is that the night has quite suddenly closed upon my task. I can see to pen no more without a candle. But without doors it is delicious; and you won't be angry, gentle reader, if I hurry forth, having such sympathy with Moore in the verse—

> " How dear to me the hour when daylight dies,
> And sunbeams melt along the silent sea !
> For then sweet dreams of other days arise,
> And memory breathes her vesper sigh to thee ! "

January, 1870.

A FEARFUL gusty (clearly a *feminine*) wind blowing! Went on the river with my youngest born ; glad to get off again. The waves ran half-a-yard high, and the savage tempest blew so lustily ! twice the mast was unshipped, and the little craft heeled over far more than pleased me. By myself I should have persevered, but I didn't like to risk the life of little Benjamin, who sat wet, but calmly unconscious of danger, with the tiller ropes in his tiny hands, as I attended to the sheet and an occasional oar. Several lots of partridges rose along the bank in places. How odd that they should choose so cold a lair on so boisterous a day ! taking the air, I suppose, as ladies after the season on the Brighton strand ; and the swans, too—four of them—for one has chivalrously detached himself, to engage with a lonely maiden some eight miles lower down the river than this (her former swain was ruthlessly murdered by some boys last year) ; they sailed about our craft so contemptuously, and saw us off, or rather off and on again, for we were driven ashore I don't know how often during the first half-hour, ere we got off, by force of wind and current. How oddly they strain their necks out to meet a gust! One could not help remarking it. It is so inelegant in so graceful a bird. I suppose it enables them to expose less surface to the impulse of the wind. As we could not ascend the stream, the little chap on landing made a merit of his mishap, and emptied his pockets of his biscuits, which he threw in morsels to the grateful birds, who, after much slobbering and sucking, to soften, I presume, the too hard outside, finally disposed of the floating feed.

This reminds me that the tomtits are in luck, and the linnets as well, for the Indian corn, which one fancied was, from its weight, proof against their purloining, having been soaked in the rain, they get in holes and corners, and against stones upon the walk, thereby speedily managing to scoop the contents of the berry at a destructive pace. All I can say is, the pheasant must look out and feed faster.

Oh! such sadness pervading the whole household; the dear old pet terrier, Vic, is no more. For some weeks she had been evidently ailing. She had also an excessive weeping at the eyes. She seemed to have caught cold through sleeping out one severe night on a mat by the lodge-door. She had been jealous, too, of another dog which had been imported into the school-room, so for some weeks she honoured me in my study with her presence, and used to sit so prettily gazing into the fire, with her head upon her paws on the fender. To the last she tried to follow the children about, but had to be carried home one day, and another afternoon she was found lying on some hay under the rick, quite exhausted. A little girl carried her in, and carefully tended her ; but all this I did not know until afterwards. When, however, the household became aware how seriously ill the old pet was, we had her put into a hot bath, and tenderly packed in a hamper before the fire. I got up early, before the servants were stirring, to see her ; and although evidently in much pain, it was quite touching to watch the sad expression of her peculiarly melancholy brown eyes as she laid her head on one side against the hamper, and seemed to be saying a long good-bye. She did not long survive, and it has cut us all to the quick. One does not know the value of a pet, to which tender associations cling, until we lose it. We had her stuffed, but the eyes were so great a failure that we have banished the case from the house, preferring the image that lies of her upon our mental mirror.

We have been unfortunate, too, with the steam-engine. We had an idle fellow imported to put it up, who, after three weeks' work, finally got the boiler so fixed that we cannot keep up steam. The worst of living in the country is, that we cannot get skilled workmen to carry out our plans, and "city mice" introduced take upon them so many airs.

This will end in the apparatus being sold again, and the horse-tackle being reverted to.

To return, however, to the spot I always delight in— the river-bank. When compelled to strike our sail and drift down home, I took the opportunity of testing the action of my precious jetties, and steered by the bank down. Quite smoothly the water lay within them, although so rough outside. (I find everybody

asking me about them now, for their unexpected
success is a puzzle.) So thoroughly effective is their
action, that I could not get my boat near the bank.
Acting as a buffer to the current on which we drifted,
they would have nothing to do with us. I shall be so
glad when the spring has come, and consolidated the
new earth upon the slopes with well-rooted grass. We
shall then be beyond the reach of tremor.

How odd it is that, despite all the wet we have had
lately, the springs have not "come home" yet. The
well that supplies the kitchen-range is lower than it
was in June.

> " As the days lengthen,
> So the springs strengthen,"

is an old and I suppose—at least from my own experience—a true adage. Why it is I don't know. One
would think that, if a fair tap were flowing in June,
an October soak would sufficiently re-supply the vessels.
In practice it is not so, however.

Alack-a-day! Since writing the above (for one stuffs
this pie at odd hours as occasion serves), such a dire
flood hath invaded us, or rather a tremendous redupli-
cation of floods — one yet more angry overriding
another. Such an onset of waters has not occurred in
this valley since 1852, bearing along with it a spoil of
all sorts from the upper country—dead carcases and
gates, and mighty trees, and, in one instance, a set of
steps belonging to a church ten miles above us, that is
built upon the bank. The boatmen were driving dangerously in their punts backwards and forwards all the
daytime that the light lasted, fishing out the waifs and
strays. One night before the flood arrived at its
highest, I got a moonlight stroll beside the rising

waters. The dense, dirty volume had been visibly swelling for hours, and was just beginning to overspread the meadow along its immediate margin, besides making insidious inroads by every hollow spot and ditch. I had some colts out, which I did not want drowned; so merely changing one's dress-boots (we had just returned from the warm shelter of a festive drawing-room — a very different climate to that to which the colts were submitted), and throwing on an Inverness cape, I hurried down to see how far it might be safe to trust the night, as our head servant, who is a stranger to these parts, and not yet used to the river's vagaries, had not thought fit to have them moved, and it struck me as hard lines to disturb at such an hour a zealous man. Well, I hurried down, and was enraptured. The long grass on the orchard slopes, kept as rowen for the ewes and lambs in spring, rustled quite crisp under my tread, for the air was frosty, and when the moon shone—a brilliant all-but-full moon—each blade glistened with a coronet of diamonds. Then the river, when I reached it, lay in a lovely lagoon, so calm, so lustrous, so lovelily reflecting at once each twinkling star—the dark hanging woods, and sharp-cut cliff. So calm is the pool that I doubt its advance upon the meadow, and have to watch by the light of the moon, where it is nevertheless most determinedly though slily stealing on through rootlet and mould-heap. You can tell the fact only by watching the gradual disappearance of some glistening leaf as it is swallowed up, or the movement of some floating twig ; and our boat there—she who played us, as I have recorded, so nearly false—floats gaily and indifferently buoyant, on the surface of a flood, which, though so treacherously still upon the one side, upon the other pours along, swishing surlily with a deep smothered sound, suggestive only of suicide.

But how after all did the jetties answer ? Perfectly. And how did the newly-made banks hold? Excellently, so long (I am bound to record all my experience) as the flood did not rise above the top of the stone, where it is built into the land. Not an atom of the newly-disturbed soil gave way until then. But when the angry waves surmounted the uppermost stones, and overran the whole plain, then, resenting the obstacles to its progress, it did wash off a good part of the softest mould, accumulating, however, a quantity at the bottom of the river between the piers. So that, after all, I am upon the whole rather a gainer than a loser. Where I had turfed the slope it did not suffer. It was only where the holes had been filled with soil and sown too late in the season for the grass to gather root. I am rapidly repairing the damage with a paring plough, taking off the rough surface of some inferior sward, which I beat and peg down, and which I propose to overlay with close small laurel twigs, which old Melon has been trimming off the avenue, stuck in flat and closely like the feathers on a pheasant's breast. Over this the water will glance, as I know by experiment already made. Next year I shall raise the jetties a foot above the mainland, and then no harm can possibly occur to the bank.

February, 1870.

WHAT glorious, bright, sparkling, frosty weather it was! It put everyone in such spirits. The bailiff merry, the labourers pitch with a will, as the empty dung-carts return rapidly over the hard fallow. We are putting a good coating on the autumn-planted potatoes, because what rich soil there was a-top when the stubble was ploughed for planting lies now nine inches deep, and their over-covering mould may be raw and insipid, as it is a field that we have not long had in possession, and the last owner did his farm but niggardly.

The river has sunk so much—probably from the binding-up of the mountain-springs—that I have been able to make a thorough inspection of the effect of the jetties, the strong mid-day sunlight showing minutely not only the material and make-up of the river-bed, but the very motes, too, floating in the air under the wall. I find that gravel has been scooped up somewhere above, and deposited in a fine sloping bed behind each pier, while between them the water rests so still, that, although there is a strong current outside, the dry broken twigs thrown in don't move on in the least. I long for March to come, that we may complete our work by sloping down the steep places of the bank, filling up what holes remain with pared rough turf from a neighbouring meadow, which has been only recently drained, and is covered with a coarse mat of sour tussock grass that no stock will touch. I shall so kill two birds. I shall defend my bank against the river by such a tough packing of the hollows, as it will get disheartened in attempting to pick out, and I shall encourage a fresh sweet springing of the pasture. The fine new mould which was filled-in during October, the angry flood made short work of when it managed to overleap the jetties. A subsequent inundation, however, was completely baffled by such packing as we did, by way of experiment, of the gaps before emptied. Once get the slope smoothed, and a fair sward upon it, and we shall have no further fear of any wash. We shall only hope that the waters will descend as thick as can be with a loamy solution from the upper country. It is very surprising to see how rapidly grass blades manage to disengage the earthy particles from the turbid sheet as it advances upon the plain. I watched it rush angrily—a very mud soup—up a narrow hollow in the field, where a fence had once stood ; but before it had travelled two hundred yards, the element was returning fast to its normal limpid condition, and became clear as crystal when it with difficulty had mounted some higher portion of the meadow.

The purchase of the mare and horse in Wales has made us very forward to our work. It is grand to have had the stubbles all deeply ploughed a month since, so that the rocky soil is getting as friable as can be. For mangold-wurzel I shall only work the ground now with a scarifier until it is opened with a double mould-board plough, for the reception of good soapy muck from our deepest fold-yard, which is hollowed out of the rock. I saw the juice running out of the carts just now, as mellow and deep-tinted as October ale. We have so much stock in the folds and boxes, that in a month's time it will be full-stuffed again. A couple of acres of cabbage having been planted during my absence in the autumn without the land having, as it should have done, a dressing of manure, the bailiff considering the bed strong enough.   I shall try the effect of sewage, and give each plant a cup of strong drink when the spring comes in, for our liquid-manure tank has long been brimful.

What a pleasant occupation it is getting the lambing-yard ready !   We shall this year make it occupy the half of a new stackyard we have established near the bailiff's bedroom window.   Having hollowed a long strip about four yards wide to the depth of 18 inches, and filled the trench with sifted dry wood and coal-ashes, we shall build a roof of straw to it and a back of wattled hurdles, along which, on the inside, deep rain-spouts will be fixed, by way of mangers.   We so manage to make a great quantity of "artificial" to drill in with the swedes.   I have some dozen porkers similarly bedded.   The hen and duck houses are all laid with sawdust, with which, too, the fattening cattle are bedded.   It does not give half the trouble that straw does in the cleaning out, and goes much further ; while we have ample use for the sheaves, there being a good part of them cut-up with hay and pulped swedes ; much, too, being strewn under the terribly high-bred pets of the establishment.   There is a special virtue in the smell of the pine-wood sawdust : it keeps off insect plagues, I think.   Talking of pine-wood reminds one of larch.   At one corner of the farm there rises at the base of a sloping arable field a conical hillock, rounded on three sides, upon the fourth attach-ing to and imbedded in the field.   What it ever can have been quite puzzles us.   It might, from its shape, have been a tumulus.   The surrounding ground is high, and a hundred feet above the level of a brook, which runs at the bottom a meadow's width below.   Rather a

T

distinguished geologist holds that over this elevated
table-land (it was not elevated then, but is supposed to
owe its rise to volcanic action) once a river ran, disem-
boguing at the point where the conical mound rises,
and which, therefore, may be simply an accumulated
deposit of drift. Some party, in old time, perchance,
had a jetty there. Anyhow, this hillock is so steep
that we cannot plough its sides ; and to plant it would
be to throw an undue shade on the adjacent corn-field.
In our despair, certainly, last year we did plant it, and
in greater despair the plantation died ; this year, then, as
the steep sides look to the east, south, and west, the
frigid north wind being well shielded off by the rising
back-ground, so that it is a hot quarter rather than
otherwise, I propose to begin at the bottom, and dig or
break it up with picks to a considerable depth, after a .
terrace fashion (as we see the hill-sides treated along
the Rhine). The outside edge of the step shall be
higher, or, in other words, the steps shall slope back
from the outside edge at an angle of ·20 deg. downwards, so that, when rain falls, it shall soak into the
sandy rock and soil at the hollows of the staircase,
instead of washing off the lips of the steps. Once
deeply worked, I expect and hope that we may make
a plot, now useless except as a rabbit-lair, of garden
value, for the raising of cabbage-plants, &c. At least,
it is worth the experiment ; while our occupation will
be as interesting as healthful.

Having occasion to open a quarry for the purpose of
making the river jetties, I observed, four feet under the
surface soil—the hole having been worked into a bank
—a regular incrustation of lime, which seemed to have
filtered through, and had gathered in cakes about the

_ayers of stone. There is a certain element of lime in the sandstone itself, which fizzes on the application of spirit of salt; but the stuff which attracted my attention is clearly an infiltrated incrustation from the surface, which I understand was dressed thickly with a compost of earth and lime some fifteen years ago. I know that lime will bury itself in time, but I had no idea it was so persevering a borer as this.

What an easy thing it is to do good! Would that we were always so inclined! Having been shown by the enterprising agent of some ducal estates in Suffolk a comfortable labourers' reading-room erected at different points of the property, I borrowed the idea, and, by the expenditure of a few shillings, boarded off half a garden-house, which has temporarily been wainscotted with matting, and is warmed by an old laundry stove. A table is erected at one corner, with a bookshelf above, and a paraffin lamp gives light. When I first broached the idea, all the villagers held off; but any night you may turn in now, between seven and half-past nine, you will find the place crowded. Each subscriber pays a penny a week. The room is managed by a chairman (elected weekly by themselves) and a committee. They are supplied with excellent coffee, at a half-penny per large cup. The profit on the sale of coffee buys them a weekly paper; besides which, between us neighbours, we put in our own half-dozen various prints every week, and they have a small select library on the shelf. They are allowed to smoke. I am delighted at the success of the plan. Whenever you may turn in, you will find a number occupied with the books, and who don't care to talk. I mention these particulars, as it is so cheap a mode of doing positive good. The plan, as

I have said, I borrowed from what I saw in Suffolk.
My sands are run, and so good-bye.

April, 1870.

THIS frost hath enabled us to get through what the
baliff calls a "sight of work." Although authorities
are agreed that upon the whole it is best to haul fold
manure on the leys and pasture during autumn, inasmuch as thereby the food has time to soak down to and
into the rootlets so that they are prepared to strike out
vigorously with the first burst of spring, yet having our
yards full we were tempted to go on top-dressing as
long as the hard surface allowed us without trespass.
Were we a green field ourselves our argument would be
that good food could come never amiss, so upon that
hint we acted, and can only hope that our wishes may
be realised by the gathering in of a grand hay crop.

The lambs are falling fast, and as yet we have been
very fortunate. The quiet dams look so comfortable in
their pens with an infant alongside. We were hurried
in our preparation at last, and so adopted a plan which
we should adhere to again from its simplicity. With a
hay-knife we cut into, or rather hollowed out, a recess
around a straw rick, into which we set hurdles at right
angles to the stack and about one-and-a-half yards apart.
Upon the portion of the hurdles that ran under the
straw we laid a tier of spare spruce boards : some small
gorse having then been pulled through the lower bars,
a long range of most comfortable pens was ready, and
that, too, in an astonishing short time.

We got our first crop of water-cresses last week. A
mistake I made in planting the bed I may as well recount for the guidance of others. I laid a floor of rich

mud for them. Instead of which I should have simply strewn gravel on sharp sand. The leaves run up too luxuriantly and lose their brown hue. The whole crop should, I am told, be lifted every spring and have their root points trimmed. But I shall be glad myself to obtain further information as to the proper cultivation of this wholesome and delicious salad. Our pool lying in a hollow, the water gets too hot by attraction of the sun rays, and makes them too soon a giant cress. I believe from what I have seen tried, that a bunch of water-cress *does* act effectually as an antidote against the depressing effects of nicotine. Either the juice of the herb or the exercise of picking it out of the fresh water quickly removed my friend's headache. Another simple effect let me record. We all know that dry earth, as well as charcoal, has the power of deodorizing. I was, notwithstanding, I must confess, surprised at the immediate and thorough success which attended cook's throwing some bowlfuls of wood ashes from the oven, after baking, down the scullery sink, which, do what we would, could never before be kept from emitting, especially in damp weather, an unpleasant odour which pervaded the whole house. They were careful never before to throw cabbage-water down. Still, do what they might, the bad smells continued. Since I desired her to throw down some ashes it has been altogether removed.

I have had much entertainment during the past week in directing a woodman to cut peeps and glimpses through the woods, which gives some exquisite little pictures of the distant landscape framed within the surrounding boughs, and which will be infinitely more effective when the foliage covers the trees again. A quantity of the superabundant young trees he has been thinning out to split into pales to fence around a rough piece of fern and bramble where the pheasants love to make their nests, and which at present is open to invasion by the pestilent curs of every passer by. One I helped him to fall; and of course knowing better than he did, and pulling the rope somewhat differently to what he desired me, got well punished by seeing a pet straight young Scotch fir snap off in two like a carrot under the weighty head of the overthrown stick. A lesson for your obstinate conceit, sir!

A mixture of good and bad luck has attended the cowsheds. One most valuable bull calf has been lost through the stupid attendant giving his dam a feed of frosted swedes. An obstinate diarrhœa took him off. On the other hand our good fortune with the ewes continues, which I attribute in a great degree to their having been very evenly kept during the last three months. It is the up and down feeding that plays the mischief with dam and offspring—now starvation, now abundance—the poor veins cannot stand such abuse. One farmer I knew lost the great part of his yearling sheep last year from this cause. Our best Guernseys have produced us fine heifer calves by a handsome young Shorthorn sire. So we must put the one thing against the other. Keep forging on against a head sea is the grand rule of agricultural life. The storm and current are sure to relax their violence in time.

We have had in the poultry-yard a singular illustration of the difficulty there is in breeding away the characteristics of any new cross one may adopt. Some years since we received some beautifully marked bantams which had been imported from Lucknow. They themselves crossed a little with some Seabright fowls, but died at an early period, owing, I think, to the strange inclemency of the weather. We saved some half-bred chickens, which have since intermixed with the Seabrights, with the effect only of rendering the succeeding hatches as they grew up more dowdy-looking and leg-feathered. These enlarged hens were very useful for sitting on pheasant eggs, and had a certain wild liking for life in the woods. Last season, however, there got mated a pair of the first cross—that is, own brother and sister—and their produce has reverted to the Lucknow sort. The shape is similar, broad, rather low and lengthy with deep feather in the legs, and a peculiar colour of the plumage. White speckled with bluish red and black represents the imported pair almost exactly. · How to go on now is the puzzle. There is, clearly, room for instructive experiment. An eminent Southdown breeder and Southdown judge, who some years ago sold off his famous flock and has since been experimenting with a cross, told me that his theory was not the usual one of taking fresh blood through the ewes and then serving the produce with a pure-bred sheep again, but to pair the half-breds. I read the other day that he has managed to produce thereby a beautifully even flock of an improved and special sort. This history of our bantams would seem to endorse his plan. I shall watch and report further results, when we have tried a variety of combinations.

We have been transplanting ripstone-pippins and filbert bushes into every wild corner on the hill. What a pull it is to live in a district where the elm, the oak the chestnut, the apple, and the walnut are really native weeds springing up in every hedgerow and on every bank at random, one might say, and abundantly! I followed my young ones just now into old Melon's fruit-rooms. How they did pocket, the old fellow bursting with delight as he looked on! And then, when the crop is on the trees, how they eat all day long between school-hours, and seem never the worse, dinner only being worse for it, as their appetites, to my sorrow, seem rather whetted than appeased!

It is no wonder that the vegetarian badger loves the district. There is such a fine fellow has his lair under a rock adjacent to this, close to which he has a raised seat, worn quite hollow on the top, like an ostrich's nest. The labourers call it his "Sunday seat." It commands a magnificent view of the surrounding country.

There has been hot work amongst the fox covers on the further side of the county, in consequence of which Mr. Reynard has migrated to our inaccessible strong-holds. You may hear him bark every evening about nightfall. One fox feasted last week on a guinea-fowl of ours, and winked his eye grandly at the traps all around, which I found the angry bailiff had soothed his wrath by setting. The red robber I love to see so stealthily slipping through the gorse, and am only vexed when, as I saw him the other day, he will keep whirling around his head, then tossing up and catching and re-tossing an unhappy rabbit, neutralizing by his conduct any sympathy on my part which might have arisen from Mr. Freeman's attacks upon huntsmen.

May, 1870.

" GOOD news from home "—nay, rather sad news from farm. I say nothing of the murderous conduct of the frost towards the young ley-planted wheats, nor of the

cruel nip it has caught the clover stems just at the back
of the neck, giving them a rheumatic twinge where the
roller had managed to bruise it. I say nothing of that,
for a good stirring with the horse-hoe, which is working
capitally, will cause the one crop to tiller, besides, that
under the surface, I find many weak seedlings just ready
to start if more genial nights would encourage them.
The wheat I don't think is after all as bad as it looks,
although several of my neighbours are, I understand,
breaking it up and replanting with barley. The clovers
too were well dressed with a coating of long manure, so
that I think they may come round, for there is nothing
like long drawers and good keep for a cold. The intelligence is unhappily of a more vexatious description. A
valuable young porcine matron, vexed I fear by the
severity of her throes, has turned cannibal and devoured
her offspring; while, on the other hand, master Reynard
has found our juicy stores out again and has appropriated
several of our darling wild-ducks. This is the more
annoying as we cannot leave them out at night now, and
the usual region of their nests is unsafe. Unluckily
they require to choose their own, and will not sit just
where the fowl-wife wishes, so we have the carpenter
building rafts to float on a pool enclosed within the fold-
yard, hoping that the red robber will not venture there.
He is, however, *sufficiently* bold, as Ciceronian authors
write. In fact he waylaid his first victim quite close to
the kennel of a terrier that, remembering former experience, I thought well to chain up in the orchard beside
the faggot-heap, under which the ducks build. It was
a curious upstanding, head-on-one-side, swaggering,
tailor-like, comical, little mallard, white as snow too
(being a cross with the call-duck), that he took first.

The bailiff and I had been looking at the bird with some amusement during his afternoon meal, and observed that by some 'means he had lost an eye, a misfortune which possibly caused his quaint air. Perhaps, too, it was with a view to protection that he haunted the neighbourhood of the kennel, keeping his extinguished light on that side, as the one-eyed hind of which there is record in Æsop's fable. Reynard is 'cute enough, and no doubt argued that where there is a kennel there is probably too a chain, and so he ventured up, choking our hero's throat by one snap of his lancet fangs, and completing his triumph by devouring the greater part of him on a neighbouring fallow. This was bad enough, and we were at once on the *qui vive*, but it happened that a few days later the children going to a low-lying meadow, beside a brook, to gather violets, came across the carcase of a vixen fox, with brush and foreleg gone, and a piece of lamb in immediate proximity. An immense forest and a large tract of rocks, inaccessible to hounds, being situate not many miles hence, the foxes breed there in great numbers, although until lately they have not troubled our hen-house. I am afraid that under all circumstances there was about our homestead a feeling of something like exultation that the thief was caught, and the ducks got their freedom again. A fortnight from that date, however, only last Monday morning, as we arrived to look round, the henwife took a mallard's gorgeous head from a cleft in a twisted pear-tree, saying, " Master Fox has been here again." On the evening before I had been watching with so much delight the love-making rambles of the various pairs as they went working about in the old grass, and sucking ever and anon what seemed especially delicious, something I could fancy between a slug and a kiss, for their bills were working together in the same spot. So, too, the cunning plunderer must have found them, and, with a feeling of undoubted glee at the sport he was to spoil, came creeping from apple-tree to apple-tree, until he got conveniently near to grab them, which he did most effectually, just cutting their necks through, and leaving the bodies behind, having possibly been disturbed, or struck with a feeling of due remorse. So the carpenter now is hard at work providing what I trust may prove a residence of safety. The cottagers under the hill tell me that they hear his lordship bark nightly. The plan they adopt to scare him from their tiny lambs is to rub them well with a ring of red ruddle around the necks. He will never touch a youngster so distinguished, they tell me. There being plenty of rabbits about, why cannot he be content therewith ? From an apprehension possibly of taking tapeworm on board, a delectable form of parasite from which these pestilent ground game suffer considerably, as we were informed by medical authorities during the Trichina discussions, and which has made ourselves resolutely set face against what we were wont to consider, when boiled, and smothered in onion-sauce, a delicate and delicious food.

In answer to some inquiries, I am happy to give the benefit of my experience in bull breeding, if the reader will take it for just as much as it is worth. If he wishes to exhibit, he must from the first do the calf well, keeping it in a box, and letting it out to its mother, or, better, to a deep-milking half-Alderney, twice or three times a day, and supplying it with meal, roots, cake, eggs, fine hay, &c. Feeding for exhibition is an art in which few thoroughly succeed, unless they

have to help them a servant who has the *inborn gift*
of knowing when and how. For it is no less, as
experience will soon show. The bull calf ought to
have a light ring put into his nose as soon as he is
weaned, and as soon as the wound is healed, the
breaking should begin. Let one man lead him, or
rather try to lead him out, for he is sure to pull back
and resist. The smart application of a switch to the
region whereby youngsters are best instructed will make
him jump on and struggle. Pat and soothe him, the man
in front holding him steadily meanwhile and walking on.
Then if he again holds back, again the smart adminis-
tration behind. One or two days of this tuition will
ordinarily bring him to lead quietly. He should then
be led and exercised daily, with many interludes of
soothing and petting.

The reader will remember Lord Byron's recipe for
dealing with a fractious flirt. "Pique her and soothe
her : soon you'll have your way." So, too, he must
conquer his Shorthorn princes. He cannot break them
in too soon. I had two gentle bulls last year, which,
being kept for home use, were not fairly broken. The
consequence was they could only be driven in company
with a cow—and not led. This, in the end, became
vastly inconvenient. A bull calf will do well on good
pasture running by its mother. They should be driven
under shelter during heat. I think, too, that there is
something in what old breeders say, that the tail of a
calf that runs with and sucks his mother on the open
is apt to be *high*. It will be noticed that they
generally suck, swaying that appendage triumphantly
in mid-air. On the field, of course, they suck oftener
than they do when kept within doors. Hence, either

the joint loosens out of symmetrical position, or at least from too frequent a repetition of the act they form a *habit* of carrying the tail high. (For further information on this head, see Aristotle's Ethics, Book II. cap. 1.) I have found no difference in disposition between bull calves reared two in a box or singly. Their boxes should be *free from publicity.* Being looked at, especially if there be a walk in front of them, irritates them terribly. I had one amiable fellow spoilt by the tricks of a lad tending a mason, whom I had occasion to employ near the box, and whom I wish the animal had pitched into primeval mortar.

I remember asking Culshaw about a bull which I bought at Towneley, and which became cantankerous. After an instant's thought he said, "Oh, it's all owing to So-and-so," naming one of his ancestry. Temper is undoubtedly inherited. I had one youngster made so quick in his temper that he was called after a distinguished auctioneer, all owing to a young lady with a white veil peeping hastily into his box through the open half-door. He started frightened to his feet, and from that hour continued fractious. I sold him, however, and the last time I saw him was with a rosette upon his brow in the show-yard, as gentle as need be. He had been put by his new owner into a secluded box, and treated by his attendant judiciously, with a mixture of severity and kindness.

Another amiable yearling having been turned into a yard for exercise, got his attention attracted by an old man who stupidly went that way to carry some straw for thatching. A few journeys passed off well. At last the animal took to follow and rub his front against the bundle. Finally, with a frisk, he upturned the straw,

and by consequence the old man too, who hobbled off
in a fright, leaving the bundle to the bull's mercy.
The animal reflecting on this issue became savagely
addicted to butting from that day. It is with young
bulls as with young boys; be firm, patient, and considerate. Promptly check any liberty taken; acknowledge and reward obedience. And now I think my
reader will have had enough of the subject.

There have been several salmon taken by anglers
in the pool under the house, but I find that there is
also there a gang of otters bent on spoil. One of the
professional fishermen informed me first. You may
hear them "whistle in the stilly night," and the mud
is covered with their cat-like tracks.

Being out early this morning, I found two of my men
hotly tearing down a bank into which they had seen a
weasel run. I disapproved and stopped them, for last
week one of the stack-yard cats caught one and killed
it, and on thrashing out a rick alongside we found no
less than fifty rats, young and old, which this foreigner
had doubtless come after. This vermin swarm had
invaded us when our neighbour cleared his granaries,
for we had been comparatively free before. The weasel
I think does more good than harm. The stoat is of
quite another sort. When we set about thrashing we
had the gardener's fruit-tree nets stretched around the
proceedings; the consequence was that not an individual rat escaped. The terriers caught every single
one, no matter where they broke, being baffled by
this fence, which they were not allowed time to gnaw
through. But I have shot my allotted arrows.

August, 1870.

"MORE enjoyable if not your own," I murmur inwardly, as I fold up to return a most tempting
advertisement of an estate in North Wales, described
as a " virgin estate," and containing besides some
three thousand acres of cultivated land, no end of
gorse hills, undeveloped slate, imagined coal-beds, innumerable wild gorges and cascades, just exactly what
one enjoys most thoroughly as a tourist in quest of
refreshment after dusty, exhaustive work in chambers,
but what one wouldn't care to invest in, considering
the trouble the development of such varied resources
must entail, unless one were in possession of such a
glorious " accumulation during minority " as Lothair
found himself possessed of when he wavered between
building a cathedral and a nest of innumerable cottages. There is a time of life at which one arrives
when trouble really does bore. Activity, mental no less
than bodily, one reads in disquisitions on the human
frame, begins to hang fire about the period when over-
trained athletes break down—that is upon the near
side of fifty. Then it is that Horatian maxims influence and Horatian pursuits absorb — deep-bodied
claret—the sound of rippling waters—the glancing,
lustrous leaves—the voice of birds—and the conscious-
ness of bills paid, with a juicy balance left. At this
period it is, perhaps, that the amateur agriculturist is
in his bloom. He has, by dint of judicious ample
expenditure, deep cultivation, minute oversight, and
unwearied persecution of weedlings, brought his land
to yield an annually improved solid lump. He can
afford to experiment in the way of thin sowing, and

has pleasure in recording his experience for the benefit
of the agricultural community at large, — amongst
whom, as amongst all pupils, there are plenty to doubt
his ability and dicta. But away with philosophic reflection; it is too hot for that. To record results. First
let me resume the old story of the autumn-planted
potatoes. What are above ground appeared much
later—as I have always found to be the case—than
the spring planted; but, when once up, they rapidly
overhauled them in the race, as though they have a
stronger propulsive power somewhere, either in their
roots finding more moisture from being lower placed,
or from the stem's muscles being firmer because of
their greater age. About one-seventh have not shown,
even yet; but when I stirred the soil with my spud,
I found lots of white tender shoots working to get
clear of their immurement. I have consequently sent
a man with a fork to loosen the solidified mould along
the line of the invisible. It would have been well if
I had run Garrett's horse-hoe over the plot in the
early spring, as I fully intended doing, but was over-
advised. What a nuisance is advice ! It is sure to
put a man wrong unless his counsellor be intimately
informed of every unknown quantity in the problems,
which can rarely be done. But I will not dwell further
on the disagreeable, except to say that henceforth I
will follow no advice that does not fit in with my own
inclination ; and unsolicited advice I will throw back
in the giver's face. But, as my temper's boiling, I had
best proceed with my story and let reflection on the
past alone. I have one pool the overflow of which
runs on to a rye-grass plot that helps to supply the
cart-stable, and around which the wild ducks build,

out of which it is impossible to shut a certain muck-yard element of stained liquor. On the bank of this I am fixing a pump, and I propose to give the potatoes a good soaking therefrom by the help of watering-cans. It will be a work of time; but, as Sutton wisely prints in his catalogue injunctions to swede-growers, " Without pains no gains." The root which produced in my man's garden over thirteen pounds of potatoes was indulged with one deep drink during the drought. Another plan I am about to adopt in my orchard was suggested in the *Bath and West of England Journal* for 1859, but which I will quote, as it may not have fallen in the way of some, while others may have passed it over. An American apple-grower writes :— " For several years past I have been experimenting on the apple, having an orchard of 2,000 bearing New-town pippin trees. I found it very unprofitable to wait for what is termed the ' bearing year,' and it has been my aim to assist nature, so as to enable the trees to bear every year. I have noticed that from the excessive productiveness of this tree it requires the intermediate year to recover itself, to extract from the earth and atmosphere the materials to enable it to produce again. This it is not able to do unassisted by art, while it is loaded with fruit, and the intervening year is lost. If, however, the tree is supplied with proper food it will bear every year; at least such has been the result of my experiments. Three years ago, in April, I scraped all the rough bark from the stems of several thousand trees in my orchard, and washed all the trunks and stems within reach with soft soap, trimmed out all the branches that crossed each other early in June, and painted the wounded part with white lead,

U

to exclude moisture and prevent decay. I then in the latter part of the same month slit the bark by running a sharp-pointed knife from the ground to the first set of limbs, which prevents the tree from becoming bark-bound, and gives the young wood an opportunity of expanding. In July I placed one peck of oyster-shell lime under each tree, and left it piled round the trunk until November, during which time the drought was excessive. In November the lime was dug in thoroughly. The result the following year was 1,700 barrels of choice fruit, besides cider from refuse. In October I manured these trees with stable manure, in which the ammonia had been fixed, and covered this immediately with earth. The succeeding autumn they were lite-rally bending to the ground with the finest fruit I ever saw, while the other trees in my orchard not so treated were quite barren, the last season having been their bearing season."

Careful treatment of the apple I have myself found to be rewarded. Our best orchard we have dressed the last two years, once with old night-soil and lime com-post, dug in at the roots, and once with leaf mould, of which the chestnut wood affords us annually a quantity. We have had grand crops both years since, and there is a good show for the coming season : I shall, however, try to lime around the stems. The trees are too old to derive benefit from a splitting of the bark.

Our youngsters have taken to bathing, and as our broad river abounds with rapids I thought it best yes-terday to inspect the scene of their enjoyment. I took down the garden syringe to give a drink to the young grass that is springing with a melancholy slowness, where I pared the broken banks. . With one end of the gutta-

percha pipe immersed in deep water, I worked away
until I was quite hot, pumping now lustily, now softly,
to the amusement of my young geese, who were splashing in a quick current just beyond my range.   " Papa's
squirting the bank," they cried with delighted ridicule.
In faith it taught me one thing, that is, to estimate the
value of a good hour's rain.   Only to watch the splashing shower absorbed so rapidly by the brown bank without leaving a trace, and considering the weight of my
steady exertion I felt more than ever a longing that
the brazen heavens would open and let down a refresher
on the parched meadow, to which we look for our winter
supply of hay.   What ever the price of this article will
be I cannot dare to guess.   Certain it is that hereabouts
there is no bottom grass, therefore right thankful am I
that I put in thirteen acres of autumn oats after wheat,
which are now in full ear, and I hope to cut when
three-parts ripened in a fortnight, so as to get in mustard quickly, with a strong dose of artificial, the
stubble being clean.   This will come partly to cut
in chaff with wheaten straw, partly to consume with
sheep.   Then, it being my own land, I shall put
wheat in again, having faith in Mr. Lawes' doctrine,
that every soil has its idiosyncracy.   This particular
plot is locally considered " to throw a capital crop
of wheat, one of the best about."   Why then not
meet its inclination?   The idea of the several soils
in various combinations being adapted to special vegetable growths bears on its surface persuasion to my
mind.   I shall at least try it, not being *tied* to the
four-course or any other system.   " Some take coffee
some take tea," is a piece of sedimentary wisdom we
owe our ancestors, which should never be lightly re-

garded, I think. So I shall indulge the land's humour
to its utmost bent.

I have had several strangers lately to inspect my
piers and their success. They are universally approved,
and will be copied in each case. Now that the water-
volume is shrunk in the river-course, the heavy, broad,
rounded banks of washed-up gravel are clearly discerni-
ble, having filled several deep holes to the brim. There
was but little damage done by the strong winter floods,
excepting to the one which stood somewhat lonely, on
a clay bottom, nor has that suffered since I erected a
second, at about thirty yards' interval, to relieve the
strain at that point, there being thereon, when the torrent is full, a tremendous blow of accumulated billows.

Grand is it to get your hay cut in the early morning.
My machine was busy at four to-day, and the swathes
(light enough, certainly) are already half withered, while
the horses, having finished for the day, are (it is not
noon) reposing quietly, after a fill of vetches. Sleeping
in the sun with wet stockings on is good for the nether
limbs of neither man nor grass.

As I went to inspect the crop last evening, I heard
over the hedge a peculiar cry of evidently a nursing
mother, somewhat resembling the turkey's, somewhat the
brown owl's. For some time I watched vainly, until suddenly it ceased, she having caught, I fancy, a glimpse
of me across the lane. Yet an infantine wailing went
on ; and on my descending through the gap I found a
little nigger of a bird, fresh hatched, which bit my
finger resolutely, and covered my hand with oil. I discovered then it was the offspring of a landrail, and, as
it would be deserted, took it home to the children,
who deposited it amongst some young pheasants newly

hatched, in and out of which it runs this morning quite lively, but with a lazy, listening look, such as one might imagine a gipsy-lad would wear if caught, upon the sudden skedaddle of poaching parents, and introduced by his captor to the mercies of the village dame.

I've been roaming, I've been roaming where the meadow grass is sweet;
And I'm coming, and I'm coming with the dew upon my feet!

This means, under exceedingly strong metaphorical language, that I went down upon the occurrence of the thaw to inspect the condition of our river bank, and to note what effect the drifting ice might have upon the protective piers, the history of which I have in these columns gradually detailed. They have now been proved to be such a thorough success that I have the greatest satisfaction in explaining minutely, for the benefit and guidance of those amongst your readers who may desire to save a swiftly-wasting bank from the undermining action of an insidious stream, not only the several points in which our plan has answered, but also the weak points that we have had to mend. In the first instance, every river-wise person that we met or spoke to when our project was in embryo said that what we had to do to save the bank was to plant " sallies "— that is, willow cuttings—along it, mentioning several instances of very successfully encouraged accumulation at several turns of the river. They always overlooked the fact that in each of these cases the gathering took place upon the slack, not the current side of the stream. There where the weaker water rested it was only too glad to have anything, stick or stone, to cling by or lean against, and let the mud drain out of its shoes. But upon the other side where the stream was wearing against its earthen barrier (as you may see a hungry, poaching old sow go trying with her snout along the lowermost rail of the prohibitive fence) planted bushes could serve no earthly purpose, save as a buffet for the river's boxing powers, like the stuffed sack upon which the ambitious prize-fighter at once burnishes his skill and builds up muscle. The sack of course gradually suffers, and would gladly I dare say, if it could, "hide its diminished head;" and, to pursue the figure even further, as upon the day of real battle the human antagonist hammered about the head gets shaky about the feet, similarly do thick shrubs suffer when subjected continually to the buffeting of the old river god; they ultimately give way and tumble over, breaking up from its solidity too the bed on which they stood, and exposing it in fragmentary shape to the force of the invading torrent, which moreover, as the too greedy school-boy, impatiently chews as well as sucks his plum. "I once tried the plan," one informant said, "and it answered splendidly until one tremendous flood came and swallowed up the whole concern." What was this but the well-known experience of the ingenious and economical old gentleman who by help of green spectacles had just succeeded in inducing his faithful Dobbin to feed on shavings and fancy it was grass, when the gentle creature died! The fact is, no greater mistake could be made than keeping a plantation on the bank you want to save, in the fond hope that its roots will keep the soil together. The ungrateful little assemblage do nothing of the sort; rather they are in a continual fret to get free, which the savage river by its worrying ultimately helps them to do. The only place in which our piers have failed to "fulfil the promise of their youth " is where the roots and about a foot of the upstanding stem, with its attaching tresses, was left uncleared at the base of the slope; but I am thankful that it was overlooked, for it has taught us an excellent lesson.   The "exception proves the rule " is a proverb which is herein borne out.

Gradually we watched the waters burrow round its holding (we were always intending to remove it, but either the boat was not ready when we wanted it, or the bill-hook, and so it never got removed, and is now hanging wearily—we can see it in the deep water—waiting until the sinking of the flood shall enable us to sever its surviving claw), and finally a solid mass of the bank, after the old fashion, slipped in to fill the hole.   In all other respects, as without exception the most prejudiced have confessed on paying them a visit of inspection, these protective fences have answered admirably.   Within them it is surprising what a quantity silts up with every flood—a process which will obviously continue until the accumulation is level with the slope of the piers, and forms one gradual turfed incline, right into the heart of what were, before building, the deep waters of a salmon pool.   Then shall the assailing stream slip over them without let or damage.

I had been long since persuaded of their general exceeding merit, but it has only been during the recent thaw that we have had the structure tested to the uttermost.   There has not been such a frost hereabouts for ten years it is said, and when once the ice-locked waters began to move it was a sight to see.   For hours, for days, and nights, with a seething sloppy sound, in one continuous flow the broken-up masses of snow-covered ice continued to move on as it were to the distant spectator a long band of frosted bridal cake. Past the extremities of our piers the current kept its sweep, and block after block, fragment after fragment, went drifting swiftly by, one just catching the other, as it came too near, what our young school-boys call "a gentle kick." Sometimes, when there was an obstacle and a stoppage lower down, the bigger members of the shoal dipped under and threw up in affrighted altitude some weaker neighbour right on end, or crushed it within the boiling mass. Still safely and surely they had been shunted off the pier point, until all of a sudden I saw one big stone upon its lower surface tremble. Then taking mean advantage of its fright, under influence of which it had staggered too near the swift outside stream, a young thickset ice-block, about a yard across and a foot deep, hit it something like a blow beneath the ear, which a second ice youngster following up, knocked the stone right into the seething abyss. This was not much after all, and so long as its surviving brother pebbles kept a judicious down-charge, as did the Duke's guards at Waterloo, there was no fear of further damage. It was only when a fellow funked and peeped to have a look that he received the retributive blow. The greater masses went contemptuously by, as if in impotent anger, until all of a sudden one monster, taking a dive and thereby mounting upon its back another equally mighty, was enabled maliciously to get a sweep of the shore above the surface of the water, and came thump against our projection, making the whole bank tremble: an alarming effect which was immediately followed up by another triangular block being similarly mounted and brought point on against our precious handywork, this time picking out a boulder which it all but dislodged. Then another, but I did not dare to wait any longer, as I was powerless to help.

Second period. Having finished one pipe, I took a stroll to see the children skating upon a frozen overflow by the river, and then went, somewhat nervously I am bound to confess, to see what effect the icebergs had finally had upon my jetties. It has been undoubtedly disastrous. Off two at least, a foot in height has been knocked, but not out of reach, and the damage can be easily repaired. From the observations I have taken it is essential that, as soon as fine weather affords the opportunity, the facing next the current should be built with mortar, or else be protected in front by a fence of stakes. At least there should be one stout post at the end to act as buffer against the recurrence of such drifting sledge-hammers. On this subject no more to be said by me, and I trust little to learn. There has been a glorious drift of sand and pebbles within each one of them. Having finished this survey, I went to the homestead to see how the cattle tied up for fatting thrive. It is the only part of the agricultural business that I don't care particularly about, and with respect to which consequently I am perpetually obliged to consult the rules of others. The distinguished M'Combie's rules have helped me most, and I commend, as a kind service to my younger brethren, the following statements which I have underlined in his little volume, to save trouble or reference. As respects the winter treatment of fattening beasts, he observes: " It is indispensable for the improvement of the cattle that they receive their turnips clean, dry, and fresh." He then recommends the storing, if possible, of the whole of the swede crop (I wish we had done so this year), but not the " Aberdeenshire Yellow (only a proportion), as they lose the relish, and cattle prefer them from the field; but I require a proportion of them for calving cows in frost. Frosted turnips make cows with calf abort; and rather than give calving cows such turnips, I would order them straw and water." This I can endorse as regards sheep too. A few frosted turnips (it was fancied the frost was out of them) were thrown to a ewe flock the other day. During the night one threw her lamb, and had to be removed. The fact is, they gripe, and the consequent straining forces out the fœtus prematurely. "However faithful in other respects, the cattle-men must have a taste and a strong liking to cattle: they must be their hobby." "Even with men of the greatest experience, the difference in the thriving of the different lots upon the same keep is great. They must not be oppressed with having too many in charge, or the owner will suffer by his ill-judged parsimony. From August till November, a man may take care of thirty cattle very well, or a few more, if the cattle are tied; but when the day gets short, twenty to twenty-five are as many as one man can feed, to do them justice. Good cattle-men are invaluable. They must not only know what to give the cattle, but the great secret, especially when cattle are forced up for show purposes, is to know *what not to give them*." "When improperly treated " (through having too much turnips injudiciously given), "the cattle scour and hove, the stomach getting deranged. It is a long time before they recover, and some never do well. We generally cure hove by repeated doses of salt, sulphur, and ginger."

" The cattle intended for the great Christmas market" (on swedes since October) "have at first 2 lb. to 4 lb. of cake a day by the 1st of November. In a week or two I

increase the cake to at least 4 lb. a day, and give a feed
of bruised oats or barley, which I continue up to the
12th or 14th of December, when they leave for the
Christmas market." "It is absolutely necessary to increase the quantity of cake and corn weekly to ensure a
steady improvement; and if cattle are forced upon cake
and corn over two or three months, it will, in my opinion,
pay no one."

For the introduction of these extracts I make no
apology. I have found the volume, *Cattle and Cattle
Breeders*, most interesting and serviceable. I will only
add that I have no personal knowledge whatever of Mr.
M'Combie, although he is doubtless well known to most
agriculturists through the lovely level black-polled heifers
he has shown, no less than by the huge bullock, which was
the wonder of London at a comparatively recent fat show.

Having hastily chewed a pickled onion and swallowed
a single glass of sherry, I hastened back to my work.
Reader, if ever you have scant time for luncheon on a
cold day, adopt the above recipe and you will thank its
author for it. While it temporarily but effectually
allays your hunger, you will find it warm your system
through. I remember many years ago attending,
amidst an awful throng, a midnight service in a Church
at Rome. At the very moment, when between the
stifling heat and the inhuman pressure one felt completely done, in nasal accents from the long throat of a
distinguished Yankee, who occupied the post of rear-
guard to me, there came the inquiry, "Guess you'd like
a cup of tea?" There is no denying that I immediately assented, without dread of possible assassination
from one whose bony frame must have found a grateful
relief in having so well-cushioned a person to lean

against. "Like a cup of tea! Certainly, if you please."
And as a nurse does to an infant, or a keeper to a mar-
moset monkey, he dabbed a lozenge into my expectant
lip-enclosure. " Thanks," I spluttered, and immediately
thereupon there commenced such a resolution of primary
elements. The little hard concentrated cake dissolving
gradually, communicated to my dry palate the refreshing
flavour of that most aromatic compound we call " tea,"
cream, sugar, and all. Voluming gradually out, as a
wreath of smoke above the discharged field-piece, it
seemed to permeate and pervade every part of one's
system, sending the blood back from the brain, and
bracing the nerves exactly as a real draught of the
imitated beverage might. Thanks to that tall Yankee
for the refreshment and comfort he gave me ; the like
of which I expect in turn from all who shall avail themselves of my own original above-mentioned specific for
intense hunger on a frigid day.

Over my pipe ! Well, then, what's the first reflection ? Why, simply that I have drifted very far away
from all agricultural subjects, excepting that onions and
grapes grow in fields, of either Egypt or Italy. This
cup of tea had an immense power of flotation, but by
dint of exceeding energy I must recover my moorings.

Reflection, therefore, No. 2. Why, simply that I
shall be glad when all these youngsters have gone back
to school.

Reflection No. 3. This winter and the condition on
their return from school of these said youngsters have
taught me a lesson I shall not forget. With the scan-
tiest possible provision in my rickyards, so scanty in fact
as long since to have brought down upon our establishment ridicule from some, and, what was worse, un-

solicited advice from others, we have managed after all to disappoint the predictions of the *cornices sinistræ*. Our boys came home with clear complexions and fat cheeks. They return pallid and puffy to school. The fact is, they thrive upon regular and measured meals. They get out of sorts upon a wasteful glut of plum-pudding, goose, beef, turkey, pears, roast chestnuts, and mince-pies. We have astonished three keen and scornful judges by an inspection of our folds. Sawdust to lie on is not pleasant to the eye, nor straw and gorse chaff in the mangers. But the heifers, cows, and calves are all fat and glossy. If we don't make our wheaten straw help us in the future to recoup the losses of the past, then our present resolution will not hold. A few spade-fuls of must, left beside the cider-mill, thrown into the heap accumulating under the chaff-cutter, and heated by a pipe of the waste steam, sends forth a teeth-watering fragrance.

Reflection No. 4. Those lambs that have fallen must have been considerably astonished on their introduction to the outside world during the last ten days. Housed, however, at night, when their dams have a good feed of crushed oilcake powder and meal, and let out on a bank of rowen during the day, they look amazingly happy, and I doubt not our admiring youngsters would be glad to change places with them until Easter (when their respective fates are very different), instead of having to return to the mercies of the Educator next black Monday. Very different is the song to-day about the passages from what regaled our ears a few weeks since with the delicious refrain:

"No more Latin, no more Greek,
No more cane to make me squeak."

Reflection No. 5. In unconscious reproof of my hard-hearted parental reasoning and declaration, a little girl has just brought in some slices of an orange from the green-house, with a whole plateful of brown sugar to modify its "bitter taste." It so happened that our one tree bore fruit in the exact number that our children are. They had, consequently, one each presented to them by Mr. Melon, and reserved until the last week of the holidays for enjoyment. How often we tell and try to convince our labourers that much more really happy their condition is than ours, the employers; for the many reasons that they have comparatively but few anxieties, so long as they conduct themselves well, so much being provided for them in the way of help over and above their wages in the shape of clothes, fuel, medicine, &c., while the larger their family the more pay they receive : in due course, moreover, each member, as he or she grows up, dropping over the nest to find an independent occupation and sustenance, and even furnishing retributive help to the parents, when their heart is in the right place. "Better is a dinner of herbs where love is, than a stalled ox and hatred therewith," are words of wisdom which often recur to us as we watch the soil-stained labourer seated by his fire-side with the little ones clustering around his knee, on which some more fortunate one has been able to secure his triumphant perch, and the mother is cooking the potatoes and cabbage for supper just flavoured with dripping or a bit of "pig meat." A crust and watercresses for luncheon, with a draught from the spring, affords more real refreshment (leaving no bilious wretched results), than oftentimes the venison haunch with turtle soup and crusted port do. This reflection (which of course no labourers endorse, since " man never is, but always to be blest")has been brought about by our repeated observation of the delight this solitary orange tree has afforded our circle so long ; in fact a full earnest share of purest Mediterranean enjoyment, through first its flowers and then its fruit, much more probably than the nobleman receives from the whole grove which his half-acre of glass encloses, not to mention the relief which lesser expense and diminished care guarantee.   The clever, well-cared-for pony gives as much gratification to its owner as the stud of horses. Happiness, in fact, hangs about upon every twig, if we only determine to see it.

Reflection—(lost the count now, and my pipe is nearly out).   It is hard lines, that this severe weather should have returned.   I just found the rooks boring into the delicious interior of the swede bulbs, while the wild pigeons are legion in the vicinity of the pheasant food, and upon my honour (I thought at first it was one's piebald whiskers one got a glimpse of) only fancy a pair of magpies, too, taking fearless advantage of the store !   All's food that comes to the net with them, I conclude, as with any other pilferers.   Talking of that, the children towards the finish of the late frost got their skating-ground mangled by some poaching rascal, who discerned a stranded salmon through a foot of ice and took advantage of the dark to mine it out. After a flood, with severe frost following, they are found not unseldom in the ditches of the meadows that adjoin our river.

No one who has ever commenced the use of steam-power upon his farm would ever do without it again. Astonishing was our inconvenience lately, when, owing

to a leak in the boiler necessitating repairs, we had to
stop a team regularly at mid-day for the purpose of
chaff-cutting or pulping.   And no one who has begun
with a small engine but would be sorry that he had
not while about it invested in a fair-sized one.   Mr.
Mechi's remarks on this subject, long since published,
we now feel to be thoroughly correct.   An enthusiastic
neighbour, who had had, too, some experience of steam
while at college, invested in a small second-hand engine
the other day with which he managed to cut up his
small stuff at a rare pace.   Unfortunately, one day he
took to exhibiting the same, some ladies having honoured
him with a visit, when he managed to blow the safety-
valve out, and the windows had to be smashed to allow
of the affrighted fair ones' escape.   So

"Beware, young man, of a musical valve."

Having re-lit, it strikes me that it is not for the
farmer to speculate.   I have just heard of a man who
will have to pay five pounds hire for bags in which his
corn has stood waiting for the rise of the market.   The
victims in this district through holding their wool have
been numerous.   One is said to have refused 2s. 2d.
for a lot which he afterwards sold at half the figure.
Talking of wool makes one think of one's head, and
thinking of one's head at our time of life leads to thinking of thatch, and thinking of thatch leads to thinking
how we shall manage, having consumed our straw, to
cover our hay-stacks this season, which we *mean* to be
numerous.   The thought strikes us ; we will carry out
our long-projected plan of felling a couple of plaguy
hedgerow elms whose long extended claws drag out the
sustenance from the adjoining soil for yards into the

field. These, sawn into thin slabs, will provide us with
the means of making a permanent shed to lift up and
down within pillars, upon the Lancashire plan, according to the depth of crop ; so out of evil shall come good.
But as to the intended abundance of meadow hay;
what mean we ? Why, last year, being over-persuaded,
we allowed the grazing of our land until March if not
April, being assured by the natives that the crop along
the river would not suffer in the least thereby. But it
did though. Dwarfed and stunted by this too harsh
treatment, it scarcely so recovered in places as to be
worth cutting. This year no ewe nor lamb goes upon
the ground; and what a top-dressing it shall have
through its harrow-shaken crevices, under guise of
guano, wood ashes, earth mould, and the like ! The
straits to which we have been put since August last
have been a top-dressing which our wits will not forget.

"We have been working like donkeys, sir, all the
morning," old Melon remarked to me just now, as I
found him blowing like a grampus, and mopping his
extensive brow. This remark had reference to himself
and his assistant. But upon it may be based some
reflections. Could he mean that they had been working reluctantly with their ears put back, and discharging
an occasional quick kick round the corner at their
nearest attendant ? Or did he mean that like the poor
faithful little thing, that you see occasionally in the
small cart with wheels rut-imbedded, they had been
struggling against hope in patient endurance ? Just so
I expect, for the employment in which they had been
engaged was wheeling some great stones from a distant
wood for the adornment and furnishing of a new fernery
upon which the Missus has set her heart. However,

donkey or not—whether Mr. Melon may have fairly compared himself or not—certain it is that I don't mean to go on much longer without the aid of one of these trustworthy carriers upon the farm. Standing about just where they are placed, in harness and the shafts all day, they are at everybody's beck and call, to do their ready service—whether the cowman may desire his feeding-hampers hauled to the distant sheds, or roots brought in, or a small additional cut of best clover-hay for the Sultana of the day, or a package for the housekeeper fetched from the town—" ready! aye, ready! " is the motto of our obedient, industrious friend. A very different sort are they, however, from the donkey of the desert. A friend of ours, who has been sent to Suez as an invalid, and who was used until two years since to lead the hunting-field through bullfinches and over brooks upon gigantic weight-carriers, is now reduced to conveyance upon a Cairo donkey; but he writes in raptures about them. The one he has purchased for himself prefers cantering to walking: hear that, ye, his English congeners! and beats any pony, he says, that he ever owned in his " ain countree." The same gentleman writes in wonder at the exceeding strength of the native porters who live on nothing but beans—a sort from which some patent pap is made in England. One instance he mentions of a load being carried by one of these men fifty yards on to a vessel, the captain of which immediately weighed it and found it seven cwt.! This sounds incredible, but our informant is not given to romancing. To slip, however, from Cairo to the Cape, we have just letters from another friend, who had been for some months hunting, and who during September and October last arranged to have the oxen belonging to some half-dozen waggons fed and tended for the period in consideration of the Kafir Chief's receiving a knife and a pair of sheets! Only fancy that, when we in England were stinting and starving to the lowest point of safety.

But this brings me to a new reflection. The hard winter months seem so rapidly waning, and the soft air of spring so near, that the holders of hay are becoming alarmed, and in Carnarvonshire lately we were offered plenty of the most fragrant quality for £4 per ton. The unreasonable charge for railway carriage, however, would add another £2 the ton to this.

By the way, one word of caution to the farming youngsters who may desire to dabble with steam. There is no possibility of persuading the men that there is any risk whatever in the management of an engine, and there is difficulty until they have had a fright or two in keeping an occasional amateur from trying his hand when the engineer's back is turned. During the frost our bailiff deservedly got a " scalding " rebuff, through the action of a half-frozen pipe, through which the steam could not force its way as swiftly as was desirable. I do not think he will repeat his experiment. But, worse than that, we had nearly a bad accident. I had taken the regular attendant away to inspect some machinery; on our return, we could hear from the road a tremendous fuss going on in the engine-house. Fortunately the carpenter had heard it, and rushed in and raked out the fire, else I don't know what might have happened. A stupid lad, who helps in the feeding, thought to be mighty grand and get the food all ready cut and pulped and steamed during the engineer's absence. As the steam arose he of course got

x 2

flustered and lost his head, whereas the steam made head, and finally blew up the safety-valve, thence escaping in dense, angry volume. The lad got such a mortal fright that when it came to the push (as he is otherwise a good fellow, and in fact got into this scrape from an over-desire to show work) we could not find it in our heart to sign the warrant for his dismissal. We shall now be able to keep all parties but the regulars from intrusion on the dangerous premises. Hitherto one could not persuade our folk that the engine was aught but a delightful toy. It had really been well-nigh a serious affair, but it is likely to be the last attempt at such freaks. It has become a positive wonder to me how it is that one does not hear of more frequent accidents than we do. I remember now, although it never struck me then, a Staffordshire gentleman, an exceedingly clever engineer, who never could, even to the last (and he was an old man), hear without an involuntary shudder the " thud, thud " of a high-pressure engine at full pace.

But let us to less exciting topics. How singular is the spread of epidemics! How absurd that, go where you will of late over England, you meet everywhere somebody complaining of boils or winking with a stye in the eye! So too of cattle-disorder. The *Illustrated London News* gave us recently a specific for lice on cattle; since that I have noticed and see everywhere the uncanny look upon the cattle which indicates the existence of this pest. Whether done well or badly, whether their hair be dry or reeking with moisture, there is still everywhere the same unpleasant, scurfy look. It must assuredly be in the air. Goose-grease, well rubbed in, astonishes the animalculæ, while it pro-motes the growth of the new hair. Sawdust, like all other forms of litter, seems to have risen to a premium ; else while the animals repose on the supply of this stuff which larch and the fir-tree tribe generally yield they keep completely clear of this nuisance. The smell of turpentine don't suit them ; it either drives them next door, as the smell of puss sends the mice, or it doubles them up to die as they inhale it.

It is very sad to see how the starlings perished everywhere during the hard weather. Down upon the flower-beds under the rain-spouts, or amidst the straw in the lofts, they turn up everywhere, seeming to have suffered more than any other bird that flies. We shall still have enough left I hope to comb the sheep's backs and gurgle their all-absorbing love-song upon the roof-ridge. Only in one instance do I quarrel with them, and that is, when they will greedily try to get possession of a hole in a willow tree upon the lawn, which our household regards as the sacred property of the nuthatch. But they soon take the hint that they are not wanted there. Let them only be caught once or twice in a horsehair noose, and after a fright be released, they will straightway cease to annoy. Blessed spring, with the tuneful birds' songs and the sweet-scented bursting buds, how soon it will be bursting upon us now. Oh ! that it may infuse a softening influence into the hard Teutonic breast, while it re-inspires with hope and energy to repair her places of spoilt loveliness the too sadly crushed capital of France !

The good old-fashioned winter we have gone through has enabled us to comprehend how much we are indebted to the frost for an increase of soil upon our fields, where the ploughing has been done in due time. The up-turned subsoil, with its occasional flakes of rock, instead of being hard and harsh, lies now in lumps of finest sandy material, which the first touch of the harrow will spread, intermingling and refreshing the old worn bed. Especially is this to be seen in the coarse conglomerate of sandstone and lime-kernels, which form a layer of our old red formation.

Being excessively attached to the famous Black Diamond pigs, one is glad to have one's approach to their habitation made endurable if not pleasant. The cleaning out produces an unpleasant atmosphere, for which, however, there is a certain cure. Get the cook to store for you the wood ashes from the brick oven in which the bread is baked, and therewith have the damp flags dusted. It deodorises at once, and were your eyes shut you would never be cognisant of the proximity of your pets' abode. As unhappily the sty, however palatially built, is not redolent of heliotrope or wood violet, this infallible specific is worth adopting. I wish the authorities of the Royal Show-yard would take a hint therefrom. I have mentioned it, but vainly, to some of them. If they would but have a layer a foot thick of burnt clay or wood ashes beneath the sod on which the pig-pens are erected, the visitors would be no more repelled, as they are under existing circumstances, by an unsavoury odour, from the delightful contemplation of a beautiful animal.

Just reminded—I must go and look at my pet quickset hedge, which was planted so carefully two years since in a trench half filled with fine mould on a deep bed of rich rotted muck. It has begun to find the full benefit of this comfort at foot, and the shoots spring amain. But the surface is choked with tangled grass, which has to be carefully cleared away soon now. One of my neighbours persists in allowing his young quick

fences to be grown up with grass, the consequence
being, that during half-a-dozen years I have scarcely
seen any improvement in height, besides that, many of
the plants have died out at the base.   In Suffolk, some
years since, I knew a shrewd farmer plant young oaks
in the fence banks at intervals of fifty to a hundred
yards.   They come in very handily for hurdle heads
and stakes of general service, without doing damage to
the adjoining crops as an elm would do.   Their idio-
syncrasy is different.   Whereas the oak goes deeply
down, doing its best early in life to get a substantial
hold, and justify its solid character as the tree of Old
England, the elm idly spreads its roots abroad, greedily
finger-like picking out and pocketing what's nice in the
soil, as a child the comfits on a seed-cake.

Of this variety of disposition you may observe abundant illustration on any shelving bank in a woodland
district where the frost has undermined and caused to
break away the enclosing soil from about the root-
mass.   There is always something on the face of nature
to amuse and instruct.   Whose life so enjoyable as the
Naturalist's ?   He that hath eyes to see, let him see.

But sweetest of all studies—even though one be not
in the technical sense of the word a Naturalist—is the
face of nature, as I am sure any one would have said
who could have been out with me at four this morning,
amidst the fragrant freshness of the fields and woods.
Having received a summons to sign, seal, and deliver
our volume at earliest convenience, I fixed the execution for to-day, and slept uneasily, I confess, upon the
thought : for is it not as though one were parting with
a long-accustomed friend, whose company one must
henceforth forego ?   Exactly at three the concert of the

birds began, and the eastern sky became streaked with
a brilliant red, indicative of Sol's propinquity, as he
struggled up through the encircling snow-white mist
with which the whole winding valley of our glorious
Wye was wrapped. Dressing at once, I descended
rapidly from our already rejoicing plateau to the immediate river-side. It was " shivering like," as old
Melon expresses it, in the lower regions at first, but
gradually a warmer influence stole upon the glistening
scene. All nature, save man, seemed awake and stirring. The rooks, which on our passage through their
demesne had gone, alarmedly cawing, into mid-air
(their first-born having lately fallen by the bullet), were
back again amidst the tree-tops. A cow lowed in the
distance. The ponies browsed upon the utmost points
of the illumined hill-side. The yellow wagtail fluttered
across the sedge. The darkling swift shot on its pre-
datory flight. The lustrous starling (that " shopkeeper
nation " of birds) worked industriously for the small
profits which a lately mown bank yielded. The
haughty pheasant-cock crowed and flapped his wings
upon the upper lawn. An occasional fish splashed
boldly. All nature seemed awake and stirring, except
the human animal, of which I saw only one specimen, a
shepherd, in the distance. The only thing reclining
was a grey goat that belongs to one of the little girls,
who is now away from home, and whom she follows
like a dog over meadow and stile. " Absence makes
the heart grow fonder," and had dulled proportionately,
it is possible, the faithful creature's appetite. But
above all enjoyable was the rippling song of the silver
stream over the gravel at our feet, and about the
margin of our pet siesta rock.

It was past five when the fishermen arrived to take up their bright, weighted night-lines, which I watched them strip of a varied scaly spoil. I then made a survey of my fields, and was in consultation with the bailiff at six.

Next having betaken myself to my study, I fell (it is to be feared) asleep—for my first succeeding recollection is of " Letters, sir, please ; " and I open one amidst the lot from our young French student, who is now at school. The following graphic description I find therein of recent enjoyment. His words I give *verbatim :*—

" Yesterday, B. and I bought twopenny-worth of cream and two fourpenny crabs. Well, we met C. in the yard, so we invited him to partake of the feast; so he came with us to the pigstye, and we ate them, constantly dipping it into the cream. We ate them in the shell mixed with cream; it *was good, just.*"

Jolly is it to be a tiller of the soil ! but jollier yet is it to be a happy boy at school!——I have but one hope left, as I regretfully lay down my pen, which is that the reader may find it in his heart to grant this medley volume the encomium which our young hopeful pronounced upon his mixed dish in the pigstye—

" GOOD, JUST !"

THE END.